PRAISE FOR *SCALES*

"In this endearing origin story, Conway (Harbinger, 2018, etc.)
hits the high notes for YA romance readers and superhero devo-
tees alike ... The author keeps her tale fun and nerdy, luring fans
toward an epic finale but also creating characters readers would
love to see grow throughout a series. This fantasy delivers a
bright tsunami of hormones and heroism."

— *Kirkus Reviews*

SCALES

NICOLE CONWAY

OWL HOLLOW PRESS

Owl Hollow Press, LLC, Springville, UT 84663

Library of Congress Cataloging-in-Publication Data
Scales / N. Conway. — First edition.

Summary:
When New York City faces the threat of an ancient evil, a teenage boy must use a magical bracelet to transform into a monster-slaying dragon superhero.

ISBN 978-1-945654-21-3 (paperback)
ISBN 978-1-945654-22-0 (e-book)
LCCN 2018961101

To Cole, Mason, and Kylie.

And to Miss Jay at Café Cornerstone—
thank you for providing the most delicious
coffees in South Korea!

CHAPTER 1

Ever had a bowl of cereal call you a loser?

That's how my day started.

Sitting alone at a table in the hotel lounge, I stared down into my bowl of Alphabet Puffs. There it was, plain as day. L-O-S-E-R. The soggy cereal bits floated innocently in my milk, like none of this had been planned ahead of time. Talk about bad omens.

I tried to ignore it. It was probably just a coincidence, right? I mean, who ever heard of divining the future out of a bowl of cereal? Cereal wasn't going to ruin this day for me.

"Morning, Koji," my dad called across the lobby as he strolled through the revolving glass door. His outfit drew a strange look from the receptionist as he made his way over to join me at the table. He wore his standard, olive-green flight suit with matching green combat boots—the same uniform I'd seen him in since…well, as long as I could remember. Tucking his navy blue flight cap into the big pocket on the leg of his suit, he flashed me a quick grin as he sat down. "Got everything packed up?"

I nodded to the two giant rolling suitcases next to my chair. "Yup. Ready to go."

"Excellent." Dad sat back and yawned, rubbing the bridge of his nose. "The traffic is murder out there. It's going to take some getting used to. Good thing we're close enough to your new school you can walk. It'll take me an hour just to get to the university. And that's on a good day."

"Did you see our new place?"

He smiled again. "Sure did. I think you'll like it. Your room has a great view. And, hey, no more sharing a bathroom. You've got your own this time."

"Sweet!" I sprang out of my chair and seized one of my rolling bags. "Let's go."

Dad followed, chuckling and rolling my second bag. After checking out of the hotel, we made our way into the chilly, early morning air and caught a cab. It took a minute or two to cram my stuff into the trunk, but then we were on our way, headed for Yonkers, where our new life was supposed to begin.

The streets of New York churned and buzzed with early morning activity as they slid past the back window of the cab. I caught a glimpse of the cabbie eyeing my dad curiously in the rearview mirror. Dad had been getting those kinds of looks basically since we stepped off the plane. Growing up as a military brat, I'd always seen Dad wear flight suits. It was the standard outfit he wore to work every day. In fact, it was weirder if he wasn't wearing it.

My dad flew F-16s for the majority of his twenty-year career in the Air Force. Basically, that meant two things. One, we moved a *lot*—more than ten times in all. And two, Dad worked nonstop. He'd always come straight from work to catch the end of my soccer or basketball games, to PTA meetings, or to pick me up from a friend's house after school. He was usually late, but I didn't mind it much. It wasn't because he forgot or didn't care. Dad worked hard to keep things going for us.

But here, Dad had promised me things were going to be different. This was going to be his last post, his "twilight tour," before he retired from the Air Force for good. As the Detachment Commander for the Air Force ROTC program at his alma mater, he was supposed to have a much less stressful schedule. That meant no more long night-flying weeks when we didn't see each other because he couldn't get home before three in the morning. No more weekends spent doing my homework in the squadron bar, eating a lunch of jalapeño popcorn and guzzling down Gatorade while he caught up on whatever mission he needed to plan to fly the next day. No more being babysat by my grandparents or living as an awkward houseguest with another family in the squadron while he went on TDY trips to Alaska or was deployed somewhere overseas.

This was our chance to finally get comfortable, get into a routine that would last, and build a life that I wouldn't have to say goodbye to in a few months.

Not that my life had been the norm for a military kid. All I had to do was take a look around and see that things were... different for Dad and me. Nearly all of the other families in our squadrons had moms at home. They brought in food and fresh meals for everyone at the office, hosted big parties over the holidays, cooked delicious dinners, came to every school play and sporting event to cheer on their kids, and made sure the family landed on their feet after the chaos of every move.

I didn't have that.

It wasn't all bad though. And it's not like I was bitter about any of it. This was the way things were, and I was comfortable with it. Sure, the moves were rough. We ate a lot of fast food, lived in hotel rooms until we found a good place to rent, and I had to overlook the few minutes here and there where Dad might come dashing in late because he'd gotten hung up at work again. I had to start over every time with a new school, new teachers, and try to build some semblance of a social life from scratch. But I knew Dad had always done the best he could on his own. We were a team. And things here were going to be different—that's what he'd promised me.

This time, there'd be no looming expectation of another painful goodbye when it was time to leave for the next base.

This time, it was forever.

It was six o'clock when our cab pulled up to the front of a narrow, red brick house with a big cement staircase out front. It stood on a quieter street traffic-wise, but there were still people strolling the sidewalks in both directions. Our new house was tall, narrow, and had three levels. A big, circular window looked out from the top floor.

I unloaded the bags while Dad paid the driver. Then, together, we walked up the front steps and opened the door. It swung in slowly, creaking on rusty hinges. Inside, dim morning light trickled through the wood blinds. The air had a funky, stale smell, like no one had been in here in a long time.

"Not bad for a rental, huh?" Dad said as he closed the door behind us. "There's plenty of space. Kitchen and living room are down here. My room is on the second floor, yours is on top. There's a little courtyard out back, too. Pretty cool, huh?"

"Yeah," I replied, peeking into the kitchen.

It was pretty nice. Old but cozy. The dark floors were weathered, and little bits of plaster had chipped off some of the walls, but everything looked clean. At least, as much as I could see through our mess of stuff. Cardboard boxes were stacked from floor to ceiling in every room like giant, brown building blocks. The couch and both recliners still had plastic wrap around them.

We had a lot of work to do.

Dad rolled my suitcase to the base of the stairs. "I had them put your stuff up there for you and grabbed a few things from the supermarket around the corner." He glanced down at his watch. "You've still got a few hours before school starts if you want to start settling in, but I need to get going."

"Right," I recalled. "One-hour commute."

He groaned, his shoulders slumping and head rolling back with dread. "Anyway, you've got all the information for your school, right? Think you can handle it?"

I nodded.

Dad dropped a set of house keys into my hand, snagged an arm around my neck, and pulled me into a gruff hug. "Good. You watch out for yourself today, okay? This place isn't like Arizona."

"No kidding. I haven't seen a single cactus yet."

He was smirking when he let me go. "All right, I'm gone. Give me a call if you need anything. Oh, and lock up when you leave."

I waved a hand dismissively. "I've got this."

His expression softened and I caught a hint of sadness flickering in his eyes. "I know you do. Have a good first day, Koji."

"You too."

I waited until I heard him shut the front door before I let out a sigh. The bad cereal omen had me worried. It didn't matter how many times I'd been the new kid—another new school filled with strangers was still daunting. And I always did something extraordinarily stupid on the first day that sealed my fate. It never failed. Sometimes it seemed like the universe was out to get me, although this was the first time it had taunted me by sending messages in my food.

I gnawed the inside of my cheek as I climbed the stairs to my new room. A new school meant a new chance and a clean slate—which normally would have been a good thing. Not for me, though. Cereal omens aside, I didn't need any extra help making myself look stupid in public. Whether it was tripping on stairs, falling out of buses, spilling mustard down my shirt, walking into the wrong classrooms, or going the whole day with my shirt on backwards, I had a long-standing track record of terrible first days. And this was my last chance, so I couldn't afford to screw it up. Whatever impression I made here was going to stick.

No pressure, right?

My new room was at the very top of the stairs, just where Dad had said it would be. Long and narrow, the room's far wall was dominated by the huge round window I had seen from outside. It had a pretty awesome view of the city. The place was bigger than my room in Arizona, which was nice, and the tiny bathroom across the hall was all mine too.

The movers had already assembled my bed frame and plopped the mattress on it. My computer desk, rolling chair, and bookshelves sat against the opposite wall. Somehow the movers got the positioning just how I liked it, with the desk in the middle and the shelves on either side. Dad must have insisted on that. I still had plenty of leftover wall space to display my vintage Marvel posters and Gundam Wing wall scrolls.

A grin wriggled across my lips as I cracked open the first two boxes, surveying all my pristinely wrapped collectable action figures. The other boxes held my comic books and graphic novels. As soon as school was over, I could start setting everything up. Visions of gaming grandeur danced in my head as I pictured my TV mounted on the wall right above my dresser. I could set up my consoles, display my inventory of classic and vintage games, and Dad could help me set up the surround sound. This place would feel like home in no time.

Weaving my way through the towers of boxes labeled KOJI'S ROOM, I looked around for one that might have clothes in it. I used the house keys to cut open a few boxes and dug around to find a nice pair of jeans, a shirt that wasn't too wrinkled, and my favorite navy blue canvas jacket. It all smelled like cardboard and packing paper, of course, but at least it was clean.

The hot water in the shower took some finesse to figure out. The handles were ancient, and I couldn't tell which one was hot or cold because the lettering had been rubbed away probably decades ago. The old pipes made weird groaning noises when I turned them on, and I got a few blasts of ice-cold water to the face before I got the balance of hot and cold right. With that trust bridge officially in embers, I made a mental note to test the temperature with my hand before getting in next time.

I dried off with a beach towel since I couldn't find the normal bath ones and hurried to get dressed. My favorite pair of black-and-white converse sneakers—the ones with my lucky *Dragon Ball Z* laces—was the perfect finishing touch to my "first day of school" ensemble. I wiped a few smudges off the toes before I went fishing through the boxes again to find my old school backpack. Lucky for me, it was in the second one I opened.

I dropped the bag on my bed and double-checked to make sure I had everything I needed: a few blank notebooks, a calculator, pens, pencils, my wallet, a spare phone charger, a little cash just in case. That should get me through the first day. I zipped up all the pockets, grabbed my phone off the desk, and charged for the door at full steam.

This was it, day one of my sophomore year, and there was no way I was going to screw it up. *Look out New York: Koji Owens has arrived.*

I threw open my bedroom door and immediately tripped. My face met the hardwood floor with my backpack smacking me in the back of my head on the way down. For a few seconds I just lay there, asking myself if this was the cereal again.

"No!" I declared and pushed myself up to my knees, whipping around to figure out what I'd tripped over. An uneven floorboard? A nail? One of my precious collectable action figures that had fallen out of a box?

Nope.

Dead center in my bedroom doorway, like someone placed it there for me to find, sat a little package about the size of my fist, tied up neatly in a purple handkerchief. A gift? Who would leave me something like this sitting on the floor?

"Very funny, Dad!" I yelled down the stairs. "You could've just handed it to me!"

No answer. Dad had already gone. There was no one else home.

A tingly, nervous, swimming feeling rose in the pit of my stomach. It was a prank. It had to be. Dad had obviously snuck back into the house while I was in the shower and left it for me.

I'd just missed it on my way back to my room. Right. That explained everything.

Picking up the package, I tossed it into the top drawer of my desk to open when I got home. If today went anything like all my previous first days at a new school, I might need something to cheer me up later. Then I could give Dad a hard time about making me trip.

I slid the drawer closed and bounded for the stairs, opting to slide the last few steps on the railing before I jogged for the door.

The front of Saint Bernard's Catholic School appeared through the tapestry of modern buildings like an ancient monument to a bygone era. The high, Gothic-style towers, stone archways, and tall stained glass windows were a stark contrast to the sleek, urban area surrounding it. It was like something straight out of a superhero movie—an academy for gifted kids that could walk through walls and shoot lasers from their eyeballs. I expected to see a charming old guy in a wheelchair waiting just inside the door, ready to hand me a spandex suit and ask me what my secret superpower was. Somehow, I doubted cereal divination counted.

I hesitated on the curb across the street, watching as a bunch of other high school students about my age wearing gray-and-red uniforms filed up the steps and through the front doors.

My mouth scrunched. Dad hadn't said anything about *uniforms*.

Actually, he hadn't said much about this place at all. Only that it was supposed to be a really good school and I was lucky to have gotten in with my grades. Dad grew up in New Jersey, not far from here, so he knew a few of the admissions council members from when he was in college.

A couple of guys dressed in the school's uniform walked past close enough to get a good look at my future attire. Pleated slacks? A blazer? They carried the same bags and even had their hair parted and combed in the same exact style. Freaky.

I swallowed hard. Was I joining a cult? My sweaty hands curled into fists. Whatever happened, I had to stay positive. This was going to work. It had to.

I took a deep breath and started toward the front steps.

A loud, scraping crash behind me made me come to a flinching halt. I turned back, staring down at a girl who'd just tumbled onto the sidewalk from the backseat of a slick black sedan. She wore the same red-and-gray uniform, and a big, oddly shaped case lay on the ground next to her.

"Hey, are you okay?" I immediately stepped over and offered a hand to help her back up. "That looks kinda heavy. Need any help?"

The girl blinked up at me in surprise. The second our eyes met, my heart started racing like I'd been electrocuted. She was *gorgeous*. Lengths of thick golden blond hair fell down her back in loose, shining curls, and her wide, upturned eyes were a dark, stunning shade of bluish green. She was like something cut straight out of a magazine—almost too flawless to be real.

She hesitantly put her small, slender hand in mine and let me help her to her feet. While she stood there, dusting off her pleated gray skirt and examining a fresh tear in one of her stockings, I darted over to grab the huge, hard plastic instrument case.

"I can manage it—really, you don't have to do that," she protested and leaned in to try to stop me. Her hand brushed mine again.

My throat went dry. Had she felt that? Our hands touching for just a moment?

I stared at her, trying to remember how to talk while my face flushed like someone had lit my hair on fire. Alarm bells screamed in my head. I had to say something—now! Before it was too late. Something cool, something suave...

"A-are you sure? I really don't mind," I croaked. Okay, not my best line, but at least it wasn't embarrassing. Progress!

She studied me for a moment, those enchanting, catlike eyes darting over my features like she was trying to read my thoughts. Then I saw the corner of her mouth twitch with a brief, faint, but glorious smile. "Okay. If you insist."

"No problem. I was, uh, just on my way inside, too. Lead the way." I grabbed the case and started lugging it along, following her up the stairs and into the school.

"I've never seen you around before. Is this your first day?" She flicked those dazzling sea-green eyes back at me again, taking another hard look at my clothes.

"Uh, yeah. Actually it is."

She opened the door to let me by first. "Welcome to Saint Bernard's, then."

The school's main hall was unbelievable. My eyes roamed the domed glass ceilings, marble floors, shiny fixtures, and sloping, red-carpeted stairs, and I slowly set her case down just inside the door so I could take it in. It was like a scene from a Victorian era film. Everything was so elegant and steeped in a sense of elegant antiquity. Basically, the last place in the world a guy like me should be going to school.

Seriously, what was I doing here? Dad was out of his mind if he thought I would ever fit in at a school like this.

I was so busy turning in circles, my jaw still slack as I took it all in, that I didn't notice the group of students watching me. That is, until one of them giggled. I stopped short, almost crashing into the golden-haired girl who had paused to watch me gaping. Embarrassing.

"You're late." A short, sprightly looking girl swaggered up to us with a coy smile playing over her features. Her auburn red hair was arranged into long, silky smooth pigtails, and her light brown eyes glittered with a few flecks of gold. "What happened? I thought you were going to let me copy your notes."

The blond girl beside me ducked her head slightly. "I'm sorry. Mom and I were…" Her brow furrowed slightly as she stole a peek at me out of the corner of her eye. "It doesn't matter."

The redhead nudged my new acquaintance and tipped her chin in my direction. "Claire, who's this? A friend of yours?"

Claire—so that was her name.

She blushed and shook her head, making her golden curls swish. "No. I mean, we only just met. He's new."

"So I see." The redhead gave a sly little smirk as her eyes traveled down to my sneakers. "Nice shoelaces."

Somehow, I got the impression that wasn't really a compliment.

"Thanks," I answered anyway.

"You should probably go to the main office and let them know you're here," the blonde suggested quickly. When she reached for the handle on case, her hand brushed mine again and I got a warm, tingling feeling in the pit of my stomach. Had she done that on purpose? No—surely not.

"I can handle it from here," she added quietly, avoiding my gaze. "Thank you very much for your help. The main office is down that hall and to the left."

I opened my mouth to reply, maybe offer my name and ask for hers, but she was gone with her redheaded friend before I could get a word out. I watched them walk away and join another group of students like I didn't even exist. The redheaded girl's laughter echoed around the room as they climbed the stairs and disappeared. No one looked back.

Well, so much for that.

I stuffed my hands into my pockets and followed her directions until I found the office where the headmaster's secretary sat behind a claw-footed mahogany desk. She peered at me over the rim of her narrow reading glasses as I walked in. Once again, I got the full-body scan—like they'd never seen someone in street clothes before. She also seemed to take a similar interest in my shoelaces.

I blushed and looked down at the floor. "Uh, hey. I'm supposed to be starting today. I'm Koji Owens."

The secretary stood and waved me over to her desk. "Yes, we were expecting you. Right this way. The headmaster would like a word with you. When you're finished, I'll have your materials ready and you can go get fitted for your uniforms." She guided me to a door at the back of the room and opened it, standing by with what seemed to be a forced smile.

I hesitated, staring at the gold placard hanging on door that said HEADMASTER in gold letters.

"You'll be just fine." The secretary's brow arched, as though she could sense my apprehension and wanted me to hurry up. "This meeting is routine. We are a small school, and Headmaster Ignatius likes to go over our rules and policies with new students personally."

"O-okay." That didn't sound so bad. I managed to smile back at her before I went in.

The secretary shut the door behind me, and suddenly I was alone in a dimly lit office. Heavy shades covered the bay windows on the far side of the room, grand bookcases arranged with leather-bound tomes lined the walls, and polished wood plaques, awards, statuettes, and weird little figurines under glass cases were displayed throughout the room. A few of them looked like the kinds of old artifacts you'd see in a museum. Some of them even looked like they might be Egyptian, not that I was an expert.

Behind another big claw-footed desk sat a stiff-looking man in a tailored suit and tie. The clear block of glass on the edge of his desk had the name GERARD IGNATIUS engraved on it in swirling letters. He was probably around my dad's age, but his cold, severe expression made him seem much older—like his features had been chiseled out of stone. His dark eyes glittered in the gloom as he scanned me from head to toe, finishing with disapproving snort. I guess he had noticed my shoelaces, too.

"Mr. Owens, I presume?" He beckoned for me to sit in the chair directly across from his.

The expensive leather squeaked as I sank into it. "Yes, sir."

He opened a thick dark red folder with a golden crest leafed onto the front and studied its contents with a pursed lip. "I understand your father is a colonel in the Air Force?"

"Yes, sir," I repeated.

"Average grades at a public high school. Below average scores on your placement tests. Average IQ, average SAT score, below-average athletic ability. Hmm," Headmaster Ignatius murmured as he flipped through the pages. Pausing, he looked up with narrowed eyes. "Your father has quite a few friends on the admissions board, I understand. That is the only reason I can logically use to justify your presence here."

My palms started to sweat.

The headmaster shut the folder and placed his hands on top of it. "Let me be clear: this school is not a joke. Not to me, and not to any of the students or teachers. There are expectations for your conduct and performance, and regardless of who your father knows, you'll be expected to meet those expectations."

"Y-yes, sir."

"You will arrive every morning on time, no exceptions, unless you have a doctor's excuse in hand. Even on those absent days, you'll be responsible for making up whatever work you miss. We enforce a strict dress code and infractions will not be tolerated. No jewelry apart from a modest wristwatch or conservative religious medals is allowed. No absurd hair colors or styles. Only black dress shoes are permitted; absolutely no sneakers or tennis shoes." He paused there, as though making a point about my footwear choice today. "You'll be given four sets of uniforms, which are to be clean, properly ironed, and without any tears or stains. These uniforms are to be worn whenever you are on school property or attending a school-related event. There are no exceptions unless another faculty member or I give you explicit permission."

I was starting to wonder if I should be writing any of this down.

"You'll be issued a bag to carry your things in. Please have it monogrammed with your name in gold as soon as possible. Cell phones and other electronic devices are to be left in your locker during school hours. We have a firm policy on this. The first time you're found using a phone in class, it will be confiscated and returned only after you've served an hour of detention. The second time will result in a meeting with your father. The third time will be suspension. Do you understand?"

I swallowed hard. "Yes, I understand."

"Excellent. It goes without saying, Mr. Owens, that we are one of the finest private high schools in the country, and we intend to keep it that way. I expect you to behave like a mature, mentally competent individual." The headmaster pulled a piece of paper out of his desk drawer, folded it crisply in half, and handed it over to me. "This is your class schedule. You'll be required to take at least one elective class of your choosing per semester. Be aware that some of these classes also hold meetings or require practice sessions that take place outside normal school hours, and you will be expected to attend. You have until the end of the day to decide your elective. Once you've chosen, come back and let my secretary know."

I glanced at the schedule quickly. Geometry, Chemistry, Economics…it all looked pretty standard. That is, until I spotted elective stuff near the bottom of the page. Fencing? Debate Team? Chess Club? Ballroom dancing? Robotics Club? Tennis?

"You are fairly tall for your age—perhaps you would perform well on the swim team," the headmaster suggested.

I folded up the paper again and tucked it in my coat pocket. "Oh, uh, actually I can't swim."

He raised an eyebrow. "Not at all?"

"No, sorry." I chewed on the inside of my cheek.

Luckily, he didn't seem to care enough to ask why. "Well, there are plenty of other options for you to choose from."

I assumed that was it and the meeting was over. But when I started to get up, the headmaster spoke again. "I understand you were involved in a physical altercation at your last school?"

I froze.

Headmaster Ignatius leaned forward to rest his elbows on his desk. He laced his fingers together and let his chin rest on them, watching me with an ominous, probing smile. "The other boy involved was sent to the hospital. You were suspended for a month. In fact, the only thing that spared you from being expelled altogether was the fact that, according to bystanders, you had been taunted and physically assaulted previously by this particular student."

My shoulders tensed. I hung my head and stared at the floor, my heart pounding so hard I could feel it in my fingertips. I should've known this would come up again.

"There are police reports, reports from the other students who saw the fight, and even one from your father. But you didn't make a statement," he said. "So in your own words, I want to know what happened. Why did you beat him so badly? You certainly don't strike me as a fighter. Or at the very least, not an instigator."

My pulse roared in my ears. Every beat made my skin feel hot and my breathing become deeper. I focused on the tops of my sneakers as I fought not to let my mind go back to that day.

"Mr. Owens?"

"He kept getting in my face and calling me names," I growled in spite of myself. "He told me to go back to…" I stopped, setting my jaw as I tried to keep my voice steady. "I-it doesn't matter. He said a lot of things. None of it matters now."

"So you hit him?"

"No. Dad told me just to ignore it; some people are just like that. But I saw him doing the same thing to another girl from our class. She'd just moved from Korea and didn't speak much English yet. He kept grabbing her and trying to scare her. I told him to stop. So he punched me in the stomach and spit on me." Slowly, I lifted my gaze to meet the headmaster's. "Then I hit him."

The headmaster and I stared at one another from across his desk while the seconds ticked by, counted noisily by the grandfather clock in the corner of the room. Every muscle in my body drew tight, and heat bloomed through my chest like wildfire. I didn't understand what this had to do with anything. It was one fight more than a year ago. I'd never gotten into a situation like that before then, and I hadn't done it since.

At last, Headmaster Ignatius leaned back in his seat and nodded slowly. "I see. While you may believe your actions were justified, you should take note that I will not tolerate any physical altercations like that at this school. Any infraction, regardless of the reason, will result in anyone involved being expelled."

I squeezed the straps of my backpack until my knuckles turned white. "Yes, sir. I understand."

"Heroics are best saved for outside the school, Mr. Owens. I can't allow street justice to prevail here," he said as he waved me off. "You are dismissed."

CHAPTER 2

The headmaster's secretary took me down the hall to a different office to get fitted for my uniforms. She left me under the supervision of a heavyset, elderly lady who peered up at me through glasses about two inches thick. I didn't understand how she could see at all. Her glasses made her eyes seem enormous, like she'd just taped two magnifying glasses together and called it a day.

She herded me toward a dressing pedestal and made me take off my coat. Then I stood with my arms spread out, trying not to move while the old woman climbed all around me with a measuring tape.

"Such a skinny boy," she muttered, shuffling away into a storage room.

When she came back, she had a pair of charcoal gray slacks, a white button-down shirt, a gray tie, and a dark red knitted sweater with the school's golden crest on the front right pocket.

"The blazers are custom-made for your measurements," she explained as she carried the uniform into a closet-sized fitting room. "You'll be given four of them, two more shirts, two more sweaters, and two more pairs of slacks. See that you get some sensible shoes and black dress socks."

Before I could thank her, she shut the dressing room door in my face and left me alone to change. The shirt was scratchy and smelled like starch. The pants were all right, maybe a little too big in the waist, but nothing I couldn't fix with a belt. When you wear a 34x36 in pants, you get used to things being either too short or too loose in the waist.

It took me four tries to get the tie on properly, and even then it came out crooked. Ties were not my thing. I'd only ever worn them whenever Dad had to attend a ceremony for work and once at someone's wedding. The sweater was the only part that didn't drive me nuts. It was soft and comfortable. The sleeves were a little too long, which I liked.

I rolled up my old clothes inside my jacket before I stepped out of the dressing room…and lurched to a halt, nearly knocking over the rack of dress shirts next to me.

The beautiful blond girl from the sidewalk was standing right in front of me, showing the old woman the fresh tear in her stockings. She stole a quick glance in my direction as I floundered, trying to steady the clothing rack so it didn't collapse.

"I'll get you another pair, dear. Just a moment." The old woman used a much gentler tone with her. Then she cast me a hard look though those massive glasses before hobbling away to the storage room again.

Suddenly, the silence was deafening. Standing alone with that girl in the small office, I racked my brain for something intelligent to say. Anything. I'd have settled for a knock-knock joke.

"You look nice." Her voice was quiet. She still wouldn't look at me for more than a second or two.

"Thanks." I almost choked.

"Are you a junior?"

"No, sophomore."

"Oh." Her brows lifted and she glanced me over again. "You look…well, maybe it's just that you're tall."

I managed a smile. "I come from a long family line of giraffes."

Her mouth quirked and she stifled a laugh. "What's your name?"

"Koji." I paused, trying to remember the rest of it. It was hard to think about anything when she was smiling at me like that.

"Nice to meet you, Koji." She opened her mouth, maybe to say something else, but the old woman returned brandishing a fresh pair of stockings and a disapproving scowl. She shooed me away from the dressing room and, after poking around at me to make sure the uniform fit properly, handed me a black leather backpack to replace my peasant one. Then she sent me on my way.

I stopped in the hall to cram my normal clothes into my old backpack before I returned to the secretary's office. I almost crashed into a girl with long dark hair who was darting out of the office as I came through the door. She stumbled back, her eyes wide and face flushed. The second it dawned on me to introduce myself, the girl darted away without a word. Weird. Was she scared of me or something? I'd never considered myself to be an intimidating guy. Tall and lanky, maybe, but not the sort anyone might flee from in terror.

As promised, the secretary had all my textbooks in a neat stack waiting for me, along with a locker number and combination lock when I returned.

"You look very nice, Mr. Owens," she offered while I loaded all my new books into my stylish rich-kid bag.

"Oh, uh, thanks." I forced a smile—despite the fact that she was staring down at my feet as though wondering why I was still wearing my sneakers with the *Dragon Ball Z* shoelaces. "So, where's second year Chemistry?"

"Left wing, second floor, room 109," she answered quickly. "Your locker is on the way, if you want to drop your things off before you go in. Good luck on your first day."

It took me a few minutes to find my way back to the main hall, and then to the left wing. After walking up and down the halls and nearly strolling into the wrong room twice, I finally found the right Chemistry class. The first bell still hadn't rung yet, so other students filed in wearing similar expressions of glassy-eyed disinterest.

I took a minute to scour the rows of lockers in the hall outside for the one that was supposed to be mine. It wasn't hard— all the gray-painted lockers had the students' names labeled on the front. Mine was still blank.

Opening the locker door, I unzipped my old backpack first. I quickly yanked out one of my notebooks and a few pencils and prepared to cram the rest of the bag into the locker. I'd deal with organizing it later, if ever.

There was just one small problem.

My locker wasn't empty.

A little package wrapped in a purple handkerchief sat in the bottom of it, like it had been waiting there for me all morning.

I dropped my bag in shock and took a step back.

Someone was messing with me. That had to be it. Someone was playing a prank. But who? I didn't have any friends here. I didn't know anyone except Dad. Was this his idea of a joke? Had he followed me to school?

I glanced both ways down the hallway to check for anyone that might be watching me for a reaction. But there was no one.

All right, fine. Time to get to the bottom of this. With my heart beating wildly, I grabbed the package out of my locker and started to open it.

The first bell rang, clanging so loudly I almost jumped right out of my dress code violating shoes. There wasn't time to open it now. I couldn't be late to my first class on my first day.

I crammed the package into my locker again and shut the door, locking it just in case. I'd have to come back for my stuff later, anyway. Maybe then I could open it and figure out who was messing with me.

I took a deep breath, putting the mysterious package out of my mind, and started for the classroom door. With every step, I struggled to muster up confident momentum. Meanwhile, the door drew closer and closer. This was it—my first chance at a first impression. I couldn't screw it up.

Suddenly, my legs locked. Faced with a Chemistry classroom full of strangers, I stood frozen in the doorway. My stomach churned with anxiety. Not this again. Sick—I was gonna be sick.

It was like this every time since kindergarten. I never got used to being the new kid. It was uncomfortable on so many levels. Maybe I could have dealt with everyone staring at me like I was from another planet, but having to stand there while the teacher made funny faces and struggled to pronounce my first name was unbearable. It was even worse if I got prompted to tell them something about myself.

"Everything okay?" a soft, angelic female voice asked.

The blond girl was standing behind me, an eyebrow arched while she waited for me to move so she could go inside.

"O-oh, yeah. Everything's fine," I lied and scooted out of her way.

"Are you sure? You look a little...green."

I swallowed and managed a squeaky, terrified laugh. "Just, uh, you know, getting my bearings. Big place, huh?"

Now both eyebrows lifted. "Was your last school smaller?"

With her captivating stare fixed on me like that, I didn't know. Where had I gone to school before? Tucson? Mars? I couldn't remember. Too late, I realized I'd never answered. I was just standing there, staring at her with my mouth hanging open.

She gave a melodic little giggle and patted my shoulder. "Well, take it easy, Koji. You'll get used to things here. Good luck." She smiled, sending me into a mild cardiac arrest, and then turned to go to a seat on the front row.

Wow. I stood enraptured, watching her float away with her shimmering golden curls bouncing at her back. There had to be a pair of white feathery wings hidden somewhere under there. Nothing else made sense.

Then I noticed—the seat next to hers was empty.

A hard knot formed in my throat. This was my chance, wasn't it? I could sit by her. It wouldn't be creepy, right? She was the only person here I kinda, sorta knew.

Another guy breezed past me into the classroom, ignoring my existence completely, and plopped down right next to her. He was tall, like me, but instead of being skinny and awkward, his biceps tested the seams of his blazer and his dark brown hair was gelled and styled to perfection. His chiseled jaw and cleft chin made him seem older. He draped one of his muscular arms along the back of her chair as he started talking to her.

So much for that.

I shuffled past them, head down so hopefully no one would see my face turning red. Shambling down the aisle of student lab tables, I dropped my bag next to the only empty seat left, in the back of the room.

The person I'd be sharing the table with didn't even look up as I sank into my chair. He wasn't a big guy, like Mr. Biceps. In fact, he was skinny like me, although much shorter. He slouched back, arms crossed over his chest as he stared up at the ceiling. The muffled, thumping rhythm of music came from the padded earphones he wore. Techno music? It was hard to tell from this distance.

I sighed and leaned against the lab table. My gaze was drawn back to the front of the room, where the girl who was quickly becoming my vision of perfection still sat next to Mr. Biceps. How could I compete with somebody like that? Sitting together, they looked like someone's idea of an experiment with genetic perfection. Nothing weird about that at all—just two deities, sitting alongside the rest of us mortals, learning basic chemistry.

"Gotta death wish or something?" my seatmate mumbled over the music buzzing from his earphones.

"Huh?"

He gave an exaggerated eye roll. "You must be new."

I stuck my hand out to shake his. "Uh, yeah. I am! I'm Koji Ow—"

"Word to the wise—stay away from the princess." The guy combed his fingers through his messy, surfer blond hair. Pivoting in his seat to face me, he pulled his earphones off to let them hang around his neck.

I tried to laugh it off, but it came out more like the panicked squeak of a chipmunk getting stepped on. "Princess?"

"Claire Faust. Heiress to *the* Camridore-Fausts." He gestured with his eyes, flicking them in the direction of the girl with those radiant curls that caught the morning sunlight like polished brass.

"Uh…"

"Seriously?" He sighed and leaned forward, resting his elbows on his knees. "Fine, it's like this. The Camridore-Fausts are famous, have been for basically all of history, or so they claim. Filthy rich, too. Their family has produced some of the world's most prestigious musicians, composers, and musical know-it-alls. Every one of them's a prodigy of some kind."

"Wow." My face flushed.

"Yeah, wow." He didn't sound as impressed. "Anyway, you better steer clear. They don't associate with commoners like us, and they won't like it if they catch you sniffing around their princess. Claire's totally out of our league. She might as well be on a different planet."

The air went out of my chest like someone pricking a party balloon.

"See that guy over there?" He pointed to Mr. Biceps. "That's Damien Blount, another spawn of the rich and famous. They're engaged."

My jaw dropped. "Engaged? Like to get married? Already?"

"Since freshman year, dude. It's one of those parentally arranged things. Word is, they've been 'meant for each other' since birth."

"Oh…" Geez. Was that even legal?

He leaned in even closer, squinting at me like he was trying to figure out what was wrong with me. "You're gonna get eaten alive at this school. What did you say your name was?"

"Koji Owens," I muttered.

His mouth curled into a mischievous smirk. "I'm Drake Collins."

I was trying to figure out if I should swap seats, run, or play it tough and hold my ground. I wasn't good at reading people— good or bad.

Before I could decide, he reached out to shake my hand. "Stick with me. I'll keep you from getting murdered on your first day."

I blinked. Was he… saying we'd be friends? No way. It wasn't never this easy for me to make friends. I tried my best to study him, looking for any evidence that he was joking or jerking me around for fun.

Drake shrugged and started putting his headphones back on, then held out a hand to waggle his fingers. "Let me see your schedule."

Ah—there it was. Ugh. I should have known.

I yanked the paper out of my pocket and held onto it with a frown. "Look, I mean, I appreciate the offer. But I'm not actually all that good at school stuff, so if you're wanting me to do your homework or let you cheat off my papers—"

"I have an IQ of 160," he retorted with a smirk, swiping the schedule out of my hand. "You know, like Einstein? So the last thing I want is you or anyone else touching my homework."

I stared at him—slouched posture, messy surfer hair, cognac-colored eyes—and tried to visualize the genius hidden somewhere under his bored expression. "Seriously?"

"How else do you think I got into this school?"

I'd just assumed he was rich like the other kids. He was wearing the uniform, after all.

"My mom's a nurse. She does fine, but we're not millionaires. I'm here on scholarship," he replied as though he could read my mind. "I am wondering how you got in here, though. Those shoelaces look about four years old, the shoes are even older, standard conservative haircut, not to mention your accent is all over the place. Diluted Southern with a touch of Korean, right? Maybe a hint of Texan, too? I'm betting you're a military kid. Obviously not rich. So what's the story there?"

"My dad knows some people," I admitted, face burning with humiliation. For some reason, it felt like a pathetic excuse. Like I'd conned and swindled my way in where I didn't belong.

"Figures." Drake was still perusing my list of classes. "We have this class, English, and lunch together. I sit in the far left corner in every one of them, so look for me there."

"So if you're that smart, why aren't you in advanced classes?"

"I am. But everyone is required to take the classes on the standard course of study. It's a school policy. So instead of taking a bunch of lame electives in the afternoon, the school has private tutors come in from the university to teach me Linear Signals and Systems Analysis, Thermodynamics, and Advanced Computer Systems classes."

I had no idea what half of those words meant. Computer—that one I got.

Drake chuckled. "Did your brain short circuit or something?"

"Sorry." I closed my mouth. "I was just thinking that I probably won't last a week here."

"You'll be fine. I doubt you're the dumbest one here."

"Really?"

He grinned darkly, amber eyes glittering with mischief. "You don't have to be smart to be privileged. Most of the student body here comes from obscenely wealthy families. You're looking at the next generation's masters of the universe. Their parents are all CEOs, politicians, or famous for some reason. But that doesn't make them smart. In fact, I doubt most of these kids could microwave a bag of popcorn on their own."

My eyes were instinctively drawn to her—the princess, Claire Faust. She sat at the front of the room, gazing out the window dreamily. The pale morning light made her skin glow like porcelain. I bet she could make a bag of popcorn. Then we could share it while we watched *Star Trek* and...

Drake snapped his fingers right in front of my nose. I flinched and shot him a glare, although I could feel my ears burning now.

"Tone it down, lover boy." He chuckled. "Remember what I said. She's Venus. You're Pluto."

Right.

He went back to scanning my class list. "So what about your free elective? It's still blank."

I sighed. "I haven't decided yet. Not swimming, though."

"Well, there's fencing, judo, ballroom dancing, tennis, soccer—"

"Yeah, I know. I read the list."

"And?"

I frowned and looked down at the top of my desk. "I'm not very athletic."

"I'm the president of the Robotics Club. You could do that," he suggested. "We have a class period for working during the day, and then we meet after school sometimes."

I forced a smile. "Thanks, but I'd probably wind up accidentally blowing something up."

"Chess Club?"

I shook my head.

"Play any instruments?"

"Nope."

Drake snorted. "Is there anything you *are* good at?"

"I like to draw. And I'm a pretty good cook. Or at least, that's what my dad says. I do all the cooking since he works all the time." I scratched the back of my head and tried to think of something, anything, that I was good at. The headmaster had really hit the nail on the head—I was the epitome of average.

"So take art then." Drake folded up my class list and handed it back over. "I hear in senior year they bring in real female models for nude sketches."

I started to blush again. "T-that's—"

"Too easy." He laughed, and I realized he was teasing me. Great. Einstein? More like a mad scientist, and I was little lab mouse scrambling through the cheese maze.

"Just do it. It'll be an easy grade if you're good at that art stuff," he said, folding his hands behind his head.

I couldn't argue the easy grade logic. And since the rest of my class load looked like it was going to fry my brain, a class like that might be the only thing that saved me. I did like to sketch. I mostly drew cartoons, comics, and things like that. I'd never tried painting before. Who knew? Maybe it would be fun.

Chemistry class got underway when the teacher, a short, stout woman, entered the room. I sat, held in suspense, for the teacher to make some kind of introduction for me, but she never did. Dodged that bullet.

I was starting three weeks after the normal beginning of the school year, thanks once again to the Air Force, so I was already behind. Drake would be my lab partner, which was fine by me. He even offered to lend me his notes so I could catch up.

That was pretty much how things went in every class for the rest of the day. I sat in the back, stood up to awkwardly introduce myself as the new kid if the teacher called me out, and hung around after class to beg a total stranger to let me copy their notes. There was so much to figure out and catch up on.

At lunch, I sat in the back of the cafeteria at the far end of one of the long dining tables. Across from me, Drake had already established that this was "his" corner of the cafeteria where he sat every day. Now I guess it was "our" corner.

I poked at the oven-broiled filet of fish served over cilantro rice pilaf and wished I knew a magic word to transform it into a cheeseburger. Or pizza. Or basically anything else.

"Don't like fish?" Drake eyed me curiously.

I shrugged. "Not unless its deep fried and in stick-form."

He laughed. "Really? Come on, the lunches here aren't half bad."

"It's got some weird sauce on it." I pushed my lunch tray away and folded my arms so I could lay my head down.

"Touchy, aren't we?" Drake asked around mouthfuls of his own food. "So how were your other classes?"

I groaned and looked up at him. "Like trying to run a marathon after I've been shot in the leg. I'm already way behind."

He grinned around a mouthful of fish. "First days always suck. Try not to sweat it."

I *was* trying. I'd been trying every year since, well, as long as I could remember. What was the point? I'd get used to it here, make a few friends, maybe even meet a girl who didn't think I was a complete dork. I'd start to fit in, feel comfortable, and then it would all get ripped out from under me. Sure, Dad said this time would be different. This time we were staying for good. But could I honestly trust that? The only thing consistent about our lives was that everything changed. Why would this time be any different? And if orders did come down to send us somewhere else, it's not like Dad could do much to stop it.

Getting attached, getting comfortable, always made things harder when it came time to say goodbye. That was the main reason I'd given up on all forms of social media. It sucked to watch all those friends I'd made and then left behind get on with their happy lives like I'd never existed. Pictures of them spending time together, group vacations or trips, always left me feeling bitter and excluded. Once I was gone, it was like I never existed.

"Hey, check it out." Drake was looking past me.

I turned around to see Claire and her friend, the redheaded girl with the long pigtails, walking by to sit together at the table behind us. My eyes met Claire's met for half a second, maybe less, and I could have sworn I saw her smile.

My heart skipped a beat.

"Why would you do that?" I whispered as I whirled back around in my seat to glare at Drake.

He was grinning wolfishly. "Cause it's funny. I've never seen anyone blush like that. Your whole head turns red."

I laid my head on the table again.

"Aw, come on. Lighten up." I felt him poke the top of my head with the prongs of his fork. "Okay, fine. I won't tease you about her anymore, you big baby. Hey, do you still want copies of my notes?"

"Yeah." I sighed. "I suck at chemistry."

"Maybe I can help tutor you or whatever."

I lifted my head, arching a brow in suspicion. "Really?"

Drake nodded. "I'm not a miracle worker, though, so no promises."

"That would be great." I smiled—not because he was offering to tutor me but because he actually *wanted* to hang out with me. I had a friend! "My house is close by. We could walk there."

"Okay," he agreed between bites of rice. "Tomorrow, though. I have a Robotics Club meeting this afternoon. We're getting ready to compete in the semifinals next month. Sure you don't want to come check it out?"

I scrunched my nose. "Trust me, you don't want me anywhere near your, uh, robot. Not unless you want to lose that competition."

"Fine, if you say so." He laughed. "Maybe we could use you to sabotage the other teams."

I couldn't resist a grin. "Now that I could probably do."

Knowing I'd already made at least one friend made the rest of the day seem less miserable. It gave me something to think about other than the growing pile of homework I had to catch up on. I went to my last two classes and didn't even mind that I sat by myself at the back of the classroom.

When it was time for my last class, the elective, I made my way back down to the secretary's office and let her know I wanted to take art.

She blinked. "Do you paint?"

I barked a nervous laugh. "Uh, well, no, but I like to draw."

"I see." She adjusted her glasses and picked up her phone, punching in numbers and talking to someone quickly about a new student joining the class.

"The art studio is in the right wing on the fifth floor. You'll see it." She handed me a slip of paper with her signature scribbled on it—a hall pass.

I stopped by my locker on the way upstairs and grabbed my other backpack and the rest of my textbooks so I didn't have to go back after the last bell rang. The mysterious little package still sat at the bottom of my locker, but there wasn't room next to all my new textbooks and borrowed stacks of notes to copy. I hesitated, then slammed the door. I'd grab it later—maybe tomorrow. Right now, I had to focus on finding my last class.

Lugging two fully loaded book bags to the top floor was exhausting. By the time I got to the top, I was panting and realizing I seriously needed to start working out, especially if these stairs were going to be an everyday thing. I wheezed my way down the hall and found the pair of double doors labeled HALL OF FINE ART.

Cracking the door open an inch or two, I peeked inside.

It wasn't anything like the other classrooms I'd been in. The room was open and airy, with one whole wall of French windows that let the afternoon sunlight pour in over the paint-spattered wood floors. Canvases covered every inch of available wall space around freestanding shelves piled with art supplies. The air had that musky, fresh paint smell. Easels positioned in a big circle surrounded a central pedestal where the teacher, a youngish man with a neatly trimmed beard, sat casually.

He smiled brightly when he saw me edging into the room and waved me over. "It's okay, don't be shy. Come on in."

I could have hugged him. That was the friendliest any of the teachers had been to me so far. "Sorry I'm late. I have a pass."

The teacher took my hall pass and crammed it into his pocket without looking at it. He nodded to an open easel. "Take a seat. I'm Mr. Molins. We're having an open discussion today about our next project. Everyone, this is Koji. He's a new student here. Try to make him feel welcome."

I gave a small, embarrassed wave before speed walking to the first open seat I saw. I felt a little safer behind one of the wooden easels. I dropped my bags and sat down on the swiveling barstool.

"Maddie, would you mind showing him the ropes until he gets comfortable here?"

At the teacher's request, the girl sitting at the easel next to mine slowly turned to look at me. Up—I should say she looked up at me, because she probably wasn't an inch over five feet. She was so petite; I would've mistaken her for a middle school kid if I'd bumped into her elsewhere. Looking at her, I got the weird feeling I'd seen her before.

She'd been vigorously shaking a bottle of blue paint, mixing it I guess, but when I sat down, she froze. Her soft, doe eyes widened as we stared at one another. For a few seconds, I thought she might say something—or pass out, because it didn't look like she was breathing. I still couldn't shake the nagging suspicion that I had seen her somewhere before.

Regardless, she was going to be my new easel neighbor. So I needed to make a good impression. I prepped my best attempt at a charming smile. "Uh, hey." I tried to sound casual. "I'm Koji. Nice to meet—"

The cap on the paint bottle blasted off like a cork from a champagne bottle. Blue paint exploded into the air. The girl squeaked in alarm as bright blue droplets spattered her face, arms, and uniform.

Silence fell over the classroom. For a few seconds, all I could do was stare at her in shock.

"I-I'm so sorry! I'll be right back!" The girl shot out of her chair like she'd been fired from a cannon and ran out of the room.

Luckily, I hadn't been caught in the crossfire. My new uniform was clean, so I leaned down to pick up the bottle of paint just as Mr. Molins came over to help clean up the mess. Judging by the amount of dried colored droplets already caked onto the floors, this wasn't the first time someone had spilt some paint. It was weirdly beautiful, like the floor itself was a piece of art.

When Maddie returned, the area around her easel was clean and Mr. Molins was back to talking about some big art project he was planning for the class to participate in. It had something to do with keeping an art journal through the year. I couldn't really concentrate on it, though, because Maddie sat next to me without a word, looking as though she were trying to hide behind her long, smooth black hair.

Hm. Maybe it was best not to embarrass her by trying to talk to her right then. That might only make it worse. I'd just wait and introduce myself tomorrow, when she wasn't still speckled with blue paint. Yeah—then we could start fresh like this had never happened.

"So start thinking about what kind of art journal you want to keep. It can be anything you like, so long as it tells the story of the year." Mr. Molins ended his lecture right as the last bell chimed. "Tomorrow we'll go around the room and discuss your ideas."

I was going to like this class; I could feel it already. With a spring in my step, I grabbed my black leather bag and started out of the room. As far as first days went, this one hadn't been so terrible. Now it would get easier. I knew where to go and what I had to get done. I could handle this. And if Drake was able to help hammer some chemistry into my brain, I might even make good grades.

"Excuse me? It's Koji, right?" A soft voice called out to me as I got to the bottom of the stairwell in the main hall.

I stopped, glancing back to see Maddie hurrying down after me, holding out my old backpack. Her face was flushed beneath the few blue smudges she'd missed, but I figured that was be-cause she'd been running to catch up.

"You forgot this." She held my bag out at arm's length.

"Oh, thanks." I took it from her and gave her my best I'm-a-friendly-giant smile. "I'm sorry about the paint."

Maddie's soft gray eyes went wide, and she ducked her head to hide behind her hair again. "No! It was my completely fault. I must have squeezed the tube too hard."

"There you are, Picasso." An arm draped over my shoulder. Drake seemed to materialize out of thin air, leaning against me with that bored yet smug grin. "Look at you, juggling two girls on your first day."

"What?" I started to protest. Sure, Maddie seemed nice and she was kind of cute, but that didn't mean I was hitting on her. When I looked back in her direction, hoping for a little support that I *wasn't* flirting with her, all I caught was a glimpse of her dark curtain of hair swishing as she darted back up the stairs. Maddie disappeared without a word.

"Nice one." Drake laughed.

"Why is she so scared of me?"

"I dunno, man. You are pretty terrifying." He quirked his mouth, then gave a disinterested yawn. "Don't worry about it. She's kind of weird anyway."

"Right. 'Cause we're normal," I shrugged out from under his arm. "Einstein and Picasso—just two regular guys."

He didn't reply as he fell in step beside me, sliding his headphones back over his ears. Drake Collins was going to take some getting used to. This whole place would. It was only the first day, and I already had the sense my new life here wasn't going to be anything like the one I'd left behind in Arizona.

I just couldn't decide if it was going to be better...or way worse.

CHAPTER 3

Dad wasn't home when I arrived back at the house. Big shocker there. He always worked late, even when he flew F-16s. I guess nothing had changed in that department.

It hadn't taken me long to figure out that working insane hours and overloading an already heavy schedule with more obligations was not something unique to my dad. That "I'll sleep when I'm dead" mentality basically summed up every fighter pilot I'd ever met, and my dad was no exception. Usually, he left every morning way before I had to get up for school and got home after I'd already finished my homework, eaten dinner, and fallen asleep in front of the TV. Sometimes I wouldn't have known he'd even been home at all if not for a sticky note left on the fridge. That was how we communicated during night-flying weeks when his hours were even stranger.

Anyway, I had hoped this new job meant he could home earlier. This did not bode well. So much for this place being different.

I tried not to dwell on that as I climbed the steps to my room, weaving through the maze of unopened moving boxes toward my bed. Kicking off my shoes, I peeled off the layers of that awful, scratchy uniform and tossed it into a heap on the floor. A loud *thunk* when my pants hit the top of the stack made me groan. I'd left my phone in the pocket. Leaning over the edge of the bed, I fished through the pockets of my slacks until I found it. Luckily, the screen wasn't cracked. If I cracked another phone screen this month, Dad would never let me live it down.

Sweatpants and my favorite T-shirt with the vintage Batman logo on the front were much more comfortable and happened to be stashed away in the luggage I'd brought from the hotel. Dressed for ultimate relaxation, I dropped my phone into my pocket and stretched, staring sadly at the empty wall where I wished my TV was hanging. I didn't dare try to set it up myself. Electronics didn't last long after I touched them—cell phones and televisions included.

My belly was growling after skipping lunch. It was time to forage. Wandering back downstairs, I rifled through the groceries Dad had bought to get us through to the weekend. He wasn't much of a shopper. I usually handled that. Frozen microwave dinners, packages of ramen noodles, a loaf of bread, some sliced cheese, a gallon of milk, a couple of bags of potato chips, and a few cans of premade soup were all I had to work with.

Everyone probably assumed me being on the skinny side had to be a genetic thing. Actually, it was most likely due to the fact that I'd been living off this crap since I was a kid. Dad couldn't cook to save his life. I was walking evidence that you could indeed survive on frozen and prepackaged food—but you weren't going to win any awards for bodybuilding doing it. My only salvation was that I had learned to cook a few things out of sheer desperation, so as soon as we got the kitchen unpacked, I was going to the store for some real food.

For now, I went with one of the frozen dinners and leaned on the counter, watching it slowly rotate while the microwave hummed happily. I wondered if Claire Faust had ever eaten a frozen dinner. Probably not.

The microwave finished with a melodic *ding*, and I went back upstairs and shut my door, prepared to wall myself in like a hermit and start studying. I put the microwave dinner down on my desk and opened my old backpack, turning it upside down and shaking to empty out the contents. My clothes, notebooks, pencils, and cell phone charger poured onto the bed.

And something else.

An all-too-familiar little package, wrapped in a purple silk handkerchief, landed on top of the pile.

Okay. This was getting too weird for me. I knew the instant I saw it that I hadn't put it in my bag. I'd left it in my locker before art class. There was no denying it now—this package was *following* me.

My hands shook as I untied it, spreading the handkerchief out on my palm. Pulling back the last corner of the shiny, eggplant-colored fabric revealed a circlet of old, worn leather. It looked like a cuff bracelet.

Dropping the handkerchief on the bed, I held the bracelet up to the light of my desk lamp. Three bands of tightly woven, dark leather held something that looked like a seashell firmly against a wide black band. The triangular-shaped shell had smooth, rounded edges like a large guitar pick, and it shimmered in the light with ghostly vivid colors like mother-of-pearl.

I grinned. Jewelry wasn't usually my thing, but this was sort of cool looking. It was way too big, though. I easily slipped my hand through it and positioned it on my wrist like a watchband. Interesting as it was, I couldn't wear it. It would fall off, and as far as I could tell, there wasn't any way to adjust it or tighten the band. Oh well. Maybe Dad could return it, or we could find someone who could resize it for—

Suddenly, the band snapped tight on my wrist.

I flailed back and tripped over my desk chair, knocking over a tower of boxes that crashed on top of me like an avalanche. The top one hit me square in the chest. Thankfully, it must have only had some of my action figures in it; anything heavier might have crushed my ribs.

I fought my way free of the boxes until I could sit up again, grabbed the bracelet, and started pulling. I yanked as hard as I could, but the bracelet didn't move. I twisted my hand, used my teeth—anything to try to get it off.

It wouldn't budge.

A cold knot of dread wrenched in the pit of my stomach. Time for drastic measures.

Darting downstairs, I began throwing open boxes in the kitchen until I found the one with the cutlery. Seizing the heavy-duty meat scissors from our knife set, I slipped the band into it and tried to cut it off.

The metal scissors cracked over the leather band, peppering my socked feet with shards. My heart thrashed in my ears as that cold knot of panic tightened in my gut.

I tried greasing my arm with lotion, but the bracelet just shifted slightly on my wrist. No way was it fitting over my hand. It was only after I'd broken Dad's box cutter trying to cut it off again that I sat back in my desk chair, paralyzed with horror and totally out of ideas.

What if it was stuck there forever?

"This isn't happening," I muttered under my breath. "It's just a bracelet. I can get it off. Maybe it's just really tough leather."

But I knew better. Something else was up. First the package had followed me around all day, randomly popping up when I least expected it, and now...

I shook my head and rubbed my forehead, pacing back and forth across my bedroom. I wasn't ready to admit the impossible. Not yet. There had to be a reasonable explanation.

With the light of my desk lamp, I studied the bracelet again. The shell gleamed innocently, shimmering in hues of purple and yellow. Then I saw it—something else rippling on its glossy surface. It looked like writing, but it was so faint I could barely see it. A watermark? Or a symbol? I had to angle the bracelet just right to even tell that it was there, and even then it was impossible to read. Brushing my thumb over it, I tried feeling for any evidence of the script on its smooth surface. There was none.

Whatever that mark was, it had been etched or pressed into the shell without leaving a noticeable trace.

"Come on, stupid," I whispered to it. "Why won't you come off? What do you want from me?"

A brilliant white light exploded from the shell. It filled my room, blinding me and sending me floundering out of my chair a second time.

By the time I hit the floor, my body felt like it was on fire. My arms and legs tingled with wild, electric heat. My spine curled as every muscle in my body flexed out of control. My lungs constricted as my body jerked wildly. I couldn't breathe. I couldn't even scream for help.

Then it was over. The light vanished. So did the pain. I sucked in a deep, ragged breath.

I screamed for help as I sat up. Only something wasn't right. My voice…didn't sound like me anymore. My voice had come out more like a deep growl.

Out of the corner of my eye, I caught a glimpse of myself in my dresser's mirror. Terror and awe rolled over me like an icy tidal wave, freezing me in place. I blinked, wheezed, and bit back another scream.

Oh no.

With a frantic breath, I staggered to my feet and faced a reflection that shouldn't have been mine. It couldn't be. There was no way.

My clothes were gone, and in their place were gleaming black scales. Each diamond-shaped scale was infused right into my skin, which was now as dark as onyx. The scales covered my hands and my forearms, contouring along my chest, back, and shoulders. More went from my waist, down my legs, all the way to my feet—which were now reptilian shaped so that I had to walk on the balls of my feet, balanced on four thick toes. Each digit was tipped with a curled talon as sharp as a shard of obsidian glass. I had similar claws on the ends of my fingers where my nails should have been.

Between a frame that rippled with corded muscle under a sheen of black scales, and features that hid behind a grafted-in mask of more scales, I was unrecognizable. Six-inch black horns poked out of my lengthy, dark hair and swept back over my long, pointed ears. I found even more horns forming a ridge down my back to the end of my, er, tail. Yep. I had a tail.

Backing away from the mirror, I wobbled to balance with my lizard legs, feet, and tail. My bare, scaly chest heaved in frantic breaths as I stared into the glowing neon-blue eyes of my reflection. My vertical pupils narrowed to hair-thin slits.

I dared to step closer to get a better look.

And then I noticed the wings.

Sprouting from my back were, two huge, leathery black wings. The tops nearly brushed the ceiling in my room and the tips dragged the floor. As if by instinct, I flexed my shoulders and chest, and the wings moved. My body tingled with wild excitement as I twitched my shoulders again, watching the wings shift and respond when I used different muscles in my back, shoulders, and chest. I had wings—*real* wings.

"T-this isn't happening," I whimpered and stumbled back, wobbling awkwardly on my scaly feet. My big wings flapped clumsily and knocked over a few more boxes.

It wasn't real. It couldn't be. This was a dream; there was no other explanation. Unless...

I looked down at my wrist, where the bracelet had been, to find that one of my scales wasn't black. Shining with the same pearlescent hue as the shell on the bracelet, one solitary scale on my wrist shimmered as white as a pearl.

It wasn't a shell. I didn't even know if it was something from this planet. But whatever it was, it had done this to me.

The longer I stared at it, the more I could sense how that single scale thrummed with energy that crackled through my veins like tongues of white fire. It made my pulse race, my muscles clench, and my spirit roar past every shred of self-doubt and fear. Whatever it was, that bracelet had awakened something deep inside of me.

But why? Why me?

Downstairs, the front door slammed. Heavy footsteps approached, coming up the stairs.

"Koji? You home?" Dad called.

Oh no. *No!* This wasn't happening. Not now.

I whirled around, knocking over more boxes. I had to hide. No—hiding wasn't going to help.

I had to leave. Right now.

I staggered across my bedroom to the big round window on the far wall overlooking the street below. Apparently no one had bothered opening it for years because even with my new physique, I only managed to wedge the rusty hinges about a third of the way before they stuck solid.

Crap. If I forced it, I might just crack the whole window off.

At the top of the stairs, Dad's footsteps stopped. "Koji? Everything okay in there?"

I was out of time and options.

Sucking in a deep breath, I squeezed, wrenched, and twisted my way through the gap in the window.

Dad was at the door, rapping it with his knuckles. *Knock, knock, knock.* "Koji?"

With one last twist, my body popped free. I sucked in a breath of cold night air…and instantly lost my balance again. I fell, tumbling end over end down the steeply slanted roof. In a frenzy of panic, I dug my clawed toes into the roof, screeching to a halt mere inches before the roof ended. My tail hung over the steep drop as I clung to the shingles, body shaking and heart pounding.

But it wasn't over—Dad was bound to notice the window was open. I still had to get out of sight before he saw me like this.

Every inch I moved made my heart lurch in terror as I crawled away from the window, clambering along the slant of the roof until I reached the gap of space between our roof and the one on the house next door. It wasn't far. Twelve feet at the most. Maybe if I jumped with my new lizard legs and angled my wings just right, I could—

My feet slipped.

I fell like a rock, straight down, and landed in a dumpster in the alley between the houses with a loud crash. Trash flew everywhere. I could have sworn I heard a cat yowl.

For a minute or two, I just lay there, sprawled on my throne of fresh garbage as I stared at the quiet night sky. Clearly I had angered some ancient lizard deity when we lived in Arizona. That was the only thing I could come up with that made even the tiniest shred of sense—divine reptilian vengeance.

But I couldn't lie there amidst the used diapers, mushy apple cores, fast food wrappers, and soggy cardboard boxes forever. Especially if my dad or anyone else decided to check out the loud noises coming from the alley. Time to move.

Grabbing the side of the dumpster, I dragged myself free of the plastic bags and empty soda cans, shaking a banana peel off one of the horns on my head. My body, despite being bizarre and feeling initially unbalanced, was strong. I hoisted myself out of the garbage and landed in a crouch, instinctively drawing my wings in close to my sides with one clench of my sculpted shoulders.

Slowly, I stood up. I flexed my lizard legs and used my claws to grip the ground to keep my balance. Then I dared to take a step...and then another. A smirk curled across my lips. I took a few more strides and then sprang, bounding from one end of the alley to the other. Twelve feet, like it was nothing at all. Every movement felt so *right*.

I glanced down at my body again, the black scales glittering like chips of volcanic glass in the darkness along my clawed reptilian haunches and lashing tail. A twist of my wrists made jagged black spines bristle along my forearms. That bracelet, the scale on my wrist, had done this to me—transformed me into some anthropomorphic spawn of bat, lizard, and teenage boy.

It was wicked cool.

Tensing my shoulders up a different way, I looked back to see my wings respond. I could feel them, move them, and spread them wide. They were as strong and solid as the rest of me, obviously made for...

Hmmm.

Widening my stance, I poured all my focus into moving my wings. Every subtle muscle twitch and contraction made them move a different way. It took a minute to figure out, and then I tried beating them. Just one, hard flap.

Wind rushed off their leathery membranes with enough force to send me staggering forward a few steps.

"No freaking way," I whispered, my voice trembling with exhilaration. "I can fly."

I tried it again, harder this time. My feet left the ground and I glided forward a few yards.

I let out a wild, maniacal laugh. "I can fly!"

Sinking down into a crouch, I coiled the muscles of my powerful lizard legs and spread my wings. My stomach did a little nervous backflip—the only indication I got that doing this was probably really stupid—right before I sprang toward the night sky.

The earth fell away, a dizzying blur of lights as I thrashed my wings harder and harder. My body burned with primal energy, fueling my efforts and sending my body surging higher. Before I knew it, all the rooftops and streetlights of Manhattan were far below.

That's when I realized I didn't actually *know* how to fly.

The mechanics had seemed so obvious—flap your wings hard enough and you're airborne. As it turned out, the subtleties of critical stuff like steering were a little more complicated. I tried to take it on instinct, but even as I frantically flapped and wobbled in the air at an awkward hover, I started to lose altitude, falling back to earth. Only this time, there was no dumpster to cushion my crash landing. Clenching my fanged teeth, I pumped my wings in another furious downward beat then spread them wide.

The wind caught them, filling the thick membranes like sails. Instinct pulled at my extremities, guiding me forward. I leaned into the wind. My pulse raced as I turned my nose into the cold night air. And then suddenly, I was soaring.

I couldn't help it; I let out a loud scream of excitement. I streaked across the sky like a black scaly comet, taking the air by storm and cruising through skyscrapers, wheeling over the Hudson River, and zipping past the George Washington Bridge all the way to the Upper East Side. The lights of the city twinkled below me by the millions, and the wind rustled my hair. I spread my arms wide, taking it all in. My senses tingled, soaking in new details I'd never experienced before—the smell of a hot dog stand miles away, the clatter of subway cars below the streets, the winking of a million stars too faint for the human eye to detect.

The world was alive all around me in ways I'd never been able to appreciate before.

And then—out of nowhere—something crashed into me.

It knocked the breath out of me, and I fell, plummeting like a meteor back toward Earth. I tried to correct myself in the air. I flailed my wings, twisting and sprawling as I fought to get my bearings back.

It was too late.

I hit the ground hard, sending dirt flying up in every direction. Spots filled my vision. Apparently with super strength came super durability, though, because even after a three-hundred-foot fall, nothing felt broken or even bruised. I sat up, dazed and spitting out mouthfuls of soil.

My head was still swimming when I crawled out of the big crater left from my impact. I barely managed to get to my knees before I fell flat on my face again, coughing and picking out bits

of grass stuck in my teeth. What the heck had hit me? I felt like
a fly that had just been mushed by a rolled up newspaper.

Blinking groggily at my surroundings, I didn't recognize
where I was—somewhere with big trees and dimly lit paved
paths. To my left was an old bridge, and to my right I could see
the lights of the city twinkling through the limbs. I could have
sworn I'd seen that bridge before. Central Park?

"You *idiot*," a girl's voice hissed. "You could have been
seen. You probably were! Are you insane? Or just stupid?"

I turned, still trying to shake the stars out of my vision, and
spotted an ominous figure marching my way. I couldn't tell
much about her, at first, but as my vision cleared, I froze. My
breath caught and my pulse stalled and started. Either I was hallucinating, or she was just like me.

Well, sort of.

Overall, her body was shaped like mine—a mixture of human and winged reptile. Brilliant blue scales adorned her skin,
fitting along the curves of her body to cover most of her arms,
chest, and midriff. Curled golden horns spiraled out from the
sides of her head, sweeping elegantly around her ears. Her hind
legs were shaped like mine, albeit a lot more slender, and instead of spines she had graceful blue-and-white fins running
down her back to the end of her tail. More fins grew from her
forearms and the backs of her legs. Even her long, pointed ears
had a finlike shape.

I gaped at her.

"You have a totem scale," she surmised, her voice dripping
with disdain. The wind rippled her long, ice blue hair as she
studied me, her eyes glowing like molten gold in the night.

"Wait." I shook my head, trying to clear it. "A totem what?"

"You don't even know what it is? Oh, for crying out loud!"
She threw her arms in the air with a growl. "That thing glowing
on your wrist? A *dragon* totem scale!" She gestured to her chest,
clawed fingers grazing over a single white scale right over her
heart. It looked exactly like mine. "You found it, right?"

Clambering back to my feet, I shook the dirt and clumps of grass off my back. "Actually," I clarified, "someone gave it to me. Three times, as a matter of fact."

Her eyes narrowed like she didn't believe me. "Who?"

"I don't know. I never saw them. Who gave you yours?" My ears perked. I took a curious step toward her. She had wings, too, but hers were smaller, sleeker, and less muscular.

She shied back and snarled in warning. The starlight bathed her scales, making them shine almost like they were wet. When I didn't come any closer, she straightened again. "I don't know," she admitted. "But I do know these totems have been lost for hundreds of years. No one finds one by accident."

"Is that so?" I shot her a challenging smirk. "How do you know they're called totems?"

Her lip curled and she gave an exasperated snort. "I don't owe you any answers. Just watch yourself, boy. No one can see us like this."

"Why not? It's not like they'd know who we were." I was pretty certain about that. My reflection, scales aside, didn't look much like my old self.

"That's not the point," she fumed. "They'll try to catch us. They'll try to take our totems. And when they figure out no one can use them except us, they'll try forcing us to use our powers to do what *they* want."

"And who are 'they,' exactly?"

She barked a laughed. "You're kidding, right? Who do you think?"

"Okay then, who are you?"

Her expression closed up, ears drooping some as she took another step away from me. "No one, as far as you're concerned. That's rule number one. No one can see you change forms—ever. If that happens, you'll lose your power forever. So it's best not to tell anyone."

"Not even each other?"

She swished her tail and frowned. "Especially not each other. If they catch one of us, they'll probably use that as leverage to find the other. This totem is mine, and no one is going to jeopardize it—especially not you."

"How do you know all this?" I tried taking another small, cautious step toward her.

Once again, her expression grew distant. "Because the person who gave me my totem also gave me information," she murmured. "It's vital if we want to keep this power for any length of time. So do what I tell you—stay out of sight." Her fins immediately bristled and she snarled again. She jumped into a wider stance, flaring her wings as though she were about to take off.

"Hey, wait!" I lunged suddenly, seizing her by the hand.

She froze, her expression blanking as she stood still, staring up at me with her golden eyes smoldering in the dark like two embers.

"I don't even know how this happened. How do I take the bracelet off? Can I even change back?" I asked as I slowly released her hand. "You can't expect me not to screw everything up if I don't know anything about what's happening to me."

With a small, frustrated sigh, she carefully slid her hand out of mine. "It isn't easy to explain. That totem, regardless of how you ended up with it, chose you. You alone can wield its power—the power of one of the four elements."

"What element?" I glanced down at the single white scale on my wrist where the bracelet had been.

"I don't know. You'll have to figure it out for yourself," she grumbled. "The more you use it, the more it will grow and awaken new abilities."

"Like...?"

She gave a shrug that made her slender, tapered wings swish. "Like I said, it depends on your element. Each one is different, or so I was told."

I glanced down at the totem scale again, my stomach flipping and fluttering with anticipation. "You said dragon before? So this is…a dragon's scale? A real, actual dragon?"

Her mouth flattened, brow crinkling with uncertainty. "I don't know. But look at us. Certainly seems real enough, doesn't it?"

She had a point. "So what about changing back?"

"That's easy. To change back you place your hand over your totem and command it to sleep. If you want to return to this form, then you command it to awaken." A claw-tipped finger suddenly appeared in my face as she tapped the end of my nose. "But you *must* be extremely careful. No one can see you change into or out of this form."

"Okay, okay."

"I mean it," she warned, distrust flickering in her glowing golden eyes. "If someone sees you—"

"If someone sees me, I'll lose my power. Relax, I got it." A grin twisted up my lips again before I could stop it. "This is awesome."

She scoffed. "It's not a toy, you know. This power is ancient. It's been dormant for centuries, waiting for the one person to come along who was worthy of it. It's not a joke."

"So what does that make us? Superheroes?"

She huffed and rolled her eyes. "Hardly. Those kinds of antics are exactly what will end with us being captured and forced to give up our totems. You've only just learned to change, and you have absolutely no control over your powers. In this form, you could destroy all of New York by accident. I've been practicing for a year, and I've only barely scratched the surface of what my totem can do."

"O-oh." My insides squirmed with a mixture of excitement and pure terror.

She turned away, preparing to leave again. Striding a few graceful steps away, the wind swirled through her pale blue hair as she spread her wings. Everything about her—the way she moved, the way her scales sparkled like starlight over a rushing stream—was effortlessly beautiful.

"Hey!" I called out. "What should I call you? I mean, if we ever run into each other again."

Her lips curled into a bewitching dragoness smile. "We won't."

CHAPTER 4

It took almost an hour to find the right alleyway beside our new house to land in. After circling the neighborhood, I finally touched down and dropped into a squat in the darkness, glancing all around to be sure no one had seen me. So far, so good.

I stood and looked down at the white scale on my wrist. Time to see if that dragon-lizard-girl was right.

Placing my other hand over the scale, I forced myself to concentrate. This had to work. Otherwise, I was going to need a superhero-style secret hideout pronto.

"Sleep, dragon totem," I whispered.

Another blinding flash of white light engulfed me. Fluttering heat spread through my body inch by inch, tingling along my skin and prickling through my chest. I took a deep breath, closing my eyes until the sensation passed. Seconds later, I was staring down at my normal, human hands again. There was nothing left of that dragon-like form except for the bracelet still strapped to my wrist.

My body sagged, shoulders drooping as I let out a shaking exhale. I was back to my old self, standing barefoot in the alleyway wearing only my sweatpants and T-shirt, like nothing had ever happened.

It seemed too easy—too good to be true. I ran my fingers through my hair just to be sure, but I couldn't find a single horn. My ears were rounded again, and my body was back to its usual disappointing scrawniness.

"Amazing," I muttered as held up my arm and brushed my hand over the leather cuff-bracelet. The white scale shimmered even in the dark, hiding a secret that, if the dragon-girl was right, had been lying in wait for a thousand years.

Just the thought made my stomach flip and my mouth go dry. Why would something like this choose *me*? Not that I was complaining, of course, but it's not like I was anything special. Drake was smarter. Mr. Biceps—Damien Blount—was undoubtedly stronger. My dad was braver than I'd ever be.

So why me?

"Koji?" Dad's voice echoed in the street at the other end of the alleyway.

Oh no.

I whirled around, looking for a good place to hide. The only spot nearby was the dumpster I'd fallen into earlier. I cringed at the idea, but before I could muster up the nerve to dive back into that vat of filth, a spotlight hit my back.

I froze.

"Koji?" Dad called out again.

I turned back, shielding my eyes from the glare of his flashlight beam. "H-hey, Dad."

"What's going on? Why are you out here? I've been calling you for hours!" His voice was tight, brimming with pending rage as he stormed toward me, panning the beam of the flashlight up and down my body. "I called your phone, the school, the police station—no one could find any trace of you."

"O-oh. Really? I was just, uh, you know, out here." I struggled to sound convincing while mentally flailing for a believable excuse. A lousy one was the best I could do. "I guess I accidentally dropped my cell phone in the garbage while I was unpacking. I had to do a little dumpster diving to find it. You must have come home right after I left. Sorry, Dad."

The flashlight beam lowered and I finally caught a glimpse of my dad's face. His brow was creased in desperation, eyes wide and frantic, and his mouth scrunched up like he was trying not to break down.

"I had no idea what happened to you, son. You can't do that to me. Never again."

My heart hit the back of my throat so hard it knocked the wind out of me. I stared back at him, realizing that I'd seen that expression on his face once before, a long time ago.

"I-I'm sorry," I stammered.

He let out a heavy sigh, wrapped an arm around my neck, and dragged me into a gruff hug. "You are the only thing that matters to me, Koji. You're all I have left, and I'm supposed to take care of you. So you can't just leave in the middle of the night like that. This city isn't like the others we've lived in. We're not living on base anymore. Something could happen to you."

I was so stunned I forgot to hug him back. By the time I thought about it, he had already let me go. "Come on, let's get back inside. I've got to call the police and let them know you've been found."

Watching my dad walk away, I hesitated to follow. In the gloom of the alleyway, the totem scale on my bracelet glistened faintly. I thought about what that dragon-girl had said—no one could know that we had these totems. No one could find out what we were or we would risk being seen and losing our powers, or being captured by the FBI and experimented on or something.

But I'd never kept anything from Dad before. We were a team, and that meant we couldn't let our communication break down. If I shut him out, kept this from him, I'd be alone with the consequences.

Was I ready for that?

"You coming?" Dad had stopped halfway down the alley and was shining the light at me again.

"Yeah, sorry." I forced a smile and jogged to catch up. The bracelet on my wrist didn't feel like a miracle anymore. That scaly blue girl was right. This was complicated—dangerous, even.

My dad couldn't handle dangerous, not when it came to me. If he found out about the totem, he would want it gone.

Dad could never know the truth. I'd have to be more careful from now on.

Once we got back inside, Dad went into the living room and started making calls to the police station and the school to let them know he'd found me. I sank onto one of the barstools at the kitchen counter and buried my face in my hands. I tried to think, but the fragrance from the two unopened pizza boxes sitting on the counter next to me was more than I could stand.

I cracked the top one open. My mouth watered. It was a circle of pure perfection—a thin crust supreme, extra bacon, and no bell peppers. My favorite.

"It's probably cold by now," Dad said when he wandered back into the kitchen.

I ripped off a slice and began stuffing my face. "I don't care. It's real food."

The barstool next to mine creaked as he sat down. He opened the bottom box, a regular crust supreme with no onions, and started to eat with me. He still wore his flight suit. He hadn't even taken his boots off yet. He must've panicked immediately when he got home and I wasn't there. A twinge of guilt made my mouth screw up.

He cleared his throat in between bites of cold pizza. "So how was Saint Bernard's?"

"Fine." I shrugged. "I have to wear a uniform and I'm probably the dumbest kid there. But they have an art class that seems pretty cool. And I think I made a friend."

Dad laughed. "Art class?"

I tore off another slice of pizza and started cramming it into my mouth so I didn't have to respond to that.

"I guess if that makes you happy," he went on. "I just wish you'd take something that would benefit you in college. That school is supposed to be the very best. I was lucky to be able to pull enough strings to get you in."

I was beginning to lose my appetite.

"Didn't you want to try a sport? What about basketball this time?"

I took one last bite and managed to swallow, but that was it. I knew where this was going. "Not really my thing, Dad. I'm already way behind, so I should probably go study. Lots to catch up on."

I shut my pizza box and started to leave.

"Koji?"

I halted at the bottom of the stairs.

"Where'd you get that bracelet? I've never seen you wear that before."

I glanced down at the leather cuff on my wrist. Excited heat still buzzed in my chest, as though the mere thought of the incredible power of the totem was enough to send subtle ripples of its energy through my body.

"It was a goodbye present from one of my friends in Arizona," I lied.

"Oh. Looks pretty cool."

I didn't answer. Keeping my head down, I hurried upstairs and hid behind the closed door of my bedroom. Everything was just as I'd left it—boxes piled everywhere, bed unmade, and the window slightly ajar. The chilly night air blew in through it, rustling my hair.

I paused to look at my reflection in my dresser's long mirror. No more scales, horns, or wings. I was just Koji—a tall, gawky, long-armed teenage guy with messy black hair, dark olive skin, deep-set eyes, and a perpetual look of bewilderment.

The glare from my desk lamp made the little scar on my jawline, right below my ear, more obvious.

Everything was exactly as it should be.

The only thing different was that bracelet, stuck firmly to my arm. I didn't bother trying to take it off again. In fact, knowing it wouldn't come off was sort of comforting. I didn't want to lose it. It felt like a part of me now.

Easing down into my desk chair, I dug through my school stuff until I found the stack of notes Drake had given me for Chemistry and English. I needed to clear my head, think about something else, and maybe try to catch up on schoolwork.

Or at least, I tried.

When I found myself staring at the table of contents of my chemistry book, I gave up. My thoughts were too scattered. My brain replayed what that dragon-girl had said over and over. This totem had chosen me after waiting for centuries for the right person. For me. And I had no idea why. That girl insisted we had to stay hidden, to keep these totems and their abilities a secret. She had good reason, but I just couldn't shake the feeling that she was wrong.

These totems had chosen us for a reason, right? Somehow, assuming that reason was just so we could take secret dragon-winged joy rides every night didn't seem right. There had to be more to it than that.

Not to mention someone had intentionally left this bracelet in places they knew I would find it. But who? No way Dad was responsible. He didn't even want me going outside on my own, so entrusting me with a power-infused bracelet I could use to fly all over New York seemed unlikely. It couldn't have been anyone from Saint Bernard's. The first time the package showed up was before I'd even been to the school, and no one knew where I lived. Who else did I even know in this city?

No one.

Pushing my notes and books to the side, I folded my arms and put my head down. For all I knew, the bracelet just materialized completely on its own. That dragon-girl had mentioned someone telling her about her totem. No one had given me any information like that.

I gave up trying to study—well, school stuff, anyway.

I had to know more. That girl said she'd been able to learn about the totems. If I couldn't get her to tell me anything, and if no one was going to offer me the same courtesy of free information, then I would just have to figure it out myself.

So I opened my computer, clicked my web browser, and got ready for a long night.

"Dude, you look terrible."

I squinted up at Drake as he settled into the seat next to mine. I must have nodded off, because it took me a second to realize I was in Chemistry class. Every blink was painful, like my eyes had been filled with sand. But that's what happens when you stay up until four in the morning, staring into the glare of a computer screen, running one useless Internet search after another. Ugh.

"I was up late," I mumbled, leaning down to make sure I was wearing my uniform. The whole morning was a blur—I couldn't even remember if I'd taken a shower or not. "Way too late."

"Doing what?"

"Studying," I lied between yawns.

Drake spun his chair to face me. "Wake up a second and take a look at this." He fanned a newspaper in my face. "It says a meteor hit Central Park last night!"

Alarm shot through me like a bolt of lightning. I snapped upright and grabbed the paper out of his hands. On the front page was a full color picture of the crater left from my crash landing after that dragon-girl had knocked me out of the sky. I gulped. "Meteor, huh?"

"Yeah." Drake's grin twinkled with enthusiasm. "It's all over the news. Social media is bursting over it. Some people even took videos, but the quality is too lousy to make out any details. You seriously didn't hear?"

"No. I had no idea. My dad hasn't got the televisions hooked up yet."

Drake arched a brow. "You don't have Facebook? Instagram? Snapchat? Twitter?"

I flushed and looked away. "Uh, no."

He leaned in closer, cutting his eyes around and lowering his voice like he was about to ask something embarrassing. "MySpace?"

"Not really my thing."

He rolled his eyes. "Well, that's not even the best part."

I peered at him over the top of the newspaper.

Drake leaned in even closer, still whispering like he didn't want anyone else to hear. "I *saw* it."

Oh no. Dread squirmed in the pit of my stomach like I'd swallowed a live snake. "Y-you did?"

"Yeah. And get this, there's no way it was a meteor. Absolutely no way."

The newspaper rattled as my hands began to shake. I quickly folded it and put it down on the lab table, cramming my hands into my pockets. "What do you think it was then?" My voice came out squeaky and panicked. Cool—I had to play it cool. Einstein or not, there was no way he could possibly know what was actually going on.

"One of two things, both of which are insane," he whispered. "Either some sort of experimental aircraft malfunctioned, which is highly unlikely. No government organization would ever run a test like that over anywhere this densely populated."

"Or...?"

"Or, and based off my own observation I think this is far more likely, what left that crater was a creature of unknown origin. It crash-landed in Central Park, but wasn't killed on impact. They didn't find a body. It must still be at large in the city. Check this out."

My pulse thundered in my ears as I stared down to where Drake was pointing at the cover of the paper. In the photo, heavily armed police officers in body armor were taping off the area around the giant crater. Meanwhile, several men dressed in nondescript black suits and sunglasses prowled around my crash site.

"Those aren't your everyday street cops. They're government officials of some sort, I guarantee it. Maybe FBI, maybe CIA—who knows. Point is, they wouldn't go to this much trouble over something like a meteor strike." Drake's cognac eyes shimmered enthusiastically. "Whatever happened, it's top secret. I think they're still looking for whatever made that crater."

A cold sweat made my body shiver. In my pockets, my hands curled into fists. The police—the government—was looking for me? That dragon-girl was right. This had already gotten out of hand. My bracelet and the totem scale had to be kept secret.

"You okay? You look like you're about to throw up." Drake gave my shoulder a nudge.

Air. I needed some air. Right now.

"A-actually I think I ate something bad this morning. I'll be right back." I bolted out of my seat and ran for the door, making a speedy path straight for the bathrooms.

I locked myself inside a stall, put the toilet lid down, and sat with my face in my hands so I could hyperventilate in private. I'd already been spotted by the FBI? Or maybe the CIA? Either way, it was bad.

Pulling back the sleeve of my sweater, I stared down at the totem scale shimmering under the fluorescent bathroom lights. I hadn't even had the thing for twenty-four hours and I was already at risk of being discovered.

After a few deep breaths, I emerged from the bathroom stall and washed my face in the sink. My reflection in the mirror startled me. My face was pale, terrified, and undeniably haunted. Dark circles hung under my red, weary eyes.

Slowly, I backed away from the sink. Somehow, I had to salvage this. I had to think. They hadn't found me yet. I still had time.

I staggered out of the bathroom, still in a daze of panic and horror, and began wandering back down the hall toward the Chemistry classroom. Halfway there, someone behind me cleared their throat.

I stole a glance over my shoulder.

There she was, my goddess, walking two paces behind me. Claire Faust might as well have been floating down the hall. Did angels float? Well, she did. Her blond curls bounced around her like spools of gold ribbon.

She gave a faint, shy smile. "Good morning, Koji."

I suddenly remembered to breathe. "Oh, hey! Yeah, uh, it is. I mean, good morning."

Crap. Not again. It was like whenever she came around, I couldn't say anything even remotely intelligent.

"Is everything okay? You look a bit pale this morning." She tipped her head to the side slightly, making those glorious curls brush against her cheek. Good grief. She wasn't even wearing makeup. She didn't need makeup. Not when her skin was so—

"Koji?"

"O-oh! Yeah. No. I'm fine. Just must've eaten something that didn't agree," I stammered like a complete moron. Someone just kill me. "Better now, though. Much better."

"That's good." She fell in step beside me. One of her sweater sleeves brushed my arm and for a moment, I forgot how to breathe.

No—I had to concentrate. Focus, Koji. This was my chance to make a good impression. I had to say something marginally interesting before we reached the classroom door.

"So, uh, did you see the news? They're saying a meteor crashed in Central Park." It was the only topic my panicked brain would default to in a moment of absolute desperation.

Her eyes darkened. "Yes. Everyone's talking about it. Some people think it's a conspiracy."

"What do you think?"

She puffed a small sigh and turned those dazzling evergreen eyes up to meet mine.

I suffered another cardiac episode.

"I think people see what they want to see, regardless of what's actually there. And whatever is there, we'll most likely never know." She shrugged slightly. "It is a little scary to think about, though. We were lucky it only hit an open space in the park and no one got hurt. If it had hit a building or someone's home, that would have been a disaster."

"Yeah," I agreed hoarsely.

"Anyway, I'm sure the media will forget all about it in a few days." She stopped at the threshold of the classroom. I almost stopped with her, until I glanced ahead to see why her expression had suddenly gone cold.

Her fiancé, Damien Blount, was watching us.

"See you around," I said as I kept walking. I even added a small, friendly goodbye wave.

Claire didn't answer. She didn't even look at me again as she walked stiffly to sit down next to her husband-to-be. It was beyond weird for me to fathom that. She was in tenth grade, like me. Dating sure, but getting *married*?

I dropped back into my chair next to Drake.

"It's a miracle. All you needed was a little chat with the princess to make a complete recovery," he teased.

I shot him a glare.

"At least she knows you're alive," he reasoned. "That's better than nothing."

"In your opinion, maybe," I grumbled. If anything, it made things worse. It would have been a lot easier to give up and move on if she'd refused to acknowledge my existence altogether. I'd never met anyone like her before. No one had ever affected me like this. Before Claire, I'd never considered myself a romantic or the kind of guy to fall for someone at first sight. But she had changed everything. And the fact she was willing to talk to me kept my flames of hope burning bright.

"You're hopeless." Drake sighed. "By the way, do you still need me to come by and tutor you later?"

"Yeah, sure. If you don't mind eating pizza for dinner. I haven't had a chance to go to the store and my dad's culinary skills are limited to microwave dinners and takeout."

He grinned. "Gee, free pizza, that sounds awful."

I gave him a forced smile. Dating troubles aside, I still had a huge problem. If somehow the CIA, FBI, or whoever might be checking into that mysterious crater in Central Park managed to trace it back to me, I'd never be able to keep my totem a secret.

I placed a hand over my wrist, feeling the lump of the bracelet hidden beneath my sweater sleeve. I was going to have to be much more diligent and careful. I couldn't take any more risks. It sucked to admit it, but that blue-scaled girl was right.

Superhero stuff was out of the question.

CHAPTER 5

D rake went on about the crater and theories about what had made it during the entire lunch period. He was determined to see it for himself over the week-end. I'd at least managed to talk him down from believing it was an alien crash site—which was a little too close to the truth for my comfort. But it was hard to come up with alternative theories that he would even consider.

"My dad has flown fighter jets for years. He said they're always experimenting with the next cutting edge piece of military technology. That's got to be it," I said.

"No way." He was rubbing his chin thoughtfully, flicking his thumb over the screen of his phone. He'd been watching the news and cruising all his social media profiles between classes, looking for updates or new conspiracy leaks. "But if it was something civilian made, then maybe..."

"Speaking of technology, uh, how's that robot thing coming?" I was getting desperate.

Drake finally looked up from his phone-trance. "You mean the Robotics Club?"

"Yeah. You said you're getting ready for a competition, right? What's that about? Is it like Battle Bots or something?"

He laughed. "Sort of, I guess. At the beginning of the year they send out these packets to all the schools that have teams.

It's got the parameters for the competition, the obstacles our robot has to get past, and a few old appliances and things we have to incorporate into our design. Then it's up to us to design and build a robot that can complete all the obstacles."

"Sounds complicated." My head hurt just trying to imagine that.

Drake shrugged. "Sort of. The actual build isn't that hard, but there's a lot of strategy to it. Some people go for speed. Others for endurance and durability. And then there's always a few who set out just to destroy everyone else's bots so they can't progress in the competition. Battle bots, as you put it."

"So which did you go for?"

The wicked, conniving twinkle in his eye reminded me a little of the main character in the old cartoon version of *How the Grinch Stole Christmas*. "All three, of course."

That smile freaked me out. So I turned my attention back to the grilled chicken sandwich on my lunch tray. At least something was going my way today—the sandwiches the school served were delicious.

I had a mouthful of juicy grilled chicken, sweet honey mustard dressing, sour dill pickles, smoked gouda cheese, and freshly baked pretzel bread when I noticed Drake had gone back to looking at his phone. So much for getting his mind off the stupid crater. I rolled my eyes and took another bite. He'd just have to get it out of his system.

Then I saw him push back one of his sleeves to scratch his arm.

From his wrist to his elbow, Drake's forearm was riddled with deep purple bruises. They almost looked like fingermarks, like someone had grabbed him hard—hard enough to leave a mark. But before I could be sure, he yanked his sleeve back down and went back to staring at his phone.

A nauseating, burning sensation scorched the back of my throat. My mouth went dry. Putting my sandwich down, I tried to think of how to ask about it without, you know, *actually* asking about it.

"So you've heard about my dad now. What's your mom like?"

He tossed his head, making his shaggy surfer hair flop out of his eyes. "She works a lot. Nights mostly. Sometimes I don't see her till the weekends."

"Oh," I said while still chewing my last bite. "That sucks. What about your dad?"

Drake flicked his eyes up to me for an instant, but his expression stayed eerily blank. "He's dead."

I choked on my food.

"Relax, it was a long time ago. It's not a big deal."

Yeah, right. "Dude, that's…I'm sorry. I didn't know."

He gave another noncommittal shrug. With his mouth locked in a straight line, like he was making a conscious effort to look as unaffected as possible, he kept his gaze locked onto his phone screen. "Like I said, it was a while ago."

So much for my subtle probing attempts. "Wow, I feel like a huge jerk now."

"Don't," he replied quickly.

I wasn't brave enough to say much else for the rest of lunch. I knew firsthand that kind of thing was always a big deal, regardless of how long ago it had happened. My mom had died when I was little, and whenever someone asked about her, all my feelings about losing her burst back to the surface. Fragments of memory—the few things I still remembered about her—floated around in my head for days like flecks in a snow globe. After a while, they settled, but it only took someone else asking about her to stir them all up again.

And that's probably what I'd just done to Drake.

The rest of the school day was a total blur. I couldn't shake that haunting sense of despair that squeezed at my chest whenever I thought about Mom. I was still in a daze when I realized I was sitting behind my easel in art class, staring listlessly at the blank canvas in front of me.

"Mr. Owens?"

I snapped back to reality with a jolt, cringing as I met the expectant stare of the art teacher, Mr. Molins. "Uh, yes. Present."

A couple of the girls sitting across the circle giggled.

"Yes, I can see that. But we're talking about our art journals now. Did you have an idea for what you wanted to do for yours?" he asked.

"O-oh." I started to panic. I'd been so busy studying for everything else and researching totems, I'd forgotten all about the art journal. I scoured my mind for something, anything, and grasped onto the first image that popped into my head—my lucky *Dragon Ball Z* shoelaces. "I was thinking I'd make a comic book."

Mr. Molins stroked his goatee. "Very interesting concept. Any ideas for the storyline? Or will it be a new short story every day?"

"No, all one story. About a superhero, I think."

Next to me, Maddie shifted in her seat.

"And it'll be like the story of him becoming a superhero and learning to live with having to split himself between what happens when he's in battle and dealing with everyday stuff."

"I see. It sounds like you're onto something there. I can't wait to see how it progresses." Mr. Molins gave a satisfied nod and moved to the next person in line. "Maddie, what are you planning for your journal?"

She sat up a bit straighter. Today her long black hair was tied into a loosely braided bun on the back of her head. A few wispy bangs brushed the sides of her face. "I'm going to do lots of painted panels that fit together into one large mosaic."

Mr. Molins nodded. "How big will the panels be?"

"I'm thinking of making them fairly small. Maybe only four- or five-inch squares." Maddie went on for a few minutes, describing the details of her idea.

As the class discussion continued, I started spacing out again. Not that I wasn't interested in what everyone else was doing for their project, I just couldn't stop thinking about Mom and Drake. And wishing I could throw myself off the school roof in dragon-form so I could feel that speed and power again. I didn't even realize that my gaze had settled on Maddie until she looked straight at me. Busted. She probably thought I was sitting there gawking at her like a creep.

Before I could try to explain myself, she leaned in and whispered, "Are you okay?" I could have sworn she was blushing a little.

I rubbed the back of my neck. "I'm not sure."

Around the classroom, everyone had begun packing up and getting ready for the last bell to ring. I should have been doing the same thing. I was supposed to meet Drake downstairs so we could walk back to my house. After our encounter at lunch, I almost dreaded seeing him now. I needed to apologize again, maybe even explain that I understood.

"I just wanted to say I really am sorry about the paint yesterday. I hope I didn't get any on you," Maddie murmured, avoiding my eyes. She fidgeted with her sweater sleeves, rubbed her shoulder, and then turned to make a mad dash for the door.

Without thinking, I stood up and grasped her wrist to keep her from running off. "Wait a second."

She halted, turning slowly back to face me with her cheeks pinker than ever. "Yes?"

"I didn't get a chance to, you know, really introduce myself yesterday," I told her. "I'm Koji Owens."

"I know," she murmured and bowed her head as though she were embarrassed. She tucked one of her wispy bangs behind her ears.

"Can I call you Maddie?"

Her wide doe eyes flicked up to look straight at me. They were such a soft, gentle shade of faded blue; it reminded me of misty gray storm clouds. "Madeline, please. Everyone calls me Maddie here because that's what my father calls me. But to tell you the truth, I...really don't like it."

"Oh, okay. Madeline it is, then." I realized I was still holding on to her arm and let her go. "I'm sorry. I'm really awkward. And weird. And lately it's like I just keep doing really stupid things."

Her heart-shaped face lit up with a grin that made her seem to glow. Her dark lashes fluttered and she edged backward a few steps, hands clasped behind her back. "For what it's worth, you seem nice to me." She tucked some of her runaway, wispy bangs behind her ears again. "See you tomorrow, Koji." With a small, shy wave, she trotted toward the door just as the bell rang.

Dad was taking *forever*.

Sitting on my bed, I listened to him shuffling around downstairs, the muffled sound of the TV in his bedroom, the pipes groaning as he ran water for a shower, and the scrape and thud of him moving boxes around until well after ten o'clock. Then, at last, everything got quiet.

Finally.

I gave it another half hour before I dared to move, just to be sure he was sound asleep. I couldn't run the risk of Dad catching me like last time. If I was going to get serious about this secret-totem business, then I had to learn how to be stealthy.

Slowly and carefully, I crept from my bed and stalked through my dark bedroom. Standing before my mirror, I pushed up my sleeves and braced myself. This was it. No turning back.

Placing a hand over the totem scale, I let my eyes roll closed as I muttered the word, "Awaken."

Even with my eyes shut, I could see the brilliant flash of white light bloom from the bracelet. Tingling chills climbed my skin from my feet to my fingertips. Every muscle in my body flexed, awakening to new strength. It didn't scare me this time, though. I welcomed it.

When I opened my eyes, my new black scaly reflection grinned at me, white fangs flashing in the gloom. My hair looked longer and wilder in this form—especially with the horns poking out of it like jagged shards of obsidian glass. My eyes glowed electric blue. I was back for round two, and this time there wouldn't be any screw-ups or giant craters in Central Park. I had to get a handle on this form and figure out my elemental powers.

I folded my wings tightly against my back, hoping to avoid scraping them against the floor or ceiling, as I went to open my window. Dad's room was directly below mine, so I couldn't afford to knock over any of the packing boxes this time.

Every step seemed to thump louder. My every breath rattled with a deep growl. I flinched as I pulled the window open and the hinges creaked and groaned.

It took some wrenching, grunting, and painful squeezing to get myself out the window. But a huff, twist, and stumble later, I was standing on the roof facing the cold air and glittering lights of New York's nighttime skyline. Free at last!

I took the sloped roof at a sprint with wings spread to catch the wind. A few clumsy wingbeats later, I was rocketing upward, soaring high enough that I hoped no one would be able to spot me. My flight was still wobbly, although not nearly as bad as last time. Practice—I needed a good place to practice where no one would be filming me.

Suddenly, alarm bells started ringing in my head. I caught the scent of something familiar an instant before the heavy *thump thump thump* of wing beats hit my sensitive pointed ears.

Someone was approaching, and I had a strong suspicion who it was.

Clenching my clawed fists, I bared my teeth and whirled around just in time to see the blue dragon-girl zooming straight at me, her expression twisted with pure rage.

Uh-oh.

"You *idiot!*" she screeched as she came at me, claws out and ready to fight.

I reacted without thinking, snapping my wings in close and diving out of her way right before we collided.

The chase was on.

I was faster and each beat of my dragon wings sent me rocketing forward with even greater speed. But the dragon-girl was far more experienced. Zipping over the surface of the Hudson, I dodged and weaved, narrowly escaping her grasp.

"What is your problem?" I snarled back at her over my shoulder.

Her reply came without warning. A wave rose in front of me, a raging wall of water aimed straight for me.

There was no time to escape it.

I smashed right into the wave. Water roared in my ears and shot up my nose. Terror overtook me in a paralyzing frenzy. I couldn't breathe. I couldn't see. I was tossed end over end, helpless against the power of the churning dark water around me.

In the chaos, one word rose like a cry from the darkest depths of my soul: *Mom.*

When I saw her face, I knew I was unconscious or maybe even dead. I was drowning...again.

CHAPTER 6

I was gonna hurl.

I didn't even have time to sit up. One second I was somewhere between death and unconsciousness, the next I was on my side throwing up about a gallon water. I coughed hard, my whole body retching. My lungs ached as I gulped in desperate breaths of the cool night air.

"You should have told me you couldn't swim, idiot." My new dragon bestie was sitting on the grass next to me, her tail curled around her legs. Her yellow eyes glowed ominously as she scowled in my direction.

"You didn't exactly give me a chance to mention it," I rasped. Pushing myself up, my head spun and my heavy wings flopped around until I could fold the back against my sides.

"Sorry. Sometimes I lose control when I'm upset. My elemental power is water," she said quietly.

"Yeah. Kinda figured that one out on my own."

"Have you figured yours out yet?" She actually sounded curious.

I raked my soggy hair away from my eyes so I could glare at her. Some of it was tangled up in my horns, too. "No. In fact, that's why I'm out here tonight. I *was* trying to practice."

Her gaze went steely. "Well, you need to be more careful! You keep messing around in the city and more people will see you. It's bad enough you left a giant cr—"

"Hey! The crater was your fault. You were the one who threw me into the ground," I growled back at her.

She snorted and the tip of her blue-scaled tail twitched angrily. "Only because you were out there showing off, making a spectacle of yourself, and putting both our totems at risk!"

"So what am I supposed to do then? I have to practice somewhere."

"Ugh! Fine. Follow me." The dragon-girl leapt up, dried leaves and twigs snapping under her feet as she strolled to the edge of the riverbank. She pointed to the opposite bank. "There."

Normally, I doubt I would have been able to see much of anything. It was pitch black where we stood facing the dark rolling waters of the Hudson. But on the opposite side of the river, my enhanced dragon eyes could see every building, street sign, and telephone pole as plainly as if it were day. Epically cool.

"You see that old building? The one with two big smoke stacks?" She gestured down the river toward the opposite bank.

I did, of course. Even from a distance, probably two miles away, my eyes easily picked out the shape of a large, rectangular red brick building with two tall stacks standing right on the edge of the bank. I crossed my scaly arms over my impressively muscular chest. "Yeah. So?"

"That's the old Glenwood power plant. It's been abandoned for years. Sometimes people use it for movie sets or photo shoots, but most of the time, it's completely empty. Locals call it the Gates of Hell." She flashed me an earnest look. "Inside, you'll have plenty of room to be a moron without anyone seeing. And since it's abandoned, it doesn't matter if you trash it a little in the process."

"Sounds perfect." I grinned. "You're gonna come teach me, right?"

"Hah! No way." She snorted, tossing her billowing locks of brilliant blue hair over her shoulder. "I only get a few hours every night to do this. I'm not going to spend it babysitting you."

I tried my very best sad, begging dragon eyes on her. "Come on. Please? Just a few nights, to get me started."

She narrowed her eyes, wrinkling her nose skeptically.

"I'll owe you one."

"Okay, okay. Three nights! That's it. After that, you forget I exist and we never see each other again. Got it?" She thrust a hand out in my direction.

I seized it before she could reconsider. "Yep. Got it. Okay, let's go." Without letting go of her hand, I spread my wings, coiled my strong legs, and sprang skyward with a yip of excitement.

She growled and hissed at me furiously as she struggled to wrench her arm away from me. At last, when her slender wrist slipped out of my grasp, she joined me in flight—after giving my tail a spiteful yank. I laughed and for an instant, I could have sworn I saw her smile. We soared side by side over the water toward the power plant, flying so low I could reach down and drag my fingers across the surface.

From the outside, the plant looked dark and abandoned. There was no civilization in sight for at least a mile or two. The city lights twinkled from afar, a distant memory. The inside of it was just as she promised—big, empty, and an absolute wreck of twisted steel and rubble. I couldn't imagine a better spot to practice.

As I landed in the center of the large atrium, I gazed up at all the dark glass windows. Some of them were smashed out, and the rush of wind from my wings stirred years of dust that sparkled in the shafts of moonlight pouring in.

The dragon-girl landed next to me and seemed to share my awe at the place. It was weirdly, hauntingly beautiful.

"So what's your hero name?" I asked as I turned to face her. "That's how it works, right? We have to have alter egos to protect our true identities."

She rolled her eyes. "Don't be ridiculous. We've been over this. No one said having a totem meant we were supposed to be heroes."

"No one said we weren't, either," I countered.

"So what do you think we are supposed to do? Fly around and stop carjackers or chase down purse snatchers?"

"Maybe."

"That would be totally reckless. The police would probably shoot us, too. I mean, look at us." She gestured to her reptilian legs and tail, and flared her tapered wings. "We don't look like heroes. We look like monsters. Anyone who saw us would be terrified."

"Fine. Do what you want. But if I can help someone with these powers, then I'm going to. Those who have the ability to make a difference in the world have the responsibility to try— that's what my dad says." I took a step back and flexed my own wings, holding up my arms to admire how my spines and scales glittered in the moonlight like chips of black glass.

Her expression softened as her molten eyes studied me carefully. Maybe my words struck a chord? Her shoulders relaxed a bit and she let out a loud sigh. "I suppose I can't stop you. But don't expect me to show up if you decide to go play superhero and get in over your head."

Something prickled in the back of my mind, like an itch I couldn't scratch. Strange—but something about her expression, the sound of her voice when she spoke those words, made me think she wasn't telling the truth.

"You're the one who keeps popping up whenever I decide to go for a flight. I'm starting to think you might actually like me a *teensy* bit." I gave her a taunting grin and winked. "Or maybe you're just a stalker?"

She made a flustered, growling, huffing sound as she turned away. "Enough chatter. You wanted to learn about your powers, right? So let's get started."

I had to give her credit. She looked ethereal, elegant, and sleek in her dragon form—but there was nothing delicate about her whatsoever. She was brutal. She was tough. And she kicked my butt all over the inside of that abandoned power plant until the sun began to rise.

By the end of our first night of training, she'd shown me all the basics of flying, how to take off without stumbling, and how to utilize the long talons on my hind legs to make landings more stable. I imagined this was how a young eagle felt the first time he took to the sky, learning to use the weapons Mother Nature had given him.

"You'll get better," she panted as she walked up to me, tilting her head to the side as she considered me with her glowing gold eyes. Her gaze halted at the white totem scale on my wrist. "Any idea what your element is yet?"

Her totem scale was on her chest, right in the center. I'd spotted it the first time we met, and now seeing it made me wonder if hers was disguised as a piece of jewelry the way mine was. A brooch, maybe? Or a necklace? It could have been a button, too, or—

"Hello? Did you hear me?"

I shook my head. "I guess awesomeness isn't an element."

She finally cracked a smirk. "Uh, no. And even if it was, I'm not sure you'd qualify."

I stuck my bottom lip out. "Hurtful."

"I discovered my element purely by accident. It happened almost immediately. I had this big fight with my parents, got too upset. I…lost control. It made all the fire hydrants down our street explode." Her gazed lowered, expression softening. "Luckily, no one suspected I was responsible. After that, I knew water was my element. I can feel it, even now, the presence of water in any form."

"So cool."

I guess she didn't mind the compliment because a faint, almost familiar smile brushed over her lips. "There's more than just elemental power, though. You'll learn to open your third eye—but that takes time and practice. It did for me, anyway."

"Third eye?"

"Yes," she said quietly. "It's another special ability unique to your totem. You'll be able to use it even out of your dragon form, but be careful. Once you open it, you can't close it again...even if you want to."

"How did you find yours?" I dared to ask. "Your totem, I mean."

Her gaze drifted up to where the sky was beginning to turn a pale shade of purple through the glass roof of the atrium. "I thought it was purely by accident. I'd just stepped outside for some air, and I found it sitting on the sidewalk wrapped in a—"

"A handkerchief?"

She nodded. "Right. It's like someone had dropped it there by accident. At first, I thought I might turn it in to the lost and found. It was wrapped up like a gift. I assumed someone would come looking for it. But I made the mistake of trying it on. It was so beautiful, I just couldn't resist."

"And then you couldn't get it off." I guessed again.

She sighed and bowed her head, brushing her fingers over the gleaming white scale on her chest. "It's like the totem and I became one. We couldn't be separated by mortal means. I was so afraid at first. I hid it from my parents and researched for weeks to try to figure out what it was so I could find some way to get it off. I didn't know how to activate it.

"Then someone reached out to me. They left a letter on my bed describing exactly what it was and how I could use it. When I finally transformed the first time, I...I couldn't imagine ever parting with it." Gazing up at me again, her brow crinkled and lips thinned, betraying the guarded desperation on her scaly face. "It's my door to a different life—to freedom I never thought I'd have."

"Tell me about it," I agreed. "In real life, I'm probably the biggest loser you'll ever meet."

"I doubt that. Just look at those muscles."

I coughed out a nervous laugh, too embarrassed to tell her that the muscles weren't exactly part of my normal everyday self. "You know, I tried doing a little research on the totems myself. I couldn't find anything."

"You probably weren't looking in the right places," she replied. "The letter told me that the totems have always been a well-guarded secret. Fear of someone who might use their power for selfish reasons has made those who do know wary of talking about them."

That was a scary thing to think about—someone flying around using their power to threaten and destroy.

"Before I received the letter, I searched everywhere for information on my totem. I even took it to a jeweler. That was who first identified it as some kind of animal scale rather than a shell or a gemstone. From there, I emailed a few photos of it to several zoologists and archaeologists who all agreed that it was some sort of reptilian scale, although none of them could tell me what kind of reptile it came from. After I got that first letter, I reasoned I needed to start looking into ancient myths and legends about dragons. I was getting closer and closer to answers. Then, once again, someone gave them to me."

"Who?"

Her expression dimmed. "I still don't know. I have a suspicion it's the same person who left the totem for me in the first place—the same one who left the first letter. Ever since then, I can't shake the feeling that I'm being watched."

Watched? Geez, that was creepy. "So what else did the letter tell you?"

"That there are four totems, one for each element, and each one can only have one wielder. After that person is chosen, the totem will stay with them until death or until one of the laws is broken."

I moved in closer. "What laws?"

"Our totems are governed by three laws. First, each totem's power is equal in strength. That means fighting against each other is almost pointless. Of course, practice and skill make a difference," she smirked at me, "but a fight between two expert totem wielders would ultimately end in a draw. One cancels out the other, in a way. Second, we can only use the power of our *full* transformation for four minutes, and after that we lose the ability to use our totem at all for twenty-four hours."

"Full transformation?"

"It's hard to explain. The information I got called it 'embracing the soul of the kur.' It's easier to think of it as a full-dragon form, I suppose."

"Full-dragon form?" My ears perked up. "Like, different from this? Like a super awesome ultra-dragon evolution?"

She shot me an irritated glare. "I don't know for sure. I haven't figured out how to use it. I mean, I have an idea. The notes I received made it sound fairly straightforward. It's just too risky to experiment with. Supposedly, full dragon form is our greatest weapon, but we have to use it sparingly."

I nodded. "Got it. What's the third law?"

"You already know this one: if anyone sees you change, you lose your powers forever. And the best way to avoid being seen changing is to protect your identity. No one can know who we really are."

"So you're smarter than me, better at flying, better at using your powers," I counted on my fingers. "And you're not worried at all about letting me fly off to save the day by myself?"

She let out a feminine, dragony giggle. "I said I would teach you, not babysit you. Besides, you just got started. Give it some time. I'm sure you'll get better."

"I've heard that before." I groaned.

Seriously, Dad had said that exact thing to me at least a hundred times since I was a little kid. T-ball, soccer, hockey, tennis, basketball, and even a junior bowling team—I had been absolutely terrible at all of it. You know it's bad when they didn't even give me the Most Improved Player award because… I hadn't improved. I sucked as bad at the end of the season as I had at the beginning.

"Maybe this is your chance to finally, truly shine then." She was smiling again.

"I hope so," I murmured. I was way overdue a shining moment. I wasn't hoping for much, really—just one small thing to be good at.

"We should get going." The blue dragon-girl started striding away, flapping her wings to artfully glide from one steel beam to another. She paused for a moment when she reached an opening in the glass ceiling, glancing back at me. "Watch yourself, boy."

"Name the noble gases."

Lying across my bed with his head hanging over the edge, Drake looked at his phone upside down. He'd been working with me for a few weeks, coming over whenever he didn't have Robotics Club meetings in the afternoons to try to coach me into catching up with all my classwork. He didn't even need the textbook or notes to quiz me for Chemistry.

I, on the other hand, suspected I was at risk for a brain hemorrhage. All my notes lay scattered around me on the floor like a bird nest, but none of them seemed to have the answers to the questions he was asking.

"Uh…krypton, like on *Superman*."

"And they call me a nerd," he muttered.

I shot him a glare. "Neon, xenon, helium, oxygen—"

"Bzzzzzzt." He made a loud buzzing noise. "Wrong. We were looking for argon and radon."

I groaned and resisted the urge to hurl a few of my notebooks across the room. "What's the point of memorizing all this if we can just use a picture of the periodic table?"

"What's the point of knowing anything?" Drake countered.

Now I had the urge to throw him, too.

"Next question. Give me the atomic number of hydrogen."

"Can we take a break?"

"It's only been an hour." He tilted his head back to look at me upside down.

"I'm starving. Why is Dad so late?" I picked up my phone to send him another text.

"So where's your mom?"

I hesitated with my finger hovering over the send button. There it was—*the* question. Ever since our awkward discussion at the lunch, I'd been treading lightly around the subject of our parents. I'd also been watching him to see if I could spot more bruises. So far, I hadn't seen any. In fact, everything seemed pretty normal. Drake was weird, like me, and we were becoming really good friends. I liked hanging out with him.

But now he'd gone and asked *that* question.

"She's dead," I answered quietly.

I could feel his gaze on me. "Oh."

"Like you said before, it was a long time ago."

His soft chuckle was hollow and humorless. "Doesn't make it any easier, does it?"

"No," I agreed. "It doesn't."

I followed Drake's gaze across my room to the picture sitting on my top shelf—the one of my family before Mom passed away. It was just a snapshot of the three of us playing in the snow. A pudgy-faced toddler, I perched on Dad's shoulders while Mom leaned in to snap the photograph. Pictures and stories were all I had now.

"Was she military, too?" Drake asked.

I shook my head. "Dad met her while he was stationed in Japan. She worked for a local real estate office part time when Dad started looking for an apartment in Tokyo. They got married less than a year later."

"She was pretty," Drake said quietly.

I stared at the picture. "Yeah, she was."

The silence grew heavy as the memories fluttered around me, an invisible snow of images, smells, and sounds that took me far away. Then I heard the front door open downstairs. Dad was home. He began calling for us to come down for food.

Halfway down the stairs I could smell it—the fragrant aroma of melted cheese, garlicky sauce, and greasy baked goodness. Dad stacked four pizza boxes on the kitchen counter and backed away while Drake and I descended like vultures.

"Sorry I'm late, boys." He chuckled and started the long process of unlacing his uniform boots. "Getting a lot of studying done?"

I was about to lie but Drake beat me to it. "Sorta. He keeps whining about it."

Dad flicked me a look of parental warning. "Well, keep after him. I was promised no Ds this year."

Drake gave a mock salute. "I'll do my best."

We gathered up our portion of the food and started back upstairs. I hoped to procrastinate as long as possible. But Drake kept his word and acted like a cattle driver, prodding me through another grueling hour of the periodic table. Two pizza boxes, three chapters of Chemistry, one chapter of American Literature, and a few hours of video games later, he finally announced he had to go home.

"Clint is gonna be furious," he grumbled as he packed up his bag.

I was still scrolling through high scores on my favorite street racing game. Drake had pretty much destroyed all of my records. He was insanely good at video games—not that I expected much else from surfer Einstein.

"Who's Clint?" I asked distractedly.

"My mom's idiot boyfriend. He basically lives with us."

His defensive tone made me glance away from the TV screen. "So what's he like?"

Drake's eyes darkened. "I can't stand him. He's supposed to be keeping an eye on me while Mom is at work during the week, but all he does is eat all our food, watch TV, and drink."

Suddenly, I had a new possible culprit for those bruises on his arm. "So why is your mom dating him?"

"I don't know." He grimaced like he didn't even want to think about it. I watched him sling his bag over his shoulder and start for the door. "Hey, I won't be able to tutor you tomorrow. I've got another Robotics Club meeting after school. We've only got a few more practices before the semifinals."

"Oh, okay. That's fine. Maybe this weekend?"

Drake gave me a nod before he left. His footsteps thumped down the stairs, and a few seconds later, I heard the front door open and close. Then the house was quiet. Dad had gone to bed a long time ago. It was late and I was tired, but I couldn't stop thinking about Drake. Was Clint the one responsible for those bruises? Or was this just a huge misunderstanding on my part? Maybe he had some legit reason for the finger-like bruises on his arm. Was I jumping to conclusions?

Somehow, I had to find out more.

My hand drifted instinctively to the totem bracelet around my wrist. I'd already finished my three dragon totem lessons. According to my blue dragon-lady friend, there wasn't much else she could teach me. I had to practice the basics, and figure out what my elemental power was. Since it would be different than hers, so I was pretty much on my own there. I tried to convince her that if we kept practicing together, it would help both of us improve. But true to her word, as soon as our three lessons were up, she'd disappeared without a trace. Now I practiced on my own in the abandoned power plant, although I kept hoping she'd come back.

And as much as I tried not to take it personally, I couldn't help feeling a little hurt that she hadn't stayed around. It was lonely without her. Besides, I still needed help. Sure, I was getting better at flying, but I still hadn't figured out what my element was or what this third eye thing was all about. The dragon-girl had mentioned she'd only discovered her own elemental power when she got really angry and emotional—so maybe that was the problem. I wasn't emotional enough or something.

I frowned and rolled onto my side, staring out across my room. All the lights were out, but the glow from the cityscape outside my window made long shadows stretch across the floor. The picture on the top shelf—the one of my parents and me— was difficult to make out in the gloom, but I could see it like it was tattooed on the inside of my eyelids. Sorrow sunk into my chest like a white-hot knife. I squeezed my eyes shut, trying to block it out. Thinking about Mom always made me emotional.

But not enough to use my elemental power, apparently.

There had to be another way, something the blue-scaled girl didn't know about. There had to be something I was missing—I just had to figure out what.

CHAPTER ~7~

Five minutes before the first bell, I threw myself into my seat in Chemistry. Drake was already there, totally zoned out as far as I could tell. He sat slumped forward, forehead on the table as he stared at his phone in his lap. Nothing unusual there.

Tossing my bag onto the lab table, I used it like a pillow while I waited for the bell to ring. Trying to balance totem training with schoolwork was really beginning to wear me down.

"I don't know how much more of this I can take," I groaned. "Good thing we aren't studying tonight. I feel like I might start bleeding from the nose if I memorize one more thing. All I wanna do is take a nap."

Drake didn't reply.

I shrugged off his silence and watched the rest of my classmates file in. Over the few weeks we'd been hanging out, I'd gotten used to his quirks. Sometimes, if he got really fixated on something he was reading or watching, he would sit for a long time without saying a word. It didn't bother me. People said I talked too much, anyway.

Mr. Biceps, also known as Damien Blount, strode in flanked by his usual group of buddies from judo class. They trolled the hallways like something from an old fifties film—only they wore judo gis instead of leather jackets, and too much hair gel. Okay, so maybe the hair gel was about the same. Just the sight of them made my lip curl. They shoved one another, laughing and cutting up on their way to sit down. I hated his perfectly styled hair and bleached white teeth almost as much as I hated that he always sat right next to Claire.

She came in after him, gliding along next to that redheaded girl. Since our encounter in the main hall, I'd learned her name was Tabitha Hunt. According to Drake, she was Claire's best friend. She was pretty, I guess, although there was something pointy and foxlike about her face. Her narrow eyes always had a cunning glint to them.

I guess it wasn't fair to judge her just by how she looked. Except for her comment about my shoelaces, I hadn't spoken to her at all, and I'd never actually caught her making fun of me. It was just a feeling I had—like she might be one of those people who'd enjoy manipulating me or making me look stupid in front of everyone else.

The bell rang and everyone cleared their desks to begin taking notes. I slid my bag off the table and rummaged through it for my notebook and pencil, already dreading the hand cramp I was going to have in about an hour. This particular teacher loved giving us dozens of pages of "crucial" notes for every lecture.

I was busy rattling pages, looking for a blank one, when I heard the teacher call out over the noise.

"Drake Collins, you need to remove your sunglasses. They are a violation of the uniform code."

I looked over at Drake. He sat perfectly still, his shoulders hunched and his arms folded on the lab table. The big aviator sunglasses perched on his nose hid most of his face. Weird. I'd never seen him wear those before.

"Mr. Collins, do you hear me? Take them off immediately or I'll refer you to the headmaster," the teacher demanded.

Everyone in class had turned to look at him now.

Slowly, he raised a hand and took off the sunglasses. His whole body trembled as he sat, his gaze locked on the lab table in front of him. Something wasn't right.

He flicked a quick glance in my direction, almost like he was afraid.

And I saw his eye.

One of Drake's eyes was black, blue, and purple and swollen completely shut.

The whole class erupted into gasps and whispers.

Words failed me. I couldn't do anything except stare at him with my mouth hanging open. Someone had given him the worst black eye I'd ever seen.

"Silence! Everyone! I said, *be quiet!*" the teacher shouted over the noise until, at last, she snatched up her coffee cup and slammed it down on her desk.

The murmurs and whispers hushed.

"Mr. Collins, pack up your things and follow me. The rest of you begin copying the vocabulary words out of chapters four and five. I don't want to hear a single peep out of this classroom when I come back, am I understood?"

I leaned over, whispering frantically, "Drake? What's going on? What happened to your—"

He didn't give me a chance to finish.

The teacher stood by the door, holding it ajar while Drake snatched his bag and nearly ran into the hallway with her.

About a millisecond after the door clicked shut behind them, Tabitha whirled in her seat to leer at me. "You two are friends, right? What happened? Did someone beat him up?"

"I don't know. He was fine yesterday." I was only half lying. After all, this wasn't the first time I'd seen him with bruises. Although a few fingermarks on his arm was nothing compared to this.

"Damien, you didn't do this, did you?" Claire started to interrogate her beefy fiancé.

He raised his hands in surrender. "Of course not! He's a weird little guy, but I don't have any issues with him. He keeps to himself. Besides, you know I wouldn't try to fight someone outside of a match. Coach would kill me, and then my dad would probably bring me back to life so he could kill me again."

She seemed to believe him. And as much as it pained me, I got the sense that he was telling the truth, too. Drake had never mentioned that Damien, or anyone else at the school, was giving him a hard time. I certainly hadn't witnessed anything like that. If anything, people seemed to either like or totally ignore him.

The rest of the classed went on whispering among themselves, joining the debate. As sick and twisted as it was, they seemed to enjoy reveling in the scandal of it. It was something new for them to gossip and speculate about.

But that was *my* friend they were yacking about.

Sinking back into my chair, I didn't say anything else while the rest of the class buzzed with excitement. One truth hung over my head and made my gut wrench with anger and regret: someone had hurt Drake. I didn't know for certain who it was, or if they could do it again. Sure, I had my suspicions about that Clint guy he'd mentioned, but no real evidence. I'd seen a hint of it before and done nothing. I'd been too nervous to ask him straight up.

I wouldn't make that mistake again. Figuring out who hurt him was officially my one and only concern—totem practice would have to wait.

Drake didn't reappear until lunch. I found him sitting in our usual spot near the back of the lunchroom, holding a big gel ice pack to his eye. There was an untouched tray of food in front of him, and he didn't even look up when I sat across from him.

I waited a few minutes before I finally dared to ask, "Are they gonna make you stay home from school?"

Drake looked at me with his good eye. "No. But I have to wear a bandage until it heals."

"Did they call your mom?"

He nodded slightly.

I didn't know where to begin. Before I could find the right words, Drake let out a growly, frustrated sigh. "Just go ahead and ask. You look like you're about to have an aneurism or something."

So I did. "Who did this to you?"

He slowly took the icepack off his eye, cringing as he ran his fingers over the bruised, swollen skin like he was trying to feel how bad the damage was. I could tell he was stalling. He kept swallowing hard. His brow drew together, furrowed deeply, and his jaw locked as though he were clenching his teeth. The corners of his mouth twitched. He was fighting, trying to hold it together.

"Drake." I leaned across the table and kept my voice down. "I'm not asking because I want to blab about it. I won't tell another soul. I'm asking because if there's something going on and you need help, I want you to know you can trust me. I know we haven't been friends for very long, but I'm gonna do whatever I can to help you."

He studied me from behind a guarded scowl, his one good cognac-colored eye searching me thoroughly. Drake wasn't an especially big guy. He was short for his age and kinda on the skinny side like I was. Neither of us looked like we were built for brawling. He had every reason to be afraid if my suspicions were true about who was doing this to him.

"It was that Clint guy your mom is dating, wasn't it? This is why you don't like him. Am I right?"

Without a word, Drake slowly bobbed his head up and down again.

I let out a slow, shaking breath. Rage like an inferno blazed through my chest, thrumming from the bracelet on my wrist. "Did you tell the headmaster?"

He shook his head, his blond hair swishing over his brow.

"Why not? Maybe they could help—"

"Clint said if I tell anyone he will make it look like Mom did it to me. He's such a liar, Koji. You have no idea. He's manipulative and always twists things around so it looks like he's innocent!" He panicked, talking faster as the color started to drain from his face. His gaze darted back and forth wildly, and his hands clenched tight on the table. "My mom doesn't have enough money for a good lawyer. They'd take me from her, and I'd wind up in some foster home or worse. She might even go to jail." He was breathing hard and his one good eye began to well up.

"Okay, okay. Calm down, all right?" I reached across to put a hand on his arm, trying to steady him before he had a total meltdown right here in the middle of the lunchroom. "We'll figure this out. I promise."

He didn't meet my eyes. "H-how?"

Think—I had to think. Looking down at the food on my lunch tray, I hoped I'd find the answer somewhere in today's roasted turkey sandwich on sourdough with a side of sweet potato fries. No such luck.

"How about you stay at my house tonight after your robotics meeting?" I suggested.

Drake held the icepack to his face again. "I can't just hide from this, Koji. Eventually, I have to go back home and face him. Besides, if I don't go back, he'll get suspicious. No—just forget it. It'll be fine."

"Fine? Are you kidding me? Look, we could talk to my dad. You know, maybe there's something he can do," I tried again.

"No! Just stop it, I'm serious!" Drake stood up suddenly and shouted, "I'm fine. I've always been fine. Just because we've hung out a few times doesn't mean you get to meddle around in my life!"

The lunchroom went quiet. Everyone stared at us. Drake's whole body trembled and his face flushed. He opened his mouth but seemed to choke on whatever he'd intended to say. Without a word, he bolted out of the lunchroom and into the hall, slamming the door behind him.

Then all eyes were on me.

I shrank down, wishing I could melt into the floor. My face felt hot, and I wanted to crawl inside my newly monogrammed book bag to hide. It took a few minutes for the normal lunchroom chatter to resume, but even then, I could still feel people staring at me.

Whatever. It didn't matter. Drake was in trouble, and I didn't know what to do. My mind raced, torn between what I knew was right and making Drake even more upset. I should tell Dad—I knew that. Someone had to get an adult involved, someone who would believe Drake and do something to help.

But Drake was my friend. I didn't want to go behind his back. He was scared and probably not thinking clearly. Once he calmed down, maybe he would agree that talking to my dad or a teacher was the best option.

At least, that's what I hoped. Only time would tell, and I had no choice but to wait.

Sitting alone, I couldn't bring myself to eat anything for the rest of the lunch period. When the bell rang, I took both of our lunch trays to the trash and wandered slowly to my next class.

The rest of the day passed in a haze as I dragged myself from class to class. Before I knew it, I was sitting in art class, staring out the window while Mr. Molins rambled about the art of ceramics.

The more I thought about it, the more I worried I'd broken some kind of sacred rule of friendship. If Drake quit talking to me because of this, I'd have no friends here at all. What then?

Mr. Molins cleared his throat as he walked past my work-station. I startled, suddenly aware that I should at least look like I was paying attention.

"Now, everyone get into pairs of two. We're going to begin our introduction to pottery today. You might want to bring an extra sweatshirt from home—just something you don't mind getting dirty since this is going to get messy. There aren't enough pottery wheels for you to each have your own, so you'll have to work with a partner."

I studied the pottery wheel closest to me dubiously. It looked like something I might break while trying to figure it out. I hadn't even begun wondering who would be my partner when I felt a soft tap lightly on my arm.

"Um, would you mind being my partner?" Madeline murmured.

I glanced around the room, noticing that everyone else had already paired off. "Sure. Sorry, looks like I'm the only choice left, huh?"

A gentle smile played over her lips. "I don't mind. Have you ever used a pottery wheel before?"

"Uh, no. But I'm betting this is a little more complicated than play dough, right?"

"Yeah, a little." She giggled, scooting her stool closer to mine. With saintly patience, Madeline walked me through how to operate the foot pedal that turned the wheel. The faster she pumped the pedal, the faster the wheel spun.

Mr. Molins gave each of us a small lump of clay and a bowl of water, then sat behind his own wheel and explained how to work with the clay. I tried to watch, honestly, but my attention was drawn to Madeline. I couldn't help it. It was totally out of my control—like gravity or the pull of an ocean tide. There was something so…serene about the way she talked.

Sitting behind the pottery wheel, her sleeves rolled to her elbows and her silky black hair in a messy bun, she patted her hunk of clay and nibbled on her bottom lip. She dipped her slender hands into the water and began pumping the foot pedal, faster and faster, her gray-blue eyes so intense and focused on the clay spinning before her. She held her wet hands against the clay, adding subtle pressure here and there. The clay moved under her hands, molding and shifting as though by magic. It was amazing.

"See?" She looked up at me, a few strands of her hair stuck to a smudge of clay on her forehead.

Oh crap. I guess she'd been talking the whole time.

"Uh, yeah, totally," I sputtered.

"Okay then." She gave a bright smile and hopped off the stool. "Your turn."

I gulped. Easing down on the stool, I started rolling my sweater and dress shirtsleeves to my elbows.

"That's a pretty bracelet," Madeline said.

My breath caught. Oh no. I'd forgotten I was even wearing it—which, according to school policy, was a violation of the headmaster's ridiculously strict uniform code. I quickly stole a glance around the classroom to see if Mr. Molins had noticed. Fortunately, he was on the other side of the room talking with another group of students.

"Thanks." I rubbed the back of my neck nervously. "Okay, so I push the pedal…"

"No, don't push it. It's not like a car accelerator. Use a rocking motion with your foot, smooth and consistent," she instructed. "Here, I'll show you."

She bent down right next to me, her shoulder brushing mine as she took my hands, guiding them in the water then carefully positioning them on either side of the clay—just barely touching the sticky, wet surface of it.

"Okay," she said. "Start rocking the pedal. Slowly at first."

Madeline's hands guided mine, and I couldn't help but notice how tiny they were by comparison. I was trying not to be extra creepy and stare at her, but I could have sworn she was blushing. Weird. I couldn't remember ever making a girl blush like that before. I told myself it was only because it was awkward to be so close and touching hands.

Then I noticed her wrists.

Right at the joint of both her wrists, her milky fair skin was blemished with scars. They seemed old and faded with time, but the skin was so raised and gnarled you couldn't miss them.

My stomach churned at the sight. My heart skipped a beat. What would leave a mark like that? The scars went all the way around her wrists, as though someone had tied her hands or handcuffed them tightly enough to split the skin.

"Okay, start rocking your foot faster now," she said, interrupting my internal frenzy. "Not too fast, though. Find the speed that feels comfortable. Let your hands just lightly graze the clay and begin adding pressure. You'll see how adding pressure, pushing, or pulling will mold it." Madeline swiftly withdrew her hands and took a big step away from me.

Oh no. Had she noticed me staring?

"I'm gonna break it or something," I warned her, trying to break the awkward tension as the ball of clay whirled faster.

She laughed a little. "You're doing fine. Just keep going."

We practiced with the clay for most of the class. Mr. Molins went from pair to pair, giving pointers and showing techniques and tools that made different kinds of ceramics. When he stopped and stared at my lopsided, pitiful excuse for a vase, however, his smile was so forced it looked painful.

"I've never tried ceramics before," I said like it was an apology.

"It does take some getting used to. Don't worry. Maddie is very good with the pottery wheel. I'm sure she'll have you cranking out top shelf pieces in no time."

Madeline bowed her head some as though the compliment embarrassed her.

Only, I knew that wasn't it.

"Actually, sir." I spoke up before he could walk too far away. "She likes for us to call her Madeline, not Maddie."

He blinked at me in surprise. "Oh?"

"Yeah."

"Very well then." Mr. Molins looked between us and smiled strangely, like he had a secret he wasn't going to tell.

When I turned to ask Madeline about it, I found her standing stiffly, her gray eyes fixed on me with a look of complete shock.

"You okay?" I was beginning to think maybe she was having some kind of seizure.

"Fine," she squeaked and instantly turned to arranging all the pottery tools that didn't really need to be arranged.

Hmm.

For the last fifteen minutes of class, after we'd cleaned up our pottery mess, everyone got to work on their art journals. Some kids worked with newspaper and magazine collages. Others, like Madeline, began to paint. I pinned a blank piece of paper to my easel and started drawing. I'd figured out what I wanted some of the secondary characters to look like, but I couldn't get the main character just right. Turns out, drawing a dragon-like superhero isn't easy.

I got so into the designs that the fifteen minutes blurred by. When the bell rang, I sat back. I still didn't like any of the things I'd come up with. I was about to crumple up the page and toss it when Mr. Molins stopped me.

"No, you need to save it," he said as he examined my work. "This is what the journal is all about, Koji. It's about recording your journey through the year. Not every piece will be perfect, just like not every day goes exactly the way we want it."

"Oh." I hesitated, glancing at the page riddled with rough sketches of dragon wings, tails, clawed hands, and scale patterns. Maybe something was hidden in there I could salvage later. Shrugging, I took the page and put it in the plastic bin on one of the shelves that had my name on it—a place for me to store all my work.

Madeline was still cleaning her paintbrushes when I returned and picked up my bag. I wondered if Drake would be waiting for me at the bottom of the stairs today or not. Probably not. The idea that I'd lost my first real friend at this school sucked. Worse than sucked, really. It felt pretty freaking horrible.

"Is everything okay?" Madeline had stopped next to me on her way to the sink, her hands full of paintbrushes and pallets smeared with vibrant colors. A swipe of bright purple highlighted one of her cheeks, matching the smudge of clay still on her forehead.

"Yeah," I fibbed. "Just tired. See you tomorrow."

My excuse sounded lame, even to me. Regardless, she didn't try to stop me as I slung my bag over my shoulder and started downstairs.

CHAPTER 8

Drake wasn't anywhere in sight as I walked my usual path through the main hall to the front doors of the school. I waited until I was outside to check my phone, wondering if he'd left me a message.

Nope. No new notifications.

I checked my phone about a dozen more times before I got to the front door of the house. Still no messages. I wondered if I should send him one, just to ask if he was okay. That would have been safe, right? Even if he was angry, I at least wanted to know he was alive.

"Hey, Koji!" Dad's voice called out as I came in the front door.

Stunned, I shambled into the kitchen to find him unpacking boxes. "Uh, hey. What's going on? Why are you home early?"

"I slipped out so I could get started settling us in. I don't know about you, but I'm getting sick of digging through boxes every time I need something. Also, I thought you and I could go to the store and get some real food."

I dropped my bag on the kitchen counter and watched as Dad went digging through one of the big boxes labeled KITCH- EN DISHES. He wore gray sweatpants and a navy blue hoodie—civilian clothes—before seven. Weird didn't even begin to describe it. *And* he was unpacking within the first month of arriving at our new place? Totally unheard of in the Owens household. It was like staring into a carnival exhibit, and I wondered if I was hallucinating or maybe having some kind of out of body experience.

"What the heck is this, Koji?" Dad held up a garlic crusher.

I smirked. "It's for mincing garlic."

"Don't they sell it already minced?"

"Yeah, but it tastes better if you do it yourself."

He raised a brow like he didn't believe me. "Whatever you say, kiddo. So how was school?"

I hated that question—especially today. Sinking down into the other empty barstool, I slumped over the counter and sighed. "Honestly, it was terrible."

He stopped unpacking and turned one of those somber, parental stares on me that always felt like a silent warning. "Did you get in trouble?"

"No, no. Nothing like that."

"What happened?"

I still wasn't sure if I should tell him. I'd promised not to blab. Even so, this situation was the kind of thing that begged for an adult's perspective. I had no idea what Drake had told the headmaster about what happened to his eye, but I was willing to bet it wasn't the truth.

I decided to play it safe. "What would you do if someone you knew was sort of in trouble, like at home, but they didn't want you or anyone else to help them?"

Dad went back to unpacking. "I suppose that would depend on what kind of trouble you're talking about."

"Like… someone beating them up."

"So, abuse?"

I looked away and began tracing the natural swirly designs in the marble countertop. "Yeah. Kinda like that."

"That's a pretty serious situation, Koji." Dad crunched up a ball of packing paper and tossed it in the open trash bag by the pantry. "Is this person's life in danger?"

"I don't know. He—er—they won't talk about it much. And today when I tried to help, he got angry. I don't think he wants to hang out with me anymore."

"Abuse is never a simple matter, and the longer it goes on, the more complicated and dangerous it gets." He was using his firm, instructive voice as he went on working. "Victims sometimes feel like anyone they reach out to will also be in danger, or that their own situation will get even worse. Fear is a powerful weapon. I think the most important thing you can do for him right now is just to be there—even if he tries to push you away. Despite what he says, he needs a friend now more than ever. It's a hard thing, getting someone to trust you who isn't used to being able to trust anyone."

"I guess so." I chewed on the inside of my cheek. "I just...I don't like standing by and watching it happen, Dad. I hate that."

He put a hand on my shoulder. "I know, son. We're a lot alike in that way. But you've got to respect his wishes, too. So just talk to him. Don't offer him any opinions or suggestions or try to tell him what to do; just listen. Sometimes listening is the most important thing people forget to do."

"You're not going to call the cops or anything, right?" I was beginning to suspect Dad knew exactly who we were talking about. "I'm pretty sure he would hate me if he found out I told someone."

"Tell you what, if you think his life is in danger and it's time to do something to stop it, then we will both go down to the police station and make an anonymous statement about it. He won't know who turned it in, and you'll feel better knowing your friend will get some help. Sound like a plan?"

I nodded. "I think I can live with that."

Dad ruffled my hair and went back to unpacking. "Good. Now come on, let's get the kitchen unpacked, and then we'll see about some groceries. I might even get a little crazy and let you pick where we eat tonight."

"Yes! Indian food. I can't wait." I drummed on the counter-top excitedly. "I'm getting samosas!"

Dad pretended to gag. "Ugh. I knew I'd regret that."

The next morning, Drake was sitting on the front steps of the school when I arrived. As soon as he saw me coming, he bound-ed to his feet and jogged over to meet me. He had a white eye patch covering his injured eye.

"Hey," he mumbled as he followed along beside me into the school.

"Hey," I muttered back.

"Sorry about losing it yesterday."

I didn't reply.

"I'm not used to actually have a *friend*, you know. Like, a real one. Most people find me weird, or annoying, or they think I'm a jerk because I'm smarter than they are—which is usually true. I'm generally smarter than everyone I meet."

I shot him a "get to the point" glare.

"Look, I know you were just trying to help. But I've been dealing with Clint for a couple of years and it'll be fine. Trust me." Drake stepped out to plant himself directly in my path. "Sometimes it gets bad, but he always backs off and everything is okay again."

I was forced to stop and look him in his remaining good eye.

"So, are we cool?"

I squinted and thought it over. Then I held my hand out. "The eye patch."

He frowned. "What?"

"Gimme the eye patch."

"Why?"

I grinned. "Best friend gets to sign it first, right?"

"Seriously? You suck." Drake groaned as he took off the patch and handed it over.

I pulled a marker out of my bag and made some quick modifications before giving it back.

Drake laughed when he saw it. And everyone who saw him wearing it after that probably thought he was insane. I'd drawn him a big googly eye on his patch.

"You think they'll bust me for a dress code violation?" He snickered as we sat down in Chemistry.

"Probably." I bent over and started digging for my notes in my bag. "Too bad it's not black. Then you'd look like a pirate."

Drake nudged me with his foot. I assumed he was just doing it to annoy me. But then he kicked me right in the ankle, so hard I almost dropped my notebook.

I sat up, ready to snap the elastic on that eye patch of his. "Hey, knock it—"

Claire was standing right beside my desk.

I choked out, "O-o-oh. Hey. Uh, yeah, uh, good morning."

Drake face-palmed.

"Good morning." She looked right past me to Drake with a polite smile. The morning light glistened off her perfect golden curls. I imagined that must have been how Venus looked when she materialized out of sea foam. "I was just wondering if I could get your help with something. I know you're pretty good with electronics and there's something wrong with the sound system in the auditorium. Would you mind coming to take a look?"

Drake's one visible eye widened. "Me?"

"I'm sorry, I know you're probably really swamped with preparations for the robotics tournament. But you're the first person I thought of when they said it was an electrical problem," she explained. "Someone is supposed to fix it tomorrow, but I really need to practice this afternoon."

"Uh, yeah. Sure. I can take a look." Drake slid me a sly glance. "If you don't mind me bringing my sidekick along, that is. I'll make sure he doesn't break anything."

Sidekick?! Oh, he was in for it now.

Claire's soft gaze met mine. I tried to restrain my pure mortification and smile—yes, I needed to smile. Play it cool. All I managed was an awkward little wave. Definitely not cool.

I heard Drake snorting back laughter.

"Okay. Meet me in the auditorium after school?"

After Claire had gone back to her seat, Drake muttered, "Dude, that was pathetic. And that's coming from someone who has never had a girlfriend."

I laid my head down on the lab table and prayed for death. "I'm such an idiot."

"Yep."

"I'm never going to get a date."

"Probably not."

"Do I even stand a chance with someone like that? I mean, am I totally out of my mind here?" I trusted him to give it to me straight. Drake wasn't going to sugarcoat it to spare my feelings.

He sighed and propped himself up on his elbow, fiddling with his phone. "All statistical probability suggests you don't have a prayer. Not a snowflake's chance in hell. But, I dunno, bizarre stuff has been happening around here lately. With extraterrestrial crafts leaving craters in Central Park, Koji Owens getting a date with the princess doesn't seem so impossible."

I rolled my head to the side enough to glare at him. "Gee, thanks."

He shrugged. "You asked."

"So you honestly think I've got a shot?"

"Depends," he said as he slid his headphones on.

"On what?"

"On whether or not you can figure out how to talk in complete sentences around her."

"You better not just be saying that to make me seem like less of a dork," I groaned.

He cracked a smile and cranked up his music. "Koji, there's nothing anyone could say that would make you less of a dork."

Before now, I'd never had any reason to wander down the halls where the dancers and musicians practiced. This part of the school was different from the rest I'd seen—it seemed even older, if that was possible. Intricate plaster scrollwork bordered the tall, cavernous ceilings, and blood-red velvety carpet covered the floor. The huge crystal chandeliers hung dark, though. Someone had already switched off the lights for the day.

"It looks like Phantom of the Opera or something," I muttered.

Drake snickered as he led the way down the spooky hallway. "Well, they do say it's haunted. And the basement is supposed to be a real mess."

We made our way up to the auditorium's main entrance at the far end of the hall. The doors were closed, but I could already hear music. It resonated with force and energy, sending pulsations and swells humming in the air. They got louder as we got closer, and when Drake opened one of the doors to let us both inside, I finally saw the source.

The grand auditorium sloped, with three sections of seating leading down to a stage just above a sunken orchestra pit. Centered on the stage, in front of a tall red curtain, sat an illuminated figure who was all too familiar to me now.

My breath caught.

Claire was perched on the edge of a black chair. Her golden hair spilled over her shoulders, dazzling in the spotlight. She cradled a cello against her shoulder, right against her neck. Eyes closed, intensity and euphoric concentration creased her brow. With one hand she pressed and pulled against the neck of the instrument, and with the other she maneuvered a long, slender bow across the strings. Every stroke made the instrument sing a beautiful, almost mournful tune in her arms.

I knew nothing about instruments, or music in general for that matter. I was pretty good at the old *Rock Band* video game, but that's about where my expertise ended. What I saw and felt while watching her perform was like stealing a peek through the doors of heaven. It stopped me in my tracks.

Drake elbowed me. "Hey, you coming?"

"Yeah." I was glad he couldn't see me blushing in the dark.

I followed him down the aisle of seats to the very front of the room, up the stairs, and onto the stage. We stood off to the side, watching Claire play through several more minutes of her song until, at last, she opened her eyes and smiled at us. Drake gave her a little round of applause.

"That's Bach, right? Suite Number 1 in G Major?"

I sort of hated him for knowing that because, well, I didn't.

Claire looked away bashfully as she set her cello aside. "Yes. Do you enjoy Bach?"

He shrugged. "Not exclusively."

"I'm sorry, I didn't see you come in. Thank you so much for doing this. I'll try not to take up too much of your time." She stood up and smoothed out her pleated uniform skirt. "Could you hear me in the back? They're saying it sounds like the speakers on the left side of the auditorium are making a buzzing sound."

"Yeah. I could hear it a little. It's like a hum, right? Let's go take a look."

Drake waved for us to follow, and together we navigated the aisles to a small room at the very back that overlooked the entire auditorium. It had a one-way glass window so we could see out but no one would be able to see inside. Not that there was much to see except for a few big, archaic-looking control panels with dozens of buttons and dials. It was like something from a vintage episode of *Star Trek*—like maybe we could land a spaceship with it.

"All righty, let's see what we've got." Drake immediately threw himself into the rolling chair at the nearest control panel, took out his phone, and plugged it in to one of the dangling wires. A funky techno pop tune started playing through the auditorium's speakers.

While he made adjustments to the sound, his fingers flying over the controls, Claire and I stood back and watched. It was awkward—for me, anyway. Standing right next to her, I couldn't look at her for more than a few seconds without feeling like a total idiot. I tried to think of something casual and not weird to say. I reached for words. Something. Anything!

Nothing. My head was still swimming from watching her play, tangled up in the bars of her music.

At last, Drake slumped back in the chair and sighed. "So much for the easy fix. This system is pretty outdated. It's probably on its last leg. But I'll try to adjust some of the wiring, and then we can try giving it the old hard reboot and see if that helps. Do you know where the breakers are?"

"I think they're in the basement," Claire replied.

"Okay. Give me like five minutes and then throw the breakers off and on again. Just once. No need to give this old dinosaur a heart attack." He was already rolling his chair away from the control panel and rolling up his sleeves.

More finger-shaped bruises covered both of his forearms. Some were greenish yellow, as though they were healing. But others were dark purple and blue—fresh.

I clenched my teeth and looked away.

"Koji, why don't you go with her?" Drake was grinning wickedly, like a mad scientist who'd just found a new corpse to reanimate, when I glanced back at him. "You know, 'cause it's dark and scary down there. And who knows, maybe this place really is haunted."

Claire giggled. "That's ridiculous! Who's saying it's haunted?"

Drake waggled his eyebrows and got back to work, climbing underneath the control panel. When we left, he was already ripping out handfuls of cables that looked like they were probably important.

"I hope he doesn't break anything," I muttered as I followed Claire back into the auditorium.

"Me too," Claire agreed. "But then again, if he does, maybe we'll finally get a new sound system installed."

When we were halfway to the stage, Drake changed the song playing over the loudspeakers. Was that... "Careless Whisper"? Seriously? I shot the control booth a dirty look—mostly because I was sure he was just making fun of me again.

Claire didn't seem to care. Either that, or she didn't get the joke. I decided to put my hopes on the latter, since the first meant I stood absolutely no chance with her.

Without a word, she led me through the auditorium and backstage. Behind the red velvet curtain, instruments, cases, and old theater props were piled everywhere. They made large, strangely shaped shadows in the gloom and it gave the whole place a spooky atmosphere. In the furthest corner of the back-stage gloom, Claire stopped in front of an old freight elevator. I'd only ever seen an elevator like it in movies. The ancient, iron-wrought lattice gate on the front had to be opened and closed manually.

Claire walked up to it without skipping a beat, opened the gate, and turned back to smile at me expectantly.

I stared at her, then at the box of death she was inviting me into. Hmm.

"Don't worry, it's fine. We use it all the time to move the heavy instruments and prop pieces," she coaxed, although something in her tone seemed off. I got that weird, tingling, itchy feeling in the back of my mind again. For whatever reason, I got the sense she didn't trust this elevator, either.

I swallowed hard. "It's not that, uh, it's just…"

Crap. I could *not* look like a coward in front of her. It was just a stupid, prehistoric, possibly lethal elevator. I could handle it. With a deep breath, I shook off the screeching alarm bells raging in my head, forced a smile back in her direction, and climbed inside.

Claire got in next to me and shut the gate, then punched the big button with a downward pointing arrow on it. The elevator began making angry grinding noises. Suddenly, the whole thing shuddered violently. I grabbed onto the closest thing for balance—her.

Oh no, I was holding her hand.

"Are you okay?" She didn't pull her hand away.

"N-ooooh yeah. Yep. I'm fine." My voice cracked.

I felt her hand squeeze mine, which was a good distraction from the antique machine slowly lurching its way down into a dark abyss. The gloom swallowed us whole. I couldn't see Claire. I couldn't see the elevator gate. I couldn't even see my own hand in front of my face.

My pulse rocketed. It boomed so loudly in my ears, I was sure Claire could hear it, too. My body went cold as memories flickered to life in the back of my brain. I shut my eyes and clenched my teeth, biting down fiercely against the fear seeping into my mind. Whispering recollections of darkness, grinding metal, water rising…

The elevator shuddered again, more violently. I bit back a yell. It rattled us like two mice in a cage, causing me to stagger. I slammed right into Claire, dragging her down with me in the process. She landed right on top of me.

As suddenly as the shaking and roaring began, it stopped. The elevator lurched to a halt. Everything became still and quiet again. All I could hear was our frantic breathing in the dark.

"What was that?" Claire's voice was small and frightened.

"You mean it doesn't always do that?"

"No," she whispered. "Was it an earthquake?"

At that moment, all I knew was that the girl of my dreams was lying on top of me. I could feel her breath on my face and the brush of her hair against my neck. I was afraid to move. What if I touched something forbidden by accident?

Good grief, she even smelled amazing.

"Koji, the elevator isn't moving anymore," she said, her voice wavering with panic as she pulled away from me. I heard her shoes scraping over the floor, the rustling of clothes, and suddenly light bloomed in the dark. Claire had her phone out with its flashlight directed at the elevator's rusty buttons. She pressed the downward one again.

The elevator didn't respond.

Claire pushed the button again, harder. She pounded on it frantically. Nothing. She tried the same on the upward button, but the elevator didn't make a sound or budge an inch.

"We're stuck, aren't we?" I asked.

The light on her cell phone panned toward me as I got to my feet. I had to shield my eyes.

"I think we are."

My thoughts went instantly to the bracelet on my wrist. I could get out. I could get both of us out of here in five seconds. Sure, normal-high-school-nerd Koji was stuck in here. But awesome-dragon-superhero Koji didn't have to be.

There was just one problem, and she was staring right at me, her beautiful eyes wide with terror.

"Koji," she whimpered and took a step back, looking around in a panic. "We can't stay in here! We have to get out!"

"Hey, it's okay." I moved closer to her. "It's going to be fine. We'll just call for help."

"No! No, we aren't! Don't you get it? No one gets cell service down here!" She was breathing hard. Her expression became wild as she backed up against the side of the elevator. "I can't be in here! I have to get out! Please! Please, let me out!"

Before I could get to her, Claire collapsed to her knees. Her phone clattered across the elevator floor, landing face up at my feet. By the light of the screen, I could still see her. She huddled against the wall, her whole body shaking as she started to sob. One of her hands gripped tightly around a pendant hanging around her neck—a religious medal depicting a female saint cradling a harp in her arms as she gazed heavenward.

I knelt down next to her. "Claire, I'm right here. You're not alone. We'll figure this out together, okay?" I put a hand on her shoulder. "That's a nice necklace. Saint Cecilia, right?"

"P-patron saint of musicians. It was my grandmother's." She bobbed her head and sniffled. "How did you know?"

"This isn't my first Catholic school. I went to another for a couple of years in middle school." I shrugged. "I'm a military kid, so we've moved a lot."

Her tear-filled eyes panned up to stare back me, her cheeks flushed bright scarlet. "I-I'm so sorry, Koji. This is all my fault."

"I seriously doubt you caused an earthquake." I brought her in close, putting my arms around her gently. She seemed so small and fragile when I held her that way.

Claire didn't answer. She curled against me and buried her face in my shoulder. My heart skipped a few beats, and I couldn't deny how my chest seemed to swell with determination. I *had* to take care of her.

"We just have to wait here for a while. Drake will figure out we're trapped. He'll get help. It'll be fine." I kept my voice steady as I dared to run a hand over the back of her head. Impossibly soft hair, like loose ringlets of golden silk, glided through my fingers. "But maybe next time we should take the stairs, yeah?"

She laughed weakly.

"Claire?"

"Yes?"

The words burst out before I could think. "I just wanted to say... I mean, I get that we don't really know each other yet. But I—"

"Hey!" a familiar voice yelled down to us. Through the iron grate on the top of the elevator, Drake panned the beam of his phone's flashlight down the elevator shaft. "You guys okay down there?"

I swallowed the shattered bits of my nerve and called back to him, "Yeah. We're good, but it looks like the elevator is stuck between levels."

"No problem, I'm already on it. Called 9-1-1, so they're on the way. Did you guys feel that? It was like an earthquake!" He had that excited squeak to his voice again—just like when he'd told me about the crater in Central Park.

I couldn't share his enthusiasm. Claire had already begun extracting herself from my embrace. She crawled over to retrieve her phone and tucked it back into her blazer pocket.

Thanks to Drake's flashlight beam, I could see the painfully forced, broken smile on her face when she looked at me again. "I really am sorry about this, Koji. But I'm glad I wasn't alone. Thank you for being my friend."

The way she said that word, *friend*, was distinct. No missing the underlying message there. It hit me like a curve ball to the face. I sat in stunned silence, gaping up at her while I tried to process what had just happened.

Basically, she'd just drawn a line in the sand between us—a line that couldn't be crossed.

The friend line.

CHAPTER
~9~

The days passed painfully slow as my world slowly faded from full color to gray. I had been officially and unquestionably friend-zoned. I stood no chance. Maybe I never had. Claire was back on Venus, and the view from Pluto totally sucked.

It wasn't the fact that she only wanted to be friends. Friendship was great, and way better than her telling me to never speak to her again. The problem was that this happened every time I started liking anyone. At least Claire had been nice about it. Usually I got the public humiliation treatment. The last girl I tried to ask out laughed so hard she spit her drink down the front of my shirt. I'd had to wear the mark of that shame for the rest of the day. Talk about embarrassing.

Was it because I wasn't handsome enough? Or because I wasn't muscular and athletic?

I shot Mr. Biceps a glare from across the lunchroom. I couldn't compete with someone like him. Even if I spent hours a day flailing around in the gym, my metabolism didn't work that way. I was doomed to be tall and lanky forever—just like Dad.

I wondered if being smarter would have helped, but one look at Drake, who was scrolling through his countless social media feeds on his phone between bites of food, answered that.

He'd never had a girlfriend either, and you couldn't get much smarter than him.

Whatever the reason, I was always in second place. And now, days later, I still couldn't concentrate on anything. Not even zipping around in my dragon form distracted me, so I hadn't bothered to sneak out to practice.

"Look, dude, it's been like a week. Get over it already," Drake grumbled as he sat across from me at lunch. "There's more to life than dating."

"I just don't understand it," I groaned. "What did I do wrong?"

"It's not about doing anything right or wrong. I told you before—this is how it is with them. They're the aristocracy and you and I are the peasants tilling the common soil."

I sighed and twisted my fork around in my mashed potatoes.

He started pinching off bits of his dinner roll and throwing them at me. "Hey, why don't you come to the Robotics Tournament tomorrow? It'll get your mind off of it. You can watch me shred my enemies with my superior robotic power *and* get a day off from school."

"No thanks." I brushed a few bits of roll off my shoulder.

"There'll be a celebratory dinner afterward for the winners. I'll print you up a membership badge, get the headmaster's secretary to sign off on it, and then you can go with us. Come on. No school? Free food? Robots destroying each other? You know you want to."

Okay, fine. So that did sound fun. I chuckled and threw some of his bread back at him.

"And hey, since you'll officially be part of the team, why don't you make us a banner?"

I raised an eyebrow. "A banner?"

"Yeah, you know, to hold up while we're competing. You can draw, right? So make it look cool." Drake went digging around in his backpack until he found a few papers printed with the designs of the robot. "Use that for inspiration."

"Okay. I'll see what I can do." I slipped the pictures into my bag and started thinking about what I could design.

By the time I got to art class at the end of the day, I had a pretty good idea of what I wanted to paint. Now I just needed the materials. Lucky for me, Mr. Molins had lots of leftover cloth banners hanging around in the classroom from last year's basketball games. He told me I could take one and paint over it.

There was just one *big* problem.

"When do you need to have this finished?" Madeline stood next to me, eyeing the huge cloth banner I'd spread out across the art room floor. It was about twelve feet long and four feet wide—the smallest one Mr. Molins had on hand.

"Tomorrow." I scratched the back of my head. "I'm totally screwed. I'll never finish it in time. Maybe I could cut it in half?"

A ripple of black hair caught my eye. Madeline had just done that hair-flip thing girls do when they tie their hair up. She managed to get it all fixed up into a big, messy bun in about two seconds. Amazing. How did they do that?

"Not *totally* screwed." She smiled brightly and rolled her sleeves up. "I'll get the paints. You get the brushes and water."

It took hours. Mr. Molins even tried helping out for a little while, just to speed things along. But soon, Madeline and I were alone in the art room, covered in paint, trying to put the finishing touches on the banner. My knees hurt from crawling around on the floor, and I could feel crusty, stiff spots on my cheeks and forehead from dried paint.

Madeline was going back through the design, putting in the final accents of white on the letters. She didn't talk much, and honestly, I didn't feel like chatting. Every time I started to concentrate, my mind went back to that look Claire had given me in the elevator.

Friend. That word was like a double-edged sword in my chest. Still, things were bound to be awkward between Claire and I now. I knew I should probably apologize for putting her on the spot like that, especially considering where we'd been at the time. Stupid, stupid, stupid...

"Hey! That looks awesome!" Drake appeared in the art room doorway, flanked with a few of his Robotics Club friends. They crowded around, praising our work and admiring the design. All the attention seemed to make Madeline uncomfortable. Her cheeks flushed and she sat back on her heels, staring down at our work as though she were too nervous to look at anything else.

"You think it'll be dry by in the morning?" Drake asked.

I gave him a paint-spattered grin. "Oh yeah."

"Excellent." He reached into his pocket and pulled out a plastic ID card, tossing it to me. "You're officially part of the Saint Bernard's Robotics Team. If anyone asks, your specialty is aesthetic design."

I examined the picture on the ID, a terrible, ancient snapshot of me from my only social media page. I didn't really keep up with that kind of stuff. "Seriously? That's the picture you picked?"

He shrugged and shot me a taunting grin. "Not my fault you haven't updated your Facebook profile in like... five years. Nice braces, by the way. They really brought out your smile."

That got a few chuckles and giggles from his group of friends. Out of the corner of my eye, I caught Madeline quirking her mouth as though she were fighting a smile, too.

I crammed the ID into my pocket before anyone else could see it.

"So all you have to do is get to school an hour early and bring that badge. We load the buses at 7:30 sharp," Drake explained as he turned around so the rest of his robotics buddies could hear him. "Got that? If you're late you get left behind!"

I'd never seen him so excited. He left the art lab with his teammates like some kind of ringleader, grinning wickedly from ear to ear. I guess the idea of blowing something up and destroying enemy robots really made his day.

I chuckled and looked back at the banner. Madeline had gone back to putting the finishing touches on it, but a ghost of a smile lingered on her lips.

"Hey, uh, thanks for this," I said.

Madeline's soft gray eyes flicked up and met mine. Some of her dark hair had fallen out of the bun and hung across her cheek. "For what?"

"For helping me with this. It would have taken me all night by myself," I clarified. "I'm sure you had better things to do tonight."

"Oh." She blinked as though she were genuinely surprised. "You're welcome."

Awkward—that was just one of many words to describe the empty silence in the air between us while she went on painting and I sat there like an idiot.

"You've seemed sad lately." Madeline spoke much more quietly now. "Is everything okay?"

She'd noticed? I guess I hadn't paid much attention to anything or anyone else since the elevator incident. "Yeah." The words spilled out in a rush. "You ever fall for somebody you know you'll never stand a chance with?"

The hand holding her paintbrush halted. I saw her mouth open slightly. Then she slowly looked back at me with a nearly desperate furrow skewing her brow. "Yes."

I didn't know what to say. I guess it was a really personal question to ask someone I barely knew. But that odd tingle in the back of my mind told me she wasn't lying. I didn't understand how I knew it, but I did.

Madeline sat back on her heels again, placing her paintbrush into one of the water jars. She rubbed her hand along her neck, like something under her collar was bothering her, and her expression changed. The light in her eyes seemed to fade, leaving behind a sense of hopelessness and sadness I hadn't expected.

"The worst part isn't knowing you'll never be with them," she continued, still fidgeting with her shirt collar. "It's knowing that when they smile, it's because of someone else. That someone else makes them so happy you might as well not even exist."

I knew who that was in my case—Damien Blount, Claire's fiancé. I didn't even know the guy and I already hated him. It was ridiculous. He'd never done anything to me. He actually seemed sort of nice, which only made it worse. It would've been way easier to justify hating him if he'd been a jerk.

"Does it get any easier?" I asked, bowing my head.

She turned away, grabbing her jar of murky paint-water and brushes. As she walked toward the sink I heard her answer, "I'll let you know."

It was snowing. Not flurries or sleet—real, actual snow.

Being the son of a fighter pilot meant we generally got moved to places where the weather wouldn't interfere with the base's flying schedule—basically, the desert or any place in the middle of nowhere. I'd seen snow on the mountaintops around Tucson, Arizona. I'd also gotten to goof off in it a little whenever we flew to New Jersey for Christmases with my grandparents. It even snowed once while we lived in South Korea.

But honestly, there's nothing like New York in winter.

I stood outside the school, watching the big flakes spiral down from a dreary gray sky. My breath formed big puffs of white fog in the frigid air and the wind stung my cheeks and the tip of my nose was practically numb. I loved it. Cold air just seemed cleaner and easier to breathe. Not to mention I'd missed the snow.

As I stood on the front steps, waiting for Drake to arrive, I recognized a few teachers and some of the other members of Drake's Robotics Club arriving. I even helped a few of them load their materials onto the bus—including the banner Madeline and I had made. Everyone was bundled up for the weather, and some of the guys had started scraping snow off the sidewalk and hurling it at one another.

At 7:25, I glanced at my phone. Drake still wasn't here. Not that it was a big deal. He still had five minutes and the snow probably had traffic backed up. Dad had been complaining about it on his way out the door that morning.

At 7:37, however, I started to get concerned.

The teacher in charge of chaperoning us to the tournament walked over to ask me if I knew what was keeping him. As club president, he had to be here. He was the one who would be driving the robot in the competition. Not to mention this tournament was all he had talked about for months. There was no way he would skip out.

"I'll have to inform Headmaster Ignatius of his absence. I'll try giving Drake's mother a call, too," the teacher said. "We can't wait forever. They won't hold the tournament for us."

As soon as she walked away, I dialed Drake. His phone rang…and rang…and rang. Then it went to voicemail.

Now I was officially worried. Drake might be running late, but I'd never seen him without his phone before. He always texted me back. He always answered when I called.

Something wasn't right.

"Good morning, Koji." I turned around at the sound of Madeline's voice. She strolled up the sidewalk, a bulky purple wool scarf wrapped around her neck and white snowflakes peppering her dark hair. "Shouldn't you be gone already? Where's Drake?"

I frowned. "I don't know."

Her brow crinkled. "He's not here?"

Suddenly, the teacher returned and started ordering everyone to get on the bus. We were leaving—without Drake.

"Hey, what's going on? We can't go without him!" I called out as I ran up to the door of the bus.

"Mr. Collins won't be joining us," the teacher replied. "I just got off the phone with his mother. He had an accident. He was admitted to Presbyterian Hospital last night."

There was a collective gasp from everyone else on the bus.

"Hospital? What? Why?" I asked, but deep down I already knew.

The teacher just shook her head. "His mother didn't give me any specific details except that he's in intensive care. So everyone, let's remember him in our morning prayers and try to do our best for him today."

I took a staggering step away from the bus and tried to breathe. My body flashed hot and cold and my chest went tight. Sick—I was going to be sick.

"Mr. Owens, get on the bus, please." The teacher was eyeing me impatiently.

No. I wasn't going.

There was somewhere else I had to be.

Madeline and the teacher called my name, trying to get me to stop as I took off down the sidewalk toward the nearest subway station.

A big male nurse seized my shoulder before I could get into the room. "I'm sorry, but it's family only."

"But I—"

"Are you family?" he demanded. When I didn't answer, he pointed back toward the waiting room. "You can wait out there."

I bit down hard and shook his hand off me, stealing one last look through the open doorway of Drake's room.

One look was all it took. I could see everything I needed to.

Drake was propped up in a hospital bed, hooked to machines that monitored his breathing and pulse. IV lines and tubes stuck out of him everywhere. His face was so bruised and swollen I wouldn't have recognized him if not for his hair. One of his arms was in a cast all the way up to his shoulder. It looked like he was sleeping, or still unconscious. He didn't stir, even when I shouted his name through the doorway.

The woman sitting at his bedside had the same white-blond hair as Drake. I'd never met his mom before, so she looked at me with confusion on her tear-streaked face. One of her cheekbones looked dusky, like maybe she'd taken a blow to the face.

The nurse managed to muscle me out in the hall and told me to sit in a waiting room again. He assured me he would let me know when I could see Drake. But sitting and waiting were totally out of the question. I'd done enough of sitting around doing nothing.

It was time to end this.

Storming out of the hospital, I searched for a good place to transform. Overhead, the sky was growing darker as thunder rumbled in the gathering clouds.

The best I could do for a secluded place to transform was the top floor of a parking deck down the street. Apparently no one wanted to park on the top with it snowing. Good enough.

I ducked into the stairwell and pulled my phone out. Drake had input his home address along with the rest of his information in my Contacts folder when we'd met and he agreed to tutor me. It wasn't far, especially not for my totem-enhanced speed. Once I had the route memorized, I stuffed my phone back into my pocket. Fury made my vision blur and my hands shake as I pulled back the sleeve of my coat. The totem scale glinted promisingly. In the back of my mind, I could almost hear the dragon-girl warning me that this was a *very* bad idea. I should just wait, try to calm down, and then figure out the right way to handle this.

Drake, beaten to a swollen pulp and lying unconscious in the hospital bed flashed through my mind. My pulse spiked. The growl that rumbled past my clench teeth had an inhuman, monstrous edge.

It was time to get my scales on.

CHAPTER 10

The wind howled at my back, filling my wings as I hurtled through the streets of Manhattan like a black scaly rocket. I'd never flown this fast or smoothly before. It was as though my powers had gone from erratic and clumsy to completely focused and razor sharp. Energy like wildfire buzzed through my veins.

I was invincible.

When I landed in front of the door of Drake's apartment building, a few people walking down the sidewalks screamed. They took one look at me and ran. Smart move. In the street, cars came screeching to a halt, horns blaring as pedestrians scrambled to get away from me.

We were a long way from where Dad and I lived. Drake's apartment building seemed run down, cramped next to similar buildings along the trash-littered streets lined with older model cars and graffiti-covered trashcans.

I halted in front of his building's door, examining the list of names printed on the intercom panel. Collins was the very last on the list—the apartment in the basement level. The front door wasn't inside the building. The basement apartment had a separate, external entrance, which saved me the effort of smashing my way through the whole building.

I sprang down into the stairwell next to the building's front door. The basement level unit had bars on all the windows. There were lights on inside.

I snarled. Someone was home, and I had an idea who it was.

I seized the door handle and flung it open, ripping a few of the locks out of the wooden frame in the process.

In the living room, propped in an old recliner with a beer in one hand and a remote in the other, sat a tall, narrow-shouldered man with a sparse, ginger beard. At first glance, I wasn't impressed, although a little surprised he hadn't jumped up at my entrance. Maybe that had something to do with the huge pile of empty beer cans next to his chair.

Clint wasn't much to look at. His pale, hairy arms were splotched with blown-out tattoos and his dull, heavy-lidded eyes gazed lazily at the television screen as he flicked from channel to channel. Dressed in sweatpants and a stained undershirt, it didn't look like he'd been out in the light of day for a while.

I was about to fix that, though.

"Clint?" I asked in my monstrous, growly voice.

"Yeah, who wants to know?" He turned to leer at me. Then his eyes went wide. His face turned white and he scrambled out of his chair.

"W-what are you?" He hurled the remote and beer bottle at me with a piggish squeal of terror.

The remote bounced harmlessly off my chest, and I showed him a toothy, devilish snarl. "Just think of me as the terrible *accident* you're about to have." My booming chuckle filled the tiny apartment as I lunged for him, snatching one of his ankles in my clawed hands.

Clint screamed and flailed as I dragged him out of the apartment and tossed him up the stairs and into the street. He bounced off the asphalt like a skipping stone over a pond.

Pedestrians shrieked and shouted as I burst from the stairwell and swooped over him, landing so that the talons of my hind legs pinned his arms to the ground. I leaned close to his face so he could see the points of my fangs and the slits of my reptilian eyes. Overhead, blue lightning snapped in the churning dark clouds, followed by rumbles of thunder. With every flash, I saw my reflection in his wide, frightened eyes.

"I don't have any money! I don't have anything!" He started to wail.

"I don't want money, you moron," I roared, digging my talons into his arms.

Clint screamed louder. "What? What do you want? I'll do anything! Just don't kill me!"

"I want you gone." I grabbed his face and forced him to look at me eye to eye. "Say it. Say you'll leave New York and never come back. Right now."

He stammered, tearfully warbling something I couldn't understand.

"Say it!" I roared louder. Tongues of lightning burst out of the clouds and struck the ground all around us so close I could practically taste electrical current crackling between my teeth.

"I'll leave! I swear!" Clint bawled.

If he was lying, I couldn't sense it. But I had to be sure—for Drake's sake.

"Good. And Clint, if you *ever* come back...I'll know. And I won't be so merciful next time." I let one of my clawed fingers drag across his cheek, leaving a fresh, bleeding cut behind. "Now, run away."

The instant I stepped off him, Clint took off down the street wailing like a madman. He tripped over the curb, fell face flat on the sidewalk, clambered back to his feet, and kept going as fast as he could.

Good riddance.

I spread my wings and let out another thundering roar just in case he had any last minute ideas about coming back later.

Suddenly, a bright light flashed in my face. It wasn't lightning this time. I snarled, whirling to face a man brandishing a camera with a big external flash mounted on the top. His camera went off again, clicking and whirring as he snapped rapid photographs of me. I cringed back, my vision spotting in the glare of the flash. What was going on? Who was this guy?

I froze at the sound of panicked shouts and screams. When I dared to turn around, I found a large crowd had gathered around me all along the street. People clambered together, leaning out of cars and swarming the sidewalks. Most had their cell phones pointed in my direction, their faces blanched with awe and fear. They kept their distance, as though anticipating I might lunge at any moment, but that didn't stop them from taking pictures and videos.

Oh no…

I was exposed. My heart dropped to the pit of my stomach. I had to get out of sight—*now*!

In a panic, I took off skyward and zipped away against the icy winds and falling snow. As I battled through the storm clouds, I caught a surging updraft and cupped my wings. I rode the frigid, howling winds, and let them carry me through the snowstorm until the familiar sight of an old building with two big smoke stacks appeared through the haze.

It wasn't home. But right then, I knew it was the only place where I would be safe.

I had messed up big time. This was worse than a crater in Central Park—*way* worse. There were pictures of me. Probably videos, too. It was only a matter of time before someone uploaded them to the Internet and then…

I shuddered, clenching my teeth. That was the scariest part. I didn't know what would happen then. Would someone recognize me? Could I even be recognized in this form? Would they come for me? Hunt me down? Or shoot me out of the sky on sight? Would I ever be safe to fly again?

I hardly knew my own reflection as I sat on the floor of the abandoned power plant, staring into a frozen puddle at my feet. But would someone else be able to tell it was me? Looking past the glowing, electric blue eyes and reptilian scales, horns, and fangs, there was always a chance someone might see regular, dorky Koji. Now that risk was greater than ever.

Suddenly, a pair of golden eyes appeared in the reflection as well.

"You." I recognized the sound of her voice—especially when she was angry.

"Nice to see you again," I grumbled.

"What have you done?" Her tone quivered with rage.

"I didn't have a choice."

She grabbed one of my horns and yanked me to my feet with surprising strength. "Yes! You absolutely had a choice. And you did it anyway. Do you have any idea what this means? The danger you've put us both in? You *idiot*!"

I pushed her hand off and bared my teeth, taking a forceful step forward. "No. You don't get to call me that."

She shrank away, body tense as her eyes searched mine. I'd never been aggressive with her before.

"You have no idea who I am or what I've been through, so you don't get to judge me," I growled. "You don't get to question the decisions I make, or tell me what I can and can't do with the power given to me. If you want to be a coward, hiding in the shadows and using your totem for weekend joyrides, that's your business. But you don't get to tell me how to take care of mine."

"They saw you," she hissed quietly, flicking her tail. "It's all over the news, the Internet, everywhere. They're looking for that man you threatened, but so far he hasn't been found."

"Good. And if he wants to keep all his arms and legs, he better keep it that way."

"Do you even hear yourself? They'll be looking for you now. Every time you decide to transform, you'll be taking a risk. If they catch you—"

"Don't worry about that." I snorted and looked away. "I won't tell them about you."

"You might not have a choice," she countered.

"I know basically nothing about you, so even if they interrogate me, it won't matter. I won't be able to tell them anything useful. You don't trust me. You don't even like me. So what do you care what happens to me now?"

Her expression darkened. "That's not true."

"Liar," I snapped when I felt the telltale tingle—and suddenly it hit me. Every time I got that feeling, it wasn't just coincidence. It was something more. "That's my third eye ability, isn't it? Ever since I got this stupid totem, I've been able to tell if someone was telling me the truth or not. You can't fool me. I can feel deception like a thorn in my brain."

She wouldn't meet my gaze. "How could I possibly know that? I've never worn your totem—I have no idea what your third eye is."

Well, at least that part was true.

"But you do know what my element is, right?"

"You should know it yourself by now. You were practically flaunting it for the cameras."

I flexed my arms, chest, and shoulders. My wings spread, causing a sudden forceful burst of wind that made the inside of the whole plant rattle. "Air."

The dragon-girl eyed me, her lips pressed together sternly. "I can't be around you anymore."

I narrowed my eyes.

"You're reckless. Reckless is dangerous, especially for somebody wielding a totem. You're going to get someone, maybe even yourself, killed." Her brow puckered into a deep scowl as she began taking slow steps away from me. "I won't be any part of it. I can't risk it. Maybe you're willing to put everything on the line for some misguided quest for justice, but I'm not."

"Fine."

Her glare went steely. She started to turn, preparing for takeoff.

I watched, my expression cold. Despite how angry I felt with her, I couldn't shake the nagging feeling that I should say something to try to fix things between us. Regardless of how differently we felt about using our totems, she was the only other person in the world I knew who could relate. She might have the answers I needed when it came to using my totem's full potential and understanding why I'd been chosen.

Not to mention I freaking needed a friend—someone that I could actually talk to about this stuff. She was smarter than I was. She'd been doing this totem-secret thing longer, too. If anyone could advise me on what to do about Drake, it was her. I couldn't accept that we weren't meant to be allies.

She paused to look back at me. "If you don't listen to anything else I say, hear this." She clenched her hands into fists. "Every time you go out there—every life you think you're saving and every wrong you think you're righting—you're risking losing your totem forever. All it takes is a glimpse, one look, and it's all over. So ask yourself if what you're about to do is worth that risk because that's exactly what's at stake. And if they find out who you are under those scales, it won't just be your life that's affected. It'll be your family's, your friends', and anyone else you care about. You'll never have any secrets again. And coming from someone who knows what that's like, trust me, you don't want that kind of life."

I clenched my teeth to keep all my angry words at bay.

"The next time you decide to fly off and play hero, just ask yourself one question." She turned her back and crouched, flaring her sleek blue wings for takeoff. "Is it for justice, or is it for revenge?"

Later that afternoon, I sat in the headmaster's office, still trying to wrap my mind around that question. The harder I looked at the situation with Clint, the less clear things became. I wasn't sure where to draw the line separating justice and revenge. Was there even a difference? In every comic I'd ever read, every movie and all the television shows I'd watched all through my childhood, it had seemed so obvious who was in the right. But now that I was chest-deep in this superhero thing, nothing was obvious except that I had no idea what I was doing.

Clint wasn't a good person. He'd deserved what happened. But did that make it right? Should I have told my Dad everything from the beginning? Should I have ignored Drake's wishes and gone to the police anyway?

Regardless, I couldn't deny how tossing Clint around and watching him tremble in fear at the sight of me had felt so… good. I knew I should be ashamed of that. I shouldn't want to hurt someone. But I had, and deep down I knew that if he ever came back and tried to hurt Drake again, I'd do worse than scratch him up a little.

My mind tangled with all the uncertainty and worry until I could barely even think about what was happening in my normal life. The headmaster was practically breathing fire when he found out I'd run off campus and ditched school. I figured I was in for detention, at the least. Expulsion, at the worst. I'd mysteriously reappeared at school at lunch without a doctor's excuse or a good explanation about where I'd been. I was half hoping the teachers wouldn't notice I'd been absent for all my morning classes. But the faculty of Saint Bernard's didn't let anything slide when it came to attendance, and it didn't help that one of them had witnessed me blitzing for the nearest subway entrance.

I hadn't taken three bites of my gourmet grilled cheese before I found myself being marched down to the office.

Sitting across from the secretary's desk, I waited in silence for my dad to arrive. Because I was a new student with a "previous record of insubordination" at my old school, the headmaster had insisted on calling him. I shuddered as I tried to picture the look on Dad's face when he got that call. It was only the second time my dad had ever been asked to come to the school because of something I'd done, but I doubted he would go easy on me. I wasn't expecting any mercy. Strike two was going to hurt.

After about an hour, Dad finally arrived. He was dressed in his uniform and walked into the office briskly, jaw clenched and eyes smoldering. He didn't even glance down at me as he approached the secretary's desk. My stomach did a series of frantic flips.

He disappeared into Headmaster Ignatius's office for a few minutes, and when he emerged, I got the *look*. You know, the soul crushing "I'm disappointed in you" look that only parents can give. Ugh. I hated the look.

Dad snapped his fingers and pointed to the floor next to him. Dragging my feet, I grabbed my backpack and went to stand on that spot.

"He'll be here tomorrow morning," Dad said to the secretary. He cut me a meaningful, icy glare before he added, "On time."

I decided not to say anything for as long as possible. Silence was safer. Dad didn't seem eager to start this discussion, either. He wouldn't even look my way until we were home, behind closed doors.

Then he snapped his fingers again and pointed to one of the barstools at the kitchen counter.

I sank slowly down into it, wringing my sweaty hands in my lap.

"All right." His voice was eerily calm. "Tell me what happened."

I blinked. "What?"

"In fifteen years you've never skipped school. So what happened?"

Just as I realized I wasn't about to be disowned, I realized I had a much bigger problem: I had no alibi when it came to where I'd been when a certain dragon-ish looking superhero had been flinging Clint around in the street. I looked at my hands in silence.

"Since you don't have anything to say, let me walk you through my morning. A teacher reported seeing you run off campus. She had her own suspicions of where you would go, so that was the first place I phoned after the school called me, at work, to inform me that my son was mysteriously absent from his first morning class." Dad placed his hands carefully on the kitchen counter between us and met my gaze with a look of subdued rage. "The receptionist at Presbyterian Hospital said you tried to get in to see your friend, Drake Collins, but you stormed out when they wouldn't let you in. That's the last anyone saw of you. So imagine, if you can, my terror as a parent when, for the second time since moving here, I'm trying to find my only child in this city!"

I swallowed hard.

"All morning I searched for you, Koji!" he shouted. I cringed and looked down at the floor when he slammed a fist down onto the counter. "And while I am, I'm getting phone calls and seeing news reports that some sort of monster has been spotted in the city, not far from the hospital. It attacked someone in broad daylight—a beast that no one could identify."

Ooooh no. My head spun and I was breathless, staring at him with eyes wide. My skin prickled as all the blood rushed out of my face. Underneath the counter, I put a protective hand over my totem bracelet.

This was it. He knew. He knew the monster was—

"Koji, what if you'd been attacked? Do you have any idea how terrified I was?" Dad yelled.

My mouth opened but no sound would come out.

"So I'll ask again: Where were you?" he demanded.

I scrambled to come up with a believable lie, but at first all I could do was make panicked choking sounds.

His jaw clenched. "Sometime today, son."

"I-I-I got lost," I squeaked. "I tried to go back to school, after they wouldn't let me see Drake. I thought I had enough time to get back to the school before the first bell. But I got on the wrong train."

I waited, holding my breath, to see if he believed me.

Dad let out a heavy sigh. "The wrong train?"

"Yeah. I'm not used to the trains—er—subways." I looked down at the countertop because I didn't trust myself to put on a convincing face. "I got confused. I wasn't thinking straight. I thought I could make it back in time."

After a long pause, Dad finally shook his head. "Well, I suppose it's good that I talked the headmaster down from sending you to detention for two weeks."

"You did?"

"I explained that you'd gone to the hospital and that you'd come to me once already about a friend of yours who was being abused. Apparently he was already aware of the situation with Drake. He took pity on you and we came to an agreement that you'd be suspended for the rest of the day instead." Dad shook his head slowly. "But that doesn't mean you're off the hook with me. I've warned you about running off by yourself in this city. I guess I need to make my point clearer."

I sank lower in my chair, unable to meet his eyes again.

"So you're grounded for the week. No video games or computer. Hand over the power cords," he said.

I flailed in protest. "What? Dad, come on!"

"And while you're at it, hand over the phone, too. You can have it only while you're at school."

I flopped back in my seat, speechless.

"I love you, Koji. I hate to play tough cop with you here, but I need you to listen to me."

I nodded, pulled my phone out of my back pocket, and reluctantly handed it to him.

He put it away and sighed. "Okay, now go get changed."

"What for?"

"I talked to Drake's mom when I called the hospital. I wanted to ask if she had any ideas where you might go. She didn't know, of course, but she told me Drake was awake. As long as we're both off for the rest of the day, I think we should pay him a visit, don't you?"

CHAPTER 11

Drake was sitting upright in his bed, talking to a nurse, when Dad and I arrived. He was conscious, but he didn't look happy. If anything he looked humiliated. After the nurse left, he bowed his head and refused to meet my gaze when we came into the room.

"You must be Koji. Thank you so much for coming by." Drake's mom stood up to greet me with a thin, fragile smile. She had the same small frame and fluffy blond hair as her son, but there were dark, tired circles under her eyes. "And you're Mr. Owens?"

Dad shook her hand. "You can just call me Danny."

"I'm Amelia," she replied.

I watched our parents looking one another over, their expressions a similar mixture of uncertainty and shyness—like they weren't sure what to say. Weird. Dad was usually at ease talking to everyone. I'd never seen him be self-conscious before, but he cleared his throat and rubbed the back of his neck, glancing my way as though he were waiting for me to rescue him from the awkward silence.

Not a chance.

"So, uh, I guess I should have introduced myself earlier. Drake has been helping Koji settle into his new school." Dad's voice cracked a little.

Wow. And I thought *I* was terrible at talking to girls.

Ms. Collins gave another quick, timid smile. She opened and closed her mouth a few times but didn't say anything.

I stole a sideways look at Drake, who was watching them with a perplexed frown. He arched a brow at me as though hoping I had an explanation. All I could do was shrug.

Parents. Who knew?

Dad finally spoke up again. "Uh, we stopped off to get a few boxes of pizza on the way. I hope you don't mind. We hadn't eaten dinner yet and figured you might want a break from hospital food."

Ms. Collins took the stacked pizza boxes when he offered them and beamed. "That's so thoughtful of you."

"Uh, yeah. It's no problem at all. Right, Koji?"

"Sure, Dad."

"I'll just go down and ask the nurses if there's anything we can drink to go with this." Ms. Collins picked up her purse and started for the door.

My dad stopped her. "No, please, allow me. I spotted some vending machines down in the lobby. How would you boys feel about a few sodas?"

I nodded and Drake's eyes flickered with interest. He gave a small shrug.

"Okay, then." Drake's mom looked a little flushed. "We'll be right back."

Once our parents were gone, Drake and I exchanged a meaningful glance before we burst out laughing.

"What the heck was that?" He laughed hoarsely. "Was your dad seriously just hitting on my mom?"

I couldn't decide which was more embarrassing—that it actually seemed like he was or that I'd been forced to stand there and watch it. "I don't know."

"That was painful! Well, now I know where your dating skills come from."

I dropped in the chair at his bedside. "Guess that doesn't bode well for me then, huh?"

"Nope."

I picked at the pocket on the front of my favorite hoodie. "So..."

"So?"

"How long do you have to stay here?"

Drake sighed. "A few more days, maybe. They said my arm was broken in two places. Spiral fracture of the humerus and elbow. Broken nose. Mild concussion. I honestly don't feel much, though. Guess that's the painkillers."

He made it all sound so...casual. *So my arm was snapped in half. No big deal.*

"I'll have to do some physical therapy with my arm. Mom said she can do it with me at home, though," he went on. "They were worried about the concussion but since I'm awake now—"

"Drake?"

He stopped talking and fiddled with the sheet in his lap.

"Have you seen what's on the news yet?"

He didn't answer, although his mouth drew up into a pinched, sideways frown as he chewed on the inside of his cheek. I took that as a yes.

"Did you know that monster? I mean, do you recognize who it was? They're saying the attack was random but I just thought, you know, because of what happened..."

Drake scowled darkly at the cast on his arm. At last, he slowly raised a frustrated glare at me. "I've spent hours going over every picture and video clip I could find online. I don't know who it was."

He was telling the truth.

Relief poured through every inch of me. Drake didn't know my secret.

"And I agree with you," he added. "I don't think it was random, either. Someone knew about us—about Clint. Someone who could change into that *thing*."

"A neighbor, maybe? Or someone here at the hospital? You said your mom is a nurse, right?"

He shook his head slightly. "I don't know. And honestly, I don't care. I'm glad they did it. I almost wish they had just killed him."

I didn't trust myself to look him in the eye anymore, so I went back to picking at my hoodie. "How come?"

"Because he might come back."

"Even with that monster lurking around?"

Drake didn't reply.

"I guess this means the alien and top secret aircraft theories are out, right? They're saying the same monster probably left the crater in Central Park."

"Yeah," he said quietly. "It's the same thing I saw flying through the sky that night. It has to be. No other explanation makes sense."

"So what does this mean?" I tried to keep my voice down in case there were any nurses lurking outside the room. "For the monster, that is. Do you think they'll try to hunt it down? Send in the FBI or something? Could they even catch something like that?"

"I don't know that, either. And I *hate* not knowing." He frowned harder. "But there's one thing I am certain of: I hope they never catch it. If that monster has any sense at all, it will lay low and keep hidden for as long as possible."

The week that followed was, without a doubt, the longest week of my life—and not just because I was grounded. Drake was still homebound, so I had no one to talk to in my classes or sit with at lunch. Claire was still avoiding me like I had the plague. Even Madeline was home sick with mono or the flu, I couldn't remember which. Everywhere I went, I was surrounded by empty seats. I felt like I might as well be on the surface of the moon.

The days grew colder, it got dark earlier, and the constant buzz of everyone discussing and theorizing about the monster made it impossible to relax. I hung in suspense, tense and waiting for someone to recognize me as the monster. But it's like I'd become invisible, which for a guy in my situation, didn't seem like such a bad thing…even if it was lonely.

At home, I couldn't play video games, thanks to being grounded. Drawing was the only way I could relieve the stress, but even that got old after a few days. I rearranged my action figures and finished hanging all my *Dragon Ball Z*, *Dragon Age*, and vintage *Ghostbusters* posters. I reread all my favorite *X-Men* comics over and over until I had them memorized from cover to cover.

At night, I listened to the sound of traffic outside, Dad watching television downstairs, and the wind howling past my window. Sleep didn't come easy, and every time a police siren wailed in the distance, my heart stopped and my body went cold at the idea they were coming for me.

But they never were.

On Friday, I looked up from my haze of despair to see a familiar face sitting in the easel next to mine in art class. My spirits soared and I couldn't suppress a smile. Madeline was back.

I sat down in my spot next to her. "Been sick?"

"Yes."

A tingly feeling prickled at the back of my mind—she was lying. I didn't push it, though. I didn't know her well enough to call her on any fibs.

"How's Drake?" She sounded concerned.

"A lot better, even though his robot placed second at the tournament. He took that sort of personally. I guess he's not used to losing."

The corners of her mouth twitched into a smile. "Well, there's always next year."

"He's coming back to school Monday." I started to ramble. It was nice to have someone to talk to again. "We're thinking about going to see a movie next weekend. You should come with us."

"Me?" Madeline blinked in surprise.

"Yeah, sure. We're friends, right?"

She hesitated, staring me down with those piercing blue-gray eyes as though she suspected I might be making fun of her somehow. "O-oh."

"If you want to, that is. It's totally fine if you don't."

"No, that's not it. I just—I didn't realize—" She stammered and then went silent. Her face had gone bright red.

"It's okay if you've got plans already," I added and gave her my friendliest "no pressure" smile. Then I took out my sketchpad. I picked out a pencil to work on my art journal, but before I could make a single mark on the paper, Mr. Molins clapped his hands to get our attention. Everyone turned to face him.

"Today we'll be working on concepts for this year's Holiday Festival booth. We've got just over a month to prepare. For those of you new to Saint Bernard's," he cast a friendly smile in my direction, "I'll explain. Every elective and club in the school gets to set up a booth on the soccer fields to help raise money to support local food banks over the holiday season." Mr. Molins sat back in his chair, crossing his arms over what I suspected was his favorite tie. It had a detailed print of Van Gogh's *The Starry Night* on it, and he wore it at least once a week. "There's also an element of competition because the booth that makes the most money for their club wins the honor of choosing the theme for the Winter Ball."

The classroom stirred with excited whispers.

Mr. Molins had to clap his hands for silence again. "So, anyone have any ideas? Face painting was a big hit last year."

Madeline raised her hand. "What if we sold papier-mâché masks? We could paint them with fall and Christmas themes."

"Couldn't we do both? The face painting was so much fun!" someone else interjected.

"What if we did one of those dunk tanks? But with paint balloons instead of baseballs!"

"Are you kidding? It'll be way too cold for that."

The class started discussing it, and I sat back to observe. I'd never been to a holiday festival before, but the more everyone talked about it, the more fun it sounded. Apparently there would be roasted candied pecans and baked goods for sale, donated from some of the local bakeries. There would also be music, dancing, a pie-eating contest, a pumpkin carving booth, and lots of games. The school's student orchestra would play audience requests in exchange for donations. The Chess Club was already working on a giant chessboard. They gave prizes away to anyone who could beat their best players, and apparently there was a huge spectacle last year when a ninety-year-old lady had beaten everyone in the club in under an hour. The Robotics Club had a famous robotic arm that people could pay to arm wrestle with, and prizes were up for grabs if you managed to beat it. I wondered if Drake would be the one behind the controls for that.

Our class finally settled on doing painted papier-mâché masks for five dollars and face painting for two.

"We'll need to make lots of masks," Mr. Molins said as he stroked his chin. "I'd guess around three hundred, at least. Can we manage that in a month?"

"Absolutely!" The class was in agreement.

Mr. Molins began doling out tasks so we could get to work as soon as possible. After our debut as master painters creating the banner for the robotics tournament, I wasn't surprised when he put Madeline and me in the group that would paint faces.

I grinned at her. "Looks like you're stuck with me again."

"How will I ever survive?" She giggled.

With fifteen minutes left in class, Mr. Molins had us work on our art journals—which was good since I had some new ideas for my comic. I reached for my pencil, but it wasn't there. Glancing up, I noticed my easel was *moving*. The wooden stand shuddered across the floor like it was trying to escape.

I frowned. Now my art supplies resented me, too? Then realized my arm was shaking, too.

It wasn't just me. The whole classroom was shuddering. All the jars and supplies on the art shelves rattled. A few of our clay pots, waiting to be painted before being fired in the kiln, slid onto the floor and shattered. The walls groaned, and I could feel the floor rumbling under my feet.

Some of the girls in the room shrieked.

Madeline had gone as pasty as a corpse. Without thinking, I reached out to grasp her arm to steady her. She took a tiny step toward me, like she wanted to hide.

The shaking stopped as abruptly as it began. Mr. Molins shouted over the confusion, trying in vain to calm everyone down.

"Was that another earthquake?" My body buzzed and shivered with adrenaline.

"I-I think so," Madeline replied.

She was lying again.

CHAPTER 12

"You invited Madeline to go to the movies? And she actually said yes?" Drake still had on a cast, so he could only wave one arm at me in dismay.

"Yeah." I glared at him over the top of my phone. I was answering her text asking where we could meet. "We've been working on this Holiday Festival stuff and I asked her if she wanted to go. It's not a big deal. She's not weird, she's just really shy. I don't get what the problem is. I think you'd like her if you gave her a chance."

"You asked Madeline *Ignatius* to the movies, that's the problem."

"So what?" I froze. "Wait, did you say—?"

"Ignatius," he repeated sourly. "As in the headmaster's daughter, genius."

"Oh...oh." I had to let that sink in.

"Yeah, *oh*. She's practically a spy!"

"She is not. And it's just a movie. We're not robbing a bank or hijacking cars." I crammed my phone into my jacket pocket and pulled my toboggan over my ears. The cold was starting to make me numb. It didn't matter how many layers I put on, the wind cut right through me. I chalked that up to the curse of having basically no body fat.

Drake must have been used to it. That, or he was wearing so many layers the cold didn't bother him. I couldn't tell thanks to the enormous, puffy coat he wore. He looked weird in casual clothes. It wasn't until now that I realized I'd never actually seen him in anything but our school uniform or a hospital gown. His black, oversized coat basically swallowed him whole—apart from his legs, which were clad in skinny jeans. He looked like an angry burnt marshmallow on the end of a toothpick.

"This is bad, I'm telling you. I've got a terrible feeling," Drake went on mumbling, kicking a crumpled soda can with the toe of his shoe.

Across the street, I spotted someone waving at us. As soon as the light changed, Madeline came trotting across the intersection to greet us. She was bundled up in a black wool coat and her usual bulky purple scarf wrapped around her nose and mouth. I could tell she was smiling because her eyes scrunched up happily as she fell in step between us.

"Thanks again for inviting me," she said. "No one ever asks me to go out like this."

Drake snorted.

I shot him a glare of warning.

"How's your arm?" She seemed oblivious to the way Drake leaned away from her.

"Better," he grumbled. "I get my cast off in three weeks."

"Oh good! So you'll be out of it in time for the festival." Madeline beamed up at me. "It looks really cool. You did a good job."

I smiled back, my chest puffing a little with pride. Drake had been embarrassed about wearing his cast to school—until I made a few modifications. I'd drawn and painted on it so that now it looked like he had a bionic arm. It was a pretty good design, if I did say so myself.

"You really think so? I was trying to mimic one of those biomechanical tattoos people get," I said.

"Oh yeah! I love the pops of green and purple. It reads very sci-fi, which I'm guessing was the whole point, right?" She nudged my shoulder playfully. It was nice to see her so relaxed and happy. At school she always seemed closed off from everyone else. Some days she barely spoke at all.

"So you like scary movies?" Drake sounded dubious, almost like he was testing her.

Madeline's eyes twinkled. "Yes! What about you, Koji?"

"Uh, yeah. Sure."

"Liar." Drake smirked. "You should see him play horror video games. He flinches even when he knows it's coming."

She laughed again. "Do you really?"

I resisted the urge to trip Drake out of spite. "No I don't."

It was starting to snow when we arrived at the theater. We hurried inside and got our tickets. I stopped to send Dad a text to let him know we'd arrived okay. He was still keeping close tabs on me even though my grounding sentence was over. Not that I was the one up to anything questionable these days. Apparently he and Drake's mom were "getting some dinner" while we were out. Dad played it off like it was nothing, but Drake and I had our suspicions. Dad had ironed his shirt, shaved, *and* put on cologne. This had first date written all over it.

On our way in to find our seats, Madeline stopped and turned to us suddenly. "You guys want some popcorn?"

"Uh, absolutely." Popcorn was my favorite, after all. And this theater had one of those self-serve butter dispensers. My mouth watered as I started to take out my wallet. "Here, save me a—"

"No, it's my treat. I insist," she said and started walked back to the lobby.

"My friendship can't be bought with salty carbohydrates," Drake grumbled as we claimed three empty seats near the back.

"Oh? 'Cause I seem to remember having to bribe you with pizza when we first met." I kicked back in my seat and sighed. "Seriously, dude. Calm down. She's nice and I've never heard her mention her dad. I didn't even know she was the headmaster's daughter until you said something." I folded my arms behind my head to watch the opening previews. "You might actually like her if you got to know her."

"Right. 'Cause you know all about her, huh? What's her favorite color?"

"Purple." I knew that 'cause she painted with it the most. Plus that scarf she always wore was purple. Seemed like a good guess.

"Okay. Favorite movie?"

"Scary ones, apparently."

"Favorite music?"

"Uh, well, she listens to some of that same techno stuff you do while she paints. Mr. Molins lets us bring our MP3s while we work. I've seen her playlist. She's got a lot of Imagine Dragons on there." I shifted around to get comfortable. Another curse of being skinny: seats without much padding are murder on the rear end.

Drake fell silent, which I took as a victory. That is, until I saw the way his eyes had gone wide with alarm. He suddenly dropped down in his seat like he was trying to hide.

"Drake, what's wrong?" I glanced around. In the dark theater, I couldn't see anyone or anything out place.

Then the opening credits started. The house lights went dark and the glow from the huge screen filled the room. I saw them. Two men were sitting in the very back of the theater, just a few rows down from us. They wore matching black suits and ties—the kind of thing you didn't expect to see at a neighborhood movie theater.

I locked gazes with one of them. His expression was cold and forbidding. My body tensed.

"You see them, right?" Drake whispered.

I spun back around in my seat and tried not to panic. "FBI?"

"I don't know. They didn't say."

"What? You've talked to them?"

"Are you kidding me? Of course not. But those same guys were standing outside my house this morning, Koji. They followed me to school. When I got home, I saw one of them talking to Mom. I hid outside until they left, but I could hear what they were saying," Drake whispered. He sat up just for a second—long enough to steal another peek at the men. "They were asking her about the monster—if she knew who it might be or if we had ever seen it before."

My palms were clammy. My heart raced out of control. Those guys had followed Drake here. They'd seen me. What did that mean? Was I going to be questioned next? What if they hooked me to some kind of polygraph machine and found out that I was really the one they were looking for?

"Are you okay?" Madeline appeared next to me, holding an extra-large bucket of popcorn.

I forced a smile, struggling to shake off my panic. "Yeah. Just, you know, excited for the movie."

She didn't seem convinced as she sat down on the other side of me and passed the popcorn. I was in the middle, so I got to hold it. All the delicious, salty, buttery smells wafted right up into my face. Unfortunately, I'd completely lost my appetite. The whole movie was a blur. I tried to watch, to forget about the two government goonies sitting a few rows behind me, but it was no use.

Drake didn't seem distracted either. He stared straight ahead with a deep furrow locked on his brow. His jawline was rigid and he chewed viciously on the inside of his cheek. If Madeline hadn't been sitting between me and the exit, I would have insisted he and I make a break for it.

But she seemed to be enjoying herself. She shrieked at all the scary parts and ate handfuls of popcorn. I caught myself watching her instead of the movie. Her dark eyelashes were really long. A few faint freckles dotted the edge of her cheek, like a mini constellation, and there were little pearl studs in her ears. When the movie got intense, she twisted her fingers in the knitting of her scarf, her eyes wide and darting back and forth across the screen with exhilaration.

It was kinda cute.

As soon as the ending credits began rolling, Drake snapped to his feet and spun around. I turned to look, too.

The two men were gone.

Somehow, that didn't make me feel any better. One glance at Drake and I had a suspicion he was thinking the same thing. Now those guys were in the wind—they could be anywhere, and we wouldn't see them coming.

The three of us stood outside the theater in awkward silence. It wasn't that late and not even close to my curfew, but I was on edge and ready to barricade myself in my room. I couldn't decide if I should tip Dad off that the FBI might be paying us a visit or not. Maybe it was better to play ignorant.

"Want to go for some hot chocolate?" Madeline suggested. "There's a good coffee shop just a few blocks away."

"Yep." Drake didn't hesitate for a second. He started walking on without us, weaving through the other people we passed on the sidewalk.

Madeline and I jogged to catch up. The two-story shop was packed, bustling with dozens of customers escaping the cold. I offered to stand in line and get our order while they looked for an empty table.

Half an hour later, and armed with a tray of three large hot chocolates, I climbed the stairs to the second level and found Madeline and Drake locked in a debate over horror movies.

"You can't say that," Drake complained. "The special effects are what make it scary. If it looks lame, then what's the point?"

"No way, Drake Collins. The *story* is what makes it scary. That's why Stephen King's works will always be the cornerstone of horror. They don't rely on fancy effects to scare you. It's all psychological." Madeline smirked confidently.

Drake narrowed his eyes. "You can't tell me you didn't think the monster at the end of *It* looked lame. Even King himself hated the adaptation of—"

"And you can't tell me that watching that movie didn't ruin clowns for you forever," she interrupted.

They both sat back in a huff—until I started laughing. Drake and Madeline looked up at me at the same time and said, "What?"

"Nothing. Just you guys." I chuckled as I put the tray down between us and took the last empty seat.

The debate continued for a few more minutes in between sips of our hot chocolate, and I was forced to choose a winner just so we could change the subject. Drake sulked when I agreed that the suspense of a scary story was worse than the computer-animated monsters.

"You're just taking her side because she's cute," Drake grumbled and crossed his arms.

Madeline's eyes widened. "You think I'm cute?"

He didn't answer, but his nose turned red as he scowled and looked away. Madeline blushed, too. I was about to tease him about it, which seemed only fair after all the crap he'd given me when it came to Claire, but the room suddenly went silent.

All around us, the other café patrons were focused on the flat screen TV mounted on the far wall. A shaky video shot from someone's cell phone began playing—one with me in the starring role. It was the first time I'd dared to watch all of it.

It began with Clint sailing out of the doorway like a crash dummy being thrown from a collision. He landed in a heap in the middle of the street. Then I emerged from the stairwell, a huge black scaly demon bristling with otherworldly power, and swooped onto him. The video went white whenever lightning popped too close. Sometimes it panned away or someone got in the way. People screamed in the background. My voice was impossible to make out amidst the chaos. Then I took to the sky and the video cut off.

A news reporter appeared on the screen, talking with some-one who had apparently been there on the street that day. I couldn't hear what they said, but the news ticker scrolling across the bottom of the screen read "NYC citizens still living in fear after unknown creature attacks."

"You think they'll ever find it?" someone at the table be-hind ours murmured.

"Humph. They say they don't know what it is, but I'm not buying that garbage. The government probably cooked it up in some lab and it escaped," an older man replied. "A genetically engineered monster they could use as a weapon."

"Or they let it loose on purpose," a younger voice suggest-ed. "Remember that crater they found in Central Park? I'd bet money that was the first time they let it out. They're trying to send a message to all our foreign enemies. Just imagine what kind of damage a creature like that could do on a battlefield."

My stomach churned and I could taste bile in the back of my throat. Me? A weapon?

"I heard it was nearly seven feet tall."

"No way. It looks way bigger than that!"

"They said the other day it must be some sort of humanoid reptile. It was probably hunting, looking for some fresh meat."

"Yeah? Then why didn't it just eat that guy, huh? No way it's just a dumb lizard. Look how it moves. It even talks. That thing is smart. I'm betting alien. It crash-landed here, left that big crater, and now they're racing to catch it before it kills someone. My brother's a cop and he said there were some sus-picious government guys creeping around both sites."

Drake shot out of his chair all of a sudden, his face pale. He muttered something about going to the bathroom and vanished downstairs.

"Is he all right?" Madeline whispered.

I leaned forward, letting my elbows rest on the table. It took everything I had to block out the rumbling conversations going on all around us—conversations about me. "It's hard to say with him."

She was quiet for a moment. Then, without looking at me, she asked, "What do you think that creature is? An alien? A monster? Or something else?"

I stared down into my nearly empty mug of hot chocolate. "Does it really matter what I think?"

"It does to me."

I took a deep breath. "I don't know. But whatever it is, I don't think it's going to hurt anyone."

"What makes you say that?"

"It would have already, wouldn't it? I mean, it obviously *could* hurt someone, if it wanted to. It had that guy pinned down, but it just let him go. It could have killed him, and some would argue that guy even had it coming. But the monster's hiding instead."

Madeline was staring right at me, studying me like she was trying to read my thoughts.

"Do you think we'll see it again?"

I shrugged.

"I hope we do."

I stole a glance at her calm, thoughtful face. "Why?"

"I don't know," she admitted with a shy smile. "I suppose I just love a good mystery."

Drake and I waited until Madeline walked out of sight down the crowded sidewalks toward the subway to catch her train home before beginning our trek back to my house. The last view I had of her was her long hair swishing in sync with one end of her purple scarf, both flecked with snow. Something about it made me smile. Headmaster's daughter or not, she was nice. I liked talking to her—even when she and Drake ganged up on me for not knowing who Major Lazer was. Totally not my fault, by the way. Thanks to my dad, I'd been raised on a mixture of classic rock and 80s hair bands. Not that I didn't like a little modern music, too, I just didn't usually pay attention to the band names.

Dad had given me some cash to take a cab home, but we still had a while before our curfew. Besides, I was hoping the cold air would help Drake chill out a little. He was still distracted and fidgety, not that I blamed him. Any sudden sound, like the screech of car tires or someone shouting at a cabbie, made him jump and start walking faster. I wondered if that was because of the FBI guys, Clint, or me in my monster form.

We didn't talk much on the way home. I'd given up trying to get him to relax by the time we reached my front steps. Not even my baiting, taunting questions about if Major Lazer had any "good" music worked. Normally, he'd have launched into a full-blown speech about how I had no taste and insist on wiping the music on my phone to make space for better stuff. This time, however, I didn't even get so much as a snort or sideways glare. Not good.

Drake and I stopped in the square of light cast from the kitchen window of my house. Through it, I could see our parents standing by the counter sipping glasses of red wine. Drake's mom was laughing and watching my dad, who was probably making a total fool of himself just so she'd keep smiling at him like that. We had a few things in common when it came to pretty girls, I guess.

"Wow," Drake whispered. His expression had gone blank with surprise as he stared into the glow of the window.

"What?"

"I haven't seen her smile like that in a long time," he replied softly. "Years. Since before Dad died." He went silent and his eyes suddenly went dark. His shoulders hunched under his poofy coat, and he looked away with a scowl. "What time is it?"

"My phone says 10:45."

"Let's give them a few minutes. We're early anyway." Drake trudged over to the front steps and sat down.

I sat beside him, and together we watched the snow fall.

"How long ago was it?" Drake asked all of a sudden, his tone somber.

"Since what?"

"Since your mom passed away."

I watched my breath turn to steam in the frigid air. "I was four and a half. So eleven years."

His voice was tight and hushed. "Five for me. You know, since Dad."

Somehow, I hadn't expected it to be so recent. He must have remembered a lot more about his dad than I did about my mom. I wondered if that made it better or worse. Or if it even mattered. Death was still death, and no one had ever taught me how to deal with not having what seemed so normal for everyone else.

"I used to have more memories of her," I admitted aloud. "But sometimes it's like I can't remember anything. The only thing that seems clear in my mind is the accident—like that moment swallowed all the others."

"How did she die?"

I shivered as the air around me seemed to get colder.

"We were driving to visit my grandparents in Jersey for Christmas. She had Christmas music playing over the radio. She loved singing. She always sang as loud as she could when we were in the car—like she was having her own private rock concert or something. She didn't care who saw." The memory darkened, and I squeezed my eyes closed, my fingers instinctively brushing over the old scar on my jaw. It was a solemn reminder that those memories weren't just a nightmare. "I remember her turning around to look at me, trying to get me to sing along with her. I was in my car seat in the back. We were driving over a bridge." I stopped. Memories strangled my voice right out of my chest. Opening my eyes, I looked down at the tops of my sneakers and waited until it passed.

"Suddenly we were going over the railing. We landed close to the bank so when the car reached the water, we hit hard but didn't sink very far. Only the front end of the car went completely under. I don't know how long it took—seconds, maybe minutes—but it felt like an eternity. The black water came pouring in through the broken windshield. Mom was under the water. I wanted to get to her—to help her—but I couldn't get unbuckled from my car seat. And the water just kept coming in. I was up to my chest, then my chin. It was so cold it hurt."

I shut my eyes tightly and bowed my head. Ever since, the feeling of water around me drove my brain into a panic I couldn't escape. My muscles seized up. I couldn't breathe. Swimming was out of the question. Even being in a bathtub was uncomfortable if I let the water reach my chest. Even after all this time, the sensation was still too much. It took me right back to that night with the dark, icy waters rising all around me.

The first responders had said Mom died on impact. But I could have sworn I heard her say my name one last time. She'd told me she loved me. That memory was the clearest of all, and I refused to believe it was just my imagination.

"The newspaper articles called it a miracle. They said I should have died. If we had crashed even a few more inches away from the bank, I would have drowned."

"You miss her?" Drake asked.

"All the time." And time hadn't made it any easier. That was a lie people liked to spread, that time heals all wounds. True, some months had been easier than others. But the empty spot in photographs, the place where she should have stood, her empty chair at every table we sat down at to eat, never went unnoticed. It was a void Dad and I didn't dare acknowledge.

"I know Mom misses my dad. But I don't. He wasn't a good person," Drake said quietly. "Good people don't do what he did."

"What did he do?"

"He lied. He lied *all* the time. To me, to Mom, to the banks, to everyone. She found out about all the debt right after my birthday. I remember because that was the day she stopped smiling." His eyes went steely. "They stayed up all night arguing. Shouting. Screaming. Mom was crying and Dad…He just wouldn't stop trying to make it sound like it wasn't a big deal. Everything he said, everything he was—it was all fake. And when he couldn't lie about it anymore, he waited until no one was home, and he…" His voice halted, as though the words burned too much to speak. He didn't have to say it, though. I knew. "He tried to make it look like an accident. He had all his gun cleaning stuff scattered everywhere. Mom thinks he did it so we would be able to get his life insurance money to pay off some of the debt. But it didn't work. He didn't fool anyone."

I hesitated to say anything. Any second now, I expected Drake would cave in on himself like a dying star and stop talking altogether. His experience, losing his dad that way, was much different than how I'd lost Mom. It didn't take Einstein to see the anger flickering in his eyes as he ground his jaw, chin trembling and hands clenched.

"The cops figured it out, of course. I heard them talking. They said he didn't even do a good job of making it look like an accident. Now Mom has to work all the time just to try to pay off all the debt he piled up. She's still carrying that burden—and he left her alone to do it all by herself." He let out a hollow laugh. "He left us… like we were nothing."

I sat, frozen in silence.

Drake sat up a little. He turned and look at me straight in the eye. The light from the kitchen window put hard shadows across his face. "Is your dad a good person?"

"I-I, uh…" Words failed me.

"If this is going to keep happening, if they're going to get serious, I just need to know that he's not like them—like Dad or Clint. I need to know he's not a liar."

"He's not," I answered confidently.

Drake glanced back, gazing through the kitchen window to where our parents were still laughing and talking. I couldn't tell if he believed me or not. It was weird that our parents were dating. Drake was obviously unsure about it. I wasn't exactly comfortable with it either. But I didn't want it to affect our friendship.

My dad grinned nervously while he poured her another glass of wine. Drake's mom did that hair-flipping thing girls sometimes do when they are bashful around someone they like. When she smiled, her whole faced seemed to glow. I could see why Dad liked her. She was pretty, and so far she seemed nice.

But she wasn't my mom.

"This is excruciating. Why are old people so awkward when they flirt?" Drake grumbled.

"I know, right?"

"It's like watching a car wreck in slow motion."

I nodded. "Worse, probably."

"It's almost as bad as watching Madeline around you."

"Hey! Wait—what?"

Drake snickered as he rolled his eyes. "The fact that you don't get it just proves my point, Koji. You're a dating disaster waiting to happen and you don't even realize it."

CHAPTER 13

B y the time the Holiday Festival rolled around, the news
had finally gone quiet about dragon monsters, conspir-
acies, and mysterious earthquakes. Normality had
settled back over New York as everyone's focus shifted to the holidays. It was almost Thanksgiving, and all my
classmates were geared up for the festival and a break from
school.

Our art class managed to get everything ready to sell our
masks and do the face painting with just enough time left to put
some extra effort into our booth's decorations. It snowed all
night, but the morning of the festival was bright and clear. We
had balloons and banners, fir trees wrapped in sparkling lights,
hay bales, and frost-covered pumpkins. Crowds filled the soccer
fields. Small groups moved from booth to booth, playing games
and buying treats while the school orchestra filled the brisk air
with music.

I was amazed how many people actually came. My dad and
Ms. Collins walked by early on and bought one of our masks
painted like a cluster of orange and yellow fall leaves. Ms. Collins even praised my mad painting skills.

Not gonna lie, as far as painting goes, I was on fire. Maybe
it was all the holiday spirit that had given my creative juices a

boost, or the two Red Bulls I'd pounded with breakfast, but I was a regular Michelangelo with my washable paints.

Madeline and I worked the same face-painting shift so we could talk. She coached me through new techniques on how to apply the more complex paint jobs. It wasn't just getting kids smeared up to look like zoo animals or butterflies. No way. This was serious, cosplay-grade stuff. We used fishnet stockings and glitter paint for scales on mermaids, different brushes for fur textures on wolves, tigers, and foxes. I didn't even need references to do spot-on superhero masks, and my Ironman design was a big hit. Even Mr. Molins seemed impressed.

"Keep it up and I'll have to tell Mrs. Kalensky about you," he threatened with a laugh. "The Theater Club is doing a production of *A Midsummer Night's Dream* this spring and I'm sure she could put you to work doing stage makeup."

It hadn't dawned on me to try something like that before. I liked the idea right away. It sounded fun to paint people up for performances—like pieces of artwork that moved.

"You've really never thought about working in film or theater before?" Madeline passed me the wet wipes so we could wash up after our shift ended. "You'd be really good at it! I can start showing you some tricks for working with prosthetic pieces if you want."

"Yeah!" I couldn't stop grinning.

"Looks like we're almost out of black and white paint again," Mr. Molins called to us. "Can one of you bring some back from the classroom?"

"I got it. Madeline's busy," I volunteered and swiped my paint-covered thumb across her cheek on my way past.

"You're so mean, Koji!" She laughed.

I took my time wandering through all the booths on my way to the back of the school. It was nice just to drink in the festive atmosphere. Inevitably, I found myself drawn toward the sound of music. The school's student orchestra had rented a full stage setup, complete with metal framework to hold the spotlights overhead. Drake had helped them with some of the wiring while they were assembling it earlier that morning. All of the student musicians were dressed in their solid black performance attire. It was impressive.

Couples swing danced while the students on stage performed a catchy jazz tune. Claire sat near the front, holding her cello with perfect elegance. Her brow furrowed with concentration as she tapped one of her feet to the quick rhythm of the song. Then, as if by instinct, our eyes met through the crowd. My heart did that crazy fluttering thing that made me feel breathless. I couldn't help it. I still liked her, even if it was totally hopeless. I didn't even understand why anymore, and part of me wished I could wipe all memory of her out of my mind. Then it might not hurt so much to see her this way, angelic and completely out of my reach.

I could have stood there and watched her perform all afternoon. At least the music gave me a legitimate excuse. Unfortunately, there were other things I had to do, so I headed into the school through the rear entrance.

Up in the art classroom, I grabbed two big bottles of paint, one black and one white. I carried one under each arm as I went back down the stairs to the bottom floor. The dark, deserted school halls felt like a museum after hours. With all the action outside, being inside alone was strangely calming. Preppy kid school or not, the campus was beautiful and rich with decades of history I could practically feel humming through the floorboards.

I started down the last hallway toward the rear entrance, toward the daylight streaming through the cloudy glass of the back door. The merry rhythm of holiday music from the orchestra drifted in, muffled by the excited sounds of the crowds. The blurred shapes of people walking past occasionally eclipsed the light from the door. I reached for the old brass door handle.

Suddenly, the earth shuddered violently under my feet.

I tripped and fell flat on my back. The paint bottles slipped out of my hands and rolled down the hall. The glass chandelier hanging above me clinked and rattled as the ceiling vibrated.

The ground rumbled and shook as I tried to get up. A horrible roaring sound, like a freight train, bore down on me. It seemed to get louder as the shaking intensified. Outside, people screamed. I stumbled and tried to keep my balance, grabbing onto one of the doors and yanking it open—

Just in time to see the orchestra's stage collapse.

The metal beams holding up the heavy light fixtures crashed onto the stage. Students dove into the crowd to get away. But not all of them made it.

Over the chaos, a voice I recognized cried out for help.

"Claire!" I couldn't stop myself from yelling. She lay less than twenty-five yards away, trapped under the metal framework.

I clenched my teeth. The weight of my totem bracelet seemed to intensify around my wrist. There were so many people—I'd definitely be seen if I went out there to help her. It would be the Clint situation all over again.

And I was 100% okay with that.

As the earthquake subsided, I took a step back into the school and let the door fall closed. A few seconds, a whispered word, and the dragon totem transformed my body.

I had to do this fast. The longer I was out there, the more people would see me. I couldn't risk getting captured, too.

Once again I ripped open the door and burst free of the school. I spread my wings and took to the air with a thunderous roar. I swooped low across the people scurrying around on the soccer fields. Everyone screamed when they saw me. They scrambled to get away, faces twisted in horror.

A large crowd had gathered around the crumpled stage. A group of people from the crowd were trying to lift the metal framework to free Claire from where she lay trapped underneath it. But it was no use. The frame was too heavy. Live voltage from the shattered lights sizzled and sparked. The whole stage was a deathtrap.

And right in the middle of it was the girl of my dreams.

I landed on the edge of the stage with a thud. The platform groaned under my added weight, threatening to buckle. As I stepped closer, the men trying to move the debris stopped and edged away. I could smell their fear as plainly as I could see the terror in their eyes. I was a monster—a wolf in a sheep's pen—and they feared my fangs.

I took a step toward Claire.

Out of nowhere, Damien Blount appeared in front of me with his arms thrust out wide. His whole body trembled as he looked up at me, blood oozing from a fresh cut across his cheek and his green eyes as wide as saucers. "No! I won't let you hurt her!"

I had to give him some credit—he was telling the truth. The aura of honesty around him was strong.

But he was still in my way.

I leaned down closer. He flinched but didn't run. "You want to get to her, you'll have to kill me first," he threatened.

All around us, the crowd had gone silent. I guess they were watching to see if I'd rip him in half.

I tilted my head to the side and tipped my chin toward the metal frame. "You look strong," I rumbled in my deep, growling voice. "Are you strong enough to lift that?"

His expression skewed with a look of desperation and defeat.

"Then get out of my way," I snarled. "I'm not here to kill anyone."

Damien slowly dropped his arms as I stepped around him and crouched over Claire. One of the metal beams had her pinned at the waist and there was a trickle of blood coming from the corners of her mouth. She was conscious but fading. When she saw me, her lips pulled into a weak, delirious smile. She must have been too out of it to realize what I was or be afraid.

I struggled to keep a fierce expression.

"Is she going to be okay? Can you get her out?" Damien interrogated as he appeared next to me again. His concern was annoyingly sincere.

I scowled. "When I lift the frame, be ready to move her. And be very careful. Got it?"

Damien nodded.

I turned back to the crowd and let out another roar. "And someone better be calling 9-1-1 instead of just taking more stupid pictures of me! Do something useful for once!"

I counted to three, then grabbed the metal frame in my clawed hands and crouched down. I flexed my shoulders to spread my wings. On three, I lifted, pressing the frame above my head. It didn't feel all that heavy in my grip, but moving it threatened to make the whole stage collapse with us on it. Sparks sizzled and popped all around us.

"Hurry it up!" I yelled. The stage shifted dangerously under my feet. I held the scaffolding up while Damien raced around to drag Claire free of the debris. More people stepped in to help him. Once they were far enough away from the stage, I let the structure fall again.

In an instant, the whole stage crumpled into a heap of twisted, sparking metal—this time with me right in the middle.

I burst out of the rubble with a roar, shaking off the power cords and shards of metal that bounced harmlessly off my powerful form. The crowd parted for me as I touched down next to the rubble of the stage. Everywhere I looked, flashes from camera phones flickered and blinked.

I glowered at my audience, who seemed to be watching me with bated breath. I guess they were waiting to see if I'd attack, leave, or say something else. They murmured to one another, whispering and speculating with eyes fixed on me. When I took a step, the entire crowd gasped and shrieked in alarm. Well, all except for the small group crowded around Claire and Damien.

"The ambulance is still ten minutes out," someone shouted. "Lay her down flat. Try not to move her any more than necessary."

"That's too long!" Damien yelled hysterically. He whirled around and stumbled, tripping over his own feet when he found me looming right over him.

Our gazes locked, and Damien froze as though paralyzed with fear.

"What are you?" he murmured.

"Someone who wants to help," I replied.

"Like you helped Clint Ackeridge?" someone shouted from the crowd.

I narrowed my eyes over my shoulder, though there were too many people for me to identify who said it. "He deserved far worse than what I did to him."

I slicked my scaly ears back, looking between Damien and the rest of the crowd distrustfully. They were still filming me. I was probably being streamed live right this second. That meant people—people like police or the FBI—would be coming for me soon. They might even shoot at me, and I wasn't sure how my dragon scales would hold up against gunfire. I wasn't eager to find out.

I had to get out of here.

Crouching down, I peered at Claire. She lay on a coat someone had spread out on the snow for her. Her face was flecked in a few scrapes, but she still took my breath away when she smiled up at me.

"Hang on, Claire." I tried to make my gruff, dragon voice softer. "You'll be okay."

"You know my name?" Her expression was mystified as she touched the scales on my cheek.

"Of course, I'm a huge cello fan." I put my hand over hers, relishing the delicate warmth of her palm against my face.

"You're...incredible."

I wondered if she could see me blushing in this scaly form.

"You should go. Fly away before they try to catch you," she said.

"Ask me to stay and I will."

Her smile wasn't really a smile at all. It never reached her eyes as she gazed up at me with a subtle desperation I didn't understand. Why was she so worried about me? Why wasn't she afraid?

"I'll be okay. Please, just go." Her voice grew quiet. "Get away from here as fast as you can."

What else could I say? In the distance, I could hear the wail of approaching sirens. Police or ambulance, it didn't make much difference. I was out of time.

I flared my wings, braced for takeoff, and gave Damien one more hard look. "Take care of her. If anything happens to her, I'll hold you personally responsible."

He didn't answer. Damien just stood there, eyes still wide and mouth hanging open, as I took off into the sky like a rocket.

The earth fell away as I spread my wings to the cold air. Clouds began to gather, as though drawn to me. The wind rushed to greet me like an excited puppy, licking at my heels and carrying me higher. If I concentrated, I could manipulate it and change its speed and direction.

So I poured on as much speed as I could. Gritting my teeth in frustration, I refused to look back to where Claire was lying, still waiting for the ambulance to arrive. I couldn't. If I saw her like that again, I'd turn around.

But my presence wasn't good for her, not in this form.

I used the clouds as a veil to hide myself while I circled the school and searched for a safe place to land and transform back. I was supposed to be in the art room getting more paint.

After almost five minutes of darting around in the clouds, waiting for the perfect moment, I zipped into an alleyway beside the school where they kept the dumpsters. With nobody in sight, I shifted back into my regular body and immediately took off back to the last place anyone had seen me go—the school. But just being there wasn't enough. If my dragon face was going to be starring on this evening's news headlines again, then I needed an airtight alibi. Ugh. They made this whole alter ego thing look way easier in the movies.

The art room upstairs would be the first place anyone might come looking for me—so that's where I went. The earthquake had done a bit more damage this time. Most of the easels had been knocked down, and paintbrushes and canvases were scattered across the floor. A few of the supply cases had toppled over, and more of our class pottery lay in broken shards on the floor.

Then I saw it: my alibi. One large, planter-style pot was still intact and perched on the top shelf of a display case. Bingo.

Leaning against the display case, I stood on my toes to grab the bottom of the pot and pull it down toward me.

I was tall, but not quite tall enough to reach the top shelf where the pot was sitting, awaiting its demise. I put one foot on the bottom shelf. A few more inches were all I needed. Just a little more. One more inch.

The shelf wobbled dangerously.

Uh-oh.

I grabbed the sides of the shelf and tried pushing it away from me.

I over corrected. The case tipped, and in a panic, I yanked the shelf back toward me to try and steady it.

The whole display case fell right on top of me with a crash.

Ceramic shards and wooden shelves smashed everywhere. The last thing I saw was the large pot I'd been hoping to drop on my own head falling right toward my face.

CHAPTER 14

I 'd never been happier in my life to have a concussion. Not only did it give me the perfect alibi, it also explained why I "couldn't remember" anything about the festival. I was useless in the eyes of the New York City Police Department, just another innocent bystander who'd been injured during the earthquake. Police officers in black uniforms were going room to room, interviewing everyone about the reappearance of the dragon monster. They asked my dad lots of questions and seemed to quickly lose interest.

I was in the clear.

My dad, however, was in a flustered frenzy. It took forever for the nurses to convince him that I wasn't going to die of brain damage. It wasn't that bad of a concussion, apparently. I was one of the lucky ones. The ER was packed with other people who had been victims of the quake, and some of them were way worse off. Bed space was at a premium, and since my injuries were minor, the hospital staff seemed eager to send us on our way.

The sharp pieces of the broken pot had cut a gash in my scalp, right at my hairline. So a few stitches and a lollipop later, I was back home curled up on the sofa. Not that they usually gave suckers to teenage patients, but I wasn't about to turn down free candy.

Drake sat cross-legged in the recliner, staring down at his phone. His mom had been called in to the hospital to help with all the earthquake victims, so he was staying with us until further notice.

"No one touches the TV, got it? It stays off," Dad warned as he marched through the living room.

"How come?" I complained. So much for seeing how the investigation into the dragon monster's identity was going.

"Because I don't want either of you getting worked up about this. You're supposed to stay away from screens on doctor's orders. I want peace, calm, and quiet. Understood?"

"Understood," Drake and I muttered in unison.

Satisfied, Dad went upstairs, and I could hear him pacing the floor of his bedroom. He was talking on the phone, too— probably to my grandparents in Jersey. They were the only ones who called to check on us once this stuff hit the news.

"The mayor has just issued a state of emergency for the whole city," Drake whispered across the room. "He's asking everyone who can to evacuate. All schools have been suspended until further notice and there's an 8:00 p.m. curfew. They've shut down the subways because some of the tunnels caved in. It's bad, Koji. They're saying the epicenter of all the quakes is the same place—a spot in the Hudson River between Ellis and Governors."

I ran my fingers over the fresh stitches on my head. "I guess it's safer if we're going to have more earthquakes. Wait, did you say *in* the Hudson?"

"Yeah. They're sending out the Coast Guard to investigate. But it's not just that," Drake said. "They think that monster is the one responsible for the earthquakes."

I couldn't disguise my frustration. "What? Seriously?"

"The earthquakes started happening around the same time he was first sighted. It's not that far-fetched to think the two events are connected." He sighed and pocketed his phone.

I hated to admit it, but he did have a point. Only I *knew* I wasn't the one causing these quakes. And I seriously doubted my dragoness friend was, either. She wanted to be as discreet as possible, so starting natural disasters didn't seem like something she'd put at the top of her to-do list.

I ran my hand over the totem bracelet on my wrist. Something else was going on. I could feel it like a tickle in the back of my mind—a sense of impending doom. I carried the totem of air. The blue dragon-girl had the one for water. So what if this was the one for—

Dad interrupted my thoughts from the stairwell. "Koji, I need you to go upstairs and pack."

"What?"

"Just do it, please," he ordered. "Drake, we're swinging by your place on our way out of town. I just got off the phone with your mom at the hospital; you and Koji are going to stay with my parents until this is over."

That was the end of the discussion.

Dad left right away to get our car out of the parking garage down the street, and I dragged myself upstairs to throw some clothes into a bag. I crammed my laptop, my picture of Mom, and a few of my favorite comics on top and zipped it closed. On a whim, I grabbed the sketchbook I'd been using as my art journal.

I flipped through the first few pages, glancing over the designs. I'd come up with some ideas for my comic. My hero character's name was Noxius. He had bat wings, wore a mask, and was nuts about a girl who was already engaged to someone else. Sound familiar?

So far, Mr. Molins was the only one who had ever seen any of my sketches and designs, and I'd been extra careful to make sure the hero didn't look anything like me. Noxius didn't need a totem bracelet to transform, either. He was older, good looking, muscular, and super successful—basically everything I wasn't.

I closed the sketchbook and sighed. Maybe working on it some more would help get my mind off worrying about everything. Drawing always helped me clear my head. Despite what my dad thought, it was more than just a hobby. Whenever I popped in my earbuds, cranked up my favorite playlist, and started to sketch, I could hear myself think without any outside interference. It was like going to a private world inside my own head where everything just felt...better.

I could use a lot of "better" right now.

When I turned to leave, I found Drake standing in the doorway, staring at me with a glazed expression. "I can't believe this is really happening."

I sighed. "It's crazy."

We stood there for a few uncomfortably silent minutes. I got the impression there was more he wanted to say, but Drake didn't move. He stood with his shoulders hunched and his hands buried deep into the front pocket of his hoodie. His brow wrinkled in a tense frown, but his mouth was scrunched like he'd tasted something bitter.

Finally, he dipped his head and let out a sigh. "Koji, I gotta ask—"

A shrill screech from outside made every muscle in my body go rigid. Were those sirens? Through my bedroom window, I could see a line of police cars and armored vehicles coming down the street. They stopped right outside our house, and police in full riot gear began bailing out of the back of one of the trucks.

Drake and I rushed to the top of the stairs just in time to hear them bash the door in with a crack that seemed to shake the whole house. I couldn't see what was going on, but I could hear plenty. Footsteps pounded through the first floor like thunder. The police officers shouted, ordering my dad to put his hands in the air and get down on the ground. Dad yelled back at them, trying to figure out why they were here.

My heart hit the back of my throat. *Me*—they were here for me. Somehow, they'd figured it out.

I started down the stairs. Dad needed my help. He didn't know about my totem. This wasn't his fault.

I jerked to a halt when Drake seized my wrist. He slowly shook his head. Together, we snuck down the stairs, passing Dad's room on the second level, until we could see what was going on by peering through the bannisters.

The police were handcuffing Dad in the middle of the living room. Two men dressed in the black suits—the same ones from the movie theater—prowled around our house like they were looking for something.

"Check him for anything out of the ordinary. Jewelry, technology, anything that seems out of place," one of the suited men said. "I want it all bagged and tagged for transport."

The police began to search my dad with a rough pat down. They took his cell phone, car keys, wallet, and anything else they found on him.

"Maybe it would help if you told me what you're looking for," Dad suggested. "I'm Colonel Daniel Owens of the United States Air Force. I haven't done anything ille—"

"We know who you are, Colonel. Just as I'm sure you know why we're here." One of the suited men approached my dad with a cold smile. "Admittedly, we don't know how you're doing it, but we know without a doubt that *you* are the creature that's been terrorizing this city."

My jaw dropped.

Dad's expression skewed with confusion. "What? That's insane!"

"You were mysteriously absent during both its appearances with the pretext of looking for your son. No one can vouch for your whereabouts except for you. The creature was first seen within days of your arrival in New York," the man pointed out in a quick, cold tone. "It appears in places where you've been previously sighted. You had a unique knowledge of the familial situation in the Collins household, and have been engaged in a romantic relationship with Amelia Collins. We like to call that sort of thing motive. You would have been compelled to intervene on her behalf."

My dad didn't say a word. Clenching his teeth, he kept his eyes focused on the suited man in front of him.

The man returned Dad's steely glare and then gestured to the police officers. "The evidence is damning. The harder we look at you, the more of it there is, Colonel. The sooner you come clean, the better things will be for you...and your son."

Before Dad could get a word out, they were wrestling him out the front door. I bit down hard. It took everything I had not to call out to him.

"Find the boy," one of the suited men murmured to the other. "Children always talk. They're much easier to crack."

I was beginning to consider doing a little cracking of my own—arms, spines, maybe a few skulls. But a policeman in a navy blue uniform rushed in. "The car is empty. The boy isn't there."

The suited man scowled. "Search the house and the school. And while you're at it, the Collins' residence as well. He won't go far. He's in unfamiliar territory here."

Drake dragged me all the way back upstairs before I could hear anything else. Back in my room, Drake locked the door while I ran to the window and watched as my dad was loaded into the back of a police squad car in handcuffs. My blood boiled. My chest thrummed with heat and a hunger for revenge that made my fingers drift to the bracelet on my wrist.

But I couldn't dwell on that now. We had minutes—maybe seconds—before the cops found us.

"Come on," I muttered. "I know where we can hide."

Drake didn't stop to ask questions.

I cracked open the circular window and scurried onto the slanted roof. Three stories below us, the cops were totally oblivious as we closed the window and climbed around to the backside of the house. We hopped easily from rooftop to rooftop of the clustered buildings, zigzagging our way for a couple of blocks until we found a fire escape we could use to scramble back down to the street.

We were standing in a narrow street between two houses, out of plain sight for now. We couldn't stay here, though. This was basically someone's backyard.

"What now? There's nowhere we can hide. They'll be watching our houses," Drake panted. "The school, too!"

I hadn't thought that far yet, honestly. I leaned over and tried to catch my breath. "Drake, I—"

Out of nowhere, the earth jolted underneath us.

It knocked me off my feet. I crashed right into Drake, toppling us both onto the concrete path.

"What the heck was that?" he rasped, eyes wide and face blanched in panic.

The ground shuddered again. It bounced me off the ground like someone was jumping around me on a trampoline. It happened again as I tried to get up. I was going to have some serious bruises.

"Are these aftershocks?" Drake was still struggling to stand.

"No." I gritted my teeth and steadied myself. "This is something else."

Add breaking and entering to the list of things I've done wrong in my life. Between the violent tremors, Drake and I rushed around to the back of the house, across the patio, and to the back door. We knocked a few times, but no one answered. Perfect.

I stood guard while Drake took a pair of paperclips out of his wallet and picked the lock. He was surprisingly good at it—

although now didn't seem like the time to ask him how he'd picked up that skill. Still, it was impressive.

The door swung open, revealing a darkened kitchen. I held my breath, waiting for someone to notice we'd gotten in. But no one did. The house was completely silent. With shades drawn over the windows and all the lights switched off, the house was dim and abandoned.

"Looks like they're not home," Drake whispered as we stepped inside, locking the door behind us.

"They must have evacuated," I agreed. "I bet half the city's sitting in traffic right now trying to get out of here."

I went immediately into the living room and snatched the remote off the coffee table. While I was flicking through the channels searching for the news, Drake's phone began buzzing in his pocket. He was getting dozens of messages.

Suddenly, he snatched the remote out of my hand and flicked the channel. The sound of shouting and the *thump-thump-thump* of helicopter blades filled the dark living room. A news anchor tried to shout over the noise of the live footage that filled the screen of something monstrous coming out of the water in the Hudson River.

Drake dropped the remote. Neither of us said a word. We stood in the gloom of the living room, staring into the glow of the television.

"The origins of this beast are still unknown, but there is speculation based on its appearance that it is a reptile," the news anchor stammered.

The monster rose up out of the churning gray water like a titan of scales and horns. It looked something like a crocodile, with a long toothy snout and small eyes, but it had longer legs and a huge, paddle-like tail. The more I saw appear out of the murky water, the less I could feel myself breathing.

The news anchor began screaming, "Oh, God help us! It's heading for Manhattan! Please, if you are in the Battery Park area, take cover now!"

"Drake?" I whispered.

He didn't reply.

"They're saying it's over two hundred feet tall!" The news anchor's voice crackled.

I cleared my throat and tried again. "Drake, I have to go."

"I know." He turned slowly to stare up at me, his expression strangely calm.

"You do?"

He rolled his eyes and went back to staring at the television. "You did a pretty good job covering it up—better than I expected, honestly. But, come on, if I can't figure out my only friend is a shape shifting, anthropomorphic dragon superhero, then maybe I need to have my IQ checked again."

"H-how long have you known?" I squeaked.

"I suspected after Clint. I knew after Claire. I was in the crowd. I saw you save her." His mouthed twitch at a smirk. "You look at her the same whether you're a dragon or not. Dead giveaway."

"Please don't tell anyone."

He spun around to face me again, his arms crossed and his expression sharp with a challenging glare. "On one condition."

I held my breath as he studied me, and then thrust a finger at the TV screen. "You go kick that thing's scaly butt and show everyone whose side you're really on."

I grinned. Easy enough. Maybe.

Hopefully.

"You can't watch me transform," I warned as I peeked outside the front door to make sure the coast was clear. So far, there were no cops in sight.

"Why not?" Drake sounded genuinely disappointed.

"I'll lose my powers if anyone sees it." I stood back from the door and rolled my sweater sleeve up to reveal the bracelet strapped firmly around my wrist.

Drake stared at it with awe, his eyes sparkling so brightly I could practically see the wheels turning in his head. "That's it? That's why you can change?"

"Yeah. Long story. I'll explain later." I made a twirling gesture with my finger. "Turn around. No peeking. Seriously. If I lose my powers because of you, I'll be pissed."

He huffed, groaned, and finally turned around.

I didn't give him a chance to consider stealing a glance. Placing a hand over the totem scale, I commanded it to awaken. The surge of ancient power rose like a whirlwind around me, consuming me body and soul. My dragon form unfolded in the gloom of the foyer, and I bumped my horns on the chandelier.

Drake couldn't resist any longer, I guess. He spun around and gaped up at my full dragon-y awesomeness.

"You should see your face." I laughed.

"You should see yours," he countered.

I already had, so I knew why he was gawking when I lumbered by to open the front door. "Stay here. If things start looking bad, you gotta get out of here. Seriously, don't do anything stupid."

He tapped his temple. "Einstein, remember?"

I took a deep breath, opened the front door, and squeezed through it. I got a running start down the front steps, flared my wings, and drew in a strong gust of wind to bear me up into the sky. The higher I got, the more of the city I could see laid out before me. The cityscape stood like mismatched black spikes against a blood-red evening sky. Smoke rose in the distance. That's where I had to go—where my enemy was waiting.

I just hoped I was up to the challenge.

CHAPTER 15

B asically, I had three goals:
One, don't die.
Two, don't let anyone else die.
Three, kill the monster as soon as possible.
Sounds simple, right? It did to me, too. But as I landed atop the Empire State Building, gripping the railing of the observation deck with my clawed hind legs, I got my first look at what I was really up against.

Spoiler alert—things didn't look so great.

The New York City skyline before me looked like something straight out of a classic *Godzilla* film. Thanks to my ultra-enhanced dragon-vision, I could see it clearly even from this distance. The giant reptilian monster stomped down Broadway, smashing into buildings and flipping cars like they were children's toys. It had carved a trail of destruction straight through Lower Manhattan.

Helicopters whirred through the air, and the distant cracking and popping of gunfire suggested someone was at least trying to stop the creature's advance, although that didn't seem to faze it at all. Guns against a creature that size seemed like throwing pebbles at a tank. The police could probably unload every gun they had at it without ever piercing its leathery hide.

The question was, could I do any better?

I'd practiced my flight and inadvertently figured out how to brandish lightning and gusts of wind, but I wasn't confident those things would do much to a creature that size. I'd never tested the full extent of those powers or my own strength.

The only thing worse than that uncertainty was the idea that I'd be charging into this fight alone. I seriously doubted my dragoness acquaintance would be eager to join me, or that the local police would view me as an ally rather than another target, so alone was my only option. Somehow, I had to get this done, and as I watched the monster's tail gut the lower levels of another apartment building, I knew I had to act now.

A police helicopter roared past me, filled with guys in heavy combat gear. They were armed with some heavier artillery—M16 machine guns like the gate guards carried at the military bases where I'd lived all my life. A couple of the officers gestured wildly in my direction, but fortunately no one took a shot at me.

Okay. Time to get busy.

I stood up on the railing and spread my wings and arms wide, letting my eyes rolled closed. I called on the power of my element again, and immediately it rose up, eagerly obeying my thoughts and desires. I opened my eyes again to see the skies darken with boiling, churning black clouds. The winds grew fierce. Bolts of lightning snapped and sizzled in the air, leaping from cloud to cloud. That, I hoped, would be enough to force the helicopters to get out of my way.

Ahead, I spotted a tank rolling into position, flanked on all sides by troops. Below, citizens screamed and ran in all directions like startled mice—climbing over cars and fleeing into buildings.

The air shuddered with a sudden blast as the tank took a shot at the monster. The artillery shell caught him square in the chest. The creature stumbled. But it didn't fall. Instead, it let out an earth-shaking roar and swung its long, crocodilian-looking snout toward the tank.

Cracks of gunfire seemed to come from all sides as the soldiers emptied their clips. Several dropped to one knee, shouldering rocket launchers and taking aim to fire. The explosives made the monster stagger in confusion, bellowing and snapping its jaws, but it never fell. I couldn't spot a single place where the rounds had pierced its hide or even left a mark. Not good.

Without warning, the beast lunged for the nearest tank. Its massive jaws opened, ready to swallow it whole. The soldiers around it dove to get away. More gunfire. More explosions. Glass shattering and people screaming. Fire and chaos everywhere I looked.

I dove head first off the top of the Empire State Building.

For an instant, I realized what I was about to do. I was just a high school student. I wasn't a soldier or a trained fighter. I wasn't a trained... anything. What the heck was I doing diving headlong into this?

Like a black-and-blue missile, I let the wind fill my wings. I surged toward the monster as it took a bite out of the side of a building as though it were a giant corndog.

I set my jaw and steeled my fraying nerves. With any luck, I would keep more people from getting hurt or killed and take that creature down.

With a thunderous roar, I dove toward the beast and its gaping maw, snapping around feet first to kick down with all my might. The force drove its jaws shut and its nose into the asphalt, cracking the street and leaving a twenty-foot-deep trench that ended just a few feet shy of the tank.

The monster lay motionless, although I doubted it was dead. After only one kick? No way it was going to be that easy.

I was pretty rattled after the impact, too. I'd just cracked the concrete street open like an eggshell with one blow, and while it hadn't hurt my leg or foot, my head was spinning as I clambered to my feet.

Shaking off my daze, I sprang off the beast and out of the trench with a burst of wind at my heels. I landed back on the street, facing the group of soldiers who still stood around the tank. Every last one of them stood frozen, gaping at me with expressions a mixture of terror and awe. I seemed to get that reaction a lot.

"Fall back now," I growled at them, lashing my tail as I stood straighter. "The choppers, the tanks, the trucks—take them all and get as many people out of here as you can! Leave this to me."

"Who are you?" one of the soldiers shouted back.

I didn't hesitate for a single second. "Not your enemy. Call me Noxius."

The ground shook as the monster stirred in the trench where I'd left it. My time was up. I yelled at the soldiers to run one last time before I dove back down into the dark abyss, teeth bared, ready for a brawl.

I honestly didn't expect the soldiers to obey. But when the crocodilian monster and I burst out of the trench, me clinging to its giant head, all the soldiers were in full retreat. Even the helicopters were whirring away to a safer distance—although I noticed a news choppers hung close for the scoop.

That suited me fine. At least now no one could blame me for being the one who started this mess. The whole world had front row seats, and I couldn't afford to screw this up.

I just had to figure out how to win.

With most of the soldiers and police busy getting the civilians out of the way, I let my full power loose, hitting the monster with everything I had. I stung his hide with bolt after bolt of white-hot lightning, summoning forth winds that pushed him back toward the river. I snapped and twirled, diving through quick aerial maneuvers to stay out reach of his snapping jaws and whipping tail. He bellowed in fury, crawling after me as fast as his legs would carry him. Every lash of his tail smashed through a building, overturned buses and cars, and ripped up streetlights and power lines like weeds.

As much as my attacks seemed to annoy and hurt him, they didn't do enough damage to put him down for good. He kept getting right back up again, long snout snapping and tail lashing. He was frustratingly resilient—and I was running out of ideas.

Suddenly, a familiar roar interrupted our symphony of chaos. My heartbeat stammered in my chest. My breath caught.

The fire hydrants up and down the street burst open, sending plumes of water rocketing into the air around us. The water massed together and formed a huge, swirling ball in midair. In the very center, I could see her.

My dragoness friend had arrived.

Her golden eyes glowed with primal strength as she waved her hands in a flourishing gesture that sent her giant water-ball rocketing forward. It hit the monster with the force of a tidal wave, sweeping out its stumpy legs, and sending it rolling several blocks toward the river.

I landed on a rooftop next to her. "Nice shot."

She snorted and nodded to where the monster was already getting up, shaking chunks of asphalt and sidewalk concrete off its back like a dog after a bath. "Not nice enough. He's doing too much damage. People are going to get hurt. We have to get him as far away from the city as possible."

"I'm open to suggestions if you've got an idea."

"Keep luring him to the river. He'll be on my turf there—maybe I can drown him."

I grinned and twitched my tail, unable to disguise my excitement. "No problem. If there's one thing I'm good at, it's being annoying."

And truth be told, annoying him was about all I could do. None of my lightning bolts pierced his hide. It was probably like getting zapped by an electric fence. It hurt him, sure, but it wasn't lethal.

I leapt off the rooftop and took to the air, zipping low past the monster and pinging him with a few more lightning bolts on the tip of his snout. He bellowed angrily and snapped at me as I buzzed around his head. Then I took off toward the river.

The monster followed with an angry growl, focused only on me. Perfect.

At the edge of Battery Park, I skidded to a halt and whirled around. Now for the tricky part. Before me, the monster approached with jaws open wide for the kill. His hide smoked, mottled with fresh scorch marks thanks to my lightning. Behind me, the rolling gray waters of the Hudson licked the shore.

My pulse sped into overdrive, sending currents of warm power thrumming through my body as I crouched. Every muscle tensed and spasmed. Setting my jaw, I braced while the monster stampeded straight for me. The closer it came, the more the ground shook. It barreled through trees and streetlights, snapping power lines like threads.

Five hundred yards…two hundred…

At one hundred yards he sprang for me, maw open wide to swallow me whole.

I shot straight into the air, snapping my wings in fierce beats and calling up a gust of wind. I zoomed over his head, down his neck, and wove through the huge, plate-like spikes that ran down his back all the way to the end of his tail.

The monster hurtled headlong into the gray waves with a crash and a hiss of dismay. At least he was away from the city. Now it was up to her—my blue dragoness ally.

No sooner had the monster submerged than a sudden swell of strong currents began dragging him away from the shore. He flailed and swished his huge, paddle-shaped tail, but it was useless. She had him now.

But I wasn't about to let her fight this out alone.

Reaching inward to the depths of my mind, I willed the full force of my winds. Once again, my power surged, obeying my whims without hesitation. Black clouds smothered the daylight, popping with bolts of lightning and filling the air with chaotic energy. Some of the clouds began to spin, rotating faster and faster until long, finger-shaped tornadoes whirled to life and formed a barrier between the monster and the city.

In the middle of the river, my dragon-girl ally called forth an immense wall of water all around the monster. She doused him from all sides, over and over, trying to bury him in the same dark depths he'd crawled out of. He gurgled and growled, snapping his jaws futilely. For good measure, I drilled the top of his head with one spiraling vortex of wind after another. At first, I worried it wouldn't be enough. Finally, the beast's struggling slowed. He sank lower and lower in the water, until at last he disappeared beneath the surface.

The waves began to calm as the dragoness lowered her hands cautiously.

I held my breath, and my ally and I exchanged a meaningful glance. Was it over? Had we just gotten seriously lucky?

The surface of the water beneath me exploded as the monster leapt into the air. Its huge jaws closed around me, massive teeth interlocking like prison bars.

It dragged me down into the water.

Beyond the monster's forbidding jaws, I could sense that we were sinking. The surface, the air, slipped away.

Out—I had to get *out*!

I slammed against the inside of the monster's jaws, floundering desperately. My clawed fingers strained at his teeth, fighting to get him to open up. He obliged—but only a little.

Just enough to let the ice cold water rush in.

Panic swelled in my chest like a paralyzing cold. Every muscle locked up. My chest constricted. The water poured over me. It hit my face, shooting up my nose, filling my lungs, and freezing me to the marrow.

I floundered in the dark water, groping for a way to keep my head above the surface. But there was no surface—no way to escape. My vision dimmed. My lungs spasmed. My arms and legs hung weightless in the water around me. My body drifted with the current, limp and helpless, as the rush of more water tossed me end over end.

Dying…I was going to die.

Suddenly, the monster's mighty jaws released their grip. Something grabbed me around the waist. An arm? My vision went black before I could see who or what it was. All I could feel was warmth—so much warmth.

And then I felt nothing at all.

I awoke with a ragged, wheezing gasp. My body lurched, jolting out of control as I gagged and threw up water. I wheezed for air between retching, my scaly form shaking.

I was alive? How? It made no sense. Someone… someone must have rescued me.

But who?

Lying back on the muddy bank of Battery Park with my body still trembling, I looked around to thank my savior. There was no one else there. I was completely alone. Out in the open water, my dragoness friend was still locked in combat with the monster; it couldn't have been her. She was fast, but not that fast.

There wasn't time to figure it out now. I had bigger, crocodilian-shaped issues to work out.

My knees wobbled as I got to my feet. Our current battle plan wasn't working. The monster couldn't be drowned. At least, not easily.

I glanced at the glowing white totem scale on my wrist. There was only one thing left I could think of to try—something not even my dragoness friend had attempted yet.

Honestly, I wasn't even sure I could do it. And even if I could, it was a huge risk. I'd only have four minutes to get this done. After that, I would be completely exposed. I'd have to find somewhere to hide and fast, before anyone figured out who I was.

Game on.

I took off to meet my ally in the air. We zipped along together, dodging the monster's snapping jaws and lashing tail. Wild savagery or complete desperation flashed in her glowing golden eyes. I couldn't tell which. Maybe it was both. I grabbed her arm to get her attention.

"Four minutes, right?" I tapped my totem scale.

"You can't," she shouted. "If someone sees you transform back—"

"One of us has to." I flashed her a smirk. "Besides, once it's done, you're the only one who can send him back down to whatever watery abyss he came from."

Her expression broke, eyebrows drawing up with what I could have sworn was despair. "I'll try to cover you. Fly as far away from us as you can when the time is up. I don't know how fast you'll change back, but you have to be out of sight."

I gave her wink. "No problem. I had a great flying teacher, remember?"

In midair, she grabbed my cheeks, dragged me in, and kissed me right on the mouth.

My mind went totally blank.

"Place your hand over your totem and offer your soul to the power of the kur," she urged after she pulled back.

It took a few seconds for my brain to reboot. At least if I died, I could say I'd had my first kiss.

"I decided on my hero name," she added with a thin, sad smile. "It's Oceana."

Before I could answer, she turned and soared off. Oceana? Even if I died, I'd never forget that name.

CHAPTER 16

My heart pounded, stalled, and started as I placed my hand over my totem scale. I hovered a few yards over the water. Despite Oceana's best efforts, the monster lumbered toward me again, walking along the river bottom. It seemed like nothing could stop him.

Except, maybe, this.

"I offer my soul to the power of the kur," I growled under my breath. Immediately, the totem scale flashed, its light piercing the darkness of the falling dusk like a nuclear explosion. My vision went white, and tingling heat spread through every muscle from my scaly dragon toes to the tips of my pointed ears.

Then it hit me—a sudden surge of power unlike anything I'd felt before. It burst through my body, twisting and stretching me as it grew more intense. My bones bent. My muscles strained. I squeezed my eyes shut and struggled not to resist.

When I dared to look again, the huge monster wasn't so huge anymore.

I'd become a creature that could match him in size, pound for pound. None of my human features remained—the totem had made me into something else entirely. Now my muscular body rippled under scales black as the night sky adorned in stripes of electric blue. Jagged black spines bristled down my back and along the backs of all four of my reptilian legs. My leathery wings were large, more powerful than ever, and tipped with jagged talons.

I'd gone full dragon. There was no turning back.

The crocodilian monster hurtled toward me. We collided in the water, and this time I wasn't afraid. With my toothy jaws open wide, I grappled him with my forelegs and snapped at his face. He hissed and recoiled, his stumpy legs too short to claw back.

We brawled and rolled, snapping and snarling amidst the lapping waves of the Hudson. He clamped his powerful jaws around my neck and I clawed at his head, raking my talons over his snout and eyes until he let me go.

We squared off as Oceana summoned walls of water all around us. There was no retreating from this death match. Overhead, my storm intensified. The lightning bolts zapped the surface of the water around us, and I willed them against the monster. Just as I'd hoped, the flashing chaos whipped him into a frenzy. He thrashed and bellowed, bristling with a snap of his long, toothy snout. Rage blazed in his eyes as he dove for me, maw open for the kill.

Perfect.

I dodged and twisted my body so I could sink my teeth into his neck. My powerful jaws bore down and my jagged fangs pierced his hide, sinking deep. The foul taste of his blood hit my tongue like sucking on an old, dirty penny.

The monster let out a shriek of pain and panic, pitching wildly. He swung his huge tail and swept out my legs, forcing me to let go and shake off the impact. *Crap!*

Just one more deep bite—that's all I needed. This time, I wouldn't let go.

I bared my fangs and paced, looking for another chance to strike. How much time was left before I changed back? I couldn't remember or even try to keep count. Faster—I had to hurry.

I dove after him and missed, landing short as he ducked to the side. Before I could recover, the creature cracked me over the head with his tail. Stars winked in my vision. Concussion number two? I shook my head, trying to wheel around so I could lunge again. But before I could get my bearings, he locked his jaws around my throat. I braced, fighting to keep the upper hand even as he began whipping his body into a signature crocodilian death roll.

A wall of water crashed around us, knocking us apart as we bounced off the bottom of the Hudson. I wasn't alone; Oceana had my back. She dipped low, drawing his focus long enough for me to get up again.

In another flash of lightning, I was on my feet and in the air. I snapped my wings into a burst of speed, skimming the surface of the water and jumping him while his back was turned. As I reared back to take another bite out of the back of his neck, right below his skull, I called forth the mightiest burst of lightning I could muster.

One last shot.

My teeth punched through his thick hide, piercing down to the soft, vulnerable parts of his body. As soon as I tasted blood, I let the lightning bolt hit me squarely on the head. The current sizzled through my body, over my teeth, and into his wound. My body screamed in pain, every nerve firing at once. But I didn't let go. I was the master of the air element. I could take it. I *had* to.

The monster's body went rigid, vibrating under the force of the electricity.

Just a little longer…

The monster stopped thrashing. His huge body went slack in my grip. The only movements he made were the erratic jerks of his muscles from the electrical current still coursing through our bodies.

I opened my jaws and let him go.

The monster hit the water, completely limp.

My vision blurred. I swayed on my feet, my footing unsteady on the mushy bottom of the bay. I blinked, trying to shake it off. Was he dead? Had I won?

A dull, tingling cold prickled across my body. I couldn't tell if it was because of the bolt I'd taken or...

Oh no. Was I out of time? How long had it been?

I staggered and sloshed toward the shore, a mountain of black-and-blue scales against the foaming water. Every step was a fight as that coldness spread over my body. My head spun, smearing the city lights and glow of the flames into an orange and red blur before my eyes.

Behind me, the dull roar of Oceana working her element droned in my ears. I had to trust she would take care of the rest. There was nothing more I could do.

I had to get out of here *now*.

I barely made it to the bank before my time ran out. My full dragon form burst like bubble made of light and I landed on the shore in my lizard-human-hybrid form again. That was a relief, but I didn't dare to hope I'd remain in this state for long. That paralyzing cold was still stretching over every muscle, turning my whole body numb.

I staggered away from the river, fighting to stay on my feet as my wings dragged the ground. Seconds—I had seconds left. I had to get to some place out of sight before I transformed back.

My body burned and my bones ached. The muscles in my arms were numb and wouldn't respond anymore.

I stole a glance back. Oceana, hovering over the water like an elegant, scaly, blue angel. She drew the focus of every chopper in the area as she made a spectacle of disposing of the monster's body. I owed her one. If she hadn't come to help me...

The air filled with a flash of blinding golden light. I gaped as the dead monster's huge body, surrounded by fountains of Oceana's water, shattered into a cloud of fine golden mist. The mist showered through the air like fireworks before dissolving into the dark, vanishing without a trace.

Wow. Had Oceana done that? Talk about the perfect diversion.

I flew sloppily, weaving and clipping the sides of buildings as I tried to stay low and out of sight. There was only one place I knew of around here where I might be safe—where I could change back and no one would see me. I could make it. I had to. The cold numbness was rising fast, threatening to leave me immobile and helpless somewhere in the open.

I kept to the shadows and long-forgotten alleyways as much as possible until I broke free of the city. Then I ducked below the tree line, following the edge of a forest as I retreated along the shoreline of the river. My vision blurred, eyes struggling to focus. I could barely make out the silhouette of an enormous building with two tall smokestacks on the top. My refuge.

Almost there.

With a final groan of pain and power, I burst through a dusty glass window of the abandoned power plant and landed in a black, scaly heap on the floor just as the dimming light of my totem scale went dark. A blink, shudder, and gasp later... I was back in my human form.

As I rolled onto my back, I could taste hot, coppery blood on my tongue. My body was so numb it was impossible to tell how injured I was. And right then, it didn't matter. I'd made it. I was alive. The monster was gone. Everyone was safe.

I shivered, although I couldn't tell if it was from relief, exhaustion, or the lingering terror of what I'd just done. What if Oceana hadn't shown up? What if I had died? Would Dad even know what really happened to me? Would anyone?

Sprawled alone in the dark, my vision tunneled as I stared up at the exposed steel beams and moonlight trickling through the smashed windows. My whole body hurt, and I couldn't hear anything over the growling, rasping sounds of my own breathing. I wondered if Oceana had made it out of sight, and where

Drake and my dad were. With my consciousness slipping, I had no way to get in touch with either of them. They'd never find me here. How could I get back home?

And what if Oceana came here looking for me? What if she saw who I really was? Maybe coming here hadn't been such a good idea after all.

But it was too late to worry about that now. As the darkness closed in, I stared up at the night sky.

For now, everyone was safe. That was something—and for me, it was more than enough.

A soft, warm palm rested against my cheek and carefully combed my hair out of my face.

Oceana? Had she found me already? How long had it been? My eyes refused to open so I could see if it really was her. My arms and legs lay heavy and lifeless. I couldn't move at all.

"Hush now, it's okay," a soft voice whispered over me. It wasn't Oceana.

"Who?" I rasped weakly.

"Don't worry. I'm watching over you."

Alarm bells screamed in my head. I *knew* that voice. I had to look. Who was it? I wanted to see!

I startled awake, bolting upright and blinking into the morning sunlight that filtered through the clean French windows. The musky scent of paint and clay made my head spin. I sat up with a grunt, staring around at the school art room floor.

How had I gotten here?

There was no one else in sight. Everything in the art room was quiet and still. Not a single paintbrush was out of place.

Standing made my head swim. I wobbled, catching myself on the edge of a stool as I reached to where a spot on my head burned and throbbed worse than the rest of me. My fingers probed a fresh bandage wrapped around my head, covering what felt like a new swollen knot on my temple. Maybe it was time to invest in a dragon helmet.

After going round after round with that giant monster, I expected I'd be a bloody pulp. But pulling back a few of the bandages on my arms revealed only a few minor cuts and scrapes. Apart from those relatively insignificant battle wounds and a weird metallic taste in my mouth—probably residual from being zapped with about a million volts of electricity—I felt strangely okay. I guess my scaly body was more durable that I'd anticipated.

I knew there were probably lots of other people who hadn't been fortunate enough to get away with just a few bumps and scrapes. Even if the monster was gone, he'd left behind a lot of damage.

As I left the art room, the eerie wails of distant emergency sirens and response vehicles echoed through the darkened building. My skin prickled as I went to the door, hesitating with my hand on the knob. I took a deep breath. Whatever was going on out there, I had to blend in. I had to protect my totem.

As I stepped out on the school's front steps, I could see smoke still rising from Lower Manhattan. It smeared over the horizon, silhouetted against the twilight. The fires and wreckage left in the beast's path put an orange glow on the horizon that rivaled the sunrise. My gut twisted into painful knots. Was my dad somewhere in that mess? Drake? Had Oceana gotten away?

Two police squad were cars lined up outside my house when I arrived back at home. I did a double take just to make sure, but there were no armored vehicles or SWAT trucks anywhere in sight. I took that as a good omen as I approached the front door.

I didn't get a toenail inside before my dad threw his arms around my shoulders and squeezed the breath out of me.

"Koji! Where have you been? We've been looking every-where!" He was sobbing and petting my hair roughly. "I thought you were dead! Drake said you two made a run for it and got separated."

Kudos to Drake for lying convincingly.

I patted Dad's back—mostly to let him know he was crush-ing the life out of me and I couldn't breathe. "Sorry, Dad. I-I hid out with some other people near the school. I saw them take you away. I didn't know what else to do, so we just ran. What hap-pened?"

"Once Noxius appeared again, I guess they figured out they had the wrong guy. They couldn't get rid of me fast enough." Dad grabbed my face to look me over. "Are you all right? How's your head?"

"Fine until you started squeezing it." I chuckled.

Dad hugged me again and started herding me back into the house. Inside, a few cops were idling around the living room. They looked up with surprised expressions when I came in.

"Koji!" Drake bounded out of the recliner.

I managed a weary smile. "Yep. I'm alive. You can call off the search party."

"Why didn't you call?" My dad loomed over me like he was searching for signs of damage.

I reached into my pocket for my phone. Honestly, I hadn't even thought about it until that moment. My clothes always mysteriously vanished when I switched forms—as well as any-thing else I was carrying on me at the time. I hadn't considered that they might be able to track or call me with my phone. To my surprise and relief, the screen was totally smashed in. I held it up as evidence. "Sorry."

Dad sighed, seeming satisfied with that explanation. "Well, at least you're okay."

"Yeah, just tired." I left the shattered remains of my phone on the coffee table and hobbled toward the stairs. "Can I go lie down?"

"Don't worry about it, Mr. Owens. I'll look after him."
Drake patted me on the back—*hard*.

I cringed.

Dad nodded and let me go, although not before hugging me
one more time. On my way upstairs, I heard him talking quietly
to the police officers, who were already packing up to leave.
Once again the case of the missing military kid had been solved,
and they had bigger problems to deal with.

Drake followed me up the stairs, practically leaping at my
heels like an excited terrier. Only when we were behind the
closed door of my bedroom did he spin me around, his eyes
wide and face flushed with excitement. "Dude—*dude!*" That
was all he could say for a few minutes.

I took that opportunity to sit back on my bed, kick off my
shoes, and crawl under my comforter. "Can we talk about it in
like four hours?"

"You just fought a freaking monster!" His whispering voice
squeaked in delight. "You…you shot lightning bolts and then
you…transformed again! You kicked its—!"

"I know. I was there." I groaned and pulled the comforter
over my head.

"So why aren't you like, I dunno, celebrating? That was the
most incredible thing anyone's ever seen!"

I closed my eyes and sighed in relief. "First of all, I'm exhausted. Fighting giant demon crocodiles, while epic, is actually
a lot of work. Second, I can't tell anyone *I* was the one who did
it. Third," I hesitated, opening one eye to look at Drake. But he
wasn't letting me off that easy.

"Third?" he coaxed.

"I think someone else knows I'm Noxius. Someone other
than you, I mean."

"Who?"

That was the worst part: I didn't know who. I gave him a
haggard frown. "If I knew it wouldn't bother me so much. I
went to a safe place to change back—somewhere only Oceana

and I know about. I guess I was out for hours. But someone *else* found me there. They must have followed me back from the battle." I leaned forward to bury my face in my hands and poke gingerly at the lump on my forehead. "They took me to the school, treated my wounds, and left. I was so out of it I couldn't tell who it was. That voice, though. It was so familiar. I know I've heard it before."

"Oh." Drake's voice had lost all its enthusiasm. He sat down on the floor beside my bed. "And you're sure it wasn't Oceana?"

I shook my head. "No. It wasn't her."

"Did whoever it was see you transform? Can you still use your powers?"

"I don't know." I clenched my teeth and looked down at the totem bracelet still clamped snuggly onto my wrist. Its luminescence was gone, like the life had been sucked out of it. That had to be a good sign, right? If I'd lost my powers, would it even still be there? Or would it just fall off? "I won't know for another twenty-four hours. Or eighteen hours or something—I don't know how long I was out for. I can't use my totem again for a day after going full dragon form like that. Oceana is going to be seriously pissed off at me when she finds out someone saw—"

"She was *awesome*!" Drake was grinning again. "I saw some incredible footage. You should see it!"

I couldn't deal with my number one fan right then. He was missing the major crisis here. I might not *be* Noxius anymore if whoever treated my wounds saw me transform back. My head pounded. There wasn't a part of me that didn't ache. I needed sleep. Then maybe I could think more clearly about all this.

While Drake rambled on and on about how awesome the fight had been, I stretched out under my comforter and let my eyes fall closed. A few hours, that was all I needed.

Before the count of five, I was out cold.

After a day, I had my answer. Or at least, part of it.

I could still transform. I tried shifting in the bathroom, just for a few seconds. A mixture of relief and intense frustration came over me as I saw my dragon face appear in the bathroom mirror. This meant whoever had taken me from the plant to the school hadn't seen me transform.

I was still Noxius.

Too bad that didn't make me feel much better. Someone knew my secret, even without witnessing it firsthand. I now had more questions than answers. Who would go out of their way to help me like that and not expose my secret? Why take me to the school? Did they know who I was? Was it one of my class-mates? A teacher? The weird old lady in the uniform office?

For once I understood why not knowing things frustrated Drake so much. Until I figured this out, I couldn't trust anyone besides him and Dad. Not that it mattered much right away. Most of the schools in the city—especially around the disaster area—stayed closed the rest of the week and straight on through Thanksgiving. I wasn't going to be seeing anyone else for a while.

That would have been great, except the university also closed, and Dad was set on keeping Drake and me under his constant supervision. Talk about exhausting. Drake's mom worked relentless hours in the hospital thanks to the monster's path of destruction. She came over to our house for a few hours at a time to shower, eat, and change out of her bloodstained clothes. Sometimes she caught a nap on the couch, but then she had to get right back to work. That's why Drake was staying with us. It made her feel better for us all to be in one place, I guess.

Thankfully, the casualties had been minimal—that's what the news channel kept saying. Only four people had been con-firmed dead, which when you looked at the damage, seemed like a miracle. It didn't make me feel any less guilty, though. I felt the weight of those four deaths like chains of iron around my neck. If I'd acted sooner, if I'd known what I was up against, if I'd been stronger—so many ifs.

As troubling as those facts and what ifs were, none of them bothered me more than the unresolved crocodile monster-shaped concerns rolling around in my head. Why had that thing attacked? Where had it come from? Would it come back? Were there others like it? Not even Drake dared to speculate.

Without a corpse left behind to investigate, no one could come up with any hard data to begin figuring any of those answers. Scientists and world leaders argued during news interviews and scholarly debates. The media went through one "expert" after another, pressing them for theories about the creature. Some thought alien. Others were convinced it was something interdimensional. Ultimately, they were all just as clueless as everyone else.

The whole world was in the dark.

Whatever the case, the damage it had left behind would cost millions to repair. One thing I could say about New Yorkers was that they didn't give up. They were stubborn—in a good way. The community was already rallying and reconstruction was well underway to fix the damaged buildings and roads.

The weekend of Thanksgiving, Dad decided we would go see my grandparents in Jersey after all. Honestly, I think he just wanted to get out of the city and away from the disaster site for a while. He didn't speak during most of the drive and kept both of his hands locked on the steering wheel, gripping it like he was in the last lap of a championship race.

Thankfully, since Ms. Collins had to work through the holiday, Drake tagged along with us and I had someone else to talk to. Unfortunately, I couldn't escape the gossip and theorizing about Noxius and his mysterious female accomplice even at my grandparents' house.

The news channels played videos of our battle almost constantly. Experts picked the footage apart frame by frame, speculating about Oceana. She had done her own little interview with the media after the battle, most likely to give me time to slip away unnoticed. I'd have to remember to thank her for that next time we crossed paths.

Some of those so-called experts thought we were evil. Others called us heroes. The commentators only agreed on two things: we had done the city a huge favor in killing that creature, and no one knew where we were now.

The police called for anyone with information about us to step forward, but no one did. Part of me wondered if Drake would ever leak my secret. Imagining that kind of betrayal made me breathless. As my closest friend, he was the only one I dared to confide in. If I lost that bond, I'd have no one.

A few days later, the military issued an official statement of gratitude for our efforts. They wanted to give us both a medal, although of course we didn't show up at the ceremony. Neither of us was dumb enough to take that bait.

On our last day in New Jersey, I sat on the living room floor at my grandparents' house, munching on my third bowl of homemade party mix, watching anime reruns, and wiggling my bare toes through the shag carpet when Drake came rushing in to change the channel. I scowled at him. He knew I was sick of watching the news.

But this was different.

The president of the United States stood behind a podium bearing the presidential seal, his face illuminated by the flashes of press cameras. Several men dressed in the same style of nondescript black suits we'd seen in the movie theater not long ago flanked him on both sides. More government goons hired to sling their muscle around.

"My fellow Americans," he began. "Tonight I've come before you to address a situation that has become one of global interest and national crisis. As many of you know, New York was recently the site of an attack by a creature of unknown origin. The city was also defended and ultimately spared from total devastation by two more creatures—also of unknown origin. These beings have declared themselves by the names Noxius and Oceana. They wield an undeniably formidable power, the likes of which we couldn't have imagined might exist outside of fiction and myth.

"After bravely fighting to defend one of our nation's most beloved cities, they disappeared as mysteriously as they arrived. Neither Noxius nor Oceana have been seen since, and as of now, I cannot offer any more information about them because we simply do not know. We don't know who they are. We don't know where they came from. And we certainly don't know what would compel them to act so selflessly on our behalf, although we are grateful.

"We also wonder why they do not reveal themselves. Many take their secrecy as a sign of guilt or untrustworthiness because we, as members of the human race, tend to fear what we do not understand. So, I speak now to those two individuals who acted so bravely and saved so many. Noxius and Oceana, help us understand you so that we do not have to fear you. We will not harm you. You have my word as president of the United States that you will not be treated as an enemy. We want only to see, learn from, and understand you. Please come forward and let yourselves be found."

As the president's speech ended, a roar of shouts, questions, and clicking camera shutters went up through the crowd of spectators. Some of them were outraged at why we were being hailed as heroes. Others were more interested in the facts, like what efforts were being made to track us down.

I closed my eyes. My thoughts got tangled up in all that senseless noise, but my third eye was clear: he was lying about how Oceana and I would be treated if we let them take us.

When Drake turned off the TV a moment later, I looked at him. He stared back with a haunted, blank expression. "So?" he whispered as he sat down next to me on the floor.

"This doesn't change anything," I grumbled quietly, glancing back through the doorway into the kitchen to make sure my dad and grandparents were out of earshot. "I'm not falling for it. I won't turn myself in, and I doubt Oceana will, either."

His brow twitched and his lips thinned uncomfortably.

"What? You think I should?"

He didn't answer.

"Are you going to turn me in?"

Drake sat up straighter, aiming a bitter scowl in my direction. "I'd never rat you out. What kind of question is that?"

I dropped my head into my hands. "I don't know. Don't listen to me. I can't even think straight right now. All I know is my third eye tells me he's not being truthful."

"Uh, what? Third eye?"

"It's a totem thing. We each get a supernatural gift to go along with our dragon and elemental powers. Mine is apparently to be a walking lie detector."

"Wow." Drake's brows rose. After everything that had happened already, I wondered how something like that still could surprise him. He rubbed the back of his neck and sighed. "I just worry, you know? The president of the United States just called you guys out personally. What happens from here if you turn him down? Do you become an enemy of the state? An international fugitive fighting for justice? And here's a better question: Where did that monster you fought even come from? Yeah, you beat it, but who's to say there's not more? What if you and Oceana aren't enough to bring it down on your own next time?"

Yeah, all very good questions that I had no idea how to answer.

I groaned and rubbed my throbbing forehead. "Oceana said there are four totems, one for each element. If another monster appears, maybe the other totem holders will, too." I knew I was grasping at straws, but what else could I do?

Drake ran his fingers through his shaggy platinum-colored hair. "Maybe I can find something about them online."

"I already tried that."

He snorted, his mouth curling into a knowing smirk. "Yeah? What did that amount to? Typing it into Google?"

My ears burned. Geez, how did he know that?

"Let the master take a crack at it." He sounded very sure of himself as he sniffed and rubbed the end of his nose. "Give me a few weeks. I'll see what I can come up with."

CHAPTER 17

I did not want to go the school dance.

Sorry, the *Winter Ball*. That's what they called it at Saint Bernard's. Rich kid lingo, I guess. It sounded fancier.

Anyway, I didn't want to go, and it wasn't because I couldn't get a date. That was usually the case for me at every school dance anyway, but it wasn't the main reason this time.

Honestly, I didn't want to watch the girl I liked go with someone else. It was bad enough to go alone, but it was way worse to stand there and watch the woman of my dreams dancing and hanging all over some other guy. Just thinking about it made me feel like I was going to be sick.

Drake was less than sympathetic to my suffering.

"You're a freakin' superhero. Have some dignity," he muttered as we walked up the stairs to our first class. Everything had calmed down enough that school was open again. "There are plenty of other available ladies at the school you can ask. What about Madeline? She's nuts about you. Ask her to go."

I balked. "She is not. Where are you even getting that? She's just a friend."

"I'm getting it from the way she stares at you like she's trying to psychically will you into her arms—or lips. Whichever comes first."

"Yeah, right. I think I would notice if she was doing that."

"Obviously not." He laughed, whirling around to walk backwards a few steps ahead of me. "So what if I ask her, then?"

"Ask who?"

"Madeline."

I stopped. "You want to ask Madeline to the Winter Ball?"

He shrugged. "Sure, why not?"

I had to think about that. She was just a friend. I shouldn't have cared. So why did it bother me? I shook my head and turned away to open my locker. "Fine, ask her."

I expected a snappy reply, but when I looked up again, Drake was already gone. I muttered to myself that it didn't matter—really, it didn't—if he asked her. He had bigger things he was supposed to be worrying about, like figuring out where that monster had come from and where the other totem wielders might be.

Two weeks before Christmas, the media finally calmed down about Noxius and Oceana. It helped that neither of us had revealed ourselves, so they were running out of experts to offer up new ideas about our origins and identities. The city continued to rebuild. Everything was falling back into a steady, normal rhythm. Dad and I were almost completely unpacked and settled into our new house, and he almost trusted me to be out of his sight for more than an hour again. Life was good.

Until early one school morning a week before the dance when I heard a shrill, angry female voice coming down the hall in my direction.

Okay, so I was eavesdropping. Not good, I know. It was kind of impossible not to, though. Claire's redheaded, fox-faced friend made a loud, whining scene outside the Chemistry classroom door, right across from my locker.

"*Not going?* What do you mean, you're not going?" she wailed. "You have to go! I've already gotten our bouquets to match. Our dresses are color coordinated!"

Out of the corner of my eye, I noticed Claire flush with embarrassment and bow her head slightly. "Damien has a judo match that night. It's the district championship, so I can't possibly ask him to come with me instead. And I can't go without him, can I? It's just a dance, Tabitha. I'm sure you'll have more fun without me than if I were to go as a third wheel."

"It's not *just* a dance. It's the Winter Ball!" She crossed her arms and huffed as she stamped her foot. "We've been planning this for months. We always double date to dances! Always!"

I rushed to cram my last textbook into my locker and shut it. I turned, about to walk away, when a certain redhead appeared directly in my path. I skidded to a halt. "Oh, uh, h-hey there."

She didn't answer. Instead, her cunning vulpine eyes studied me with penetrating force. Something about that look made me feel like a piece of meat about to be devoured.

Tabitha seized my uniform tie like it was a dog leash and dragged me over to stand with her and Claire. "What about this nerd? I doubt he's got a date."

Ouch, my pride.

"Uh, I-I, w-what?" I stammered.

Claire straightened, her expression closing as she avoided my eyes. "Tabs, that's really not—"

"You're friends with him, aren't you?" Tabitha demanded.

"Yes, but—"

"So go as friends." Tabitha waved a hand in the air dismissively. "I'll explain everything to Damien. I'm sure he'll understand, especially since you already have your gown and everything."

"Uh, what's going on?" I interrupted.

"You're going to take Claire to the Winter Ball. But only as a friend of course, so don't get too excited." Tabitha smirked proudly between us and tapped the end of my nose. "And with a little preparation and personal grooming, you might even pass as a gentleman."

"You're forgetting something," Claire chimed in softly. "He might already have a date."

Tabitha cackled. "Seriously? Him? Who would possibly want to go with *him*?"

Ouch, my pride again.

"What do you say?" Tabitha still gripped my tie as she narrowed her eyes on Claire. "It's this or sit at home feeling sorry for yourself."

Claire's gaze drifted up to meet mine for a fleeting second. That guarded, cautious smile reappeared on her lips just as briefly. "Very well, then. Just as friends. And only if Damien says it's okay."

Tabitha squealed victoriously and released her death grip on my tie. "Perfect! I'll take care of all the details." She spun around to poke me in the chest one more time. "You be ready at 7:00 p.m. sharp. We will send the limousine to pick you up first."

I smoothed my tie back out and tuck it under my sweater. "Limousine?"

She rolled her eyes. "Please tell me you at least know what a limo is."

"Yeah! I just, uh, I've never ridden in one before."

"Riiiight. Of course you haven't. Just… try to make yourself presentable. Dress shoes only." Tabitha bumped her shoulder lightly against Claire's and giggled, like it was some kind of inside joke between them. I got the impression I was the butt of that joke.

The bell rang and Tabitha swaggered into the classroom, leaving Claire and I standing in an awkward silence.

"I'm so sorry about that, Koji," she said quietly. "If you'd rather not go, I can explain to her—"

"No," I insisted. "It's fine, really. Besides, something tells me I do not want to be on that girl's bad side."

Claire's face softened with a genuine smile. "She's not all bad, I promise. She means well. She just comes off a little…"

"Intense?"

"I was going to say bratty."

I laughed. "Well if it makes you happy and keeps me off her naughty list, I'd be honored to go with you."

"Can I see your phone, then?" She held out her hand.

"What for?" I dug around in my back pocket until I found it. Dad had bought me a new one as an early Christmas present after what had happened to the last one.

"So I can go through all your pictures and make sure you're not cheating on your girlfriend to take me to a dance," she quipped.

I choked.

She giggled and flashed me another smile that made my brain scramble. "So I can put my number in your contacts, silly. I'll send you the information for your tuxedo."

Her number—I was getting *her* number! It took everything I had to keep a straight face. Cool, I had to play it cool. No big deal. This was not a date.

"There," she said as she handed my phone back. "Let me know if you have any questions."

"Just one, actually."

Claire blinked in surprise. "Yes?"

"Is Damien really going to be okay with this?"

If there'd been any light in her soft, sea-colored eyes, it went out like a dying star the instant I mentioned his name. Her shoulders sagged ever so slightly, and her eyebrows crinkled with a hint of distress. "Yes. I don't think he'll mind. He isn't the kind of guy who gets jealous easily."

Unfortunately, I didn't have to worry about whether or not she was telling the truth. Thanks to my third eye, I knew better than anyone that she was.

"Ah, that's good, I guess." I pocketed my phone and started walking with her toward the classroom door.

We both hesitated at the threshold. I didn't want to go in. I liked this—getting a second to talk to her again. We hadn't been alone like this since the elevator. She was different without Tabitha or Damien lurking around her.

I fished desperately for something intelligent to say. "I, uh, I'm glad you're going to go to the ball. I heard about what happened at the festival. I was worried you might be too injured to go anywhere."

Suddenly Claire's cheeks blushed bright red. She fidgeted with the hem of her sweater. "O-oh. No, I wasn't hurt badly at all. They said it was just shock, mostly. A bit of bruising and a cracked rib—nothing serious. I feel perfectly fine now."

Her reaction made me want to fish a little more. "Lucky someone came along to save you, huh?"

Yeah. Right. *Someone.*

She nibbled her bottom lip, flashing a flustered smile in my direction. She quickly looked down again, as though she hoped no one else would see it. "Yes. Very lucky."

My heart began to race. What did this mean? Was it possible? Did she have a crush on, well, not *me*, but Noxius me? Not that she knew he and I had anything to do with one another. Still, it was a part of me, right? So that counted.

"Just between you and me, I think it's pretty awesome you got to see him up close." I chose my words carefully.

Claire's fidgeting intensified. "Just between you and me, I don't think he's the terrible monster everyone seems to suspect he is."

"Oh?" Now we were getting somewhere.

"No, not at all. He was so gentle to me, Koji. So kind and so warm. I've never felt—" She stopped talking abruptly, her gaze catching on something in the classroom. I followed her line of sight to find Damien and Tabitha gesturing for her to come sit between them. Without another word, Claire swiftly turned away and left me standing there to go sit with her friends.

It didn't matter. I was on cloud nine. Maybe she didn't like me. But Noxius had made an impression.

I still had a chance.

Not gonna lie, I looked good in a tuxedo.

Call it a perk of being tall and lean, but I made a suit look pretty darn suave. Standing in front of my dresser mirror, I straightened my bowtie, adjusted the white handkerchief in my breast pocket, and picked a few pieces of stray lint off my sleeves. Perfect. One passable gentleman, coming right up.

Dad and Ms. Collins were teary eyed as they forced Drake and me to stand together and take some pictures. It was weird since neither of us had our dates with us. Drake's mom had persuaded him to get his hair cut, which he sulked about. But since he was taking Madeline Ignatius, the headmaster's daughter, she insisted. Dad tried his best to help him out, but calling Drake's hair "Point Break style" hadn't helped his cause.

"My ears are cold," he complained as he tried in vain to fluff his hair up a little on the sides.

"It'll grow back in a few months," Dad tried to reassure him as they walked to the car. Dad had offered to drive him to get Madeline and drop them off at the school, where I hoped I'd get to see them later.

I, on the other hand, waited on my limo.

It was strange to see Dad walking away with some other kid, his hand resting on Drake's shoulder like he was, well, you know, his parent or something. The sight made a confusing mixture of emotions swell in me. Drake was my friend. But that was my dad. Where was my shoulder pat? My good luck handshake?

Ms. Collins stood next to me on the front steps, watching them drive away. She smiled at me nervously, which I returned when I realized it was just us left. We hadn't spoken all that much. Not one-on-one, anyway.

"You look very nice tonight, Koji," she said. I knew the tone. Adults all used it when they intentionally try to say or do the right thing even when they were uncomfortable. My dad used that tone a lot when he asked about my drawing.

"Thanks." I gave her what I hoped was a reassuring grin.

She cleared her throat and took a tiny step closer to me. "I haven't gotten a chance to thank you for how kind you've been to Drake. Before you came along he just locked himself in his room for hours on end. I'm glad you two get along so well."

"He didn't have friends before?" Seemed strange to think of him being alone, especially since he seemed comfortable around all his Robotics Club peers.

Her sigh put a puff of white fog into the cold air. "Not really. Not close ones, anyway. I know it's been hard on him. Drake idolized his father. Losing his hero that way changed him. For a while there, it felt like our lives completely unraveled. And then Clint..." She swallowed stiffly, as though trying to keep her emotions in check. "I know you're too young to appreciate this, but as parents we spend a lot of time drowning in our own regret and guilt over you kids. We feel like nothing we do or say is the right thing. We worry any little mistake will scar you for life." She hesitated for a moment, her lips thinning as though she'd said too much. "We try so hard to keep everything in the big picture together that sometimes we forget to see the tiny details that are missing. I didn't see how lonely he was until you came along. I didn't see a lot of things. I hope one day Drake can forgive me for that."

"I don't think he blames you for anything," I said.

She looked down, her expression uncertain.

"For what it's worth, we do see how hard you guys try. You and Dad, I mean. And even if we never say it, we know you're working hard for us."

"Sometimes it seems like we're trying too hard at all the wrong things," she added quietly, her voice catching.

"Drake loves you a lot, Ms. Collins," I tried reassuring her.

Her eyes shimmered with moisture as she stared up at me. "Your father is a very good man. He loves you more than anything in the world, Koji."

I leaned over and wrapped an arm around her shoulders. It was easy—especially since she was shorter than me. I hugged her a little. "For the record, I don't mind if you guys are dating. It's good. Dad hasn't been serious with anyone since Mom died. But I'm just saying this as a personal disclaimer: don't ever let him grill anything. Ever. He will try to tell you he can, but I'm telling you he's lying his head off. He can't grill or cook *anything*."

She laughed and gave me a little side hug in return. "Thanks for the warning, Koji. I'll keep that in mind."

CHAPTER 18

As I stepped out of the limousine at Claire's house, my hands were shaking like crazy, and it wasn't from the cold.

The Camridore-Faust home was like something from a fairy tale, picture book. It had cone-shaped towers and everything. The hedges were manicured to extreme perfection, cut into identical square shapes and dusted with a fresh layer of untouched snow. A tall iron fence separated the property from the rest of the city, and Gothic stone gargoyles sneered at me from lofty pedestals as I walked up to the front door.

I didn't even make it to the top step before a man in a solid black suit and tie opened the front door. A butler, maybe?

Then Claire stepped out.

I almost tripped backward down the stairs at the sight of her. A huge, totally undignified grin spread over my face, and there was absolutely nothing I could do about it. I didn't even care if she saw it.

In a gown of sparkling midnight blue, she was the picture of elegance with her golden curls pinned into a cascading bun. She looked at me and smiled—I mean *really* smiled. It made her eyes shine and her cheeks flush slightly. She bent slightly to pick up the long train of her gown before she walked toward me, descending the staircase with all the grace of a true princess.

The simple golden necklace around her neck caught my eye as it sparkled in the light. It didn't seem to match the rest of her fancy ensemble. When she turned to face me, I recognized the religious Saint Cecilia medal she always wore.

"You look…" I couldn't find the right words.

She laughed softly. "Thank you."

I offered her my arm to walk her slowly down the stairs. Drake had spent hours talking me through all this several times. I had to escort her, make sure she didn't trip, and open doors for her like a gentleman. If I could make it through the night without doing something stupid, I'd chalk this up as a huge win for Team Koji.

Once we were loaded into the back of the limo, we set off to pick up Tabitha and her date. Matthew Richards wasn't her boyfriend. She reminded everyone of that every five minutes or so—not that I felt too bad for him. Tabitha was a handful. Matthew seemed like a nice guy, though. Apparently, their parents worked together at the same prestigious law firm, and I wondered if they had the same arranged marriage situation brewing that Claire and Damien did.

In their matching dresses, Claire and Tabitha did look pretty incredible. Tabitha's dress was the same style as Claire's, only it was deep red instead of blue. Claire's bouquet had white and blue roses, while Tabitha's was white and red. No wonder she had been so nuts about making sure Claire went.

They both wore their religious medal necklaces—gold and glittering. I recognized Claire's as the one her grandmother had given her, but I'd never noticed Tabitha's before. Engraved on its gleaming surface was a relief of a small boy and a rooster. Honestly, I didn't think much of it. A lot of the girls at school wore medals since it was the only kind of jewelry allowed. Some of the guys wore them, too.

While Claire and Tabitha reapplied their lipstick and checked one another's hair for imperfections, Matthew and I chatted about school. He didn't go to one, which was weird considering his family's financial status. Apparently his parents in-sisted he have one-on-one private tutoring at home. He didn't get out much.

"I'm pretty good with languages. I'm learning Russian, Mandarin, and Japanese," he said with a nervous smile.

"Wow. That's impressive."

He laughed hoarsely and rubbed the back of his neck. "It's no big deal. And you can just call me Matt, by the w—"

"You mean you don't speak Japanese?" Tabitha interrupted. "Wasn't your mother from Japan?"

I gaped at her. "Uh, yeah. She was. But she died when I was little, so…"

"So what about her family? You must have relatives in Ja-pan, right?"

"Uh, well, I've never actually met my maternal grandpar-ents and I've never been to Japan. Who told you all this, anyway?"

She smirked and flashed Claire a knowing look. "Drake has Calculus with us. He's always going on about you."

"Only when you're teasing him," Claire chided her calmly. "He's very loyal."

"And very annoying," Tabitha grumbled and rolled her eyes. "He's so cocky—like just because he's a genius, he thinks he's better than everyone else."

"Well, if he is a genius, then he is better, right?" Matt said. The comment got him an icy glare from his date.

"Drake Collins is an irritating little dork," Tabitha fumed, flicking me a frosty glance, too. "No offense." There was an edge to her tone, almost like she was hoping I would disagree.

I did, of course. And any other time I'd have been happy to jump to Drake's defense. But I didn't have the natural capacity for spitefulness Tabitha did. Not to mention my third eye told me she wasn't being completely truthful. Maybe it was just a show? Or maybe she was just trying to bait me into an argu-ment? Either way, I wasn't falling for it.

Instead, I sat back in my seat, staring at the toes of my polished black dress shoes until our limo cruised to a halt in front of the school. The building was lit up for the Winter Ball with hundreds of sparkling white lights. Glittering strands wrapped around the pillars, the doorframes, the trees, and the handrails along the walkways. More were arranged around the hedges out front, and wreaths of evergreen fronds and deep red poinsettias hung on every window. The fresh blanket of snow made the scene look like a Christmas postcard.

Matt and I got out first and helped the girls up to the front door. There, one of the teachers checked to make sure we were registered guests, and then let us inside.

The school's main hall was adorned with every kind of holiday decoration I could imagine—including a huge Christmas tree, wreaths of pine and holly over every doorway, and big bundles of mistletoe hanging from the all chandeliers. We stayed in the main hall for a "cocktail hour" before the doors of the largest ballroom, usually reserved for fencing classes, opened. Servers dressed in white walked around offering sparkling cider and punch—nonalcoholic, of course—and appetizers. Word around the punch table was that after their glorious victory at the Holiday Festival, the Theater Club had selected A Christmas in Paris as this year's theme.

When the ballroom doors opened, I saw why everyone was so excited about it. A tall replica of the Eiffel tower sparkled in the middle of the ballroom, covered in hundreds of white lights. Around the ballroom, faux iron lampposts held flickering candles, and a steady light trickle of white confetti from the ceiling mimicked snowfall. They had hired a professional DJ to supply the music, and it was an artist I actually knew. This wasn't your everyday school dance.

I had to admit, it was impressive.

As soon as I got inside, I couldn't stop myself from looking around for Drake and Madeline. I hoped we could all hang out for part of the dance at least, but I hadn't seen them anywhere during the cocktail hour. From where I was standing, I couldn't spot them anywhere in the ballroom, either. Were they even here? Surely they wouldn't ditch me and go to see another movie without me.

My gaze wandered back to Claire, pulled as though by gravity. She stood beside me, but her expression made it seem like her thoughts were a thousand miles away. The distant fogginess in her eyes was unmistakable as she slowly panned the ballroom—she was looking for someone.

But who? Damien?

An elbow jabbed me in the ribcage. "Don't just stand there. Ask her to dance," Tabitha commanded in a whisper.

"What? Now?"

"Yes, now. Go on," Tabitha snapped.

Nearly tripping over my own feet as I turned to face her got Claire's attention. I blushed as I straightened, smoothed my tuxedo jacket, and offered her my shaking, sweaty hand. "Do you, uh…" Once again, my voice tangled in my throat. Smooth, Koji, very smooth.

"Want to dance?" she guessed.

I grinned and gave a sigh of relief. "Yeah."

She placed her gloved hand in mine. "Sure."

I managed to lead her to the dance floor without throwing up from anxiety. So far, so good. My heart kicked violently in my chest as I put a hand on her waist and she stepped in close enough that I could smell her perfume.

"Do you know how to waltz?" She spoke quietly against my cheek.

I closed my eyes, my face drawn instinctively closer to hers so that we could talk without shouting. "Yeah, sort of." I'd been to enough military balls and banquets that I could stumble my way through a formal dance if I had to. But my partner had never been the most beautiful girl in the room.

We spun slowly around the dance floor amidst the other couples, and I got lost in her bottomless blue-green eyes. I couldn't stop myself from imagining that she was mine and I wasn't just a stand-in for some absentee fiancé. I wished I could tell her I deserved her more than he ever would, but that wasn't true. Not really, anyway. He had more money, better looks, a distinguished family, and the promise of a bright future. What did I have? An embarrassingly huge collection of comic books, every vintage *Transformers* action figure ever made, and the same pair of black-and-white Converse sneakers I'd worn since eighth grade. None of that was going to impress her.

Regular, average Koji was never going to be enough.

Her gaze wandered across the ballroom again. She was definitely looking for someone. Tabitha? Damien? As the song came to an end, I finally got up the nerve to ask.

"Are you looking for anyone in particular?"

Claire flinched. Her eyes snapped back to me, as wide as saucers, and her cheeks turned bright scarlet. "No!"

"No?" I knew she was lying.

She took a small step back, her expression dimming. "I'm sorry. There was someone I'd hoped to see. It's ridiculous, really. He would never come here. It's a silly hope."

"Who?"

She swallowed hard. Her gaze drifted up, meeting mine for a fleeting second. One look was all it took. Somehow I just knew.

"Noxius?"

Her cheeks flushed darker and she pressed a hand over my mouth. "Don't say it so loud, please."

I couldn't decide if I should be happy or frustrated that she was crushing on my alter ego. "Yeah. Kinda doubt he'd come to a school dance."

"I know. It's ridiculous to even want that." She bit her lip. "But I do. I find myself hoping to see him more and more these days."

"Because he saved you at the festival?"

Her hands slipped from around me as the music faded to silence. She didn't look up at me again as she stepped away, her
brow crinkled with what seemed like embarrassment and shame.
Our song was over, and somehow it felt like it had never even
begun.

As I followed Claire back toward Matt and Tabitha, I finally spotted Drake and his date entering the ballroom. To be
honest, Madeline caught my eye first—well, mine and the eye of
everyone else standing in the room. It was impossible *not* to notice her.

My heartbeat stammered and stalled as she stepped into the
ballroom. In a gown of rich dark purple with a narrow corset
bodice and a voluminous skirt, Madeline was breathtaking. Her
delicate features seemed to glow, probably highlighted by some
makeup, although it wasn't thick or overdone like a lot of girls
did it. Her long black hair hung down her back and over her
shoulders like silk, complementing the black lace gloves on her
hands. The thin golden collar around the base of her neck caught
in the twinkling light of the Eiffel Tower. It matched the cuff
golden bracelet on her left upper arm and the small stud earrings
in her ears.

Our eyes met, and I got a weird tingly feeling in my chest
that I didn't understand. What was this? The tingling moved to
my stomach and my throat went dry. Suddenly, the collar of my
shirt felt too tight.

Madeline smiled at me brightly from across the ballroom.
My stomach did another backwards handspring.

I smiled back, even though my heart was racing.

Then, her eyes panned to my right and her whole demeanor
shifted. Her eyes darkened. Her mouth became stiff, and her
brow creased with distress.

I glanced to my right to find Claire glaring back at her with
an identical expression of revulsion. I frowned. What was that
all about? I'd never seen them interact before, and this was
just…uncomfortable.

Taking Madeline's arm, Drake led her across the ballroom to meet me. The two girls didn't say a single word to one another. Even when Tabitha and Matt joined us, it was still awkward. I had to break the icy tension in the air. Only Drake seemed totally unfazed by the hostility crackling in the air between Claire and Madeline.

"You guys look great," I tried.

Drake tugged at the collar of his tux and scowled. "This thing itches."

"Not used to the finer things?" Tabitha made it sound teasing, but I caught the flicker of mischief and malice in her eyes.

"I suppose not. Just like I'm sure you're not used to getting As on any of your Calculus exams," he retorted.

Claire's cheek twitched with a smile as she looked down.

Tabitha, however, was *not* smiling. Her nostrils flared a little, and her jaw tightened as she clenched her teeth.

"Maybe we should dance again?" Matt suggested. His efforts to diffuse the situation were obvious—like watching him throw himself on a social grenade. Poor guy.

"Yes, run along and dance." Drake wafted a hand at Tabitha as if sweeping her away. "You've only got a few hours to convince some idiot in here to marry you when you graduate so you'll be set for the rest of your life. Better hurry."

I cringed. Too far, Drake.

Tabitha's eyes were wild as she moved in to stand nose to nose with Drake, which was possible because they were both really short. "What are you saying? That I'm a gold digger just because I wouldn't be caught dead dancing with someone like you?"

He grinned wolfishly. "As if you could handle a dance with me."

"Hah," she scoffed. "I can handle anything that comes from you, Drake Collins."

"Prove it, then." He suddenly stuck a hand out to her, offering to dance. "If your date doesn't mind letting me borrow you long enough to defend my honor."

Matt raised his hands in surrender and slowly shook his head.

No one said a word as Drake dragged Tabitha away—first to the DJ booth, where I can only assume he made a song request, and then out onto the dance floor. The intro to an energetic Latin-sounding song started to play, and the other couples glanced around, confused. What kind of song was this to play at a school dance? Could anyone here even dance properly to this kind of music?

Drake threw off his tuxedo jacket and rolled up his sleeves, then immediately whipped Tabitha into a brisk spin. He caught her in a dip, lowering her until her hair brushed the floor before he snatched her up again. Tabitha's face flushed bright pink as he spun her again, bringing her back against his chest and guiding her into the first steps of a sultry tango.

Holy. Crap.

Next to me, Claire covered her mouth to stifle a laugh of surprise. Matt was grinning ear to ear.

The music kicked into a fierce, sultry beat and their dance intensified. Tabitha blinked at Drake as though dazed, but suddenly her expression sharpened into fierce determination. Her eyes smoldered as she glared back at him and whirled around to seize his hands and join in the dance.

All I could do was stand there, gaping at Drake and Tabitha in total shock as they moved through a fancy, complicated, and steamy tango. Their smooth, calculated movements were flawless—like they'd rehearsed this beforehand. Only, I knew that couldn't be the case. I'd never seen Drake do anything like this. He hadn't even wanted to come to the dance in the first place.

It was impossible to tell that now, though. He whisked Tabitha through suggestive pose after suggestive pose like it was nothing, his expression focused and serious and eyes blazing with quiet vengeance. Tabitha's look of defiant ferocity cracked with surprise whenever he jerked her in close enough that their noses brushed, or lifted her easily into a deeper dip with a hand planted firmly on her thigh.

When the dance ended, the ballroom erupted into applause. Even the teachers and chaperones cheered. Drake and Tabitha stood panting, still glaring at one another from inches away. Although, from where I stood, she looked a lot more breathless than he did. Drake cast her one final smug glance from head to foot and turned to swagger back over to us, picking up his tuxedo jacket on the way.

CHAPTER 19

The evening wore on, and as much as I wanted to talk to Claire about her interest in a certain scaly superhero, it almost seemed like she was avoiding me. She stood off to the side, talking quietly with Tabitha or Matt, and occasionally cast a smoldering glare at Madeline out of the corner of her eye. The tension between them was like a thick, poisonous smog. I needed to find out what was up with them.

I waited, biding my time until Claire went to the bathroom with Tabitha. Madeline had already left to dance with someone else. Now was my chance.

I slid over to Drake and nudged him with my elbow. "What's up with Claire and Madeline?"

He stared at me like I'd grown a second head. "You seriously don't know? How long have you been at this school? And you don't know about the rivalry?"

"What rivalry?" I had a feeling I was going to regret that question.

"It goes back to their parents," he explained. "Our headmaster and Claire's dad absolutely hate each other. They've forbidden Claire and Madeline to speak to one another."

"But why? Why do they hate each other?"

"Something about an accident? I'm not sure, exactly. The story's different depending on who you ask. All I know is those girls will never get along and you are totally screwed, my friend."

I scowled. "Why am I screwed?"

"Cause you love one and the other loves you." He laughed like he found my misery entertaining. "It's like a Greek tragedy waiting to happen."

Not funny. This was exactly why I hadn't told Drake about Oceana kissing me during our battle. I was honestly trying not to read too much into it. I figured she probably thought I was about to die a horrible death, so why not give me something nice to think about while that crocodile monster gnawed on my innards.

Anyway, it's not like I liked Oceana. Not like *that*. She was a friend, an ally, and someone I knew I could trust—nothing more. That kiss didn't mean anything.

"I don't love Claire," I mumbled as I stared back out across the dance floor.

"Oh?" Drake's brows shot up. "Since when?"

I shrugged, a little embarrassed I had spoken the thought aloud. That wasn't an easy question answer. Sure, I had liked her, and I still did... at least, I thought I did. I wasn't even sure about that anymore. She seemed to have feelings for my alter ego. So why not the real me? I might not always be Noxius— one glance while I was transforming could change that—but I'd always be Koji.

I decided to change the subject. Thinking about girls too much made my brain hurt. "So what did Madeline say when you asked her to come here with you?"

Drake was scratched at his shirt collar again. "She asked who you were going with."

I winced. "Seriously? Sorry, man."

"Forget it—I didn't take it personally. Dances are stupid."

"Speaking of dancing...I have to ask, where did *that* come from?"

"What?"

I arched an eyebrow. "The tango."

"Oh." He smirked and rubbed his chin proudly. "I had to take ballroom dancing last year as one of my electives. Mom said it would be a 'good experience.' It sucked, of course, but turns out I'm pretty good. At least, that's what the instructor kept telling me. He wanted me to stay on and compete. As if I have time for that." He shrugged and shot me a cunning grin. "You should take it next year."

"Uh, no thanks. I'll leave the fancy dance moves to you." I chuckled.

"It impresses the ladies, even if school dances are the worst kind of torture for someone of my incredible intellect."

I snorted. "At least there's free food."

"Yes." His cognac eyes sparkled at the mention of it. "Free food is always a good thing."

Drake ate a lot of the free food until Madeline dragged him away to dance again. Since he'd advertised his mad skills in front of the whole school, she wasn't the only one lining up to force him into another elaborate display. I couldn't tell if he liked the attention or not. Mostly, it just seemed to fluster him. He grumbled and stalked around, acting like he didn't want to be bothered. But whenever a girl asked him, he obliged without complaining. Granted, none of the other dances made quite the impression the first one had. And every time he danced, I noticed Tabitha watching him with her eyes narrowed and expression sour.

Interesting…

Whenever Tabitha was off with her date and Madeline was nowhere in sight, I summoned all my courage and asked Claire to dance a few more times. She always said yes, but each step was more uncomfortable than the one before it. She never stopped looking around, and I could tell her mind was elsewhere. On Noxius, I assumed. My thoughts simmered with frustration. I—Noxius—was standing right here in front of her. Why couldn't she see it?

Why couldn't she see *me*?

The night wore on, and with every passing hour, I found myself agreeing more and more with Drake's opinion that dances were stupid. I had thought going with Claire would be a chance to get to know one another, become actual friends. But her obsession with Noxius kept her distracted. Finally, I quit asking her to dance.

I told her I was going to the bathroom—which I did—but only so I could talk myself out of actually having Noxius show up to my high school's dance. How lame and totally irresponsible would that be? No, I couldn't risk it. There were too many people here. Too many chances that someone else might see or figure out my secret. I had a responsibility now. This city might need Noxius again.

When I emerged from the bathroom to find the ballroom mostly empty, I realized it was that point in every high school dance where the couples split off and sneak away to be alone. Not a good time for someone like me. This was when I usually went home to play video games, eat an entire bag of Funyuns, and wallow in my loneliness. My curfew was up in an hour anyway. Maybe it was time to call it a night.

I sighed and lingered in the doorway, watching Claire from afar as I tried to decide if it was even worth it to say goodnight to her. Would she even notice if I left? Probably not.

I was supposed to ride back home with Drake and Madeline. Or rather, Dad was going to be waiting at the front of the school to pick us up, drop Madeline off at her house, and then take us home. Drake was staying over since his mom had to work tonight. I doubted I'd have a hard time convincing Drake to leave early. But I couldn't find him or Madeline anywhere.

When I finally found Drake, it was on the other end of Tabitha's mouth—literally. Hiding in a dark corner in one of the nearby classrooms, Drake had her pinned against a dry erase board, his mouth against hers, while she ran her fingers through his hair.

Yikes.

I shuddered and slowly backed out of the room without making any noise. Too bad I couldn't erase the last ten seconds from my memory.

Seriously? Tabitha? She probably had fangs, for crying out loud. I shuddered again.

Making my way through the school, I passed the ballroom where Claire and Matt were talking—probably about where Tabitha was. Good luck with that one, guys. Claire didn't even look my way when I passed; I might as well have been invisible. I told myself that didn't matter. She wanted Noxius. And she couldn't have him unless she wanted Koji, too.

I wandered through the main hall, hoping Drake and Tabitha would be done soon. My listless gaze wandered over the festive, sparkling holiday decorations. Hundreds of ornaments, most made of white and gold glass, hung from a twenty-foot Christmas tree in the center of the hall. I stopped to stare up at it for a moment. I couldn't look at a Christmas tree without thinking of Mom. This month made twelve years since…

I shook my head, gritting my teeth against the familiar pain rising slowly in my chest. I couldn't think about that now. Not here. With a deep, steadying breath, I turned to go out the front doors of the school.

I wasn't the only one looking for an excuse to leave early. Madeline sat on the front steps, her long purple gown pooling around her. She had to be cold—the air was freezing and her shoulders were bare—but she didn't seem to be shivering.

I took off my tuxedo jacket and walked up behind her to place it around her, just for good measure.

She blinked and flinched away, startled as I sat down next to her. "Koji?"

I smiled. "Hey."

She glanced at my jacket around her shoulders. "But won't you be cold?"

"Not as cold as you, I'm sure," I replied.

"I suppose you're right about that." She sighed.

"Why are you sitting out here all by yourself?" I cringed as soon as the words left my mouth. Dumb question. Her date was inside making out with someone else. I wasn't sure if she was aware of that fact, and I wasn't about to tell her. Although, according to Drake, if she did like me then maybe she wouldn't have cared regardless.

"I should ask you the same thing," she answered quietly.

I sighed too. There was no short answer for that.

She pulled my coat around her tighter. Suddenly, I felt her weight settle against my shoulder. "Is this okay?" she whispered.

I closed my eyes and smiled to myself. "Yeah."

"Your date might not like it," she pointed out.

I bowed my head slightly. "To be honest, I'm not her real date. I'm not even her second choice. She came with me because Damien is at a judo tournament, and I just happened to be standing nearby when Tabitha was convincing her to come with a friend. Lucky me, huh?"

Madeline was quiet for a long time. I hadn't intended to tell her a sob story. I wasn't fishing for her pity. For some reason, it seemed like whenever I talked to her, the truth just came pouring out of me before I could stop it.

"Want me to tell you a secret?" she whispered again.

"Sure."

"My feet are absolutely killing me." She giggled and pulled up her skirt just a little so I could see. Her small bare feet were sporting the most complicated looking pair of high heels I'd ever seen with straps and sequins everywhere.

"Ouch." I arched a brow at her. "Haven't your toes been freezing this whole time? You can't even see your shoes in that dress. You could have worn bunny slippers and no one would have known."

She laughed again. "It's a girl thing, I guess."

"Well, no offense, but some girl things are stupid." I got up and knelt down on the step below her.

Madeline's laughing smile melted into a look of shock as I started taking those awful shoes off her feet. It took me a minute to figure out which buckle would loosen them, but eventually I tossed them aside and slipped out of my own shoes so I could lend her my socks. When I was finished, I sat my sockless self back down on the steps beside her. "Better?"

"Y-yes." Her whole face had turned scarlet.

"Good."

"Koji, if I wear these down the sidewalk they'll get dirty and wet."

"It's okay," I told her. "I'll carry you."

"You'll...carry me?"

"Hey, I may be skinny, but I'm stronger than I look." I flexed a little.

Madeline nibbled her bottom lip as though suppressing a smile. "If you say so."

"You know," I suddenly recalled, "I don't think we danced together tonight."

She quickly looked away. "It's okay. I didn't think your date would like it if she saw us dancing together."

I frowned. Standing up, I offered her my hand. "And what if I don't care about what anyone else thinks? Would you dance with me?"

"Koji." She said my name so softly I barely heard it. When she took my hand, I helped her up. Together we walked down the front steps of the school to the sidewalk.

"These socks are going to be ruined," Madeline warned.

I wrapped an arm around her waist and pulled her in close, so she could stand on the toes of my dress shoes. "That better?"

She opened her mouth like she was going to speak, but nothing came out. Not a squeak. Not a gasp. She stared straight ahead, right at my chest, while her arms found their way shakily around my neck.

Madeline Ignatius was so tiny and petite, she could stand on her tiptoes on my feet and still barely reach my chin with the top of her head. It made dancing with her like that easy. I spun us around in a few circles, humming and singing along to the music playing inside. I had to make up a few of my own lyrics. It made her laugh, which was well worth the embarrassment on my part.

She gazed up at me with the holiday lights sparkling in her soft gray eyes like stars. Some of her dark hair brushed around her cheeks. My stomach did a crazy flip, and tickling heat bloomed in my chest. It was freezing, but I could barely feel it. All I could feel was how my heart pounded into overdrive every time her skin brushed mine.

Her smile was so infectious, I couldn't look at her without smiling back. When she laid her head on my chest, it was impossible for me to deny it—I loved the way she made me feel. She saw me even when I felt invisible.

"Koji," she murmured as the song began to end.

"Hmm?"

"I know I shouldn't say this. I know you like someone else, but I don't know if I'll ever get the chance to say it again."

Panic stirred in the pit of my gut. I had a good idea what was coming next. The way her voice trembled, her soft gaze catching mine while her shaking hands clenched at the back of my shirt.

What if Drake was right?

No. I couldn't do this. Madeline was my friend. I mean, sure, she was smart, creative, warm, and…and…

I swallowed hard.

Before Madeline could finish, a sleek black car pulled up to the curb right next to us.

The smile on her lips vanished in an instant, snuffed out like a candle on a stormy night. An expression of fear crept over her delicate features, slowly draining the color from her face. She wrenched away from me so suddenly it nearly knocked me over.

The rear door of the car opened and a man stepped onto the snowy sidewalk. Headmaster Gerard Ignatius was the last person I expected to see at the dance. He took a few stiff, awkward steps toward us with the help of a cane and stopped, a cold stare fixed on his daughter.

I'd never seen him walk around the school before. Come to think of it, I'd never seen him leave his office. The way he moved, with abrupt jerking motions, made it seem like the effort caused him pain. His jaw was set and his eyes smoldered, as bitter and relentless as the winter wind. Nothing about his expression softened when he stared down at Madeline, who scrambled to stand before him with her head down submissively.

"Did you not see that I called you?" he growled sharply.

Madeline's whole body tensed and cringed away slightly, like she was expecting to be hit.

Without warning, anger like a roaring storm rose within me. "It was my fault," I interrupted.

"No!" Madeline turned on me, her face blanching with terror. Her wide eyes searched mine for a second, as though silently pleading with me to stay quiet, before she scrambled to her father's side. "He's lying to look chivalrous."

"Is that so?" Headmaster Ignatius stared me down, a frigid smile curling across his lips.

I glared back at him. I couldn't justify it beyond a feeling of pure instinct, but something about him put me on edge. He had an indifferent, almost otherworldly darkness in his gaze, like a menacing alien inspecting a captive he intended to experiment on. Maybe I could have shrugged it off if it was only me he looked at that way—but seeing him regard Madeline like that? It was too much.

"You know how it is with these lower class people," she murmured through a painfully forced smile. "They all think they'll be the one to appear as a knight in shining armor."

I couldn't disguise my shock. What was going on here? I'd never heard Madeline talk like that before.

The headmaster's lip twitched and that inky darkness in his eyes glinted like fire lit obsidian. "And are you a princess in need of saving, my Maddie?"

Her eyes met mine—soft, gray, and swallowed by despair. "No."

It was a lie.

"Then let's go. We'll need to have a long discussion about you ignoring my calls." He wrapped his long fingers around the back of her neck. Her whole body tensed.

"Wait," she said suddenly and began taking off my tuxedo jacket. She held it out to me stiffly. "This is yours."

As I reached for it, something caught my eye.

For a single second, the faint light from the twinkle lights caught on that golden jewelry she wore. I didn't think much of it, at first. But a wink of light off her arm band made me pause. There was something pearlescent set in the band's center.

A single white scale.

I sucked in a sharp breath like someone had just drop-kicked me in the gut. Was that a—?

Madeline didn't react. Perhaps a second wasn't long enough for her to notice what I'd seen, or she didn't recognize the shock on my face for what it was. Either way, she just kept that awful, thin smile pinched firmly on her lips as she climbed into the back of her father's car and shut the door.

With the low, purring hum of the car's engine, she was gone.

Madeline Ignatius had a totem scale.

I'd seen it, plain as day, right there on her arm. But how? I didn't understand. How could she have one and I not notice it until now? Had she been wearing it all this time? Or had she just gotten it recently? Had she transformed already? Surely I would have seen her if she had. But did that mean Madeline was Oceana?

It didn't make a single shred of sense. How could she be Oceana and me not realize it?

There was another possibility, though, and one that made even less sense to my frazzled mind. That crocodilian monster hadn't come from nowhere. Someone or something had sent it here. What if that someone was Madeline?

No. That couldn't be true. Madeline was my friend. She was kind, gentle, and shy. She'd never do anything like that.

Right?

Maybe I had been mistaken. Maybe it was just a gem or shell that *looked* like a totem scale. Yeah. That could totally be it. It made way more sense than thinking one of my best friends would summon a monster to destroy the city and get innocent people killed.

I set my jaw against the cold, wrenching sensation of dread squirming in my stomach. Was I being naïve? Did I really know her at all?

I staggered back up the steps to the school. Help—I needed help. Or did I? I didn't know what I needed. The instant I touched the handle the school's front door swung inwards. Drake stood on the other side, his mouth, jaw, and neck smudged with traces of lipstick.

"Was that the headmaster's car? Did Madeline just leave?" he panted. "Wasn't she supposed to go home with us?"

Anything I tried to say died in my throat. Rage built in my chest, stoking fires of insanity in my brain. I was a spark away from doing something especially stupid.

Drake took a nervous step back. "Koji, are you okay?"

My fingers slowly curled into fists. "I have to go after her."

"Who?"

"Madeline," I snarled and spun around. "I have to transform. Right now."

Drake chased me down the sidewalk. "What's going on? Your dad is gonna be here any second! What am I supposed to tell him happened to you guys?"

"You'll think of something. You're a genius, remember?" I strode for the nearest dark alley—the one I'd used to transform after the Holiday Festival disaster. I rolled up my sleeve, exposing my totem bracelet.

"Koji, wait! Can you at least tell me what's going on?" Drake yelled. "You can't just bail on me like this without telling me what this is all about! If I'm going to be running defense for you, protecting your identity and giving you alibis, you at least have to let me know what's really going on here."

I stopped. He was right. I needed his help. Dad wasn't going to like me disappearing like this again. Our stories had to match up.

So I told him what I'd seen: the pearlescent scale in Madeline's arm bracelet as she got in her dad's car and the feeling my third eye had given me when she said she didn't need help.

Drake looked like he might be sick. "She's Oceana? And she's been right here under our noses this whole time?"

I sighed. "I don't know. It's possible. My scale is on my wrist when I transform, and Oceana's is on her chest, so I always thought her totem would be a necklace, not an arm cuff." I rubbed my forehead with the heel of my hand. "But I don't know specifically how the totems work. Hers could be different. I've never seen another totem-wielder other than Oceana, so it makes sense. Plus, in the last battle, she... kissed me."

His eyes widened. "Oceana kissed you?"

"I thought it was just because I was about to do something that might get me killed. You know, like a farewell-type thing."

"But that would mean Madeline knows you're Noxius, right?" Drake rubbed his jaw thoughtfully. "That doesn't add up. Are you sure it was a totem scale?"

"I only saw it for two seconds. Why are you asking me? Wasn't she your date? How could you *not* notice?" I countered.

He started to get defensive. "It's not like I studied her that close. Girls always wear gaudy, weird jewelry to dances."

I held up my arm to show him my bracelet. "Okay, but *this* is important. Seeing anything that looks like this scale on someone else is a big deal."

"Why? What does it matter if she's Oceana or another dragon-girl?"

The truth was sour on my tongue. "Because if she isn't Oceana, then she's probably the one responsible for that monster that nearly destroyed the whole city and killed four people. She certainly didn't help out the day of the disaster."

He shook his head slowly as he stared at the leather band around my wrist. "I don't know. I'm sorry, I didn't pay any attention to it."

Great. So neither of us could say for sure that's what it was—but I was *almost* positive. I grumbled under my breath and turned away, gnawing on the inside of my cheek. "There's only one way to know for sure."

"Why don't you just ask her on Monday?" Drake suggested. "Flying off now, when the heat is already on you, isn't going to help."

"Yeah. Sure. That's a *great* idea. 'Hey Madeline, are you secretly a superhero? 'Cause I am!'"

"At least you'd know if she was lying or not, right?" His brow furrowed as though he didn't appreciate my sarcasm. "You've been lying low all this time to keep your identity safe. If you transform, the media and authorities will be all over you in minutes."

"And if she isn't Oceana? What then? The point is not to tell anyone else about this—especially now that the freaking president is breathing down my neck," I fumed. "If I ask her that, she'll know I'm Noxius. I can't risk it."

"So we're screwed," he concluded.

"Very screwed," I agreed. "I don't have a choice. I have to know, Drake. If she's not my friend, she might be my enemy, and an enemy who can call up creatures like that is not one I want in my blind spot."

Drake bowed his head, his mouth scrunching with dissatisfaction. "Just try not to get into trouble."

"You'll cover me with Dad, right?"

He offered a worried, halfhearted smile. "Maybe you can tell when I'm lying, but I haven't met an adult who can. As far as I know, Madeline went home with her dad and you've been kidnapped by Oceana."

CHAPTER 20

Drake turned his back so I could transform. Luckily, since he'd already been to her house once this evening, he was able to tell me exactly where Madeline lived. The Ignatius home wasn't far from the school, only a few miles by air. I could be there in minutes, seconds if I pushed it.

I left Drake standing alone in the snowbound alley as I zoomed skyward with a burst of icy wind. I flew low, trying to track down the route their car might have taken when it left the school. Unfortunately, finding a black car in the constant river of city traffic wasn't working.

And flying low drew too much attention.

Cameras flashed and people called out to me from the street below when I landed atop of St. John's Cathedral. Some cheered. Others yelled curses. Not that I didn't understand their fear—I must have looked like a wicked black gargoyle perching on the eaves—but hadn't they seen my fight with the croc-monster? I'd nearly drowned myself to save this city. Didn't that mean anything?

Apparently not. I guess if the news channels said I was a bloodthirsty alien monster, then that's what everyone believed.

Scanning the streets in every direction, I spotted more and more cars stopping and curious onlookers stepping out to point and pull out their phones. I couldn't keep this up forever. The police were probably already mobilizing.

But where was Madeline?

My heart pounded, thrashing in my ears and throbbing in my palms. I *had* to find her. Whenever I closed my eyes, that awful, empty smile she'd given me right before she left flashed through my head. Like something terrible was going to happen to her and there was no hope for anyone to save her.

Not true.

I could save her.

Closing my eyes, I took a few breaths before I took off again—this time for the Ignatius house. When I landed out front, my body tensed as I studied the ominous house crouching in the shadows of several large oak trees. The French-styled chateau stood alone, separated from the modern buildings around it by a tall, iron-wrought fence topped with sharp points. This was where the headmaster of our school lived? It was like something straight out of a horror theme park.

Suddenly, my pulse stalled.

The Ignatius car was parked in the driveway—empty. Only a few yards away, the front gate was ajar, and all windows in the house were dark.

Was Madeline in there?

I made my way cautiously past the gates, up the short cobblestone drive, to the front door. It was standing wide open, too.

I hesitated in the doorway, peering into the intense gloom of the house. Doubt muddied my resolve. Should I change back? If I came here right away, the headmaster might figure out I was Noxius. Then again, if his daughter really had a totem, what's to say he didn't already know? What if he was the one who'd given it to me in the first place?

My mind swirled with uncertainty. Going in without my dragon form on felt like going in unarmed. I wasn't sure if my scales would deflect a knife or a bullet, but I was positive my human skin wouldn't. Better safe than sorry.

I steeled my nerve and crossed the threshold, striding through the open door with my wings tucked at my sides.

The inside of the house was no less disconcerting than the outside. Throughout the large entryway, big glass cases held bits and pieces of pottery, statues, and artifacts. Reproductions of Grecian and Egyptian statues stood against the walls, as though to guard the cavernous hall. It was like being in a museum after closing time…only this place had a very *particular* theme.

Every single one of the artifacts, works spanning thousands of years, from ancient Chinese tapestries to Nordic woodcarvings, depicted dragons. There were winged dragons, serpentine ones, and every shape in between. Some were breathing bursts of flame. Others rose from churning ocean waters. Every single relic in the hall bore the image of a dragon.

A cold pang of dread hit the back of my throat. No way this was a coincidence.

Directly ahead, two sweeping staircases met in the center of the foyer underneath a massive unlit chandelier. The long talons on my dragon hind legs clicked against the stone floor as I turned in a slow circle, trying to take it all in. My breathing echoed in the cavernous ceiling far overhead.

A rustle caught my keen ears.

Whipping around, I nearly crashed headlong into a huge marble bust of a guy in Viking-style clothing. I stumbled back, staring up at the statue. The Viking man held a fistful of lightning bolts while he grappled with a woman who was a snake from the waist down. Something about the Viking seemed so familiar. Then I saw it.

Around his wrist was a cuff bracelet—one that looked a lot like mine.

"It's rare that relics such as this are created, let alone survive to be found by the next generation of totem-holders." I recognized Headmaster Ignatius's voice immediately. I turned to find him at the base of one of the staircases, leaning against his golden-tipped cane. At first glance, I'd assumed he was another one of the statues. Had he been watching me the whole time?

His cane made a *click-scrape-click* sound as he walked toward me.

"This is perhaps the most impressive piece we have found intact," he continued, pacing past me as though my draconic form didn't intimidate him in the slightest. "A stroke of luck, really. Without this accurate rendition, I doubt I would have found your totem so easily. Generally speaking, after a wielder perishes, his totem is broken down and made into a new artifact, usually a mundane piece of jewelry, by his comrades or loved ones."

I narrowed my eyes at him and growled.

"It's the same with them all. Well, most of them, anyhow. Any effigies of bearers are usually destroyed in an effort to hide the existence of the totems. The bearers become legend and then, eventually, mere myth. Your totem, however, endured as it was worn by its previous wielder."

I guess that answered a few of my questions. He knew exactly *what* I was. But did he know who?

I bared my teeth. "Where's Madeline?"

He smiled, his dark eyes twinkling with amusement. "You really care about her, don't you? So selfless. So brave. Always ready to throw yourself into a fight at a moment's notice just to defend others."

"You don't know anything about me." I growled, taking a threatening step toward him. "What did you do with her? Where is she?"

His smile widened into a toothy sneer. "You're mistaken, Koji Owens. I know *everything* about you."

My stomach lurched and for a moment, my heart stopped. Oh no. He knew who I was.

Steeling my nerves, I lashed my tail and took an aggressive step forward. "Tell me where she is!" I roared, letting a current of white-hot electricity sizzle off the tips of my clawed fingers. "If you hurt her, I swear—"

"You'll do what? Are you going to attack a crippled old man in his own home? I doubt your friends in the media would look amiably upon something like that," he sneered. "You're already on thin ice with them. You saved New York from certain destruction and yet are still one misstep away from being the public's most wanted criminal. Human fear is a fickle yet undeniably powerful force."

My thoughts swirled like a vortex. Something about this wasn't right. Headmaster Ignatius knew what I was, but he wasn't scared of me at all. He'd been waiting for me in the dark, doors open, almost like he wanted me to come here. Why?

He hobbled toward me with that menacing grin still on his face.

I took a calculated step backward.

As soon as I moved, he lunged with alarming speed, spinning his cane like a weapon. The golden tip glowed, sending a burst of power through the room that rattled the chandelier and left me reeling. Before I could react, he pushed the glowing tip of the cane right against the center of my chest.

The impact sent a tingling chill through my entire body. My feet went numb, and then my legs. I strained to move, but it was as though someone had frozen my feet to the floor. I flapped my wings and roared, fighting to get away. Nothing. I couldn't move an inch. My feet, my legs, and now my waist—they were all turning into solid gold.

Headmaster Ignatius grinned as he backed away from me, leaning heavily upon his cane again. Between his fingers, I could see the light of a shining white scale set into the cane's handle. A totem scale? How could that be? What element could be responsible for this? The only ones left unaccounted for were fire and earth.

…Right?

"Time is always against us," he said as he turned away. "But it favors me today. Soon you'll be just another relic collecting dust in my foyer. Another totem lost to time." His laugh echoed through the foyer. "This city is ours, Koji. We won't stand for any usurpers. With you out of my way, Oceana, as the silly girls calls herself, will go back to being the useless coward she was before. But in time, she will serve us, too."

I lifted my arms to try summoning a burst of lightning— anything to save myself. Nothing happened. My thoughts were sluggish, as though my grasp on my elemental power was slipping through my fingers. I reached inward, stretching to find that power hidden deep within. It was no use. I was helpless.

My arms were already frozen in place, encased in gold. My wings and chest began to go numb as well. Only one thing on my body hadn't changed: my totem bracelet. Instead of turning to gold, it remained on my arm in its normal, leather bracelet form.

My lungs spasmed, tingling as I fought to take a breath. "You won't get away with this!" I roared with my final breath. My last scream died in my throat as my neck, jaw, and face went numb.

Unending, smothering darkness closed around me like I was being squeezed inside a giant fist.

Then, a flicker—the tiniest spark—sparked in my vision. Suddenly I felt life return to my body.

I took in a deep, desperate breath as my body went slack. I crumpled, falling into someone's arms. My head lolled and my vision swam as my body trembled. Something cold and wet touched my back. Snow?

I squinted, trying to focus my hazy vision on the person bending over me. I could smell the crisp outside air, tinged with frost and car exhaust, and hear the distant rumble of traffic.

As I lay on frigid earth, I could sense someone's body heat next to me. It was so intense. Too warm to be human. A gentle, scaly hand cupped my face.

"You'll be okay now," a female voice murmured over me. "You can't look for me anymore. I can't come back now. Just forget me. Forget I ever—"

A deafening cry pierced the air like the shriek of an eagle. It was one I knew all too well.

"What did you do to him?" Oceana bellowed with rage. The earth shuddered under my back as she landed and walked toward us.

I needed to move, to stand up. The best I could do was roll onto my stomach and push myself onto my hands and knees. I choked, still wheezing for every breath. My vision swerved, giving me only brief glimpses of my human hands in the snow. The trees seemed to spin around me until, at last, I managed to spot the figures of two monsters standing over me. One of them was a smudgy bluish shape. Oceana? I blinked hard, trying to clear the haze.

Finally, I saw her. My blue dragoness ally. She stood, bristled and snarling at the figure next to me—another sleek dragoness with scales of red, orange, and yellow. Warmth rolled off her like I was crouched before an open furnace.

"Who are you?" Oceana demanded.

A sudden burst of heat hit my face. I turned away, shielding my eyes. Then a shockwave sent me spinning away from the orange dragon, who roared in challenge.

I rolled, thrown by the blast of her elemental power, until I smacked against the base of a tree. The impact and cold snow on my face helped to clear my head a little. I squinted back up the hill into the blinding light of combat between the two draconic beasts.

It was already a brawl.

Oceana brandished melted snow, weaving her element with lethal elegance. I'd seen her fight like this before. But the other dragoness…she was as terrifying as she was gorgeous, with white hot flames crackling off her lips and the golden light of an inner fire leaking through her red scales. Her long yellow hair parted around black, spiky horns that formed a crest like a crown of volcanic glass on her head. Her eyes flashed, as red as coals, and her sleek red wings sent waves of heat surging through the night.

They clashed in the air, sending out another explosive shockwave that plowed up the ground and sent snow, dirt, and rocks flying in every direction. A plume of fire shot past my head, blazing so close it singed off a few of my eyelashes. Panic and adrenaline took over. I scrambled behind the tree, flexing my still tingly limbs. I could move them again. There were no traces of gold anywhere. Had the red dragoness saved me?

I peeked around the tree.

Oceana drove in hard, willing a wall of water to smash against a fist made of raw, white-hot flame summoned by the other dragon-girl. They strained against each other, fire, water, and steam spouting off in random directions from where their two elements made contact.

This was no place for human Koji. Somehow, I had to stop this before the police and news teams rolled up and we all got caught. The last thing I needed was to deal with police firing at us while some reporter accused us of burning down Central Park.

My list of options was short, though. Option one? Easy. Transform, try to call off Oceana and detain that red dragon-girl, and try to figure out what the heck was going on.

No, I couldn't risk it. My identity was becoming more difficult to protect by the day. The red dragon-girl might have some clue that I was Noxius, but Oceana didn't, and I wanted to keep it that way. I'd have to try something else.

Cue option two, and quite possibly one of my worst ideas of all time.

I ran straight at them, waving my arms in the air and yelling like a maniac. "Stop! You have to stop fighting!" At the top of the hill, my legs got tingly and numb again. I went face down into the snow—right in the middle of their battle.

Well, that was it. I figured I'd either be drowned or burned into a Koji-shaped ash stain on the snow. But when I pulled myself up to my hands and knees, I was shocked to find my idiotic plan had actually worked.

The two dragon-girls crouched on either side of me, snarling and hissing like angry lionesses. Oceana's gaze fixed on me and I instantly went stiff. Now I understood why people were so afraid of us. She loomed over me—a giant, scaly beast with glowing yellow eyes and a body that radiated ancient power. I could only hope I looked that cool as Noxius.

"What did you do to him?" she hissed, glaring at her opponent again.

Behind me, the red dragoness snapped her teeth defiantly but didn't reply. Her features were different, warped by the power of the white totem scale glinting on her arm, but I knew her all the same. Somewhere underneath all those red, inferno-hot scales, was Madeline Ignatius.

I started to reach out to her. After all, she was the one who had saved me, right? Somehow, she'd brought me back from whatever horrible death her father had banished me to. A prison of gold.

The second I moved, she snapped her wings out and took off with a blinding rush of crackling flames.

All I could do was sit there, watching her disappear into the night like a shooting star. Why would she run like that? Where was she going? I wanted to chase after her. I could, and I'd probably catch her easily with Noxius's speed.

Then a giant scaly hand landed on my shoulder.

"Are you all right?" Oceana asked. "Did she hurt you? Can you stand?"

I suddenly remembered I was supposed to be, you know, at least a teensy bit scared. I sat up and backed away from her, feigning a look of terror I hoped was convincing. "Y-you're—"

"Not going to hurt you," she said. "Do you know who that was?"

I hesitated, thought for a second, and then slowly shook my head. "She just...took me. I stepped outside to get some air at a school dance and then *whoosh!*"

Oceana frowned. "I see."

"There are three of you?" I could barely believe it myself.

Her gaze tracked the sky where Madeline had disappeared. Her brow furrowed deeply underneath her blue scales, and her lip pulled up in a snarl that exposed one of her pointed incisors. "I guess so."

"What now? Where's your, uh, partner? Noxius, right?"

"I don't know." She glanced up at the sky as though she were hoping to see him—er, me—swooping in. "But you need to go back home. Your family is probably looking for you. Do you know where you are?"

I took a moment to glance around. "Central Park?" I guessed.

She gave me a charming dragoness smile. "Good luck, then. Try not to get kidnapped again, if you can."

"I'll do my best," I promised.

She flexed her wings, preparing to take off, when I remembered something.

"Hey! Wait a second." I staggered back to my feet.

She glanced over her shoulder at me.

"Can I, uh..." I blushed and took out my phone. "Can I have a picture with you? I didn't get a picture with my date to the dance. But this would be really cool, too. I'm a big fan."

She rolled her glowing yellow eyes. "Are you kidding?"

I put on my best begging face. "Just one picture. Wouldn't hurt to get some good press, right?"

She snorted. "I suppose not. Your date won't be jealous, will she?"

I forced myself to keep smiling through the painful twinge in my chest. "Nah. To tell you the truth, she barely knows I'm alive. I think the only reason she agreed to go with me is because someone else made her do it."

Oceana's brow perked as though that surprised her. Then she came striding over to drape one of her arms around my shoulder. She leaned down so we could take a quick selfie. And at the last second, she turned her head and planted a kiss on my cheek as the camera flashed.

I didn't have to pretend to be embarrassed as I thanked her. With a picture like that, I guess no one could accuse her of being a vicious beast who killed on sight.

It was also the first dragon selfie ever, for the record.

Ankle deep in the snow in my sockless dress shoes, I watched her soar away. As she disappeared into the night sky, I realized that was the second time Oceana had kissed me—even if she wasn't aware of it. And let's face it; both of them were totally sympathy kisses.

I was beginning to wonder if that was my only hope for ever getting a girl to kiss me.

As soon as I was sure she was out of sight, I collapsed back onto my rear end in the snow. I yanked the bowtie out of my tuxedo collar and rubbed the back of my throbbing head. Whatever Headmaster Ignatius had done to me, I'd been helpless to stop it. I could have been stuck like that forever. I was as good as dead until Madeline—

I cringed. Just thinking about her made me grit my teeth and clench my fists. Why would she just leave like that? Wasn't she on our side? We were all supposed to be on the same team here, weren't we? Why would someone give us these totems just so we would fight one another? It made no sense.

Regardless, I knew her secret—and she knew mine. We were both totem wielders, but something else was going on. Headmaster Ignatius had a totem scale, too, and I was willing to bet it didn't have anything to do with the elemental powers of earth.

I needed answers.

But first, I needed a cab…and some ibuprofen.

CHAPTER 21

My story of being kidnapped by Oceana so I could help her out with her "bad press problem" won Dad over after a lot of panicked explaining on my part. It was the only thing I could come up with, especially when I added in how Drake had mistaken our departure from the dance as me being kidnapped. His story wound up complementing mine pretty well. We were both in the clear as far as parental interrogations were concerned.

Drake could barely wait to interrogate me. He gnawed in the inside of his cheek, flicking me frantic glances when no one was paying attention. Neither of us could concentrate on the video game flashing over the TV screen while we waited for Dad to go to bed.

Once the house got quiet and we were tucked in for the night—me in my bed and him on an air mattress on the floor—he flopped over to glare at me. "What the heck happened?"

I tried to tell him, to explain every detail, but when I got to the part where Headmaster Ignatius had hit me with that weird totem-cane of his, my voice started to shake. I shuddered, remembering how it had felt as my whole body turned into gold. I'd only felt that helpless one other time in my life. Those dark memories drew my gaze up to the picture of my mom sitting on my bookshelf. This time had been worse only because Headmaster Ignatius had challenged me in my scaly form. When I felt most invincible, he'd brought me down with a single touch.

"Wait—he had a totem scale *in* his cane?" Drake interrupted. "The one for earth? Why would that turn someone into gold?"

"I don't think it would," I murmured. "Whoever told Oceana there was only four of them must have lied. There's a fifth one, and maybe more that we don't know about."

Drake rolled over on the air mattress again. It made loud, rubbery, squeaking sounds against the hardwood floor like someone wrestling with a pool float. "So then he's got to be the one who brought that monster into the city, right?"

"I guess so. Maybe. I don't know." He hadn't outright admitted that he had been responsible for that incident, but he definitely seemed the most likely candidate.

"I can't believe Madeline has the fire totem. Are you sure it was her?"

My eyes fell closed. If I thought about it hard enough, I could remember exactly how she'd looked in that form. A terrifying mixture of magnificence and fire-breathing rage. "I'm sure."

"But wait." Drake's head popped up over the edge of my bed. "Ignatius said that the totems were put into jewelry, right? Like your bracelet and Madeline's arm cuff. We can only assume that Oceana's is like that, too."

"We talked about that once," I recalled. "She said she couldn't get hers off either."

"So totems are fixed to an item that wouldn't come off once it chose you. A piece of jewelry or something similar. But a cane isn't like that. You don't wear a cane, and it would be easy to get rid of if you wanted to."

"Well," I clarified, "he did say *most* of them were like that. His must be the exception."

"So it's safe to assume his is not a normal element. It didn't bond to him like the others do to their wielders." Drake's head peered further over the edge of the bed. "Hey, are you okay?"

I wasn't. I felt sick to my stomach about it all. I was out of my depth in more ways than I could count. Everything was beginning to spiral out of control. Ignatius was up to something, and he didn't want me to interfere—I just had no idea what he might be planning. And what would he do to Madeline for helping me escape?

I rolled over and turned my back. "I'm fine."

"I'll figure it out, Koji. Listen, tomorrow we'll go to my house. I'll show you what I've found. It's not much, but with this new information, maybe I can get some real answers."

Drake had been pretty quiet about his research into the totems—not that I was worried. I figured he'd tell me what he'd found when he was ready. But regardless of what he'd found, my thoughts were too scrambled to even wonder about it. Madeline was all I could think about. She was still out there somewhere. Her dad was my school headmaster and he'd tried to kill me. I had to go back to Saint Bernard's on Monday and face him like nothing had happened. I had to sit right next to Madeline in art class. How was I going to do that?

"The photo with Oceana was pretty clever," Drake muttered. He'd gone back to lying on his air mattress. "Unusually clever for you."

"Gee, thanks."

"You want me to send it to a few of the news stations? I could do it anonymously, not that it would matter. Your dad already got arrested once, and he's reported you missing like, what, fifty times now? The police probably have him on speed dial. As soon as they see your face in that picture they'll be knocking the door down to question you. Then again, maybe it is a good idea for Noxius and Oceana to get some good press for a change."

I thought about it. That's the real reason I'd taken it in the first place, not just to avoid being grounded again. Reaching over onto my nightstand, I pulled my phone off its charger and looked at the picture.

Then I deleted it.

"No," I decided aloud.

"What?" Drake sounded surprised. "I thought you wanted to clear your names with the public."

"I did. But now..."

"Now what?"

"Now that I'm thinking about it, if there are other totem users out there who aren't using their powers for good, then maybe it's best for the public to be a little scared of us after all." I sighed. "I don't know what Headmaster Ignatius is planning, and I don't know how Madeline ties into all of it, but Oceana is right—protecting my identity means protecting Dad, you, your mom, and anyone else I care about. A picture like that puts me too close to the spotlight. I need to lay low, keep my head down, and figure this out."

"What are you gonna say to Madeline?"

I pulled back the sleeve of my sweatshirt. The totem scale shimmered temptingly in the moonlight that poured through my bedroom window. It held so many secrets; so many ancient mysteries that were waiting right at my fingertips, but were still out of reach.

"I don't know. But I think I know who gave Oceana all that information about the totems. Madeline is the key. She knows a lot more than she's ever let on. Somehow, I have to convince her to tell me."

"Yeah. Good luck with that," Drake muttered. He got quiet for a few minutes, and then I heard him start to snore.

I tried to sleep, too. I tossed and turned for hours. Every position felt comfortable for about a minute before I got restless again. Across my room, I could just barely make out my mom's face in the photograph sitting on my shelf. I thought about her, about that night in the cold, dark water. My last few seconds with her had been filled with so much terror, and yet all I could think about was how gentle her voice had been when she said my name.

"Koji...my sweet boy. It's okay. Don't be scared. You're going to be okay. Mommy loves you."

The next morning was a Saturday, and also the first day of our Christmas holiday break. It was bizarre before my feet ever hit the floor. I woke up to the smell of food—delicious breakfast food—coming from downstairs.

No way that was Dad's cooking.

I got up and stepped over Drake, who was still snoring like an old chainsaw on the air mattress. As I crept downstairs, I heard Christmas music coming from the sound system in the living room and laughter in the kitchen. Dad and Ms. Collins were standing around the kitchen table together, sipping mugs of coffee and talking. Ms. Collins still wore a set of scrubs covered in pink and white snowflakes. Her pale blond hair was tied up in a messy bun and dark circles rimmed her eyes.

When she noticed me standing awkwardly in the kitchen doorway, her expression brightened with a smile. "Good morning! You're up early. Your dad was just telling me about your adventures last night."

"O-oh," I stammered. "Yeah. It was, uh, interesting."

"We've got breakfast. Sausage and blueberry pancakes." Dad hoisted his coffee cup in my direction.

"I made them," Ms. Collins added with a wink. Looks like she'd taken my advice about not letting Dad anywhere near the cooking. Good call.

"You should show her that picture," Dad suggested. "The one with Oceana. It's pretty cool."

I blushed. "Uh, well. Actually, I deleted it."

"What? Why?" they both asked at once.

I shifted uneasily and scrambled for an excuse. The truth leapt out of me before I could come up with one. "I didn't want anyone to start asking questions. They already arrested you once, Dad. If it's all the same to you guys, I don't want the police coming here like that ever again."

Their expressions of complete surprise were eerily similar—and a little exasperating. Was the fact that I had thought this through really that surprising?

Okay, don't answer that.

Dad ruffled my hair and chuckled. "I suppose I can't argue with that. Hey, Amelia thought it might be a good idea for all of us to get out a little today. You know, soak in the holiday spirit. What do you say? You up for a little shopping? Maybe some ice-skating?"

Me on skates in any form was asking for an impromptu trip to the emergency room. But, then again, Ms. Collins was a nurse. And this was my first Christmas in New York. It would have been a shame not to give it a try.

I smiled and went to start heaping pancakes and sausage onto a plate. "Sure. Sounds good. Drake and I wanted to go over to his house tonight and maybe play some video games, too."

"We should just make a day of it, then. We can order dinner for everyone." Ms. Collins beamed.

Even Dad seemed to like the idea.

"It's settled, then. I'll run home and get cleaned up. Do you mind bringing the boys by in a few hours? We can take the train from our place." Ms. Collins gulped down what was left in her coffee mug and grabbed her purse off the table. "Be sure you all bundle up warm! It's freezing out there today."

Dad walked her out. Even though they were around the corner in the front foyer, I could see their reflections in the hall mirror. Ms. Collins gave my dad a quick kiss on the cheek before she wrapped her scarf around her nose, pulled a fluffy white toboggan over her head, and dashed outside.

Dad stood in the doorway and waved as she left. For a few extra seconds, he just watched her. That's when I saw it on his face—the look.

He liked her. I mean, *really* liked her.

My insides scrambled. Frantically, I tried to decide how I felt about that. Cool, I had to keep it cool. No need to freak out.

Dad still had that misty glint in his eyes when he came back in to pile food onto his own plate and sit down across from me at the table.

I cleared my throat to get his attention. "So, she's pretty great, huh?"

His eyes narrowed ever so slightly. He knew I was up to something. "Yeah. She is."

"So, you gonna ask her out?"

He choked on his pancakes. After some coughing and sputtering, he shot me a look. "Son, we've already been to dinner a few times."

"I know. I mean like a real, serious date, though."

He put his fork down carefully. I could see his brows beginning to rumple together, making a triangular wrinkle right at the top of his nose. "She and I have talked about it. We agree that, whatever this is, we'd like to take things very slow. She's just gotten out of a long, rough relationship, and I haven't dated in a while. It wouldn't make much sense for either of us to rush into this."

"Oh." I pretended to be totally occupied cutting my pancakes into perfect triangles before smothering them in syrup. "Guess that makes sense. You'll just have to hope no one else comes in to plant their flag first."

His eyes narrowed further. "What's that supposed to mean?"

"Like you said, you've been out of the dating game for a while. It's pretty brutal out there. The competition is stiff. If you like her, you better make your move before someone else does."

He pursed his lips unhappily. "That's ridiculous. Where do you even come up with this stuff?"

I shrugged. "Take it from a professional second-placer—plant the flag."

The four of us spent the day shopping, ice-skating at the Rockefeller Center, and taking in the sites of New York at Christmastime. I only crashed into two people while skating, which was good compared to my previous attempts. No one had to be carted away in an ambulance. Win-win.

When he thought no one was paying attention, I saw my dad start holding Ms. Collins's hand. It started while they were skating but continued while we walked past the shops and took photos at Times Square. Our last stop was the top of the Empire State Building, and I had to pretend like I'd never been up there before ever. It's kind of hard to fake that reaction, but it is different when you're not in a form that can fly. Thankfully, Dad was so distracted "planting the flag" he didn't seem to care what I did as long as it wasn't life-threatening.

I wasn't sure Drake had even noticed until he leaned over to me at the end of the day and muttered, "Is it just me, or are they extra cozy?"

I stifled a laugh. "Seems like it."

He pulled a disgusted face. "Gross."

"Like you and Tabitha?"

Drake's eyes went wide and his cheeks turned bright red. "You saw?" he rasped in a panicked, squeaky whisper.

I made the same disgusted face back at him. "Believe me, no one is more sorry about that than I am."

After dinner, Dad and Ms. Collins settled in to watch one of the Christmas specials on TV while Drake and I retreated to his bedroom. We were going to "play video games." Also known as researching totem facts.

It dawned on me as I crossed the threshold that I'd never actually been in Drake's room. It looked like the inside of a mercenary spaceship whose sole occupation was acquiring and repurposing old electronic parts. Wires, cables, computer monitors, keyboards, and circuit boards covered every surface. Some were in heaps against the walls, while others were actually mounted on the wall. When he flipped his light switch, little LED lights illuminated the cramped space—centering around one extremely overloaded computer desk. A small, unmade single bed was crammed against the wall like an afterthought.

I had to pick my way carefully across the floor to find a place to sit. "Nice, uh, room?" I wasn't sure this workshop qualified.

"Try not to break anything." He plopped into his desk chair and switched on the largest monitor. "In fact, it's probably best if you just don't touch anything at all."

"Agreed." I put my hands in my pockets just to avoid the temptation. "So what is all this stuff?"

"I build computers, small electronics, and some other stuff in my spare time," he replied as he started hammering away on the keyboard, his fingers flying over the keys like he wasn't even trying to make real words.

"Bombs?" I joked.

"Tried that once. Mom freaked out when I blew up the bathroom in second grade, so now I can only do the explosive stuff at school sometimes."

My laughter died in my throat. My best friend was an evil genius.

"Okay, so here's what I've got." He wheeled over a few feet so I could see the screen. "I've hacked into a few different government databases, some museum files—basic stuff. At first I couldn't find anything. Let's face it, you can't just run a search for 'dragon totem' and hope to find useful intel."

I blushed because that's exactly what I'd done.

"So instead, I decided to hack the FBI files."

My jaw dropped. "You did *what*?"

He ran a hand through his platinum hair proudly. "Come on, like it's hard?"

Cold sweat beaded on my forehead. "You're gonna get us both arrested! No one caught you, right?"

"Relax, I'm not a newb." Drake rolled his eyes. "They don't arrest people with my skills, they *hire* them. Okay? They wouldn't arrest Michelangelo for painting on the Popemobile, even if he wasn't invited to."

I rubbed the back of my neck and tried not to hyperventilate. "O-okay."

"So anyway, between all the data about alien landings, Bigfoot, and who shot Kennedy—I found this." His fingers flew over the keys again and brought up images of several old documents, some of which looked like they might have dated all the way back to medieval times. Most of it was faded beyond legibility or written in some ancient, foreign language. But the pictures were clear. The documents had illustrations of four beings, all with bat-like wings and the mixed features of human and reptile.

"It was easy to find once I hit the right keywords. These FBI guys have been snooping around, so I looked at recently accessed files. These came right up. Look at the different time periods, Koji. These are from all over the world. There's the Han dynasty in China—that's around 200 BC. Greek, Egyptian, Roman, Nordic, Medieval Europe, Aztec—there's traces of these beings throughout history. You look at each piece of evidence individually and they seem totally different—they describe the totems and dragons in different ways. But if you stand back and look at all these historical depictions of gods, goddesses, and creatures of myth all at once, then you start to see the big picture. These totems have been all over the world. They've been around since the dawn of time."

"It's just like Headmaster Ignatius's house," I said quietly as I leaned closer to the screen. "He's collected artifacts with dragons on them from all over the world."

"In some cultures these beings, or dragons, were viewed as evil. They were powerful forces of destruction. So those totem wielders must have used their power for their own gain." Drake continued scrolling through the documents. "But in other cultures they're viewed as benevolent. They were the forces of good—protectors. Check this out. I thought it was nothing at the time. After all, you were sure there were only four totems until recently. But now…"

He brought up an image of a Grecian piece of pottery. It was chipped and faded, but the painting on it showed four human figures. One held lightning in his hand, another was a man surrounded by waves of water, one was a man brandishing a fistful of flames, and the last was a woman covered in leaves and flowering vines. In the center, there was one more figure. This one was different from the others. He stood in the center of a golden circle along which all the figures of the zodiac were arranged. On his head rested a circlet, like a crown, with a gleaming gem in the center.

My breath caught. Was that a totem scale?

"Who is that?" I pointed to the man in the circle.

"Aion," Drake replied. "According to Grecian mythology, he's the god of eternal time."

I swallowed hard. "Is time an element?"

Drake's silence was disturbing. I watched him scowling at his screen, his expression wrinkled with uncertainty. Together, we stared at the photograph of the pot.

I'd never considered that time might be an element that could be wielded or manipulated. I wasn't even sure what that would look like. Would it let someone summon giant crocodilian monsters or turn people into gold?

I guess Drake was wondering the same thing.

"If there is a totem scale that allows someone to control, freeze, or rip holes in time and drag giant monsters through—I think we can agree it is the most dangerous of them all," he murmured. "It would be even more dangerous if that totem didn't work like the rest, where it could only be used by one person. I'm only guessing here, but perhaps that's why the totem wielders in the past have been so careful to cover their tracks and erase their existence as best they can. They wanted to keep the time totem from falling into the wrong hands."

My voice shook, coming out as a hoarse whisper. "There has to be some way to stop it. There has to be something we can do. If Headmaster Ignatius really has the ability to control time, he's already tried to destroy the city once. We have to—"

"Talk to Madeline," Drake interrupted. "It's her father doing all this. She probably knows better than anyone what he's up to. You have to talk to her, Koji. You have to get her on our side. If he let a monster loose once, what's stopping him from doing it again?"

"Me," I realized aloud.

"What?"

"Oceana and I. We're the only ones able to stop him. That's why he lured me to his house—so he could freeze me in gold. He wanted me out of the way. He said it himself: Oceana's not a threat on her own. She and I are the only chance this city has."

Drake studied me in the glow from his computer screen. "Then you better warn her. And you better talk to Madeline before it's too late. She's sympathetic to your cause; she wouldn't have saved you otherwise. So find her before she changes her mind or Ignatius takes her out of the equation altogether."

I squeezed my hands into fists. "I will."

CHAPTER 22

Finding Madeline Ignatius was easier said than done. Going back to her home wasn't an option, although it would have been the most obvious place to look. I wasn't going to chance it alone; I had no interest in being turned into a gilded, dragon-shaped coat rack again. But before I got Oceana involved, I wanted to give Madeline a chance to explain herself. So I had to find her on neutral territory, sometime when she was alone. The problem was, with school closed for the holiday, I had no idea where to begin looking.

After all my normal attempts—calling her, messaging her, even sending her an email—failed, I got desperate. I worked up the courage to at least walk by her home, but there was no one there. The gate was bolted shut, the front door was closed, and curtains blocked all the mansion's dozens of windows so I couldn't see inside.

Madeline was nowhere to be found.

My only hope left was to find her at school after the holiday break was over. If I couldn't talk to her there, I'd have to go to Oceana. I couldn't keep putting it off. The longer I waited, the greater the risk that something might happen before I got the opportunity to warn her.

I decided to give it until the first Monday back at school after the holidays—just one week. Then I couldn't put it off anymore.

The bleak, cold winter days dragged miserably. I couldn't get into any of the festivities, not wholeheartedly, anyway. I jumped at every sudden sound, cringed whenever Dad turned on the TV to check the news headlines, and tossed and turned all night. Every distant whine of police or fire engine sirens set my pulse racing and my body shaking. Had Headmaster Ignatius struck again? Was another monster rampaging through the city? Was Oceana all right? Where was Madeline?

I couldn't even muster up the will to mock my dad when he shocked himself and nearly fell off the ladder while hanging Christmas lights on the front of the house. Drake was there to pick up my slack in that area, though. Having him around felt normal now, as though he were a part of the family already. I couldn't decide if that was a good or a bad thing, and honestly, I didn't have the extra brainpower to spare worrying about it. Figuring out what to do about Madeline consumed my every waking thought.

Still, it was going to suck big time if I got used to him being there and then our parents stopped dating or got into an argument and refused to see each other again. Then what? Were we supposed to take sides? Or did we just go on and pretend the whole dating thing never happened? Would Dad still let him come over and hang out?

On Christmas Eve, a little normality returned. Drake and his mom had left a couple days before to visit relatives in Philadelphia. My grandparents drove in from Jersey to have Christmas dinner, and the house was filled with the familiar chaos of Owens family holidays. My grandmother scolded Dad for sneaking bites of the food before it was ready, while Grandpa snored loudly in the recliner in front of the TV. A John Wayne marathon filled the living room with the resonances of the Wild West. Ah, family tradition.

I passed the evening on the couch, flipping through one of my favorite comics and sipping on a mug of my grandma's signature homemade hot chocolate. I dare you to find someone who can make it better than she can. It's the best in the world.

After dinner, we settled in around the Christmas tree to open gifts. I got some new socks, a wool coat, a couple of video games, and set of earphones that had the cool noise-canceling feature. After everyone else had finished opening their presents, Dad passed me another gift. It had been tucked behind the tree, out of sight.

"From Ms. Collins," he explained with a secretive smile.

I cocked an eyebrow. Money was tight for them, wasn't it? She didn't have to get me anything. "Did we get Drake something?"

Dad's smile widened. "I got it covered, don't worry."

I tore away the shiny wrapping paper to reveal a decent-sized tackle box, which seemed weird since I had never been into fishing. But when I opened it, my throat tightened. I sat motionless on the floor, staring at the contents of the tackle box, unable to make a sound.

For a moment, all of my worries and responsibilities vanished like fog dissolved by the morning sun.

The tackle box was filled with brand-new, special effects character makeup and tools. Everything I'd ever need to start learning how to do stage and cinema makeups was stocked inside. A full set of paints, brushes, adhesives, prosthetics, sealants, and even molding wax I could use to make scars or skin modifications were organized neatly inside the trays, drawers, and divided sections.

I'd never owned anything like this. I'd never even thought about asking for it. Dad wasn't a huge fan of my artistic interests, which was okay. He was an engineer—not to mention a fighter pilot. He excelled in all things math and science, so art was like a foreign language to him. I understood all that, but it still stung to have him dismiss the things I enjoyed as less important or as time-wasting hobbies that would never get me anywhere in life. Art, drawing, and painting were the only things I'd ever felt confident doing. And this was the first time an adult had ever really supported my interest in them.

"Koji? Are you okay?" Dad leaned over my shoulder to peer into the box. "What's all that for?"

"It's for learning to make stage makeup, like for movies and stuff."

"Oh," he said, a hint of skepticism in his voice. "Looks pretty cool."

"Yeah." My voice was husky and I swallowed hard, trying to keep my eyes from watering. Even if Dad didn't really understand, I didn't care. This was the best present anyone had ever gotten me.

We celebrated New Year's with Drake, Ms. Collins, and my grandparents. Rather than battling the crowds in Times Square, everyone agreed it was better if we stayed in to watch them all on TV. Grandma and Drake's mom worked for hours on a big fancy dinner, filling the house with delicious smells and girlish laughter.

I should have been happy. It was supposed to be nice, having everyone together like that. I couldn't remember the last time there had been that many people sitting around our dinner table. Probably never.

But school started again soon—and that's all I could think about.

Headmaster Ignatius.

Madeline.

Oceana.

While everyone else feasted and made dinnertime small talk, I was busy wrenching my hands under the table until my palms were sweaty. My foot wouldn't stop tapping. My fingers traced the outline of my totem scale under the sleeve of my sweater.

Just one more day. Patient; I had to be patient.

"Koji, are you feeling all right?" Ms. Collins asked as she refilled my glass of soda. "You've been so quiet tonight."

From across the table, Drake's eyes flickered up from where he was stuffing his face with buttery crescent rolls. We stared at one another for a half a second, then quickly looked away. My stomach writhed like I'd swallowed live snakes.

"I-I'm fine," I mumbled, forcing a smile.

"He's just worried about exams," Drake piped in.

Okay, so that wasn't completely untrue. We had midterm exams a week after the holiday break, and my Chemistry grade was hanging by a thread. It was only because of Drake's tutoring that I was passing at all.

"Better hit the books then," Dad warned. "We had a deal, remember? No Ds this time."

I sank lower in my seat. Great. As if I didn't have enough to worry about already, now I had to try and study, too.

I didn't notice when the clock struck midnight, and I was oblivious to the celebration that followed. The fireworks, cheers, and explosions of confetti seemed muffled and distant as I sat on the end of the couch, staring at the toes of my socks.

Even after we said our goodbyes to Drake and Ms. Collins and everyone settled in for the night, my body refused to relax. I couldn't sleep. So instead, I watched the moonlit shadows move across my floor and counted down the hours until morning. I was already dreading the next day. Twenty-four more hours of waiting, and every second was agony.

On January second, snow fell in thick white sheets as I left for school almost two hours early. I stood outside on the school's front steps, in the exact spot where Madeline and I had sat together, and waited to see if she would arrive. The school doors opened and I got strange looks from the janitor and secretary when they arrived.

The morning wore on. My classmates filed past me, hurrying into the warmth of the building to get out of the snow and bitter wind. I'd lost the feeling in my nose a while ago. The ten-minute bell rang, then the five-minute one.

I waited until the absolute last second to finally give up. If Madeline was coming to school, she was either late or had snuck in through a different entrance. After a quick dash by my locker, I threw myself down next to Drake in Chemistry and tried to concentrate on something—anything—else. I opened my textbook and started reading over the first chapter again. Atoms and elements to the rescue.

A commotion in the front of the classroom caught my attention. I peered up from my book to where Tabitha crooned loudly, making a noisy spectacle. It got the attention of every girl in the room, who all flocked over to Claire's desk to huddle around her.

I glanced at Drake for an explanation.

"It's official now," he murmured. "She got the ring."

"What?"

He raised his left hand and waggled his ring finger.

Oh. *That* ring.

"Damien popped the question on Christmas morning, or at least that's what I heard."

"Tabitha told you?" I guessed.

His cheeks colored slightly and he scrunched his mouth as he glared back down at his phone. "She texts me sometimes, okay? It's not a big deal. Anyway, supposedly the ring is four carats. Someone said it cost over fifty grand."

I folded my arms and laid my head down on my desk.

"Sorry, man," Drake said. "I did warn you."

Yeah. He had tried to warn me that liking her was moronic and completely hopeless. That was basically the essence of who

I was as a person, so it's not like I was shocked at this turn of events. That wasn't what bothered me, though. How could she agree to marry another guy if she had real feelings for Noxius? That just seemed hypocritical. Not that I had any room to judge. Maybe she had other reasons for saying yes.

But still…

I told myself it didn't matter. I was over her. I had bigger problems to deal with, anyway.

At lunch, I stuffed my face full of the school's delectable broccoli, cheddar, and ham soup served in a soft bread bowl. It was like a warm, tasty food-hug. I ate two helpings and chugged a can of coke before I noticed Drake looking at me weird.

"What?"

"Hungry there, buddy? Or just eating your feelings?"

I groaned and licked my spoon of any remaining morsels. "Can't it be both?"

When Claire walked by to sit with her friends, I saw it. You couldn't miss it. The light struck that giant diamond ring and practically blinded me. I glared back down at my empty food tray.

"Isn't there a school rule against jewelry?" I growled under my breath.

"Says the guy wearing an ancient super-power-giving bracelet." Drake chuckled. "She's practically New York royalty. The rules don't apply to her. You, on the other hand, better keep your sleeves down."

He had a point there.

Drake put down his phone and folded his hands on the table. "Look, can I ask you something and you not freak out on me? Just hear me out and actually think about this for a second."

I eyed him down skeptically. "Okay, what?"

"What do you like about Claire? I mean, besides that she's pretty and popular? What do you know about her that makes you think being with her would make you happy?"

I opened my mouth, ready to make a snappy argument—but the words just weren't there. I didn't know.

"No offense, but you don't know anything about her, do you?"

"She's nice," I tried to sound convincing. "She plays the cello like an angel."

Drake rolled his eyes. "Pretty much everyone knows that about her. Even news reporters who have interviewed her for ten seconds know that. I'm taking about the real details, the stuff that matters. What's her favorite color? Favorite flavor of ice cream? What kind of movies and music does she like? What makes her sad? What cheers her up? What makes her laugh?" He paused and leaned his elbows onto the table, leveling a series gaze in my direction. "Wouldn't it make sense to actually learn some of that about her before deciding you're in love with her?"

"I never said I loved her," I reminded him with a scowl.

"Fair enough." Drake sighed. "Look, all I'm saying is that you've been pining after someone you don't even know. What if you don't have anything in common? What if she hates video games? Or thinks comics are stupid? Or would rather die than go see a *Star Wars* movie on opening night? Is that someone you'd want to be in a serious relationship with?"

I sank back in my chair in utter defeat.

"Now forget about the stupid ring and start focusing on what matters, like finding Madeline before she and her dad turn the city into a pile of rubble."

Right. Now wasn't the time to be losing my focus.

My last hope for seeing Madeline was at the end of the day. When I arrived in Mr. Molins's class, I hesitated in the doorway and scanned the room from one end to the other. Everyone was getting out paints, brushes, sketchbooks, or ceramics materials. It all seemed so ordinary, like just another day.

But Madeline was nowhere in sight. Her easel and stool were vacant and untouched.

On my way to my easel, my gaze hung on the spot on the floor where I'd awoken after my fight with the crocodilian monster. Of course, no one knew I'd been here. Well—no one except...

Realization nearly made me fall off my stool.

Madeline. She *must* have been the one who had brought me here that night, tended my wounds, and left without a trace.

Beside me, her stool remained empty through the rest of class as Mr. Molins gave with his lecture on the proper techniques for using pastels. After his demonstration and instruction, he started his usual rounds through the class, walking the big circle of easels while everyone practiced on their own.

My heart just wasn't in it today. I tried to sketch something out, to work in my art journal, but nothing would come. It was like trying to force one more drop out of an empty soda can. It didn't matter how hard you shook it. My mind, heart, and spirit felt bone dry.

The canvas before me was still empty when Mr. Molins stopped by to check on me. Lucky for me, he didn't seem all that interested in my pastel work—or lack thereof.

"Koji, I wanted to ask you about something." He stroked his goatee thoughtfully. "Remember I mentioned Mrs. Kalensky's Theater Club is doing a production this spring?"

I nodded. "*A Midsummer Night's Dream*, right?"

"Yes. She and I spoke about it this morning, and she's interested in letting you try your hand with the stage makeup and even help with some of the costume designs. If you have the time after school, of course."

Did I have the time? Between school and my secret life as a totem guardian, I sort of doubted it. Superhero work wasn't just a weekend gig, as it turned out.

"I'll ask my dad if he minds," I replied. That seemed like a safe excuse. If I couldn't swing it, I'd have a legitimate reason.

"Perfect." Mr. Molins smile and patted my shoulder. Then he glanced over at Madeline's empty workstation. "Have you heard anything from Miss Ignatius? It's not like her to be absent without an excuse."

My heart sank. "No. I was just wondering the same thing. I'm kind of worried about her."

His brow creased with uncertainty. "I'll phone the office and see if they've heard from her."

"Will you let me know if she's all right?" I asked.

"Of course. Stop by my desk after class."

I wasn't all that surprised that Mr. Molins couldn't find out anything about where Madeline was. According to him, both she and the headmaster had called in sick that morning. They'd likely be out for a few days.

Out sick? Yeah, right. No way that was true.

Unfortunately, that was my last shot at tracking her down. I'd done everything I could to find Madeline. Now I had no choice but to take the matter to Oceana. Tonight, I'd go to the old abandoned power plant and hope she spotted me and followed me there. We had to talk about the headmaster and what we could do to stop him before he used that cane-totem again.

Drake had a meeting after school with the Robotics Club, so I went to my locker and prepared to walk home alone. I spun the dial, opened my locker door, and went to cram a few of my textbooks in wherever they would fit.

An envelope sat on the top shelf with my name written on the front in dainty, girlish handwriting.

I glanced both ways down the hall, checking for perpetrators. No one had ever left anything inside my locker. Well, except for a certain package almost six months ago.

Suddenly, it hit me. I stood motionless, staring down at the note. All the dots connected in my head, fragments of information finally falling into place. They revealed truths like constellations hidden amidst the chaos.

I knew where my totem had come from.

Opening the letter, I hurried to unfold it with shaking hands. There was only one line written on it in that same curly handwriting:

Glen Span Arch. 4 p.m.

I crammed the note in my pocket and checked the time. It was almost 3:15 p.m. Even if I took cabs and subways, I barely had time to get there.

Slamming my locker closed, I stuffed my arms into my coat, slung my bag over my shoulder, and started running down the stairs for the front door. I dodged and wove through the crowd of other students leaving the school, taking the stairwells two and three steps at a time. Halfway across the front sidewalk of the school, someone called out my name.

I screeched to a halt right on the curb and looked back.

Claire was running out the front doors after me. "Koji! Wait up!"

I stopped, unable to hide my total bewilderment as she stood before me. All her lovely golden curls blew around her face in the winter wind as she sent me a breathless, almost worried smile.

"I never got a chance to…I mean, I forgot to say thank you the other night," she said. "For taking me to the Winter Ball, that is."

"Oh." I almost wanted to walk away right then. I didn't have time for this right now.

"It's just different, you know?" Her expression crumpled slightly, seeming flustered and unsure. "I'm not used to it."

"To what?"

"Guys, people, anyone here—no one just does something nice for me because they can or want to. Not in my experience, anyway. You have to understand, Koji, I've never met anyone like you before. Most of the people in my life all have—"

"An ulterior motive?" I guessed.

She let out a breath of relief and bobbed her head. "Yes, precisely. So I didn't mean to seem ungrateful, or like I didn't want to be there with you."

I swallowed hard.

"When I realized you'd already left to go home, and how distracted I must have seemed all night, I see now how unfair that was to you. I'm so sorry, Koji. You've been nothing but kind to me and that was an awful way for me to treat you," she said softly. "I hope you'll let me make it up to you."

"Nah, you don't have to do anything like that. Really, it's not a big deal." I managed a nervous smile.

"It *is* a big deal. I've never had a normal friend before. Not that there's anything wrong with normal people, or that you're normal—Ah! I mean you are! That's not what I mean!" Her eyes went wide, her cheeks flushing as red as ripe apples. "What I mean is, I've never had a real friend before. Someone who just wanted to spend time with me because they liked me. Even Tabitha. I mean, we're friends, but we probably would have never even spoken if our parents hadn't insisted on it. We don't have much in common. Does that make sense?"

I covered my mouth so hopefully she wouldn't see me trying not to laugh. "Yeah. I get it."

"You're laughing at me." She looked down gloomily. "I mean it; I want to make it up to you. To prove to you that I'm not the miserable brat you must think I am now."

"What did you have in mind, exactly?"

"There's a charity gala event. I have to attend because it's for my parents' work at the New York Philharmonic-Symphony. My father is the president and my mother is the music director. It's not a ball—more like a fancy cocktail party attended by the most snobbish, stuffy, boring people you can possibly imagine."

"Sounds super exciting."

"Oh, absolutely." She smirked for a brief second before quickly glancing down again. "I was hoping you would go with me."

"Me?" I stammered. "What about Damien?"

"He already has plans. Although, honestly, I think he's just digging for an excuse since he hates these sorts of things. Not that I particularly enjoy them myself, but I don't have a choice. I have to be there to support my parents." She slowly raised her gaze, her lovely features glowing with a small, hopeful smile. "They said I could bring a friend instead. So will you go with me?"

A few weeks ago, I would have been on my knees praising the heavens for this chance. Another night out with her? It had to be a miracle. But now, everything was different. I hesitated, my mind tangling around what this actually meant. I couldn't get Madeline's face out of my head.

"Koji? Is everything okay?" Claire asked.

I suddenly remembered there was an important question I was supposed to answer. "Oh. Yeah, no, I'm fine. I was just wondering if Damien is really going to be okay with me taking you out again. I mean, not that we're going out. It is out—but not *out* out. It's not a date."

Smooth, Koji. Real smooth.

Claire tilted her head to the side slightly, one of her slender brows lifting as though she weren't convinced. "If you don't want to go, it's okay."

"No! No, I'm good. It's totally fine. I mean, yes. I'll go." I pulled at my necktie. All of a sudden it seemed too tight. "When is it?"

"Tonight," she replied. "At 7 p.m. I know it's short notice, but you don't need to wear a tuxedo. Just a suit and tie will do."

I was internally screaming. Four hours from now? How was I gonna pull this off? I started clenching my hands in my pockets, gripping the note from my locker tightly. The clock was ticking.

"Okay, I can manage that." I cleared my throat nervously. "Look, I gotta go take care of some stuff beforehand. Where should I meet you?"

Her smile brightened beautifully, like morning sunlight breaking over a hilltop. "I'll send a driver to come pick you up at your house. Is that okay?"

"Sounds good." I was already backing away when I waved. "See you tonight."

I didn't hang around to see if she waved back. I turned and broke into a mad sprint for the nearest subway station.

CHAPTER 23

I was late.

Six minutes late—which wasn't that bad considering how far I'd traveled without using my totem to get there. But still. As I wheezed and sprinted the last few yards down the narrow, icy pathways to the Glen Span Arch, I was terrified six minutes late was too late. Sweat dripped off my nose when I finally jogged to a halt in front of the iconic stacked-stone archway in Central Park.

I turned in a slow circle, panting and gasping. There was nobody in sight. Not a single soul in any direction. Just the little mostly frozen creek flowing under the arch and me.

No. *No!*

I rubbed my face and growled through my teeth in frustration. If Madeline left me that note, she was probably long gone by now. Why had I stopped and talked to Claire? Those few minutes had been the difference between getting here on time and blowing off my last good chance to find Madeline.

I trudged underneath the arch to get out of the wind so I could think. My nose and cheeks felt chapped from the wind and sweating made me even colder. It was starting to get dark already. If I was going to get back home before Dad, I needed to leave soon. Leaning against the stony side of the arch, I shivered as I tried to figure out my next move. I had to talk to Oceana and explain everything before—

"I was beginning to think you weren't coming," a soft voice called.

She appeared out of thin air like a ghost, standing on the other side of the archway with the cold evening wind catching in her long black hair. She walked toward me slowly, her graphite-colored eyes focused, cautious, and searching me without blinking. I could see tension in the way her brow was creased and her mouth fixed into a thin, hard line.

"Madeline," I gasped in relief. "I was so afraid something had happened to you, that he hurt you or—"

"Koji, I asked you here to warn you," she interrupted. "You need to get your dad, Drake, and his mother, and you have to leave the city. You have to go today, Koji. Right now."

"Why? What's going on, Madeline?" I moved in closer and grasped her arm before she could escape. I could feel the metallic shape of her arm cuff beneath her thick winter clothes.

Her gaze flickered, becoming wild and desperate as she tried to wrench away. "Stop it! Please! I-I can't tell you anything else. They may already know I'm here."

"Who? Your dad?"

Her expression skewed painfully. Tears in her eyes as her chin trembled and her arm went slack in my hand.

"It was you the whole time, wasn't it? You're the one who gave me my totem. You kept leaving it in places you knew I'd find it. You did the same thing for Oceana, right?" I moved in closer and tried to keep my tone calm. She was already scared. I didn't want to make it worse. "And then you made sure we had enough information about them to fight whatever your dad threw at us. You were the one who moved me from the abandoned power plant to the school and treated my injuries."

"Yes," she answered quietly. "It's because of my third eye—I can sense who should be totem wielders and where each totem wielder is in the world."

"So why?" I gently pulled her in closer. "Why help us if you're on his side? Talk to me, Madeline. You know you can trust me. I'd never do anything to hurt you."

Her mouth scrunched uncomfortably and she swallowed, as though the words were too bitter to speak.

"I know about his totem scale. I know he wields the power of time. What's he planning to do with it?"

"Koji, please don't," she begged. "You have no idea what you've gotten into—what he's capable of. It was only because my totem allows me to negate his power, to melt the gilded prison of time, that I was able to save you before. But there's so much I still don't know—so much they won't tell me. I don't know if I can save you again." She shrank away, her chin trembling. "I'm so sorry. I shouldn't have gotten you involved."

Grabbing one of her hands, I pressed it against my chest firmly. "Stop that, Madeline. It's not your responsibility to save me. You're my friend. We should be fighting this together. So tell me what your dad is after and how we can beat him."

"We can't," she answered in a fading, broken voice. "The totems are all balanced so that no one can overpower another. Their abilities cancel one another out—except for the Scepter of Time. It was created first, and its power is far greater than any of the elements of chaos. Only the combined power of all four of the other totem scales can suppress it. You need them all. Alone, you and Oceana will not be enough."

"Elements of chaos?" I frowned. "What does that mean?"

She shook her head, cringing as though she were too afraid to say anything more.

"And what about you? Are you going to fight for him?"

Tears rolled down her flushed cheeks as she met my gaze. "I can't choose. He's my father, Koji. He's all I have in the world. I can't just leave him. You can't ask me to choose between him and—"

A sudden screeching, booming, teeth-rattling roar ripped through the air like a crack of thunder or the roar of a beast. Only, it wasn't either of those things. This was a sound I knew all too well.

Leaning out from under the archway, I spotted the silhouettes of four F-22 fighter jets flying low toward the horizon.

"What was that?" Madeline whispered.

I'd seen this kind of display before because it got used whenever there was a terrorist attack or a threat to American safety. The president was daring Noxius and Oceana to appear again. It couldn't have come at a worse time. "A show of force," I said. "Apparently the president is tossing down the gauntlet."

Madeline gripped the front of my shirt. "Please, you have to take everyone and go, right now," she begged. "Even if I fought with you, we don't have the earth totem. My father has been searching desperately for it for years. It's the only one that is still unaccounted for. Without it, we have already lost."

I whirled around. "No! I refuse to accept that."

"Koji—"

"If there's one thing you need to know about me, it's that I do *not* run from a fight. Not now, not ever. And if your dad wants to hurt anyone in this city, he's going to have to get through me to do it."

Madeline's expression hardened. Her brow furrowed and her eyes blazed with fiery anger as she reached up and seized my face in her hands. She yanked me down and kissed me right on the mouth.

"You are such an idiot, Koji Owens," she growled against my lips.

"Takes one to know one." I grabbed her by the arms and dragged her in closer so I could kiss her back. I couldn't explain it. It just felt right. And it was over far too soon.

Madeline slipped away with a strange, sad smile. "Old rivalries die hard," she said, turning away. "And some hatred runs too deep to be easily forgotten."

"What?" I called after her. But she was gone.

I stood in bewilderment, my lips still ablaze from her kiss and my mind completely boggled. What old rivalries? What did that have to do with anything?

Oh. Crap. She'd just given me the answer.

I knew what Headmaster Ignatius was going to do.

"Hello?" Drake finally answered the fifth time I called him. He sounded out of breath. Weird, since he was supposed to be at a Robotics Club meeting.

"Drake, we've got a big problem. I need your help. Where are you?" I tried to keep my voice down as I took a seat on the subway near the back of the car.

"I'm—"

"Who is it, Drakey?" a female voice whined in the background. "Is that that sneakers guy you always hang out with?"

Okay, that did *not* sound like Robotics Club. And did Tabitha seriously not know my name?

"Are you with Tabitha again?" I rubbed my eyes to get the image of them making out in the classroom out of my head. Yuck. "Never mind, don't answer that. I don't want to know."

"You mentioned a problem?" Drake mumbled like he was embarrassed.

"Yeah. It's Ignatius. I know what he's after and where he's going to strike next." I glanced down at my phone's screen for a quick second. "It's almost five now. We've got two hours until things get messy."

Drake's tone had gone serious. "What do you want me to do?"

"I want you to tip off the FBI. Tell them something's going down at the New York Philharmonic-Symphony Orchestra's gala tonight."

"What?" He panicked. "Seriously?"

"Then I want you to send a message directly to the president. Can you do that?"

The line crackled like Drake had dropped the phone. "I think so. Yeah. Maybe. I'll try. Could take me a few minutes."

"He needs to know that Oceana and Noxius are coming. We're going to be the only thing standing between Ignatius and the public execution of the entire Camridore-Faust family. If he tries to send in troops or air support, tell him not to fire on us. We're not the enemy," I said. "You can give him that message, right?"

"Shut up, I got this," he retorted. I could already hear the sounds of fingers clattering loudly on a computer keyboard in the background. "Einstein, remember?"

"Good. I've got to get ready. Once you get them the message, find your mom and get to a safe place."

"What about your dad?"

"I'll handle that."

"Hey, Koji?"

"Yeah?"

"You sound freaking awesome, you know that, right?"

I smirked and hung up.

Dad was walking in the door from work when I barreled down the stairs, dressed for the gala. I'd quickly ironed the only suit and tie I owned. It was snug across the shoulders, and it wasn't quite as spiffy looking as a tuxedo, but it would do. I didn't expect to be wearing it long, anyway.

"Going somewhere?" Dad glanced me over while he took off his coat.

This was it. The moment I'd been dreading since first grade when a freckly girl called me cute during the parachute game in PE.

I had to tell my dad I was going on a real, actual date.

Okay, so it wasn't *technically* a date. But in order to dispel his suspicions about why I was sweating bullets right now, that was the excuse I was going with. Him believing I had pre-date jitters was preferable to him finding out I was marching into battle against my archenemy.

I guess having an archenemy made me a legitimate superhero now. Awesome.

"I, uh, I've got a date tonight," I explained as I stole one last glance in the hall mirror and straightened my tie. "If that's okay, I mean."

It was hard not to take my dad's look of genuine surprise personally. Yes, it was shocking that I—Koji the Super Nerd—had a date.

"Yeah. That's fine," he replied. Then I saw him grin. "So, are you going to plant the flag?"

Until that moment, I hadn't even thought about it. It made me smile in spite of myself. "Nah. Not this time."

"Why not, son?"

I tried to think of how to explain it, but the words didn't come easy. Claire and Madeline couldn't have been more different. As much as I had liked Claire, part of me understood she had always been out of reach. It had nothing to do with money or social status, or even her feelings for Noxius. She wasn't the one.

Madeline was different. She'd grown to be my friend and someone I felt I could trust. She'd known I was Noxius all along, but it didn't seem like that was the reason she wanted to be around me. It was hard to tell what her motives were. All I did know for certain was that being with her, painting with her, and talking to her, and even kissing her under that archway had felt right. Being with Madeline was like coming home.

"Dad?" I looked at him squarely. "How did you know Mom was the one?"

His expression slackened as though I'd caught him off guard. "I didn't have to try to impress her by pretending to be something I wasn't, or like things I didn't like. She had this way of always putting my mind at ease. I could be myself with her, and I knew that wouldn't change the way she felt about me."

"Oh."

"Basically, I knew your mother didn't like me in spite of my quirks—she liked me more because of them," he said. "If that makes sense."

I sighed deeply. It did make sense. It was like all the winds of worry and uncertainty rushed out of me at once. "That's why, Dad. I'm waiting for that, too."

I grabbed my coat and started for the door. Before I opened it, I looked back to smile at him.

Dad grinned. I could have sworn his eyes were a little misty. "I'm proud of you, Koji. Be safe tonight. You saw those jets fly over this afternoon, didn't you? It's been quiet lately, but we can't be too careful. And be back by eleven, okay?"

"Right. See you at eleven." I was about to leave. My hand twisted the knob.

It hit me like a semi truck. Guilt. Terror. Doubt clamped down over my throat and paralyzed me. How could I not tell him? I should tell him what I was, what was about to happen, and warn him to leave with Drake and Ms. Collins. If something happened, if I didn't make it back, he should know the real reason why.

My only consolation was that the Philharmonic was far enough away from our house that he might not be in any immediate danger when everything went down. That is, unless he knew I was there on a date. Then he would most definitely come charging in to find me.

I couldn't let that happen. If I couldn't contain whatever Headmaster Ignatius had planned, then I'd insist the local police start evacuating everyone.

"Everything okay?" He sounded concerned.

I bit down hard against everything I wanted to say. "Yeah. Everything's fine," I lied. "We're just going to go get some dinner nearby and take a walk. I won't be far away."

"Okay. You've got some money, right?"

"Yeah."

"Be nice," he warned. "Make eye contact. Hold the doors for her. Pay for her meal. Got it?"

"I know, I know."

He nodded. "Have a good time."

I stepped out into the cold evening air and let the door close behind me. Right on cue, a sleek black SUV pulled up to the curb in front of our house. The rear window rolled down, revealing Claire's smiling face. She waved me over, inviting me to join her.

I took a deep breath.

No turning back now. The wheels were already in motion, Claire was waiting, and the FBI would be there to back Oceana and I up—that is, unless they just decided to shoot at anything with scales.

Either way, there was a storm on the horizon.

And I was about to step into the eye of it.

CHAPTER 24

The New York Philharmonic building, with its tall glass windows, bathed the front courtyard and fountain in golden light for the event. Men in black suits escorted ladies wearing glittering cocktail dresses or long silk gowns up the front steps. Flocks of paparazzi gathered around a velvet-carpet pathway that led inside, their cameras blinking in the night. Ahead of us, celebrities and famous musicians filed past the flashing cameras, occasionally pausing to pose, smile, or talk to a reporter standing on the sidelines. Some even signed autographs.

I escorted Claire, surprised that having her touching me didn't make my heart race even though she was stunning as always. She walked beside me, her strides as elegant as they were effortless. With her head held high and her silver sequin dress trailing behind her, she shone like something from another world.

I, on the other hand, felt like I was going to throw up. It took all my mental faculties not to trip over my own feet and drag her down with me, face-first into that red carpet. She'd made this sound so nonchalant, like just some family barbecue her parents had tossed together for charity. Now I was standing next to Grammy and Academy Award winners.

When we finally reached the front door, I leaned in to whisper to her, "You said this was nothing fancy."

Claire winked and gave a coy little shrug.

Maybe it wasn't for her. I might have been upset at being painfully underdressed if I hadn't been too busy gawking at everything. Inside the building, more famous guests grouped together talking amongst themselves, snapping photos, or being interviewed. I swallowed hard. What was I even doing here?

Suddenly, one of the press interviewers stepped into our path and shoved a microphone toward Claire. "Miss Faust, can we expect a performance from you tonight?"

I jerked back in surprise.

Claire didn't even blink. Maintaining a gentle, ethereal smile, she replied, "I'm not at liberty to say. This year, my parents decided to keep the performances of all the participating artists a surprise for their guests."

"And who is this young man escorting you this evening? Is it true you're engaged to the Blount Pharmaceuticals Corporation heir, Damien Blount? Where is he tonight? How do you feel about the media's treatment of the vigilante Noxius after recently being rescued by him? Do you have any idea who he really is?" The interviewer pressed in, asking more questions than I could keep track of.

I glanced at Claire. The mention of Damien's absence and her encounter with Noxius must have hit a kink in her paparazzi-proof armor. Her smile began to fade, her soft blue-green eyes clouding over with disappointment.

"That's enough for tonight. We should be getting to our seats," I interrupted as I muscled my way between them. The interviewer tried to shout around me to get one last answer. I made sure she didn't get one.

"Thank you," Claire said weakly as I steered her over to a quieter corner of the room.

"No problem. One good thing about being a nobody is I don't have to care what anyone else thinks, right?" I gave her a confident smile.

"Koji, you're not a nobody." Her expression drooped some, her lovely doe eyes drifting down toward the floor as though there were more she wanted to say.

I almost asked. She hadn't seemed all that happy since the appearance of that giant rock on her finger. I would have thought she'd be thrilled. Her future was set, right? She already had a career, a family legacy, money, and now a husband-to-be. Was there anything she wanted she couldn't buy or use her family connections to get?

"There you are, Claire." Another woman approached us, although she didn't look like a member of the press. She was tall and thin, wearing a formal black gown and a string of shining pearls around her neck. The pale aqua color of her eyes and delicate rosy flush of her porcelain cheeks reminded me of someone.

"Hi, Mother." Claire stepped out to embrace her. "Where's Father?"

"Oh, you know how he is at these things." The woman laughed softly. "This is his opportunity to schmooze and show off. He'd never pass that up."

Suddenly, her piercing gaze fixed squarely on me. "And who is this?"

"Mother, this is Koji Owens." She took my arm. "He took me to the Winter Ball, remember?"

"Ah, yes. My goodness, Claire. If he keeps stepping in to pick up Damien's slack, we're going to have to put him on the payroll." There was a frosty, cutting edge to Mrs. Faust's tone, almost like she was testing me somehow.

"I dunno if you can afford me." I tried to laugh it off.

Mrs. Faust narrowed her eyes ever so slightly. "Charming. Tell me, Mr. Owens, do you play any instruments?"

The question sounded like an insult—like she knew the answer already and this was her subtle way of reminding me of where I stood in the social pecking order here. There were two little problems with that attempt. First, I didn't actually care where I stood, and second, I didn't scare easy.

"I play a mean kazoo," I replied.

Beside me, Claire coughed and covered her mouth to hide a giggle.

Mrs. Faust's probing smile faded a bit. "I see," she said dryly. "Well, I should go find your father." Her eyes flickered dangerously in Claire's direction, like an unspoken warning, before she went gliding away in her high heels.

"I'm so sorry about that, Koji," Claire murmured as we started for the concert hall.

"Don't worry about it. She's just being protective. I can't say that I blame her. Here I am, taking you out for the second time while your fiancé plays hooky. And now that she's seen how unwittingly charming and handsome I am, it's only natural she'd be worried I might steal you away from him." I grinned and pretended to straighten my tie.

Claire giggled again and rolled her eyes. "Oh yes. I can hardly resist."

"But I'm not the one she should be worried about, am I?"

She froze for a second, and her face paled slightly as her eyes went wide. She looked away immediately, like she was too ashamed to meet my gaze.

"There's that look again. You always make that face when someone mentions Noxius."

"I know." Her voice was barely more than a whisper. "I've tried forgetting about him. It's stupid to think anything could ever happen between us. I don't even know who he really is."

I edged a bit closer. She wanted to know, and part of me wanted to tell her. Even if I didn't see her that way anymore, I wondered how she would react. Would she be shocked? Disappointed? Or would her perception of me—regular, normal Koji—change as well?

"What is it about him, Claire?" I asked.

Her gaze held mine, and something about that guarded, almost frightened expression on her face struck a chord in my brain. I'd seen that look before, hadn't I? Maybe it was just a recollection of our awkward encounter in the elevator.

Claire bowed her head and refused to answer.

"What if, in real life, he's not who you expect? What if he's an even bigger nobody than I am?"

"That doesn't matter to me, Koji." She snapped a glare up at me, defiance blazing in her eyes. "I don't care who he is. He could be the school janitor and it wouldn't make any difference—I'd love him just the same!"

My jaw dropped. What? Love? She *loved* Noxius?

I struggled to keep my reactions under control. But hearing her say that made my pulse clash in my ears and my blood run hot as the fires of anger stoked to life deep in my chest.

Especially since my third eye verified she was telling the truth.

Because who Noxius was *did* matter. He was standing right in front of her, had been for months, and she couldn't even see it. She didn't love me. She only loved what the totem made me.

Did that even count?

A shrill scream tore through the Philharmonic lobby. For a few seconds, everyone went quiet, looking for the cause. Quiet murmurs rippled across the crowd. The camera flashes stopped.

Suddenly, I smelled it—something was burning. Black smoke poured from the concert hall doors into the lobby. Claire gasped and gripped my arm.

It was instant chaos. The building fire alarms buzzed, and more screams broke out as everyone began running to escape out the front entrance. Overhead, the interior sprinkler systems activated and dumped cold water over the crowds pushing to get out.

I seized Claire's hand and rushed for the doorway too. Behind us, fire roared through the building. It moved strangely, hesitating and surging almost as though it were a living thing set on herding the scattered guests out of the building.

Not that the outside was any safer. Claire screamed as a wall of flames rose up like a tidal wave, surrounding the Philharmonic grounds and cutting us off from all sides. There was no way out.

The frightened crowd of gala guests panicked in their fiery cage. I tried to protect Claire from the worst of it as everyone pushed and shoved, looking for a way out. There wasn't one. We got squeezed to the edge of the group. A sudden gasp went up from the crowd, and Claire squeezed my hand tightly, a look of terror in her eyes.

At the edge of the fountain, about twenty feet from us, a man in a pristinely tailored suit leaned against a cane. Behind him, crouching on the edge of the fountain, a familiar red-and-yellow dragon-girl stared out at the crowd, her eyes glowing in the night like smoldering coals. My heart wrenched in my chest, leaving me breathless.

Madeline?

Red-hot tongues of fire licked off her hands as she stood, her wings unfurling. A rumbling snarl from her lips made flames crackle over her pointed fangs. Several people in the crowd around us cried out, their horrified screams splitting the night air. The crowd drew back at the sight of her, leaving Claire and I exposed.

I set my jaw. Why was she doing this? Was she really going to help her dad kill people? On my wrist, I felt the weight of my totem scale like an anchor.

Madeline's head snapped in my direction. For an instant, our eyes met through the turmoil. She saw me holding Claire's hand. Her expression skewed, flashing between shock, pain, and pure rage in a matter of seconds. Her hands clenched, making the flames crackling around her hands burn white-hot and surge up to her forearms.

"Where are you, James? Come on out. We have urgent business to settle," Headmaster Ignatius called across his captive audience. He raised his head slowly, a wicked smirk curled over his lips. "It's long overdue, wouldn't you say? Maybe you thought I'd forgotten after all these years."

I held my breath. Seconds ticked by like an eternity. Beside me, Claire stood frozen as though holding her breath.

Then one man stepped forward from the rest of the crowd. He had a tall, stoic-looking frame and a short, salt-and-pepper colored beard trimmed neatly along his jaw. He held his head up proudly as he stood in front of Ignatius with a disapproving scowl. "Gerard, what is this? What have you done?"

"What have *I* done?" Ignatius shouted, his body jerking and face flashing scarlet. Behind him, Madeline hissed, lashing her long tail as she flared her wings. A wave of heat rolled off her body, hitting me like a blast from a furnace.

I let go of Claire's hand and slipped a hand under my shirt-sleeve to touch my totem scale. I just needed a chance, a good place out of sight, and a second to transform.

With his chest still heaving with manic, panting breaths, Ignatius stood straight again. He gripped his cane so hard his knuckles blanched, and a vein stood out against the side of his neck. "An interesting question from you," he seethed. "You took something precious from me. You owe me a debt, James. You owe us both. So now I've come to collect—with interest. Fyurei, bring him to me!"

He raised his cane, and I felt every hair on my body prickle at the sudden swell of power humming in the air. Madeline swooped forward with a piercing roar, sending a wave of horrified screams through the crowd. In an instant, she snatched Mr. Faust off the ground by his neck and dropped him at her father's feet.

"*No!*" Claire screamed. She broke away, her hand wrenching out of mine as she ran toward her parents.

All eyes were on Ignatius, Mr. Faust, and Madeline.

This was it—my chance.

I slipped to the back of the throng of panicked guests and ducked behind one of the big cement columns at the front of the building. Secluded? No. Out of sight? Sort of. Would it work? Crap, I hoped so.

I clapped a hand over my totem scale and bade it to awaken. A chilling rush of wind and flash of light called forth my element in an instant. Black scales masked my face and climbed my limbs. Wings flexed from my back as my entire body reeled, primal power unfolding with a thundering roar.

I emerged from my pathetic hiding place as Noxius. With one beat of my wings, I rocketed over the panicked horde. I landed between Ignatius and Claire an instant before she reached him, lightning sizzling over the spines along my back.

"Fancy meeting you here." I gave them all a toothy, dragon smile.

Headmaster Ignatius seethed. "Stupid, foolish, meddling boy! You should have known better than to challenge me alone again. I will not be so merciful this time. Fyurei, bring him down!"

I grinned wider. "What makes you think I came alone?"

Right on cue, the signature *thump-thump-thump* of helicopter wings filled the air with a wild burst of wind. My cavalry arrived in the form of one Blackhawk and two Apache helicopters—courtesy of the president of the United States. I'd have to send him a thank you fruit basket. Well, as long as they didn't shoot at me, too.

The choppers circled, and a voice over a loud speaker commanded Gerard Ignatius to release his hostages and surrender immediately.

As if it would be that easy.

"I surrender to no one," Ignatius sneered and raised his cane again. The round end that held the totem scale began to glow. My body jerked, flooded with adrenaline and panic at the sight. I could sense that raw power swelling in the air, just as it had before he turned me into gold.

I didn't stick around to get a front row seat to whatever he was about to do. Whirling around, I grabbed Claire by the waist and took off for the Metropolitan Opera next door. Lucky for us, that building wasn't on fire, too.

I put her down on the roof and started to go back.

Suddenly, she grabbed my big, scaly hand. "Noxius," she pleaded. "Both my parents are down there. Please, you have to save them!"

I gently brushed her hand off. "I will. You stay here where I know you'll be safe. Understand?"

"Y-yes." She nodded.

I could feel the lie like a thorn in my mind. She had no intention of staying there. There wasn't time to worry about it now, though.

Below, Ignatius used the head of his staff to draw a glowing golden circle in the air. It burned brighter, pooling light in the center like a floating mirror in the air. The earth shuddered under the force of it, rumbling as though it might shake every building in New York apart.

An enormous, scaly, snarling head emerged through the circle as though it were a portal to some other world.

My heart dropped. Oh no. Not this again.

Six snakelike eyes peered around at us, each one as big as a beach ball. Four huge nostrils flared, drinking in the cold New York air. The beast snapped its insect-like mandibles and stuck the rest of its long neck through the gateway. Then came a foot, then a leg. More and more of the monster squeezed through the portal and stepped into the middle of Manhattan.

"I'm getting rather good at this!" Ignatius let out a maniacal laugh. The crowd before him scattered like mice, trying to find anywhere they could to escape within the confines of the fiery walls Madeline had kindled around the Philharmonic.

I cursed under my breath.

I'd seen a beast like that in some of my old fantasy books. It was a wyvern—a dragon with two leathery wings instead of arms and a long tail tipped in jagged spikes. That wouldn't have been an issue…except that it was colossal. It was pound for pound as huge as the crocodilian creature had been. The beast broke the fountain in the center of the courtyard with one stomp of its foot. I watched in horror as it spread its humongous wings and took to the air, sending up gusts that sent the military helicopters scattering for cover.

Their retreat was only temporary, though. I watched the choppers immediately regroup and begin pursuing the creature into the sky. They opened fire with every piece of artillery they had. Cool as that was, I doubted guns would do much except distract the creature.

Luckily, a distraction is exactly what I needed.

I dove off the rooftop and hit the air at turbo speed, charging straight for Ignatius. I braced for impact, ready to hit him as hard as possible and hopefully knock that cursed scepter out of his grasp.

Something else hit me first.

Fyurei struck hard, knocking us both through the front glass windows of the City Ballet Theater on the other side of the courtyard. We flew through the lobby, snatching chandeliers off the ceiling and cracking the marble floor as we landed in a brawl. She tried to get her hands around my neck. Her expression had gone utterly feral, and the heat of her presence made my eyes water.

I'd never hit a girl before, but there's a first time for everything. After all, she started it. I reared back a fist back and let her have it.

One hard sock to the face, right across the cheek, sent her rolling off me. I jumped up and flared my wings, showing her a snarl with all my spines and claws bristled for combat. "Back off," I thundered. "I don't want to fight you! It doesn't have to end this way!"

"Doesn't it?" she hissed back. "I saw you with her. You manipulated me. You used me, just like Father said you would. You made me believe you cared—just so you could get closer to her. Just so you could make yourself out to be a hero!"

She spread her own arms wide, summoning a burst of fire that rolled off her and threatened to scorch me to ash.

I crossed my arms and braced for impact, drawing on my own element to deflect her attack with a blast of wind.

"No! I don't feel that way about her anymore. I don't know if I ever did," I roared. "But if I have to stand at her side to protect innocent people from your dad's insanity, then so be it! How can you fight for him? Look what he's doing! He's trying to murder people, Madeline!"

She surged toward me again with flames crackling along her talons. I met her in the air, our powers colliding with a shockwave that blew out every piece of glass in the building and threw us in opposite directions.

My head swam from the impact as I staggered to my feet again.

Fyurei was already up and prowling in my direction. Before she could get up to retaliate, an oddly familiar sphere of water doused her and snuffed her flames.

Oceana landed beside me with a proud smirk.

"Don't look at me like that," I snorted. "You're the one who's late."

"It's not like you sent me an invitation. Besides, I had a bit of a mess outside to clean up first. In case you hadn't noticed, the whole block *was* aflame." She narrowed her golden eyes at Fyurei. "I assume that's her doing?"

My growl would have to be answer enough. Fyurei was back on her feet, her clenched fists crackling with flame. The sight of the two of us, standing together ready to fight, made her whole form ignite like a living torch. She shrieked and took off out of the theater like a fiery comet.

"You go after her," Oceana ordered as she crouched for takeoff. "I'll take care of that madman with the fancy stick."

I seized her wing before she could leave. "Be careful. You can't let him touch you with it."

She scowled and snatched her wing away. "Why?"

"There's no time to explain it now. Just trust me. Attack him, do whatever you can to stop him and save the Fausts, but don't let him touch you with that cane!"

CHAPTER 25

Fyurei was fast.

But I was faster.

She zipped through the city, barely fifty feet off the ground. Any lower and we'd be dodging streetlights. She cornered sharply around buildings and zoomed down avenues, sending civilians scattering in terror. All around us, the city blazed with combat.

I knew the sound of jet engines roaring in the night. I'd heard that sound my entire life. I could even tell the difference between some of them. Without even a glimpse, I knew there were at least four of them making tactical attack passes, engaging the humongous wyvern flying overhead.

"Madeline, stop!" I yelled at the top of my lungs. I doubted anyone else would hear me using her real name in this madness, but maybe she would.

She did.

Without warning, Fyurei whipped into a quick somersault flip, changing direction in midair to charge me head on. I didn't back down. With the winds at my back and the skies sizzling with my power, I collided with her in the air. The impact sent out a blast of fire and lightning that blew out the sides of the buildings around us and left lampposts smoking like burnt up matchsticks.

We wrestled in the air, clawing and kicking, until at last I got a lucky shot in to her jaw. Her head snapped back and I saw her expression go blank, as though she were dazed. Before she could regain her senses, I grabbed her shoulders and bore her down to the ground, smashing us both into the middle of the street with a primal yell.

I pinned her there as she kicked and fought. Cars swerved around us, horns blaring as she screeched and unleashed wave after wave of heat that seared at my scaly hide and blazed over my wings. Every nerve in my body screamed in agony, begging me to pull away.

I wasn't about to let her go until she knew the truth.

"Do it! Burn me alive!" I yelled down at her as she pitched and flailed against me. "Kill me if it makes you feel better! I'll die saying the same thing: *I didn't use you!*"

She screamed and pressed a clawed hand glowing with white-hot heat against the center of my chest. It burned like a branding iron.

I couldn't breathe. My body spasmed and my vision tunneled and blurred. I couldn't think. I couldn't even scream. The pain was too much.

Then the pressure on my chest was gone. But the damage was done.

Through the agony of the burn, I met her gaze. The heat rolling off her body rippled the air. She jerked her hand back, her expression stricken with shock and terror.

"I wouldn't...do that to you, M-Madeline," I slurred. "You know I wouldn't. I-I would never hurt... someone I love."

Something snapped in my brain, as though all the wiring had been cut. Suddenly, I couldn't feel the pain of Madeline's heat anymore. My vision went dark and my body went slack. I fell forward into something soft. Warm arms squeezed around me and I heard the broken, rasping breaths of someone sobbing against my ear. Madeline?

"I'm so sorry, Koji," she cried. "You'll be okay. Everything will be fine now, I promise. I'm going to fix it. Just please hang on. Please don't leave me."

I felt the cold of the pavement as Madeline gently laid me down. Her frantic, weeping breaths moved further away as her heavy footsteps retreated, lost to the roar of the battle in the sky.

I reached for her shakily, but it was too late. My arm dropped back to the ground. Lying on my back in the middle of the street, all I could do was listen to the mayhem around me—gunfire popping, the thumping of the chopper rotors, the screech and roar of jet engines, the wyvern bellowing in rage, sirens in the city streets.

I closed my eyes and let the noise wash over me. Was I giving up? Or was I just dying? I couldn't even tell the difference. Fear crept in, rising higher and higher. I was scared—drowning in the chaos.

Koji, my sweet boy. It's okay.

The sound of Mom's voice echoed through every corner of my mind like a tolling bell. Adrenaline poured into my body. My muscles went solid, tingling back to life. My eyes popped open, focusing on the night sky. Overhead, my storm clouds still rumbled, flashing and sizzling with bolts of lightning.

Don't be scared. You're going to be okay. Mommy loves you.

I sucked in a deep breath. The sensation of raw pain from the burn on my chest rocked me to the core. Fury-like chaos roared through my veins. I yelled in agony—and in relief. I could feel it again.

I was down but not out. This fight wasn't over.

My wings flopped limply at my sides as I forced myself to roll over and get on my hands and knees. Up. I had to get up. Right now.

I dragged myself to my feet and flexed my chest, arms, and back. My powerful wings snapped open, sending out a burst of wind that flattened nearby parking meters.

There was only one objective on my mind now. I would end this, whatever the cost.

I pressed my hand against the totem scale on my wrist and whispered, "I offer my soul to the power of the kur."

Piercing light bloomed from the totem scale. It swept over me and took away my pain, molding and stretching me into my full dragon form. The instant the searing energy coursed through my body, I launched myself into the sky.

I didn't have a single second to waste.

Now that I was a beast of comparable size, I crested the skyscrapers in a few powerful beats of my wings. From a few blocks away, the wyvern spotted me. It let out a howl of fury as it surged straight for me. I answered with a battle cry of my own, driving more and more power into every beat of my mighty black wings.

Two F-22 fighter jets rolled in on either side, joining me in aerial formation. Their engines roared, and both pilots gave me a confirming thumbs-up. They were following me in for the attack.

I'd never felt so cool in my entire life.

I clashed with the wyvern in the air over Central Park, clamping my jaws around his throat. I prepared to give him a taste of my lightning, the same way I had the crocodile monster. One good jolt and maybe I could bring him down.

Before I get a good grip, he swung his spiked tail and whacked me across the eyes. I let go, snatching back with a roar of pain.

He dove at me, his toothy mandibles open wide to rip my throat out.

A sudden plume of fire scorched his hide and sent him reeling. I drew back, wary of the blistering flames.

Another giant dragon joined the battle, scales as red as fresh blood and a ridge of tall, slender black spines bristling all the way down her back. My breath caught. Madeline? She'd gone full-form, too?

She attacked the wyvern mercilessly, pinning him under another blast of her fiery breath.

Shaking off the blow to my head, I charged headlong back into the fight, lightning sizzling and popping off my open jaws. We had to get him on the ground. If we could pin him there, he'd be within range of ground fire and an easier target for our air support. We could contain the damage to the rest of the city, too.

So I went for one of the wyvern's wings full-force.

Fyurei had him distracted. He never saw me coming. I swooped in and broke one of his wings at the shoulder with a single powerful crunch of my jaws and sharp jerk of my head. The creature screeched and kicked, floundering with his one good wing and swinging his tail like a medieval mace. The bulbous, spiky tip struck one of the F-22 jets and sent the air-craft flipping through the air end over end. Not good. I watched the aircraft fall, waiting for the pilot to eject.

He didn't.

I didn't hesitate—I dove straight after the jet, summoning every bit of speed I had. The jet spiraled, smoking and streaking toward the ground. I threw myself the final distance with a des-perate cry, jaws open wide.

I caught the tail of the jet in my teeth about a hundred feet shy of the ground. As soon as my jaws clamped onto the metal, I reared back, kicked my legs out, and flared for an emergency landing right in the middle of the park.

It took a second for the dust, snow, and trees to settle.

Picking the jet carefully out of my mouth, I held it up to my huge dragon eyeball like a little kid's toy. Inside the cockpit, the tiny pilot was giving me a shaky thumbs-up. He was okay.

I gave him my best dragon smile, terrifying as it probably was, and placed his jet, right side up, on a grassy spot in the park. Then I turned around to get back to business. I still had some wyvern rear end to roast and an evil headmaster in dire need of reeducation.

I charged forward, senses primed and nerves steeled for round two. My pulse roared in my ears, supercharged by the power thrumming through my body. With my wings open for flight, I leapt into the night sky—

And that's when my four minutes were up.

This was not going as planned.

Frankly, that could be the title of my autobiography. Or at the very least, I needed to consider a title change for my comic book art journal. *This Went Way Better in My Head: The Koji Owens Story.*

As my face met the frozen grass of Central Park, the power of my totem blinked and waned. Crap. Because of last time, I knew I only had about a minute in my dragon form before I would be regular Koji again.

What could I do now?

Spitting out rocks and dirt, I stood and turned in the direction of the explosions rocking the night sky right over the Philharmonic building. Overhead, Madeline scorched the wyvern's side with another stream of fire, and F-22s did passing strafes, bombarding him with artillery. They had him on the run—so my remaining seconds had to be spent on our final problem: Ignatius.

Hurling myself into the sky, I managed a clumsy flight to a clump of trees right next to the Philharmonic building. I flared for landing just as the last bit of my elemental power slipped away. I dropped the last few feet out of the sky and hit the ground like a rock, bouncing off a few tree limbs on the way down.

Rolling over, I hauled myself back up to my feet. I had to hurry. Every second had to count.

I staggered toward the courtyard and into the glare of a helicopter's spotlight. The Blackhawk circled Ignatius and Oceana's battle as they squared off. She stood between the insane headmaster and the Fausts, lip curled in a defiant snarl. Everyone else had gone, escaping into the night after Fyurei's fiery walls had been doused by Oceana's arrival.

Huddled beneath a dome of Oceana's water, Mr. and Mrs. Faust were safe for the moment. But for an old guy with a cane, Ignatius wasn't making this easy. He brandished his totem, spinning his cane and sending out bursts of golden light like comets in the night. Whatever the blasts struck froze, turned to solid gold.

Oceana dipped and dodged, evading some of his assaults and throwing up bursts of water from the fountain to deflect others. With her golden eyes flickering and her teeth bared, she swished her long tail and coiled her powerful legs. "Is that the best you can do?" she hissed.

"Hardly." Ignatius snickered, raising his glowing totem skyward. I knew where this was going. He was about to open up another portal.

Enter me: the barely conscious idiot with a death wish, dragging the dead weight of my limp wings behind me. I figured I had about five seconds before Ignatius realized I was there. So I took a deep breath and ran like a maniac, jumping over the crumbled remains of the fountain and landing right on top of him.

The impact knocked both of us to the ground and we went rolling across the cement in different directions—me toward Oceana, and him toward the fountain. It also sent his cane clattering across the courtyard.

We sat up at the same time, blinking at one another in a daze.

My gaze snapped toward the cane. I had to get to it first!

Ignatius was closer and had already started crawling for it, cursing under his breath. But his crippled leg put him at a disadvantage. Oceana didn't wait for my cue. She leaped into the air and dove for it. I had no chance of getting there first in my weakened state, but I wasn't about to give up and stumbled to my feet, lurching forward.

Oceana snagged the cane an instant before Ignatius's stretching fingertips could brush it. But as her scaly hand closed around it, her triumphant smile seized into a grimace of pain. Her agonized scream tore through me like a bullet to the brain, the pitch getting higher and higher until Ignatius, laughing, snatched the cane from her frozen grasp.

She collapsed, wheezing and cradling her hand.

"Fools." Ignatius laughed as he grasped the cane in both hands with a triumphant sneer. "Wielders of the elemental totems cannot touch the totem of time without experiencing unspeakable pain. A clever trick, isn't it? Intended to keep any one of you from becoming too powerful since this totem chooses no wielder."

He shuffled closer to stand over me, whipping his cane into a flourishing spin. I stiffened, my breath catching as he pointed it right at me, the tip mere inches from my nose. A cold pang of fear shot through my body. One touch was all it would take.

"Any final words before I dispense with you, boy? And don't worry, this time I'll make sure your fate is much more… final." He smiled triumphantly.

I glared up at him, curling my lip into a defiant snarl. "Just one," I said with a hoarse, growling laugh. "*Duck!*" With the last of my energy, I threw myself into a desperate leap—away from Ignatius.

Fyurei and the wyvern hurtled through the air like a firework and smashed into Ignatius. I dropped into a frantic roll, avoiding being reduced to a charred skid mark on the cement. Golden light bloomed around us, flashing like the birth of a star as the wyvern vanished.

I cringed and shielded my eyes, but my heart hit the back of my throat. Madeline had done it! She'd killed that thing!

As soon as the light dissipated, I lowered my hand. My teeth clenched and panic sent chills down my spine. Oh God.

Before me, Madeline and her father lay sprawled a few feet apart at the bottom of a crater left by the wyvern's crash landing. She was back in her human form, and Ignatius had let go of the cane again.

Neither of them was moving.

"No! Madeline!" I shouted as I climbed, tripped, skidded— basically fell—to the bottom of the crater. After kicking that stupid cane as far away as possible, I dropped to my knees beside Madeline. My hands shook as I carefully rolled her onto her back. Her eyelids fluttered, soft gray eyes staring foggily up at me.

I scooped her up and held her close against my scaly chest. It hurt. The mark she'd left with her incinerating touch was still raw and smoking. I wasn't sure how that would translate to my human body. But right then, I didn't care. She was alive. That's all that mattered.

"Madeline?" I rasped. She was battered, bruised, and bleeding from cuts and small wounds all over her body.

"Did anyone see me transform?" she whispered weakly.

"No." I swept my clawed fingers gently over her brow, brushed her hair away from where it had gotten stuck in the blood from a gash on her forehead.

"My father, is he…?"

I flicked a quick glare down at him. His chest moved up and down as he breathed. "Alive."

The corners of her mouth pulled weakly at a smile. "And you?"

"Am seriously pissed that you think I'd go straight from kissing you to chasing someone else," I growled softly as I leaned down to press my lips against her forehead.

She raised her hand to touch the black scales on my cheek. "Stay strong, my Noxius," Madeline whispered. "My Koji."

Wait, why did that sound like goodbye?

Madeline went still. Her head lolled against my shoulder. I shook her slightly, called her name. She didn't answer.

God, no. She couldn't be dead. I could *not* lose her.

The last of my power melted away before I managed to I crawl out of that hole with her in my arms. My human body was much more fragile, reeling from all the blows I'd taken and drained because of using my full dragon form. As I put Madeline down in the rubble of the Philharmonic courtyard, I crumpled to my knees. My vision swerved and spotted. I couldn't help her. I couldn't even hide myself. Someone would see—they'd figure out who I was.

Suddenly, a strong arm wrapped around my torso and hoisted me to my feet again.

"Have you completely lost your mind?" Oceana chastened with a fierce scowl. "Get out of here before someone else sees you."

"But she's—"

"I know what she is," Oceana warned. "I'll look after her. Just go—*now!*"

CHAPTER 26

I awoke to the soft beep of a heart monitor keeping pace with my pulse. I knew that sharp, excessively sanitary hospital smell as soon as I breathed it in—even before I felt the crunchy, starchy sheets around me. Everything hurt— my arms, my legs, but especially my chest. Opening my eyes, I squinted into the dim fluorescent light as my vision swerved in and out of focus. A few hard blinks helped to clear things up.

"Koji!" my dad cried out. He was standing over me, his eyes bloodshot and his chin dusted with several days' worth of stubble.

Yikes. How long had I been out?

"W-where—?" I started to ask, only to find my throat ached like I'd swallowed a mouthful of crushed glass.

Another face appeared above me. Ms. Collins leaned in with a teary, relieved smile. "You're in the hospital, Koji. You're safe."

My dad gripped my hand tightly and stroked my head. "The rescue team working the disaster site found you near Lincoln Center. You've got some bad burns from the fire."

Panic flooded my body. The heart monitor beeped faster. I couldn't remember—after pulling Madeline out of that hole everything blurred. What had happened? How had I gotten here? What about the scepter? And Ignatius? And...

"M-Madeline," I rasped. "Where is she? Is she alive? W-what happened?"

"Shh, Koji, you need to calm down," Ms. Collins crooned.

Dad put a hand on my cheek and steered my gaze to meet his. "It's okay, son. You're safe here. Once the police have asked you some questions, we're going home. There was a lot of damage and people got hurt. They just want to be sure they find the people responsible. Try to rest for now, okay? Everything will be fine."

I didn't need my third eye to tell when he wasn't telling the whole truth. I could see his worry in the tired creases around his eyes and the way he kept checking his watch—like he was waiting for something.

I was scared to find out what.

My free hand moved across the bed to touch the comforting weight of my totem bracelet. Whatever had happened, I'd managed to transform without being seen. It wouldn't be there otherwise, right? And my third eye was working, so I was still Noxius.

For now.

Ms. Collins helped me lie back down and brought me a cup of water. After that, the pain in my throat wasn't quite so bad and I could talk. Still, no one could answer my questions about where Madeline Ignatius or her father was. In fact, it was like no one even knew they had been at Lincoln Center at all. When a doctor in a long white coat came in to see me, he examined my wounds and asked how I felt. He seemed especially curious about how I'd gotten the hand-shaped burn on my chest. Lucky for me, feigning amnesia wasn't that hard when so much of what had happened was a blur.

"Your injuries aren't serious enough that you'll have to stay here more than a day or two," the doctor assured me. "We just have to monitor that burn to make sure there are no signs of infection. After that, you'll be dismissed with instructions to keep the wound clean and make sure you take the antibiotics properly. I'll prescribe some pain medication as well." He nodded, casting Dad and Ms. Collins a parting smile before he slipped out of the room.

The hospital got quiet as night drew in. Only a few night shift nurses roamed the halls, checking in on patients and administering medications. Ms. Collins went home to make sure Drake was doing okay. She promised to bring him to see me in the morning. With the beeping heart monitor gone and dad sitting silently in the chair beside my bed, the silence felt heavy. Dad had hardly left my side all day, but I could tell he was exhausted. He probably hadn't left this room since I was admitted.

"Go home for a little while," I insisted. It took some convincing, but he finally agreed to at least shower, change clothes, and bring us both something better to eat. Besides, I'd be fine for an hour or two.

Once he was gone, I could finally think. Alone in the darkness of my tiny hospital room, I stared out the window at the blinking city lights. I couldn't remember much after Madeline had gone limp in my arms, no matter how hard I focused. Oceana was there—I did remember that. Staring into her glowing golden eyes was the last image I could recall.

I cursed quietly and pushed the button that lowered my bed into the flat, sleeping position. I might as well rest. Maybe that would help my mind recover that lost information.

I'd almost succumbed to my exhaustion and the haze of the medications when I heard the door click open. Light from the hallway spilled inside around the tall shape of a broad-shouldered man.

Ignatius? Had he found me here?

I clenched my teeth against the stretching, burning pain in my chest as I forced myself to sit up. Every muscle in my body tensed at once. I gripped the bed railings, braced and ready for a fight. If he wanted to take me down while I was injured, I wasn't going to go down quietly.

"Relax, Mr. Owens, I'm not here for you," a man's voice said smoothly.

Something about his tone was familiar, but it wasn't until he stepped into the faint moonlight ebbing through the window that I recognized him.

The FBI agent who'd arrested my dad stood before me, wearing the same nondescript black suit and tie. I remembered his face right away from when he and his men had kicked down our front door and later followed Drake and me to the movie theater.

He gazed down at me, his expression cold and calculating— like an eagle trying to decide whether or not to let a mouse live or rip it to shreds. His eyes were pale and cold like arctic water, and his chiseled features weren't any friendlier when set in bold relief by the pale sterling light.

"I see you remember me." He sounded amused, though his face remained serious. "So you were at your home the day your father was detained."

"I've been a lot of places lately," I managed to reply despite the agony from the burn on my chest.

"You're a clever young man. Your teachers describe you as kind but unremarkable. Average. Normal. Your friends, although fiercely loyal, can't disagree with that description."

I narrowed my eyes. "Is there a point to all this besides just insulting me? You're here to arrest me, aren't you? I'm a minor. You can't interrogate me without my dad here."

The agent's thin mouth curled into a smirk. "I doubt you would want your father present when I ask the questions I've come to ask."

He had me there.

I thumbed the incline button on my bed, raising it so I could relax against it. "Okay, then. Ask."

"We've assembled a solid alibi to explain your presence at the Lincoln Center disaster site. As far as you or anyone else at that scene is concerned, you were another innocent civilian victim. You were found by a fire department rescue team twenty yards from the Philharmonic building with burns suggesting you were injured in the initial attack and lost consciousness attempting to flee to safety."

The agent walked slowly to stand at my bedside, the heels of his shoes clicking over the linoleum floor. "That is the truth you will tell if you are asked about what happened by anyone, including the police."

I narrowed my eyes. "You mean…?"

"That's correct, Mr. Owens. As of this morning, the president of the United States has acknowledged that both you and Oceana are important assets to American public safety and have proven yourselves as allies worthy of our trust. While I may not agree with letting two teenagers roam freely while in possession of incredible power from an unknown origin, I must defer to his judgment in this. I am obligated to follow his commands. I hope you'll prove me wrong, but understand that I will be watching you *very* closely, Mr. Owens."

"What about Gerard Ignatius?" I asked. "Where is he?"

"He's been moved to a military medical center for questioning and observation. His injuries are serious—not surprising considering his fragile physical condition prior to his attack at the Philharmonic—but not believed to be fatal. If he is able to regain consciousness and recover, then he will be held accountable."

"He's in a coma?"

The agent nodded. "We are unsure if this is a direct result of the incident or something caused by the artifact. The effects of exposure to those items, such as the one you wear so casually on your wrist, are still unknown."

I clenched my fists, feeling the weight of my totem bracelet again. He made a good point, and one I hadn't considered before. Was there any side effect to using these powers? "The scepter—where is it?"

"The artifact has been taken to a secure location for further research."

"To be examined by 'top men'?"

The agent's stony expression cracked into a brief, subdued smile. "Something like that."

"I still don't get why he did it," I murmured. "Why attack those people? Why try to destroy the city?"

"Until he awakens and is interviewed, I can't say with any certainty," the agent replied. "But our initial investigations have suggested that Mr. Ignatius has been in a questionable state of mind since the tragic death of his wife. Perhaps exposure to the scepter, as you call it, warped his grief into vengeance."

Grief over losing his wife? Did that have something to do with the rivalry between him and the Fausts? How could that possibly justify murdering innocent bystanders who got caught in the chaos?

The agent reached into his pocket and took out a small black cell phone about the size of a credit card. I'd never seen one like it before—not something you could pop into a local store and buy off a shelf. He placed it on the bed next to my hand. "This is a secure line, completely untraceable. The president is offering it to you as a gesture of good faith. An olive branch, if you will. If you know of another impending attack, he asks that you contact us."

I placed a shaking hand over the phone. "Okay."

He nodded and began walking toward the door. At the threshold, however, he stopped and glanced back. "Also, the pilot from the F-22 that you snatched out of the air is alive and unharmed. I thought you might want to know."

"Good." I closed my eyes. At last, I felt like I could breathe freely.

Except for one thing.

"What about Madeline Ignatius?"

The agent paused again with his hand on the doorknob. "She has not yet been found, but a search for her is underway. If there's anything you can tell us about her whereabouts—"

"There isn't." My third eye told me the agent wasn't lying; they really didn't know where she was. I didn't, either, but I wasn't going to help them find her.

"Of course." I could hear a smirk in his voice.

"And Drake? Are you going to arrest him?"

"Mr. Collins has been under our close observation for some time now. His recent actions, while highly illicit, were not surprising to us. A boy of his intelligence and skillset is a valuable resource—not something we plan to dispose of lightly. Tossing him into a juvenile detention center would be a waste."

"He said that you guys would rather hire him than send him to prison." My mouth twitched at a grin. Guess Drake had been right about that. I wondered if his "skillset" included his tango dancing abilities.

"Perhaps, if he manages to keep his priorities in order." The man turned and opened the door slowly. "My name is Agent Ellison Kirkland. Rest well, Mr. Owens. I'm sure we'll be seeing one another again very soon."

Three weeks later, I was sitting next to Drake in first period Chemistry like nothing had happened.

Well, sort of.

I'd finally managed to convince Dad that there was no reason I couldn't go back to school. Drake had been faithfully helping me keep up with my classwork from home, but that couldn't last forever. I had to go back.

Under my uniform, I still had a bandage on my chest from the burn, which looked like it was going to leave a nasty, puckered scar. It itched worse thanks to my starched button-down shirt. Or maybe that was just my nerves.

Facing the stares of my classmates who had all heard about my miraculous survival from the Philharmonic disaster was unnerving. Not to mention I had to walk past Headmaster Ignatius's empty office. Worst of all, I would have to sit next to Madeline's empty easel in art class.

I couldn't shake the feeling that she wasn't coming back. Not this time. But hope always dragged my gaze away, panning the halls and corridors in case I spotted her.

Of course, I never did.

I struggled even more than usual to concentrate on any of my work. I forced myself to eat lunch. I pretended to be excited to be working on the theater production. Soon, I told myself, it wouldn't be so hard. Soon it would feel natural and normal again. Soon I wouldn't have to force every smile. Soon I wouldn't have to pretend that I was okay.

I just didn't know when "soon" actually was.

It was even harder to ignore the whispers. Everywhere I went, I caught murmurs of gossip about the rivalry between Ignatius and the Fausts. There was no escaping it, and the more I heard, the more confused and conflicted I felt about it.

If the rumors were true, then Mr. Faust had harassed, bullied, and overworked Madeline's mom while she worked at the Philharmonic. She'd been his public relations specialist, overseeing the advertising, publicity, and news coverage for the whole symphony. It was a stressful job on it's own. When Mr. Faust was accused of stealing some of the symphony's funds, he and his wife had found evidence that showed Mrs. Ignatius had actually stolen the money.

Naturally, she hadn't taken the news well. No one could agree on whether or not she'd actually done it or if she was being framed. In the end, it didn't matter.

A week later, while driving home from work, Mr. Ignatius had gotten the call that his wife had been found dead in their home…by their five-year-old daughter.

It was an intentional overdose.

The rumor was that Gerard Ignatius was so shocked by the news that he lost control of his car. He'd accidentally swerved into a lane of oncoming traffic. The wreck left his body crippled, which was bad enough. But losing his wife left his mind hopelessly entangled with hate and rage for the Fausts.

Grief was a state I knew all too well. I'd felt that pain, too. Losing someone you loved wasn't an agony you ever got used to. You wanted someone—anyone—to blame. Even if the rumors were true and the Fausts were guilty, did that justify what Ignatius had done? Or any of the things he'd tried to do?

I knew the answer was no. But the more times I heard the story, the harder it was to blame him for losing it and trying something desperate in a grand attempt at justice. No wonder Madeline hadn't wanted to abandon him.

Every time my thoughts circled that concept, Oceana's words after I dealt with Clint echoed in the back of my mind. What was justice? What was revenge? Where did you draw the line between the two?

I had no answer for that. Maybe there wasn't one.

After school let out, Drake asked me to wait while he ran to the Robotics Club room to pick up a few things. He and his club-mates were working on yet another robot, although this one wasn't for a competition. Drake was trying to make his own version of a high-speed aerial drone outfitted with a high-definition camera. I couldn't imagine why he'd want something like that, though.

I sat on the front steps of the school and watched the traffic roll by while I waited for Drake to return. The sight of every fancy black town car made my heart jump and my hands twitch, wondering if Madeline or her father would suddenly step out of the back seat. How long would that last? Would I ever see her again?

Suddenly, someone plopped down on the steps right beside me.

Claire Faust cast me a quick glance but didn't say a word. With her curled golden hair blowing around her face and one of her hands resting on her cello case, she sat and watched the cars roll by with me. For a long time, neither of us spoke.

To be honest, I hadn't given her much thought since the incident. I'd heard that she, her mother, and her father had all survived the attack without any serious injuries—which was good. I was glad she was okay. But I didn't really have anything to say to her after all that.

"Koji?" Claire asked quietly.

I met her soft, sea-green eyes.

"Are you okay?"

I swallowed, looked away, and forced myself to lie. "Yeah."

Claire was quiet again for a moment. Then I felt her gaze studying me carefully. "I was thinking about everything today. Do you remember what you asked me at the gala? You asked what it was about Noxius that I loved."

I did remember that much.

"I realized later that I never answered you."

Claire scooted around so she was facing me. One of her warm hands reached out to take mine with startling strength. She was tougher than she looked. Her fingertips were callused, probably from playing her instrument.

"I love that he's enthusiastic and courageous, even if he's a little impulsive sometimes. I love that he does everything he can to protect the people he cares about, and that he never backs down from a cause he believes in—even if no one is standing with him. I love that he puts the needs of others before his own, and that he's a little bit silly." She gave my hand a firm squeeze as her gaze became intense. "And most of all, I love that he's you, Koji."

My heart skipped a beat. Panic swirled in my brain like a tornado. She knew? But how? How could she possibly have seen me? Or had she figured it out some other way?

Claire smiled gently as she slid her hand away from mine. "Don't worry, your secret is safe with me. And I know you don't feel the same way. At least, not anymore. I missed my chance, and it's my own fault for not seeing it sooner."

I choked on every word that came to mind. What—how—when—?

As Claire got up to leave, she flicked her hair over one of her shoulders, picked up her cello case, and gave me one last, broad grin. It spread over her face from cheek to cheek, putting dimples on either side of her mouth and making her whole being seem to glow. It made her blue-green eyes sparkle like sunlight on the ocean.

It was the first real, totally uninhibited smile I'd ever seen from Claire.

Speaking of sunlight—the warm glow of the sunset caught on her gold necklace and made it shimmer brightly. It was the Saint Cecilia medal she always wore, the one her grandmother had given to her. Usually it was tucked under the collar of her uniform sweater, but today it bounced freely against her chest. The sun had reflected against something fixed to the back of the pendant as she turned away. Something glossy, smooth, and shiny like pearl.

Or maybe like a totem scale.

"Claire!" I called after her.

She didn't stop. She strode proudly down the steps of the school, a spring in her step as she held her head high and turned her face to the warmth of the first touch of spring wind. She paused, her shoulders heaving with a deep breath, before she climbed into the back of an expensive black car. In a matter of seconds, she was gone.

"Hey, so did your dad say anything to you about spring break?" Drake called out as he came jogging up beside me. "Mom said he suggested we take a road trip down the coast. To Savannah, right? I hear they have good seafood."

I didn't move.

"Hey, what's wrong?" He leaned around to peer up at my face. "You look like you saw a ghost or something."

My body relaxed as I sighed, unable to resist a huge smile that spread over my lips. "No, not a ghost." I laughed under my breath. "Just a friend."

"A friend?" Drake balked. "Yeah, right. I'm your only friend. Who else comes by on weekends to try and salvage your pathetic Chemistry grade? Not to mention keeps your epic secret and lies to your dad for you all the time so you can run around saving the school princess. I think I've earned superior friend status."

I gave him a shove as I started ambling down the sidewalk. "Superior friend status? That's not even a real thing."

He jogged to catch up. "Sure it is. It means I get to borrow your comics any time I want *and* you have to help me test out the drone. I want some in-flight action coverage of your next battle."

"What?"

"Don't worry, I'm pretty sure it'll work," he assured me.

"This better not involve gasoline, or jet engines, or anything explosive," I warned. "It doesn't, does it? Seriously, I've got enough problems without your gadgets blowing up around me."

Drake grinned impishly as he fell in step beside me. "Guess you'll just have to wait and see."

ACKNOWLEDGEMENTS

Whew! What a ride that was!

First, I am SO excited to be sharing Koji's adventure with you! He is a character near and dear to my heart, and I hope you'll enjoy watching the rest of his story unfold as much as I have. There's so much excitement, adventure, and many more epic battles yet to come!

I'd like to give Jenny, Chelsea, Jamie, Cristy, Caylen, Tamilyn, and the rest of the spouses of the 25th FS at Osan AFB all my love. For me, writing this book hit home on a whole new level because Koji's story is the story of so many military kids out there—our kids—who are challenged in ways most people can't even fathom as we move around the world. You ladies were my rock during what we all know can be a challenging and difficult time spent living overseas. Ladies, I see you. I see your courage and heart, your selflessness and enduring love. I know you are all fighting the hard fight to make hotel rooms, rentals, apartments, and even the belly of airplanes feel like home. Having you all cheering me on from the sidelines is what keeps me going on those tough days! Not a day goes by when I don't miss you all so much.

I would like to give a huge THANK YOU and extra-big hug to Emma and the rest of the wonderful staff at Owl Hollow Press for helping bring his adventure to life! You guys have been so supportive, amazing, (and incredibly patient) and have gone the extra mile to make this book special. It has truly been a pleasure working with you, and I have so much respect for all of you. Thank you for being awesome!!

I'd also like to thank my agent, Fran, for continuing to support and push me to be the author she believes I can be. There are times (more lately than ever) when I feel myself slipping and falling to despair. But Fran is always there to talk me back into the ring so I can keep fighting for my dream. For all you do, Fran, thank you so much!

As always, I'd like to give my love and thanks to my fan club, the Legion, my team of beta readers, and last but not least—to my husband, family, and close friends. You guys continue to blow my mind with your overwhelming support, love and enthusiasm. I wouldn't be able to do any of this without you!

NICOLE CONWAY is a graduate of Auburn University with a lifelong passion for writing teen and children's literature. With over 100,000 books sold in her *DRAGONRIDER CHRONICLES* series, Nicole has been ranked one of Amazon's Top 100 Teen Authors.

A coffee and Netflix addict, she also enjoys spending time with her family, practicing photography, and traveling.

Nicole is represented by Frances Black of Literary Counsel.

Find her online at www.authornicoleconway.com and here:

#SCALES